****
Monroe Doctrine

Volume I
****

By James Rosone and Miranda Watson

Published in conjunction with Front Line Publishing, Inc.

Copyright Notice

©2021, James Rosone and Miranda Watson, in conjunction with Front Line Publishing, Inc. Except as provided by the Copyright Act, no part of this publication may be reproduced, stored in a retrieval system or transmitted in any form or by any means without the prior written permission of the publisher.

ISBN: 978-1-957634-33-3
Sun City Center, Florida, USA
Library of Congress Control Number: 2022902479

Table of Contents

Chapter One: Jack in the Box	5
Chapter Two: Task Force Dupre	16
Chapter Three: The Age of AI	29
Chapter Four: Down Under	40
Chapter Five: Belt and Road Initiative: Phase One	47
Chapter Six: Space Junk	50
Chapter Seven: Big Data	54
Chapter Eight: Sun Tzu – Art of War	57
Chapter Nine: Foreign Aid	62
Chapter Ten: For the People	69
Chapter Eleven: Project Ten	83
Chapter Twelve: Project Chengdu	94
Chapter Thirteen: Cuba Libre	106
Chapter Fourteen: Spy Games	119
Chapter Fifteen: Prisoner Swap	128
Chapter Sixteen: Big Reveal	143
Chapter Seventeen: Kompromat	176
Chapter Eighteen: Miami Heat	190
Chapter Nineteen: Chess, Not Checkers	201
Chapter Twenty: Escalation	209
Chapter Twenty-One: Pawn for a Bishop	214
Chapter Twenty-Two: Blockade	223
Chapter Twenty-Three: Snake Eaters	233
Chapter Twenty-Four: Don't Mess with Texas	239
Chapter Twenty-Five: Murphy's Law	257
Chapter Twenty-Six: Dragon Fire	270

Chapter Twenty-Seven: Angels in the Sky	276
Chapter Twenty-Eight: Death Dealers	282
Chapter Twenty-Nine: Black Unicorns	292
Chapter Thirty: Collateral Damage	301
Chapter Thirty-One: Preparations	319
Chapter Thirty-Two: Vipers, Vipers, Vipers	323
Chapter Thirty-Three: The Long March	327
From the Authors	352
Abbreviation Key	355

Chapter One
Jack in the Box

Monday, October 25, 2024
Type 909D Merchant Raider
Mid-Atlantic
Roughly 300 Miles Away from US Eastern Seaboard

The calm sea masked the deadly cargo hidden in the Panamax freighter as it steadily moved closer to Norfolk, Virginia.

"I sure hope this works. If not, we're dead," the executive officer declared, so softly only he and the captain could hear.

"It will work," Senior Captain Tsai whispered back. "For all intents and purposes, we are just a cargo ship on our way to port." He paused, waiting for what he'd said to sink in. "Make sure that once we fire off our missiles, you have someone paint the new name on the ship," he ordered. "It's imperative that we conceal our identity for as long as we can after this attack."

"Yes, Captain. I'll personally see to it," the young officer noted. He appeared a bit calmer after their short conversation.

Tsai felt proud and nervous as his merchant raider approached their launch point. After nearly two weeks, they were finally within strike range. They'd been heading toward their target along the same international shipping routes as every other cargo vessel traveling from the Port of Thessaloniki to the Norfolk International Terminals.

While outwardly this was a Panamax-sized cargo ship, it was secretly the key to the Chinese Navy's ghost fleet that was about to wreak havoc on the West. The ship appeared to be a Greek-flagged cargo ship bringing goods from China to Europe, then from Europe to America, and then from America to China before it would repeat the process.

Tsai hoped this mission would have a real impact on the war. *If we get lucky, the Americans might even decide a war with China would be too costly to pursue*, he thought. *Who do the Americans think they are, anyway?* The US dictated what countries could operate in the Caribbean and South America, and then they had the audacity to run spy ships and planes along the coasts of China. Of course, they'd freak out if someone did the same to them.

"Captain, we are nearly at the launch point. When should we uncover the missile launchers?" asked the weapons officer.

Tsai turned to the younger officer, the glow of his computer screen illuminating his face. "When we reach ten minutes from the launch time," he answered. "Verify your missiles have their coordinates for their specific targets."

"Yes, Captain," the young officer responded as he pecked away at his keyboard.

Tsai looked at the officer manning their communications terminal. He had his Toughbook open and the satellite cable from outside connected to it. They were connected to DragonLink, the indigenous satellite network China had built to provide low-cost to no-cost satellite internet to the world. Interlayered within the satellite infrastructure was the Chinese military's newest way to covertly communicate across the globe in real time.

Tsai mused to himself about the passage of time. Somehow time seemed to be dragging on, while simultaneously they seemed to be marching into history at warp speed. Tsai didn't quite know how to explain this feeling welling up within him.

Finally, he announced to the bridge crew, "In ten minutes, we should receive our final set of instructions—a pair of messages that will change the course of history."

The young lieutenants manning the communications and weapon systems smiled at the announcement as they waited for the opening salvos of the war against the West.

****

Joint Battle Command Centre
20 Kilometers Northwest of Beijing, China

President Yao Jintao examined the ocean map of the Pacific, the Panama Canal Zone, the Caribbean, and the Mediterranean. He saw a string of red icons denoting known locations of American warships. He also spotted two groups of interest. One was the *Liaoning* battle group as it approached Central America. The other group consisted of three green icons denoting the merchant raiders who had steadily moved into their firing positions.

"It's not too late to stop this, Mr. President," Han Jinping whispered.

Han, the Foreign Minister, had opposed Project Ten from the beginning. He had argued they should stay the course and not provoke the Americans while they continued to silently build their navy and strengthen their economic grip on the rest of the world.

Yao turned to look at his longtime friend and confidant. "Han, we've been over this. Jade Dragon war-gamed this out. By striking the Americans first, we will cripple their military. It will be years before they rebuild and recover from this attack."

"Mr. President, our merchant raiders are nearly in position," announced Fleet Admiral Wei Huang, the head of the Chinese Navy.

"We are ready to initiate the first phase of the attack, Mr. President," explained Dr. Xi Zemin, the head of Project Ten and the architect of Jade Dragon.

President Yao Jintao turned to face his chief scientist and military advisors. "October 2024 marks a historic first for mankind, and China. Today, for the first time in history, an artificial intelligence tool will be used as a first-strike weapon against an adversary." The President paused for just a moment as he let his words sink in before giving the official order that would change the world. "Commence Operation Dragon Fire."

Xi smiled smugly as he walked over to the computer terminal, shooing away the operator. This had been his dream for nearly thirty years. If anyone was going to unleash an AI on the world to start a war, it would be its creator.

Xi's fingers danced across the keyboard for the briefest of moments before the final prompt appeared. It asked him to confirm he wanted to execute the plan.

Turning to look for the President, Xi saw the man had walked up behind him.

The leader of China leaned down as he said, "This had better work, Doctor. Commence the attack."

Oh, this will work…and when it does, I will be the one who will rule China and the world when it's over, Xi thought as he nodded and clicked on the execute button.

In the blink of an eye, a ground base's laser communication system uploaded the command and shot the code from the bowels of the JBCC to the DragonLink satellites high above. Once the microsatellites received the message, they transmitted the kill code to a single cellular tower owned and operated by a company called American Tower.

The cell tower had been recently modified, using a Huawei router with an embedded malware code that would systematically infect a single industrial control unit in every cellular tower owned by American Tower. The code would then spread to the rest of the cellular networks across the United States in the span of minutes. Once the infection was complete, a final kill order would be given, which would corrupt the power relays—allowing more power to cross the circuits than the systems could handle, and physically burning out some of the critical components.

When that last order was received, every cell tower in America would cease to function until the burned-out components were replaced. A set of simple eighty-cent parts would cripple America's cell networks until they were swapped out.

With the first of many Easter eggs in place, it was now time to start the first of a series of attacks that would destroy the militaries of the West and cement China's role as the dominant world power of the twenty-first century.

****

Peterson Air Force Base
Colorado Springs
0100 Hours Mountain Time

"General, are you ready to head back to the mountain?" asked Colonel Conrad, or Connie to his friends and fellow fliers.

General Anita Barrett had taken the first night shift watch so her deputy commander could spend another evening with his young family, since her own kids were all grown.

Yawning, she replied, "Yeah, I'm ready. I found my go bag. You know, the SecDef thinks the Chinese may not back down. That's why he's having us lock the mountain fortress down later this afternoon. Personally, I think once we start gliding some fighters and bombers around Cuba, they'll take a hint and know we aren't joking around. They need to leave."

Connie nodded. "I hope so. When will the fleet start sortieing from their bases? I think once the Chinese see the Navy encircle the island, they'll really get the message. That's what caused the Soviets to back down last time around, when they tried to place missiles on Cuba in the 1960s."

Barrett reached for her coffee and took a long gulp. "Two days. They're still taking on provisions and doing final maintenance checks. The Marines reinforced Guantanamo a few days ago. The rest of them will start boarding their ships in about a week to head down to Florida."

Connie blew some air out his lips. "I sure hope the Cubans and the Chinese realize we aren't messing around. I really don't want a shooting war with them, but if they think we'll let them set up military bases ninety miles from our border, they have another thing coming."

"Right now, I think it's all posturing," Barrett countered. "In another day or two, an agreement will be reached to allow everyone to save face and move on. The Chinese economy is in the toilet, just like the rest of the world. They aren't in a situation to wage a war, let alone a war with us." Grabbing her go bag, she called out, "Come on, Connie. It's time to head out to the flight line and catch our ride back to the mountain. The crew here has things covered."

The two of them walked out of the command building to a waiting vehicle that would take them to a helicopter standing by to fly them to Cheyenne Mountain. Barrett didn't like leaving the watch commander alone for more than an hour. She had come back to her office on Peterson to grab a few items before they sealed themselves in. She had no idea how long this standoff could end up lasting.

Their helicopter had been in the air for a couple of minutes when she received a message from the pilots telling her someone from the mountain was trying to reach her.

She grabbed for one of the helmets and put it on.

"This is General Barrett," she said loudly over the noise of the helicopter.

"General Barrett, this is General Landers. We received a FLASH priority message from the NSA. They're saying there's a cyberattack underway against the nation's cellular network. Less than sixty seconds later, the National Military Command Authority issued an order for all military installations to go to THREATCON Delta. I have to seal the mountain. How far out are you?"

Holy crap, this can't be happening…

Barrett grabbed one of the pilot's shoulders. "How far out are we?"

"Two minutes."

"You need to get there in less than a minute. *Now!*" she screamed.

The pilot dove the helicopter down to the deck as he increased speed. They were now racing to reach the mountain before it was sealed.

"Landers, the pilot says we'll be there in a minute. Give me a few minutes to get inside before you seal the place up. I have no idea how long it could be before we're able to open back up."

Landers replied, "I'll give you exactly three minutes, General. Then I have to seal the mountain."

The call ended, and Barrett felt a burning anger building inside her. *This better not be the opening move of a new war...*

Moments later, the pilot yanked up hard on his controls, flaring the front of the helicopter as they bled off their speed. He skipped landing on the pad and settled down right in front of the entrance. There was a vehicle waiting for them.

Barrett and Connie were out of the helicopter and in the vehicle in seconds. The driver sped them away before they even had a chance to close their doors. They raced down the tunnel at an ungodly speed for being in such a tight, narrow space.

As they approached the blast doors at the end of the tunnel, they could see they were already halfway closed and continuing to pull together. People were rushing in, being waved in by the security forces airman standing next to the door.

The driver slammed on the brakes as he approached the entrance, scaring the hell out of everyone. Barrett and Connie bailed out of the vehicle, running and stumbling their way to the blast door, which was now almost completely shut. The two of them slid inside, moments before it would have crushed their bodies.

"Thank God you made it, General Barrett. Please, come with me," a security forces captain said.

The trio ran through the corridors until they reached the command center, where Major General Landers was on the yellow phone, the hotline directly connecting him to the National Military Command Center or NMCC—the command room in the heart of the Pentagon. This was the same room that could order a full nuclear strike if ordered by the President.

Landers pulled the receiver down to his shoulder. "They're about to move us over to a secured video teleconference in a second if you want to take your seat."

10

He pointed to a table with a very wide computer screen and three chairs sitting in front of it. One was for the North American Aerospace Defense or NORAD Commander, one for the operations officer, and one for the watch commander.

Barrett took her seat as the monitor came to life. Instantly she saw a feed from the NSA, CIA, DHS, SOUTHCOM, SOCOM, the NMCC and the PEOC. There was also a feed that suddenly appeared from Air Force One. When that last feed popped on, she knew the Secret Service must be in the process of getting President Frank Alton airborne. That meant the VP would be the one in the PEOC—that or the President's cabinet.

Moments later, the respective directors or their deputies started appearing on the screens. There was a lot of chatter coming from the various stations until someone from the NMCC muted everyone.

"This is Brigadier General Pike. I'm the duty officer at the NMCC. I will provide a short briefing of what we know. Then the meeting will be handed over to the President and the Chairman of the Joint Chiefs to discuss."

Everyone from the various outstations all nodded, paying very close attention, anticipating the critical nature of what was about to be shared. The fact that it was the middle of the night only added to the gravity of the situation.

"Twenty-eight minutes ago, we received a message from the NSA, alerting us to a concerted cyberattack on the nation's cellular network. It cannot be confirmed that this attack originated out of China; however, it has the fingerprints of their hacker tool sets. At this point, we initiated THREATCON Delta. Seven minutes ago, a second series of cyberattacks took place against our power grid." Murmurs could be heard from some folks on Air Force One before someone on that end muted their line.

General Pike continued, "I want to assure everyone, it wasn't an attack on the entire grid. It was an attack on the power plants and transmission nodes that provide power to our military facilities in Hawaii, Alaska, Greenland, Virginia, Iowa, Florida, and Texas. Please note, this was not a full nationwide blackout. This was a very targeted attack on the power grid to these specific military facilities."

Before the general could elaborate any further, the missile launch warning alarm blared and lights started flashing around Barrett and the command center.

"Sorry to interrupt, General Pike. We're receiving a missile launch warning from Pine Gap and our CONUS early-warning systems," Barrett announced forcefully. She turned away from the screen to start barking orders, not realizing her side of the line was still unmuted.

"Where are those missile launches coming from, and do we know what kind of missiles they are?" she demanded.

The action officer relayed, "The 20th Space Control Squadron at Eglin's Site C-6 is reporting multiple cruise missile launches from several Chinese warships in the Gulf of Mexico." A short pause ensued as the officer held their hand up to indicate that they were receiving more information. "Ma'am, the PAVE PAWS early-warning systems are now tracking multiple ballistic missile launches originating from previously suspected DF-15 launch sites on Cuba."

"General, those missiles appear to be tracking toward Texas, Louisiana, and Florida," an Air Force major called out.

Barrett sat back down, whispering to herself, "They're going for our air bases."

"*What!*" screamed the President from Air Force One.

In that moment, Barrett realized everyone on the conference call had heard the interactions in the command center. She turned to face President Alton. "Sir, I believe this is a preemptive attack on our fighter and bomber bases across the southeast. The only viable military target we have in Louisiana is Barksdale Air Force Base. It's a B-52 base and the head of the Air Force Global Strike Command. I'll bet the missile heading toward Texas will eventually track toward Dyess Air Force Base, a B-1B base. Both Florida and Georgia have several fighter bases and command-and-control facilities as well."

The President shouted some obscenities before demanding to know what they should do next.

The National Security Advisor, the Chairman of the Joint Chiefs, and the Pentagon watch officer were all advising Alton to alert those bases and see if they could get any of their bombers under shelter or in the air before the cruise missiles hit.

"General Barrett," the President finally said over the shouts of advice and information being thrown at him. "Move us from DEFCON 4 to DEFCON 2. Order our remaining bombers to get airborne with nuclear weapons, and order our silos to begin spinning themselves up for possible launch orders. If any of those missiles are nuclear, we must be ready to respond in kind. In the meantime, do we have the exact location where those Chinese missiles originated from?"

Turning to look back at the large monitor on the wall, General Barrett saw a couple dozen tracks originating from a small group of Chinese warships northwest of Cuba in the Gulf and a few locations on Cuba proper. She relayed the coordinates to the President and the Pentagon.

The Chairman of the Joint Chiefs advised, "Mr. President, I recommend we order our naval forces in the Gulf to engage and sink those Chinese warships before they can fire additional missiles. I also recommend we send some Tomahawks at those ground base systems on Cuba that fired on us. For all we know, they could be reloading those launch vehicles to hit us with a second wave of missiles."

President Alton sat back in his chair for a moment, a conflicted look on his face.

"Damn it! They struck first! We need to hit them back! What's there to think about?" shouted the President's Chief of Staff angrily.

General Barrett cleared her throat as she pulled a phone receiver down to her shoulder. "Excuse me, Mr. President. I'm on the phone with the CO of the USS *Hue City*, the task force command ship in the Gulf. The CO is telling me their AEGIS systems aren't tracking any missiles heading toward the US from those Chinese vessels or Cuba."

"That can't be possible," interjected General Pike at the Pentagon. "I'm looking at the missile tracks from the various early-warning systems and our satellites. Their AEGIS must have a gremlin or malfunction."

No one said anything for a moment as they tried to figure out what this meant. General Barrett raised the receiver to her ear, asking them to run a diagnostic on their equipment.

The President's Chief of Staff spoke loudly to cut through some of the chatter. "General Barrett, if the *Hue City* runs a diagnostic on their system, how long will that take, and how close will those missiles be to their targets?"

She relayed his question to the captain of the ship. "Sir, it'll take them close to five minutes to run a full diagnostic. As to when will those missiles impact? In two minutes, they'll be outside of *Hue City*'s ability to interdict. But, sir, it's not just their ship—the other two *Arleigh Burkes* with them aren't tracking any missiles either. It would appear it's only our ground-based radar and satellites tracking them."

"None of this makes sense. Why would the Chinese launch a preemptive attack on us like this? What do they have to gain from it?" the President said aloud to no one in particular.

"Mr. President, we don't have time to figure out why they would launch an attack at us. In less than two minutes, those missiles will be out of range for our ships to engage. We need to start shooting them down now," the Chief of Staff said urgently.

More loud chatter broke out, both on Air Force One with the President and the advisors with him and among the people at the Pentagon and NORAD. Everyone was trying to voice their opinions on what President Alton should do next.

"Enough! I need a minute to think!" barked Alton.

"We have less than sixty seconds to engage those missiles or they're gone!" one of the officers said forcefully from the Pentagon feed.

The President scrunched his eyebrows together in anger and frustration. He clearly wanted more time to think this problem through, but there wasn't any more time left.

President Alton finally looked up at the NORAD screen. "General Barrett...order the *Hue City* to engage those missiles."

General Barrett lifted the receiver to her ear and relayed the order. The airborne early-warning and control or AWACS plane on station over the Gulf started relaying the satellite feed and early-warning radar feeds they were getting from NORAD to the naval ships. Now they were seeing what the President and his advisors saw.

"Mr. President, I recommend we launch a counterattack. Take those enemy ships out and hit those launchers before they can either reload them or relocate them to fire more missiles," Admiral Thiel said with perhaps a bit more forcefulness than he should have.

President Alton slumped in his chair, looking defeated by the situation. He nodded in approval after a few seconds. "Fine. Take them out. Make sure they can't hit us any further."

Admiral Thiel then turned to look at Barrett. "Order the *Hue City* and the *Burkes* with her to engage and sink those Chinese warships. They're also to engage those ground launcher sites with their Tomahawks immediately."

General Barrett took a deep breath in and held it for a moment, almost not comprehending the orders from the President. They were officially attacking the military forces of the People's Republic of China.

Chapter Two
Task Force Dupre

Gulf of Mexico
USS *Hue City*

"Sir, I say again, USS *Barry* Actual requests—"

"I heard you, damn it. Very well," Commander Michael Dupre snapped, more harshly than he'd intended to. The junior officer of the deck was just doing his job. Standing from his chair, he took the handset from the JOD.

"*Barry, Hue City* Actual, send it."

In the two weeks since the aptly named Task Force Dupre had been thrown together, he had tried to express to the captains of the more modern *Arleigh Burke* destroyers that when it was ship-to-ship comms, he wanted to forgo typical Navy formality. The fact that they ignored him validated his suspicion that they didn't respect the *Hue City*.

He couldn't blame them. *Hue City* was old, and as more than one junior sailor said in hushed tones, she was haunted. Of course, he didn't believe that—despite his superstitious upbringing in Louisiana. The Navy desperately needed to replace the *Hue City* and all her sister *Ticonderoga* cruisers, but in true Navy fashion, the brass had wasted two decades on pipe dream "Charlie Foxtrots" like the *Zumwalt* class.

Shaking the frustration from his head, he focused on what Commander Ziegler of the *Barry* was droning on about.

"*Hue City, Barry*. We have confirmation of four Type 52D Luyang III–class destroyers north by northwest of Cayo de Buenavista, Cuba."

"*Barry, Hue City*. Very well," Dupre acknowledged.

"Helm, plot your course to intercept, all ahead full."

"Plot my course to intercept. All ahead full, aye, sir."

Dupre had received orders to chop his task force from the Carrier Strike Group Twelve, set sail at best speed into the Gulf of Mexico and close with any Chinese warships they found. They were now less than two hundred nautical miles from the lead Chinese destroyer.

In the briefing with the admiral prior to his departure, it had sounded like unicorns and rainbows to lead his own task force. But the *Hue City* was the weak link in the task force, and Dupre knew it. He could barely keep pace with the newer and faster *Arleigh Burkes*. The captains of the

USS *Barry* and *Laboon* were rising stars in the destroyer community. At one point he had been a rising star in the *Arleigh Burke* world. Then his mouth and inability to suffer fools had seen him cast off to the world of aging and ignored cruisers. This command was like last year's Christmas present. The Navy in its infinite wisdom had yet again opted for younger and faster.

I should have joined the Coast Guard, thought Dupre.

For all his griping, Dupre actually loved this old "*Tico.*" She was old and beat up, but she was like a comfortable pair of sneakers. He knew in his bones that, if push came to shove, this old girl could fight. Driving this fact home was Lieutenant Clarissa Price, in his opinion the best tactical operations officer in this or any navy.

She was sharp, driven, and capable of multitasking on a level that made his head spin. During war game scenarios, she and her watch could assess and prioritize targets almost as fast as the ship's computer. She was his ace in the hole, and the reason the *Hue City* had gotten this assignment. For all intents and purposes, the Gulf of Mexico belonged to Task Force Dupre.

****

Lieutenant Clarissa Price knew she was a bit of a taskmaster. She ran the combat information center or CIC hard. She was constantly running her personnel through their paces. She ran scenarios, drills, and system checks throughout every watch. If each watch didn't meet her time expectations, there would be hell to pay.

From the moment she had set foot aboard the *Hue City*, she'd fallen in love with it. A previous chief petty officer or CPO who'd worked for her in the CIC had told her, "Where there's a will, you'll find the *Hue*." That had stuck with her, and no matter what, she wouldn't let her division or her ship down. Commander Dupre was another matter. She found the man insufferable. She'd heard him called "The Crazy Cajun" before she'd reported for duty aboard the *Hue City*.

When she'd reported in, she had done so in proper naval fashion, wearing a crisp uniform, with orders in hand. She'd stood at rapt attention and presented herself. He'd had his feet on the desk, listening to country music. When she'd seen him spit in a Gatorade bottle, the disgust on her face had been obvious to Dupre, which had made him laugh.

He'd glanced at her Annapolis ring and asked her what year she'd graduated. The sudden change in topic had thrown her off. That was Commander Dupre in a nutshell—he always kept you on your toes. When she thought she had a handle on the man, he threw a curveball at her, or went astern full and kept changing rudder direction.

In the two years she'd worked for him, she had never been able to get a read on the man. It infuriated her to no end. The only time she had even come close to getting to know the man was at a port call in Singapore. He'd invited some of the junior officers to the Goodluck Beer House on Haji Lane. Most had declined as they didn't want to get drunk in front of the boss. She'd seen it as a challenge and charged in headfirst. After a couple of hours, it was just the two of them. She found his charm to be unnerving; he was a completely different man off the ship.

It had absolutely floored her when he'd told her she was one of the best officers he ever served with. At first, she'd thought he was making a pass at her, which wasn't uncommon for an attractive woman in the Navy. No matter how many sexual harassment and rape prevention PowerPoint briefings they sat through, men were still men. She'd hardened herself to it, to the point of being numb.

When she'd realized he was being sincere, she'd blushed, cursing herself for again being caught on her heels by this man. Since that night nearly a year ago, she had considered him a friend and mentor, but he still annoyed her.

She stood from her station and walked around the CIC to make sure the sailors of her watch were all focused. God help the sailor who nodded off at their station.

Looking at the various monitors and the big board in the CIC, she saw something odd. The Electronic Warfare Control and the Tactical Information Coordinator flickered for a few seconds. She looked at every screen she could see, and all seemed to have the same glitch.

Lieutenant Price called out, "Attention in the CIC. All stations perform immediate diagnostic."

As the sailors responded to the new orders, she went to the wall and picked up the phone.

"Captain, TAO," said his Tactical Action Officer.

"TAO, Captain. Send it."

"Captain, CIC reports a system glitch. All our screens were garbled for approximately seven seconds. I ordered a diagnostics to be run on all stations."

"TAO, Captain, very well."

****

Commander Dupre placed the phone back in its cradle as he digested what his TAO had just told him. Pausing for a moment, he picked up another phone for the ship-to-ship communication.

"*Barry, Laboon, Hue City* Actual."

Both ships responded. On a hunch, he asked if they'd experienced any system glitches. Both ships reported they had, at precisely the same time as the *Hue City*.

"*Barry, Laboon*, very well. Run your diagnostics and report back your findings."

He hung up the phone and sat back in his chair. His initial reaction was to ignore it. After all, his ship was over twenty years old. But the Flight III *Arleigh Burkes* weren't, and for all the ships to experience the glitch simultaneously was damned odd. He couldn't write this off to random chance.

Dupre picked up the phone again and instructed his communications officer or COMMO to send the information to Fleet HQ.

****

Cape Cod Air Force Station
6th Space Warning Squadron
Joint Base Cape Cod

Major Mario Espinosa had been on shift for two hours. He paced around the operations center, trying to wake up. The first hours on shift were the worst. He glanced at the two other airmen on watch with him. They were typical geeks. Both wore glasses and had complexions that screamed, "My girlfriend lives in Canada; you wouldn't know her."

They were also incredibly smart, even brilliant at their jobs. But when it came to a twelve-hour shift looking at objects in synchronous and geosynchronous orbit, conversations with them were as exciting as watching paint dry.

He cursed his luck that he couldn't get a shift with First Lieutenant Childs. He cursed the fact that he couldn't muster the guts to even talk to her. Brushing that aside, he glanced up at the two one-hundred-inch displays at the front of the room, then down at his watch.

"Hey, guys, the International Space Station is about to pass overhead again."

It had become a running joke on their watch that when the ISS passed over them, they'd recite the intro monologue to *Star Trek*. He had known Staff Sergeant Tate was the bigger nerd of the two the first time they'd done it, when Tate had played the soundtrack to the original series from his Non-classified Internet Protocol Router Network or NIPRNet workstation. The icon representing the ISS blinked on screen and the two younger airmen stood as Tate pressed play. In unison, they all started, "Space: the final frontier. These are the vo—"

At that moment, every screen in the room flickered for a few seconds. The three immediately forgot about *Star Trek*.

"What the hell was that?" Tate asked.

"Beats me, is your system rebooting?" inquired Technical Sergeant Bishop as he opened his systems manual to begin the functions check process.

Major Espinosa was on the phone, checking with his counterpart at Beale Air Force Base in California before calling Site 6 down at Eglin.

Responding to a question from Beale, Espinosa said over the secured hand receiver, "Yes, our systems flickered. All of them. I don't want to get all geeked out, but every system in the room did."

Espinosa held up his hand to quiet Tate and Bishop, who were starting to talk a bit too loud. The two settled down and looked at him while he finished the call.

"OK, you two run a full system diagnostic. Beale reported the same glitch. I'm calling Eglin next and then I'll check in with NORTHCOM. I'll call the boss and let her know."

Espinosa learned Eglin had the same problem, which meant this wasn't a random glitch. No way three of their sites would be reporting the same system issues at the same time. Reaching for the phone that would connect him with NORTHCOM, he pressed the speed dial to reach Lieutenant Colonel Patricia Benson, his boss, when the alarms wailed.

The large wall screens that displayed a view of the world around the United States started blinking in a couple of different areas in the direction of the Caribbean. This signaled missile launch detection warnings.

Espinosa dropped the phone, oblivious to the fact that Lieutenant Colonel Benson had picked up on the other end.

"What the hell?" he demanded, looking at Bishop.

"Sir, multiple launches detected!"

"How many? From where?" Espinosa could feel himself losing his bearings as his body dumped adrenaline. He stopped long enough to take a deep breath to regain control.

"Sir, the missiles appear to be sea-launched, roughly fifteen miles north-northwest of Cuba."

Before Espinosa could reply, Tate interrupted, "Sir, I've got multiple new missile launches originating from Cuba."

"Designate those tracks and alert NORAD!"

Espinosa picked up the phone from the floor and updated his boss. She said she was alerting the other operators on standby to head into the office to assist them and that she'd be over there in a few minutes to help him as well.

Just as he hung up the phone, every phone in the watch center started ringing. Each time he answered, there was an immediate demand for information and then confirmation that this was real. Every US early-warning and detection system had reported the same tracks, to include their satellites. The number of missiles heading toward the US had increased rapidly until it leveled off at two hundred.
****

Gulf of Mexico
USS *Hue City*
Task Force Dupre

Commander Dupre had just lain down, figuring he'd try and catch a couple hours of sleep while he could. He was just drifting off to sleep when suddenly the 1MC sounded the general quarters alarm.

"General quarters, general quarters! All hands, man your battle stations! Set Condition Zebra. This is not a drill!"

Dupre reached for the phone next to his bed and called the CIC. "TAO, what the hell is going on?" he said groggily as he swung his feet over his bed and began the process of putting his trousers on.

"Captain, we received a FLASH priority message from NORAD. They detected multiple missile launches from Cuba and three Chinese Type 52s off of the northern coast of Cuba," Lieutenant Price answered immediately.

"What the hell?! Hang on, I'll be there in a couple of minutes. Out."

As Dupre walked out the door of his room, the hallway was filling up with people running to their various stations.

The master chief petty officer or MCPO of the *Hue City* caught up with him as the two of them rushed to the CIC. As Dupre moved down the tight corridors, his master chief yelled out behind him, "Make a hole!" The sailors, realizing they were in the way of the captain, parted like the Red Sea for them to run the rest of the way to the CIC.

Barging into the room, Dupre shouted, "TAO, give me an update!"

Lieutenant Price answered immediately, "Sir, NORAD and their early-warning systems are still showing multiple missile tracks originating from those PLA destroyers and some land-based launchers heading toward the US. However, our systems aren't showing anything to verify what they're saying."

Dupre almost did a double take at what Lieutenant Price had told him. Snapping out of his momentary surprise, he asked, "What do you mean we aren't detecting them? How's that possible?"

Lieutenant Price took a breath and tried to explain. "Sir, all we know right now is NORAD's early-warning systems, including the PAVE PAWS out of Cape Cod and Eglin's Site 6, which can track cruise and ballistic missile launches from the Gulf, picked up two hundred missile tracks ninety seconds ago."

Scrunching his eyebrows together, Dupre countered, "Whoa, what? They're tracking all that, but we're tracking nothing on AEGIS? That's not possible."

Lieutenant Price seemed as dumbfounded by the situation as he was. "Negative, sir, AEGIS is clear. We detected no launches."

"This makes no sense. We need to get a verification of launch, Lieutenant!" ordered Dupre.

"Aye, sir," responded Price.

****

COMDESRON 40
Naval Station Mayport
Jacksonville, Florida

Commodore Charles Mathison, the commander of Destroyer Squadron 40, had returned to his desk after getting his third cup of coffee for this shift. He hated the graveyard shift, but as the commander, he needed to do it from time to time. He didn't want to model his command style on that of his direct boss, Admiral Levison, the deputy commander of 4th Fleet—the guy loved the sound of his own voice and routinely made life tough for those who worked for him. Levison also generally didn't do unpleasant things if he could have his underlings do them instead..

Mathison opened the slide deck one of his staffers had sent him, wanting to give it a quick check before he forwarded it to the admiral's desk for the morning brief. *Ugh, slide six is using Arial when it needs to be Times New Roman—are they all using the wrong font?*

Then one of the night shift staffers burst into his office, startling him. "Sir, you need to come to the operations center. We just received a FLASH message from NORAD. They're reporting two hundred missiles were just launched from the waters off Cuba, and from the island!"

It's way too early in the morning for this be a prank, he thought as he grabbed his cover and headed down the hall to the operations center.

When they entered the squadron operations center, every wall-mounted OLED monitor displayed the missile tracks from the vicinity of Cuba, heading right for the American underbelly.

Mathison didn't hesitate in the least once he saw what was happening. "Get me Task Force Dupre, *now*!"

****

Gulf of Mexico
USS *Hue City*
Task Force Dupre

"I understand your orders, ma'am," Dupre replied to General Barrett. "We are one hundred and ninety nautical miles from the launch points and showing no missile tracks on our AEGIS or on the *Laboon* and *Barry.*"

Dupre was on a video call with the 2nd and 4th Fleet admirals, the ones that had been able to get on a video call, and the DESRON 40 Commodore, along with the NORAD Commander.

General Barrett forcefully responded, "Commander, my understanding is you reported a computer glitch on all three ships in your task force not more than thirty minutes ago. It's very conceivable that your systems have been compromised. The entire North American early-warning system is tracking two hundred cruise and ballistic missiles heading toward the southern United States from the location of those Chinese warships and several locations on land."

"Commander Dupre," the 4th Fleet admiral cut in, "those enemy missiles will be outside of your engagement envelope in less than sixty seconds. POTUS has ordered you to engage them now. They're still trying to decide what to do about the enemy warships and those land targets, but the CNO is pushing the President to order a counterstrike on them. You have your orders, Dupre. Don't let us down."

Nodding, Dupre reached over for the handset. With everyone on the call still watching him, he ordered his TAO to engage the enemy missiles with the targeting data fed to them from CONUS.

The ship shuddered briefly as the magazine of SM-2s took flight after the cruise missiles while a set of SM-3s went after the ballistic missiles.

The NORAD Commander placed the hand receiver down as she returned her gaze to him. "Commander Dupre, POTUS ordered a retaliatory strike against the Chinese ships and those sites on Cuba. Please confirm you received your new orders and execute them immediately."

"I received and confirm attack orders. Will execute immediately." Commander Dupre grabbed for the phone next to him. "TAO, POTUS directed us to attack those ChiCom warships and those launch sites in Cuba. Spin up a targeting solution and package for the task force. I'm on my way to CIC now." He turned back to the monitors. "If you'll excuse me, I need to return to CIC to oversee our counterattack. Admiral, I'll reestablish contact in the CIC."

Dupre shook his head as he left the wardroom. *One of our radar systems is right…I just hope it's theirs, or we're about to start a war with China…*

When Dupre entered the CIC, he saw Lieutenant Price waiting for him.

"Sir, we located the Chinese warships and we received the coordinates for the sites in Cuba. All targets are programmed, and Bulldogs are ready to launch on your command. *Laboon* and *Barry* report their targets are programmed and weapons ready in all respects, sir."

Dupre paused for a moment, thinking about the gravity of what he was about to do. Then he commanded, "Fire!"

He echoed the command to the *Laboon* and the *Barry*. The deck plating shuddered as their missiles left the vertical launchers and streaked into the sky toward their targets. On the monitors in the CIC, he watched each missile as it shot skyward and then arched into its flight track toward four Chinese destroyers and the island of Cuba.

Dupre said, "I'll be on the bridge, Clarissa. Stand by for possible counterattack by the enemy warships."

The sailors stepped aside as he left the CIC.

Lieutenant Clarissa Price followed him into the passageway so the two of them could talk privately for a moment. The fact that he'd called her by her first name seemed to have upset or surprised her.

Price asked, "Sir, if we're at war, what do we do now?" Her question was desperate for a reassuring answer, yet Dupre didn't have one.

Looking at her, he calmly said, "Now, Lieutenant…we fight."

She nodded, then turned to head back into the CIC while he went to the bridge. Dupre reflected on the situation. The task force had fired sixty-five cruise missiles at the Chinese warships and the land-based targets. He had trained for this his entire adult life.

Despite the years of training and having ordered the firing of his weapons at targets in Syria and Iraq, he felt a wave of sadness wash over him. Something about this just didn't make sense. He was about to be responsible for the death of hundreds of Chinese sailors and soldiers. He'd also fired the first shot in what might become the Third World War…

No matter what happened now, history would remember his name and what he had done today. That thought made him sick to his stomach.

25

****

Type 909D Merchant Raider
Mid-Atlantic

"That's it! We received the message. Authenticating now," called out the communications officer excitedly.

"XO, let's open the safe and authenticate," Captain Tsai announced as he went to the small vault on the bridge.

Tsai entered his code and the safe popped open. He reached in and retrieved the only two plastic keycards. Walking over to the communications officer, he placed them on the table. The XO looked at the authentication code from Command and compared it to the two keycards. Once he found the one that matched, he broke it open and pulled out the code and the small metal key that would fire the missiles.

The XO took a few seconds to verify the codes, nodding in satisfaction. "We have a valid launch order," he said, then handed the papers over to the captain for verification.

Tsai looked at the two papers and read them over. A grim look settled on his face as he turned to his weapons officer. "Lieutenant, prepare the missiles to fire."

This single order set into motion a series of actions across the ship. On the bow deck, the double stack of shipping containers pulled apart to reveal the three hundred and fifty vertical launch tubes. While the front of the ship performed its transformer trick and became a full-blown missile ship, the targeting officer fed in the final targeting data from Jade Dragon into the missiles' targeting and flight computers.

The XO's eyes grew wide as he stood behind the targeting officer's shoulder and saw the number of missile groups and targets being downloaded. Given these missiles were going to hit during the wee hours of the morning, it would come as quite a shock once they landed.

Group One: Eight missiles, Naval Submarine Base New London, Connecticut

Group Two: Two missiles, Defense Intelligence Agency facility on Joint Base Anacostia-Bolling, Washington, D.C.

Group Three: Two missiles, Andrews Air Force Base, Maryland

Group Four: Four missiles, NSA Headquarters, Ft. Meade, Maryland

Group Five: Eight missiles, Pentagon, Arlington, Virginia
Group Six: Six missiles, CIA facility, McClean, Virginia
Group Seven: Four missiles, CIA facility, Herndon, Virginia
Group Eight: Eight missiles, National Reconnaissance Office, Chantilly, Virginia
Group Nine: Thirty-two missiles, Langley Air Force Base, Hampton, Virginia
Group Ten: Sixty-eight missiles, Norfolk Naval Facility, Norfolk, Virginia
Group Eleven: Thirty-two missiles, Naval Air Station Oceana, Virginia Beach, Virginia
Group Twelve: Forty missiles, Joint Base Charleston, Charleston, South Carolina
Group Thirteen: Twelve missiles, Hunter Army Airfield, Savannah, Georgia
Group Fourteen: Fifty missiles, Fort Stewart, Hinesville, Georgia
Group Fifteen: Twelve missiles, Naval Submarine Base Kings Bay, St. Marys, Georgia
Group Sixteen: Fifty missiles, Ft. Benning, Columbus, Georgia
Group Seventeen: Twenty missiles, Naval Station Mayport, Jacksonville, Florida
Group Eighteen: Twenty missiles, Blount Island, Jacksonville, Florida

"This is a huge list of targets, Captain. We will kick up one hell of a hornet's nest with this attack," commented the targeting officer.

As the data from Jade Dragon was loaded into the missiles, it designated each one inside the targeting group to hit a specific target. Some missiles were redundant to offset the chance that one or more might get shot down, but each missile had its own unique purpose.

"How many missiles are we firing?" asked Tsai as he observed the progress status on the missiles inch closer to one hundred percent.

The XO looked at the control screen. "A total of two hundred and ninety-two missiles have assigned targets. That will leave us with fifty-eight missiles for follow-up attacks if we are not sunk or captured in the next couple of days." The XO gulped as he realized he shouldn't have said that last part.

Turning to face him, Tsai snapped, "Do not take a defeatist attitude with me or anyone else on this ship, Commander. Is that understood?"

The tension on the bridge was thick. The men anxiously awaited the orders to attack soon, cognizant that they might not live for very long once they launched.

Tsai's XO hung his head low, realizing his mistake.

Softening his tone, Tsai turned to look at his bridge crew. "Listen, we will do our duty to China. Our leaders gave us every tool possible to help us survive the next few days and weeks. But make no mistake, whether we live or die, we will hit the American intelligence and military with a blow so hard it will make Pearl Harbor and September 11th look like a pinprick. Our single attack may very well knock the Americans out of the war before it even has a chance to start. You all should feel pride in being selected to take part in this mission, for it will be talked about in the annals of history for hundreds of years to come." Captain Tsai spoke with real conviction in his voice.

"The missiles are ready, Captain," announced the targeting officer.

Turning to look at the young man, Captain Tsai lifted his chin up a bit as he exclaimed, "Fire!"

The missiles fired every three seconds until all two hundred and ninety-two missiles were gone. While a cloud of missile exhaust consumed the ship, the crew went to work covering the missile launch tubes and repainting the sides of the vessel. Their pilot and navigator found a new cargo ship lane seventy miles to their northeast, and the ship headed toward the new shipping lane at flank speed. If they got lucky, they would be able to tuck themselves into a new shipping lane without anyone being the wiser.

They would then make their way back toward Europe, hopefully undetected until they received their next set of orders for their remaining missiles.

Chapter Three
The Age of AI

February 2017 – Seven Years Earlier
Alibaba AI Division
Shanghai, China

Dan munched on a Tunnock's tea cake and checked his personal email on his phone before he got back to work. He saw a message from the hotel he'd booked last night for his upcoming trip to Macau. He had planned to meet up with some friends for a weekend of drinking and general debauchery. Unfortunately, the email informed him that he could not stay with them. His social credit score had fallen too low.

Seeing that rejection really ticked him off. This was the third hotel to deny him a booking in the last couple of days. He'd gotten lucky finding a plane ticket, but he was striking out hard in getting a room at one of the high-end casinos. His friends in Singapore and Hong Kong were pestering him to know which hotel they should meet him at. He still didn't have an answer for them.

Frustrated by yet another denial, Dan reached for his noise-canceling headphones and put them on. He wanted to shut out the world around him and focus on solving a problem with a line of code some of the senior analysts had been unable to fix for weeks. Sometimes he felt like he was surrounded by idiots. It wasn't that they weren't good programmers. They just didn't seem to have the ability to come up with something novel and unique. You couldn't teach a program how to interpret data and then use that interpretation to perform a specific set of objectives if you couldn't allow your mind to think outside of the box.

An hour into his work, his headphones were suddenly removed, the music he'd been listening to still blaring out of them.

He turned to see who had touched him without his permission. The face of his immediate supervisor, project manager Joseph Chung-Hsin, hovered over him, staring at him angrily.

"Ma Yong, I need to speak with you in my office. Oh, and turn that music off!" He turned on his heel and headed to his office, not waiting to make sure Dan was following him.

Sighing, Dan turned his music off and got up. *What have I done now?* he wondered. *And why can't he call me by my Western name, Dan, or even Dr. Ma? Is it too much to ask of them to call me by the name I want to be called?*

Walking into his supervisor's office, Dan saw there was another person waiting for them. His boss's boss, Zhang Lou.

"Please sit down, Ma," his supervisor told him, and the three of them took a seat at the table in his office.

"Have I done something wrong? Is my work not up to standards?" Dan inquired hesitantly. He had only been at Alibaba's artificial intelligence division for a year, so he was still technically in his probation period.

"Hello, Dr. Ma. It has been a while since you and I last spoke. My name is Zhang Lou, though you may call me Lou if you prefer. I like to be as informal with my staff as possible," the older man offered with a warm and inviting smile.

Dan wasn't sure why the head of the department wanted to speak with him, but it was obvious he had done something wrong or he wouldn't be here.

Lou continued, "As you know, Dan, I am the managing director for this unit. I oversee *all* two thousand employees that work in this unit. Unfortunately, I do not get to spend as much time with each of you as I would like. However, something about you was brought to my attention. I felt it important enough for me to take some time to speak with you privately about it."

Here we go, Dan thought.

Lou then opened a folder he had in front of him before continuing. "Prior to this meeting, I took some time to review your background and examine some of your recent work. I must say, your work is impeccable, and your academic credentials are impressive."

Dan lifted his chin up a bit with pride at the compliment.

Lou continued, "When your family sent you abroad to receive your education, you left Shanghai to attend the University of Oxford's department of computer science, where you graduated with top marks. You then went on to become a distinguished honor graduate in your master's program in the same department."

Lou eyed Dan for a moment before he added, "Your file says you turned down spots in PhD programs at both Oxford and MIT to pursue a PhD at Carnegie Mellon University in machine learning. Why did you make that decision?"

The question caught Dan off guard. No one had asked him that before. It was customary to get your PhD from a different university than your lower-level degrees. He also hadn't told anyone he'd turned down the Oxford and MIT positions.

Dan replied, "It was a hard choice to make at the time. But I felt the artificial intelligence program at Carnegie was a better program. The person who would ultimately become my academic advisor was working on a special program for the American Department of Defense. What he shared with me about machine learning and what the future of AI would look like in ten years fascinated me. I wanted to learn from the best, and by all accounts, he was the best in the field, so I opted to pursue my PhD there, as opposed to MIT or Oxford."

Grunting at the answer, Lou continued, "Your advisors and professors said you were by far one of the most gifted minds in the field of artificial intelligence they had seen. I hope you understand that was a big reason why we specifically recruited you to join our firm and my department. But we are also starting to face a problem with you that needs to be addressed."

Crinkling his brow, Dan said, "A problem? What sort of problem? You said earlier my work is excellent."

Lou waved off his concerns about work with his wrist. "This isn't about your work performance, Dan. You are a gifted and exceptional employee. This is about your social credit score. Would you say you have struggled a bit socially since you have returned to China? You had, after all, been living abroad for nearly ten years. A lot has changed in that time."

Dan tried not to chafe at the mention of his social credit score, which had taken a serious hit in the last four or five months. It was perhaps the most aggravating experience he'd had to deal with since he'd moved back to China—this recent hotel bookings denial being a case in point.

Dan sighed as he commented, "I apologize about my social credit score, Lou. I realize it has taken a hit the last few months. I will admit, I have been having some challenges readjusting to life in China. As you know, I lived in the UK and then the US for the last nine years. Things are obviously different there than they are here. I will try to do better."

Lou appeared to be sympathetic, even if Joseph, Dan's immediate supervisor, was not.

"Dan, the social credit score is becoming increasingly important in China. Right now, there is still some leeway in the system. There will come a time very soon when there will be no leeway. As it stands, your score is so low we cannot send you on a business trip for the company. As a matter of fact, with the new guidelines coming out in the near future, we would probably have to terminate you because you'd become blacklisted," Lou explained calmly.

Lifting an eyebrow at this revelation, Dan immediately countered, "What? I'm sorry, Lou. What exactly have I done that would rise to that level? I'm the most knowledgeable person in the company when it comes to machine learning."

Joseph then looked down at a folder Dan hadn't noticed earlier, explaining in a softer tone than Dan had been expecting, "Dan, in the last ten months, you've received nineteen social infractions. Here are a few things that caused you to become labeled as a 'problem.' Three months ago, you made a reservation at a restaurant and then you failed to keep it."

"Whoa, are you saying I could be blacklisted because I failed to keep a restaurant reservation? I tried to call them to cancel the reservation, but I had a problem with my cell phone," Dan protested defensively.

Joseph nodded in agreement. "Yes, you were also three days late in paying your cell phone bill. They suspended your service until you paid it." He held up a hand to forestall Dan saying anything else as he continued. "Two months ago, you left a derogatory comment on a computer science chat board about something utterly unimportant. Several people reported that comment and it was flagged for review.

"Later that same month, you were captured on a red-light camera in your Tesla, failing to yield to a traffic light. Three days ago, you received a citation for eating on the subway."

Joseph then lowered the paper as he shook his head in disappointment. "These are only a few of the infractions you've received since you started here." He paused for a second, letting some of that information sink in before he continued.

"Dan, none of these infractions is serious on its own. But when you add them all up, they become an issue. They become a pattern of behavior that needs to be addressed. That is why the social credit program was developed. Each infraction negatively affects your standing, until eventually, it flags you in the system. Once you are flagged, your social profile is reviewed. A reviewer then determines if you should be blacklisted until you are able to change your behavior."

Dan sat there dumbfounded. He knew the social credit situation was starting to become a big deal, but he hadn't paid much attention to it. His motto had been work hard and play harder—something he'd learned in America. Apparently, that wasn't acceptable behavior here in China.

At this point, Lou stepped in. "Dan, we are telling you because we want to help you rebuild your social score so we can get you back on the right track." Lou paused for a second before adding, "You are a brilliant man, and I want to have you work on a very special and sensitive machine learning program. But before I can do that, we need to help you break some bad habits you learned in America and rebuild your social score. To that end, I need you to understand this social credit system is serious, and very real. Second, if you understand that it functions like a game, it'll be a lot easier for you to accept it and then find ways to manipulate it to your benefit."

"Manipulate? How so?" asked Dan.

"OK, right now, your score is in the gutter. But there are easy ways for a person like yourself to get out. Unlike most people, you are paid a very healthy salary. If you begin to donate large sums of money to dozens of different charity organizations in Shanghai and around the country, those donations will be reported as positive social contributions. Doing this monthly will immediately boost your score. Second, if you donate blood once a month, it'll be annotated as a positive contribution to society. Third, if you volunteer to assist certain organizations, those also get counted as positive engagements."

"So, you're saying I should start doing some of these things now and work on keeping my nose clean," Dan replied.

Lou and Joseph both nodded.

Lou explained, "We have big plans for you, Dan. I want to get you back on the right track. Here is what we will do to help you. First, you will sit down with the same financial advisor both Joe and I use. He will get your financial house back in order. He'll get your bills all set up on autopay and make sure you never get dinged for something as silly as a late payment.

"Second, we will arrange for you to teach a single class on computers and artificial intelligence at an underprivileged school. This will help you bring your score up as this school will give you a positive report each week. Third, we have identified eight charity organizations you will start providing money to on a monthly basis. This will generate eight additional positive interactions a month in addition to the teaching job.

"If you follow this regimen we are outlining for you, we can get you removed from the "problem child" list within a couple of months. In three to four months, we'll be able to get your score up to an acceptable level. In six months, you'll be in the top tier like us. Then I can get you moved onto this new machine learning collaboration program. Is this something you are willing to do?" Lou asked.

Dan took in a deep breath. He'd honestly had no idea that his social score situation had warranted an actual intervention. The fact that they were this willing to help him, though, made him feel incredibly blessed to be working for Alibaba.

Dan looked the two of them in the eye. "I will. You have my word. I will do my best to stay clean and follow this plan."

Joe and Lou both smiled, pleased that their intervention appeared successful.
****

The BAT Laboratory
Shanghai, China

Standing before the most powerful men in China, Dr. Xi Zemin, the chief scientist for the BAT laboratory and arguably one of the world's leading experts in machine learning, explained, "Mr. President, as an avid chess player, you understand the importance of being able to anticipate your opponent's next move and the five or six moves after that. As Sun Tzu once said, 'Do not engage an enemy more powerful than you. And if it is unavoidable, make sure you engage on your terms, not your enemy's.' I believe we have created a tool that can do just that."

President Yao Jintao narrowed his eyes a bit as he countered, "That is a bold claim, Doctor. Please explain this a bit further."

Xi nodded. "Mr. President, in the private sector, Alibaba, Amazon, Baidu, Netflix, and Google created a software algorithm that can anticipate, almost predict, consumer behavior. This has led to enormous economic growth and profitability in these organizations and within the broader economy. This is the power of machine learning."

Xi continued, "When that technology is coupled with social media platforms, the economic growth and profitability become exponential. *But*, if we pair machine learning with a deep understanding of behavior analytics, we can create a weapon more powerful than any naval ship or stealth fighter our country or adversary can field."

President Yao held a hand up. "Dr. Xi, perhaps you can explain this concept of machine learning you are talking about and how the government of China can leverage it to achieve our global ambitions."

Smiling at the opportunity to expound further, Dr. Xi excitedly explained, "Yes, Mr. President. What we have been doing with machine learning in our social credit program is giving the algorithm access to the electronic data we have been collecting from the users on the system. By creating a series of what we call deep neural networks, which are computer programs that function and operate much like the human brain, we created an algorithm that learns more and more on its own. You see, our algorithm is in the process of learning how to automatically improve its assessments and understanding of human behavior through improved experiences."

Before Dr. Xi could continue, someone from the Ministry of State Security interrupted to ask, "So what you are saying, Doctor, is that the machine you created is moving from the position of receiving and interpreting information to taking that information and making predictive analyses of future behavior based on past user actions."

Xi excitedly nodded. "Essentially, yes. It's kind of like learning how to ride a bicycle, if you will. In theory, a child or adult understands the concept of using their legs to push down on the pedals. They know if you do this, it will spin the wheels and that will in turn propel them forward. But once they sit on the bike and have to put that theory into practice, they now realize the importance of balance—a new concept they had not known, observed, or experienced when they watched other people riding a bicycle.

"You see, this concept of balance was something that could only be learned through experience. In the case of machine learning, we couldn't preprogram certain functions. The algorithm needed to experience them in order to learn from them, much like a person does when they first learn how to ride a bicycle. At first, the person falls a few times. Each fall usually causes them to feel physical pain if they hurt themselves or emotional pain or embarrassment if they are laughed at. Those experiences are then integrated into the brain, which learns not to make those same mistakes as it tries again.

"This is what we call a neuro loop. The brain knows the basic functions, but now it is integrating new experiences into those basic functions, thus expanding them until the individual is able to ride the bike successfully. That is what we have been teaching our algorithm to do with the social credit system. It is absorbing all this information and then learning from it, identifying bad or corrupting behavior within society and then developing a system or process to be applied to the person to change the corrupt behavior into publicly acceptable behavior. This is an example of applied artificial intelligence."

Interrupting him, this time one of the president's advisors commented, "Let me know if I am understanding this correctly. The AI you created is using machine learning to become smarter, thus moving beyond the current tacit or narrow AI currently in use around the world? This is what allows your AI to better understand people and their behavior better, correct?"

Xi nodded. "Yes, that is correct. We built the basic algorithmic code—kind of like having a five- or six-year-old child. Now we need to allow it to learn so it can advance to the next level."

The advisor responded, "You are implying that as your algorithm is fed more data, it will grow and learn. Its ability to observe human behavior will in time allow it to accurately identify ways to change or manipulate that behavior. If *we* provided the algorithm the desired outcome, it could design a series of actions to achieve those outcomes?"

Xi smiled at the advisor. He got it. "That is exactly what I am saying. The social credit system is the first step. What I am proposing we create is so much greater than this. Something that will revolutionize the world and humanity. If I may make another reference to Sun Tzu—he talks about the nine variations or nine contingencies one must plan for. I believe there is a tenth contingency he could not have been aware of during his day and age. That is machine learning and applied artificial intelligence."

General Li Zuocheng, the head of the People's Liberation Army, leaned forward in his chair. "Perhaps you can explain the military applications of this to me. How well could it develop war games against potential adversaries, and why would your AI be any more accurate than our human war planners? I ask not to suggest your AI does not have value, but a machine is not a human. It still does not fully understand human emotion or the irrationality of people."

XI nodded. "That is a valid point, General. What we have done with the social credit program is given our machine a basic framework from which to understand people and human behavior. Let us look at it this way. The AI we want to build needs more than just a brain. It needs a knowledge base. It needs memories. We can create the smartest machine in the world, but if it doesn't have memories of how humans reacted to situations or facts, it will never be able to really learn or anticipate future human behavior and thus how a person or adversary may ultimately respond."

President Yao Jintao said, "This is why the social credit program was so fundamental to your AI project, isn't it?"

Xi nodded but did not say anything right away.

The President continued, "But the social credit program will only take us so far. It will only understand what our people who live in our culture are able to think or how they react to things going on around them. How will you teach your machine to deal with the *West* if the only knowledge base you have to draw upon is our own society?"

A smile crept across Xi's face. "Facebook's founder, Mark Zuckerberg, realized that the real value of his company was its user data. Knowing what their users watched, shared, and commented on allowed them to create incredibly effective marketing products and services they could then sell or allow users to promote and sell their own products across their platform. Mr. Zuckerberg also realized this data would only grow in value as more people joined his platform. Knowing this, he set out on a mission to bring free Wi-Fi to the world.

"Similarly, SpaceX's Elon Musk wants to colonize Mars. However, space exploration is incredibly expensive. One way he's working to solve this cost factor is to develop Starlink, a constellation of satellites that will provide high-speed internet to the world for a price. While his service isn't free, he's picking up where Zuckerberg left off. If we offer up DragonLink to the world for free, we will be able to monitor all the traffic that flows across it. That user information can then be fed directly into our servers, giving our AI even more data from which to learn."

One of the President's advisors commented, "You are talking about an incredibly expensive endeavor, Doctor. Do we even have the technology capable of doing all of this yet?"

"On our end, yes. We have most of what we need. What I need from the government is a large, secured place for us to build this super-AI and then the resources to build the brain for the machine," Xi explained.

No one talked for a moment as all eyes drifted to the President. Ultimately, he would be the one to decide if the government would go all in on this.

President Yao steepled his fingers. "Sun Tzu also said, 'The skillful employer of men will employ the wise man, the brave man, the covetous man, and the stupid man,'" he told Xi. "Which one of these categories you will ultimately fall into, we shall see over time. For the moment, you have convinced me of the value your proposal could bring to China. I will grant you the resources needed to build this machine under one condition. This AI you are creating—it needs to be designed with one and only one intent."

As the President paused, everyone waited with bated breath to hear the condition. "This machine must be built to enable China to dominate and control every aspect of the world. This is not some altruistic project for mankind you will build to solve world hunger or find a cure for cancer."

President Yao continued, "Right now, there are two things standing in the way of China's greatness. The first is us. We are addressing that with our social credit program, to build and condition the type of society that we need to dominate the world. The second is the West, led by the United States. The Americans, in particular, stumble across the world stage like a drunken bully, demanding the world bow down to them. We must use this AI to defeat them, to supplant them as the foremost superpower in the world. You have one year to build the bones of this project. From then on, you and your team will be in a race against the clock to continue delivering results."

Before the President ended the meeting, he asked, "Dr. Xi, what are we calling this project of yours?"

Xi thought about that for a second. "Project Ten, in honor of the tenth contingency, which Sun Tzu would surely have included had he known about this technology."

President Yao replied, "Very well, Dr. Xi. Project Ten has one year. Do not disappoint China…do not disappoint *me*."

With nothing more to be said, the President walked out of the room along with two of his trusted advisors. Xi and his team of researchers from Baidu, Alibaba, and Tencent, the AI superpowers of the world, had been given the green light. Now they would have to deliver.

Chapter Four
Down Under

August – 2018
Sydney, Australia

Professor Hank Iverson, the current director for graduate studies at the computer science department at the University of Oxford, prepared for a week of death by PowerPoint at the latest conference on advancements in AI. He dropped his bags in his room, then went to the hotel lobby, where he spotted a face he hadn't seen in years.

Walking toward the familiar man, he called out, "Dan Ma, is that you?"

The Asian man turned around with a drink in his hand and smiled. "Well, I'll be. It's good to see you, Professor Iverson. I wasn't expecting to run into you," Ma "Dan" Yong replied happily.

"Please, call me Hank. You know, occasionally they let me leave the university," said the professor with a chuckle. "How are you doing, Dan? What have you been up to?" Hank took a seat at the bar next to his former student.

"I'm doing well, Hank. When I graduated from Carnegie in 2014, I went back to Shanghai. Things have been good."

"Ah, that's great, Dan. I was curious where you would ultimately land. Stay in the US, come back to the UK, or go back to China. If you don't mind me asking, why did you decide to go back?" Hank probed before getting the attention of the bartender and ordering a local beer.

"That was actually a tough decision. I was offered a position at Microsoft that I really wanted to take. But my parents are getting up there in age. They still live in Shanghai, and as I'm the only child, I felt it my duty to go back there to help take care of them. They did put me through university, after all."

"Yeah, that makes sense," said Hank.

Dan finished off his bourbon and motioned for another double. Hank took a couple of long drinks from his beer, downing a third of it in one go before putting it down.

"Hey, easy there, old man," Dan joked as he sipped on his double bourbon.

Hank laughed at the comment. He placed an order for a club sandwich before continuing, "Where are you working these days? Are you still pursuing machine learning, or did you go on to something new?"

The bartender brought Dan his own lunch, ratatouille, which was apparently a specialty at the Sofitel.

"I took a job with Alibaba. They have a big AI department. You know, looking at consumer behavior and then figuring out how to get the right product in front of the right person. That kind of work." Dan took his first bite of the French peasant dish and smiled like someone remembering their grandmother's cooking.

The two ate for a few minutes, not saying very much, before Dan commented, "You know, I almost didn't make it to this conference, but I'm glad I did, or I wouldn't have run into you."

"Oh, Alibaba keeping you too busy to come to these conferences and stay abreast of the changes in the field?" asked Hank between bites of his sandwich.

Snickering at the comment, Dan answered, "Ha, I wish. No, I bought a new Tesla a few months back and I have a bit of a heavy foot. Without even realizing it, I ended up racking up half a dozen speeding tickets in a week. It dragged my social credit score dangerously low, to the point where I almost couldn't come on this trip."

Hank did a double take at his former student. "Are you serious?" he asked skeptically. "They almost didn't let you come to a conference because you got a few speeding tickets—that seems a bit heavy-handed, don't you think?"

Dan called out to the bartender to give him another double before downing the glass. "It's been a bit of an adjustment these last few years. It's the strangest thing, Hank. Freaking *Skynet* literally sees and monitors everything you do in Shanghai, from your interactions online, to whether you pay your bills on time, to whether you speed or get a citation from the police for jaywalking. If Alibaba wasn't paying me what they are, I doubt I'd stick around. I'd probably go work for Amazon or something."

"Wow, that's…interesting," Hank replied. "I've heard about the surveillance state in China. I figured it must be similar to what we have in London. But it sounds like yours is a bit more intrusive."

Dan shrugged. "It's a big game. Once you accept it as the new normal, you learn to play within its rules."

"Yeah, I suppose. Do you guys really call it *Skynet*?" Hank asked in reference to the *Terminator* movies the Americans seemed to love so much.

Dan laughed. "No, they don't call it that. I call it that. It reminds me of that book you told me about, that one written by that guy George Orwell, *1984*. Did you know that book is banned in China? I have a secret copy I brought with me, but you aren't allowed to buy or sell it in China."

Hank countered, "Well, you wouldn't want the everyday citizens to read a book like that. They might get angry and question the government."

Dan laughed again, now clearly feeling the effects of three double bourbons. "Hank, no one questions the government. This new program I'm working on, it's incredible. When we're done with it, the things we'll be able to do with it will blow your mind away. It will change the world."

It took him a few minutes, but Hank remembered Dan had been a bit of a party guy at Oxford. Hank noticed that about nearly all his students from China. They were exceptional students, but they liked to drink and party when they weren't under the watchful eye of the state. Hank figured it was their way of letting loose.

Before Hank could inquire any further, Dan finished his food and left some money on the bar to cover both of their meals. "I'll catch you at the conference tomorrow, Hank. It was good catching up, but I've got to get some rest if I want to go party it up tonight and still be functional for tomorrow."

Hank nodded and took a bite of his sandwich while Dan headed off to his room.

****

Next Morning
Sofitel Conference Room B

Hank sat in the rear third of the room, listening to a lecture on machine learning and human-computer interaction, when Dan sat down in the chair next to him, his hair still wet from a shower or the pool.

"Morning, Dan. Did you have a fun time last night?" he asked softly, trying not to interrupt the others who were listening to the speech.

Dan looked a little tired but alert. Snorting at the question, he replied, "You know, I was so damn tired I ended up sleeping through the night. I woke up half an hour ago."

"They must be working you hard, then," Hank replied softly.

Dan shrugged. He pulled a Tunnock's tea cake out of his bag and nibbled at it.

"You still hooked on those things?" Hank asked.

"Everyone's got to have that thing that helps get them in the right working mode. I just happened to have found mine at Oxford," Dan explained.

The lecture continued for another thirty minutes. The speaker was going on about the advancements in machines learning from humans and how the two were interacting with each other in laboratory environments.

Dan leaned over. "This guy's information is so dated. We're light-years ahead of what he's talking about."

Lifting an eyebrow, Hank countered, "Dan, can we skip this afternoon's lectures and you and I go out and have some fun? I'm getting burnt out working on this research project at Oxford, and frankly, I would love to bounce some ideas off you."

After thinking about it for a moment, Dan nodded. The two of them got up and headed for the lobby. They flagged down a cab and climbed in.

"Where to?" asked the driver.

"Royal Botanic Gardens," Hank replied.

"A park? Sounds like you had this all planned out, Hank," Dan said hesitantly.

"Remember at Christ Church, when you used to ask me about the future of artificial intelligence? How can we know if it will be used for good and not for nefarious purposes? We would stroll along Meadow Walk toward the boat clubs along the Thames," Hank reminisced.

Dan smiled at the memory from long ago, then nodded.

"When I have a tough problem I need to figure out, I like to surround myself with nature. Sometimes the peacefulness of it all ends up bringing clarity to the chaos of the problem," Hank explained.

It took them a few minutes of fighting traffic to get to the park. When they arrived, the two of them began meandering through the trails.

Dan finally asked, "So, what's your tough problem you wanted my advice on, Hank?"

"I'm working on a new AI project with the Metropolitan Police, but I'm not sure I should be," the professor explained.

"OK, so what are they doing that you seem to have a problem with?" inquired Dan.

"The Met, as you know, have hundreds of thousands of surveillance cameras all over London," Hank said, and Dan nodded in acknowledgment. "Over the years, they've improved their skills at taking the image of, say, a burglar or other criminal and then plugging their face into the system. Using an algorithm we helped create, they're letting the facial recognition software monitor all the cameras across the city until one of them finds a match. Once the suspect is found, a nearby police officer receives a text message with the person's face and location. It's effective at combating crime."

"Sounds like they're doing a good job. So, what's the dilemma on your part?" asked Dan, not sure where this was going.

"You work at Alibaba, so you're using your AI to better understand consumer behavior. Like what a consumer is looking for, what are they buying—if they buy x, then they are more likely to also buy y and z, so you can build a microtargeted ad to get a product in front of them. Right?" Hank inquired.

Dan nodded. "Yes. We learned a lot of this from how Amazon built their system. For instance, when Google AdSense first came out, Amazon was the largest consumer of keyword marketing. Eventually, once Amazon had built a large enough platform, they were able to start doing that themselves. At Alibaba, we replicated that system. I suppose the only real difference between our two companies is we have access to a much larger demographic of users and consumers given China's population."

Hank explained, "The Met want my help in creating a predictive behavior analysis program. They want me to build a program that will allow them to identify people who may be *about* to commit a crime. This way they can move officers to intercede or be there when it happens. One, I'm not sure it's totally possible to create something like that, and two, I'm not sure we want to create a society where we have AIs anticipating our actions before we take them."

Dan contemplated Hank's dilemma as he made his way over to the Botanical House to buy something warm to drink. Australia was in the midst of its winter season, even if it was a sunny day.

When the two of them had their coffees in hand, they continued their walk, further away from people. Dan finally replied, "I think that is unfortunately the direction AI is heading, Hank. Even in China, with our social credit program, it's almost like that already. The government monitors everything we do, and we're graded on how we handle things, positively or negatively. If we handle them negatively, then we lose points, like any other scoring system."

Hank responded, "But we're talking about something much bigger, much more dangerous than a social credit system, Dan. We're talking about predictive behavior analysis. An AI that can predict with fairly good accuracy what someone will do and then have the government intervene."

Sighing, Dan replied, "I get what you're talking about, Hank. But you're thinking too small about how this technology can and will be used. You're looking at predictive behavior on an individual level. Imagine that kind of capability on the national level. A government with a tool that can predict the impact of their decisions before they make them. Look at it this way—most countries will only push something, anything, so far before they stop. Like the South China Sea. My country will only push things so far because they're unsure how the Americans will respond. But what if we could create an AI that could tell us with a certain degree of accuracy how the Americans would respond to certain actions? How emboldened would that make a country if they had that kind of crystal ball?"

Whistling softly, Hank countered, "That'd change the world, that's for sure. I think we're still a long way from being able to do that. You'd need to have a quantum computer just to be able to crunch that kind of data. I mean, the volume of data required to develop and then run the various modeling simulations would be zettabytes."

Dan smiled briefly. "When Project Ten—um, when something like that comes online...I mean, when a quantum computer is available and they can create something like this, it'll change the world."

Hank looked at Dan quizzically. "What do you mean by Project Ten? You guys working on something new and cool like that at Alibaba?"

Dan blushed, realizing his slip. "I—it's nothing. I'm not supposed to talk about certain projects. Corporate espionage and all. You know how it is. First to market is everything in the tech world."

Hank tried to set Dan at ease by changing the subject. "Yeah, I get it. Hey, so enough work. I think you helped me understand what I need to do with this project. You're right—it is coming. What we need to focus on is creating rules and policies for how it's used. Take away the fear of the unknown and then figure out how we can use it for the good of humanity. So, tell me about your parents. How are they doing, and when will I get a chance to meet such wonderful people?"

Dan's posture relaxed as he responded, "They're doing great. As to meeting them, let me know next time when you're in Shanghai and I'll organize a family dinner at my place. I decided to make life easy on my parents and got a flat in the city. They have their own room, with a separate living room, and I have my own half of the place. It's really nice. You'd love the view."

Hank smiled happily as he responded, "That sounds great, Dan. I have some vacation time I want to take around the holiday period. Maybe I can spend a few days in Shanghai. I always wanted to see the city. I'd also like to see Hong Kong and Macau while I'm at it."

Dan got excited. "Oh man, if you're going to Macau, count me in. I'll check my own schedule. Maybe I can get them to let me take a week off and show you around. It's easier to navigate China when you have a tour guide and translator." The two of them continued their stroll through the park and then headed toward the iconic Sydney Opera House.
****

Later that evening, Hank logged back in to his special email and typed up the following message:
> Source confirmed existence of Project Ten.
> Project Ten sounds like it's either active or near completion.
> Rapport has been fully established. Source has invited me to stay with him in Shanghai. Will spend a week with me touring Shanghai, Hong Kong, and Macau in December.

The rest of the conference was enlightening professionally, but that wasn't Hank's reason for being there. MI-6 had carefully choreographed his chance encounter with Ma Yong to acquire this very information.

Chapter Five
Belt and Road Initiative: Phase One

October 2018
Caracas, Venezuela

"Mr. President, with this agreement finalized, we can accelerate the construction at the port and begin the infrastructure modernization program," Foreign Minister Han Jinping declared as the two men shook hands.

It was a beautiful September morning as President Javier Moros smiled while photographers snapped photos of the two men shaking hands. The agreement they had signed was lucrative as well as historic for both nations.

When the photographers finished, Javier motioned for them to go to his office, where they could talk privately. Minister of Foreign Affairs Andrea Rodríguez and Minister of Defense and General-in-Chief Adán Chávez stood near President Moros's office door, waiting for them. They both had broad smiles on their faces. The two of them had worked hard on this enormous trade and military aid deal for years.

The four of them walked into the presidential office and then to a private study that connected to it. Once inside, General Chávez proceeded to pour everyone a glass of champagne to celebrate.

"Now, if the Americans don't interfere in the implementation of this agreement, we might finally be able to turn Venezuela into the economic powerhouse of South America we ought to be," Foreign Minister Rodríguez said. She was not a fan of America, angered by their continual attempts to keep her country under their thumb.

Minister Han smiled at the comment. "We have the Americans tied up in a trade war with us as they negotiate a new trade deal. I am confident that our activities with them, along with the trouble we can have North Korea and that belligerent Iranian ayatollah stir up, will keep them sufficiently distracted from our trade deal."

President Moros raised his glass of bubbly to that.

Minister Han proudly announced, "Over the coming weeks, ten thousand guest workers will begin work on the infrastructure projects so we can get your oil and mining operations back up to optimal levels again. Building that new highway and rail line connecting Ciudad

Bolívar and the new port facility being built at Maiquetía alone will increase trade and commerce by hundreds of millions of dollars. The new highway and rail line connecting Maiquetía and the oil refineries at Puerto La Cruz will be crucial to restarting your energy sector."

Minister Rodríguez raised an eyebrow at how fast the Chinese were apparently moving. "You still plan on employing the tens of thousands of Venezuelans in these projects as well?" she pressed.

Han smiled at her. "Of course. We are bringing in specialists, engineers and skilled labor that will fill in any gaps in your own workforce. Beijing is particularly interested in getting the refineries up to one hundred percent as soon as possible. We want to increase the daily production of oil from the 2.3 million barrels per day to six million if possible."

President Moros countered, "As long as China will continue to guarantee a price of fifty USD per barrel, we will increase daily oil production as high as Beijing would like."

With oil costing twenty-seven USD per barrel to produce, this trade agreement with China would net Venezuela one hundred and thirty million dollars per day. This amounted to a hundred-and-nine-billion-dollar oil trade deal, an increase in GDP of nearly a hundred percent. Once the new Coltan mines started producing, that would add another seven to ten percent to their GDP.

"Beijing will buy as much oil as your country is willing to produce. Anything that lets us avoid having to deal with the Middle East is a welcomed addition," commented the Chinese Foreign Minister.

"When will your people begin construction on the airports?" asked General Chávez, eager to start the modernization of the military.

"In a couple of days, General," Minister Han explained as he sipped on his champagne. "We have engineers and specialists that will arrive at the Tomás de Heres Airport to begin expanding it and building it up. Once that's completed, they'll begin getting the mine area cleared and everything ready for the miners to start work; they are scheduled to start later in the month."

"The jobs these new projects create will really help our economy," President Moros commented. "But how will we hide your military activities from the Americans?"

"We'll keep them distracted elsewhere," Han replied with a flick of his wrist. "Besides, we are not building any Chinese bases. We are merely providing your military with foreign military aid to purchase Chinese-made equipment instead of that Russian garbage. It only makes sense that we would provide military trainers to teach you how to operate the equipment you are buying. To do all of that, we'll of course need to help you rebuild some existing military bases or maybe even build a few new ones."

"I like this plan," General Chávez announced. "What bases do you want to build first, and where are you suggesting we place them?"

"I will leave that up to General Yu Zhongfu. He arrives tomorrow along with fifty other military advisors. They will tour the country and start making their assessments on where these new facilities should be built. Once they have that figured out, we will bring more workers in to start construction on the projects."

Foreign Minister Rodríguez asked, "How many Chinese workers are you intending to bring to Venezuela to help with all these projects?"

The others looked at Han to see what he would say next.

"Fifteen thousand the first month. Then another eighty thousand over the next six months."

"Whoa, that's a lot of people. Aren't most of these jobs from all the projects supposed to go to our own workers?" asked Minister Rodríguez.

"They are, and they will, Minister. But you have to understand—there is an incredible amount of work that needs to be done and not a lot of time to do it in. We cannot wait three years for your refineries to be rebuilt or get back up to one hundred percent. We need them running now, so we will send specialists to help make sure the work gets completed. Same with the highways, rail lines, ports, airports, and military bases. If we use only your people to accomplish this, it may take years to finish it. Our people know how to build things quickly. This is important because, once the Americans do figure out what's going on, they may cause problems. We want these projects completed before they can place any further hurdles in our way."

The group talked a bit longer about some of the finer points. It was starting to dawn on the Venezuelans that a lot of Chinese nationals would soon be living in Venezuela. So long as the money continued to flow and the jobs were created, though, none of the Venezuelan officials really cared.

Chapter Six
Space Junk

OneSpace Research and Development Center
Beijing, China

Dr. Xi Zemin looked at a computer monitor showing the latest deployment of the DragonLink satellites. They now had more than one hundred and forty satellites blanketing China and its territorial waters.

Shu Chang, the CEO of OneSpace, proudly announced, "We have officially brought secured and reliable internet to every square meter of China."

Smiling at the announcement, Xi commented, "That you have. When will you be able to move to phase two?"

"We should have phase two completed by 2019. The Pacific, Caribbean, South America, and India will then have steady, free, and reliable internet themselves," the CEO said excitedly.

Xi smiled inwardly, knowing that the data riding across the DragonLink internet would be fed directly into his project. Their AI would continue to grow in knowledge and power, until one day it would be able to govern not only China but the world. He felt like the child he had been waiting for had been born.

****

Three Months Later
The Mountain
Northwest Beijing, China

It might have been a hot and muggy July, but deep under the mountain, the workers building the world's most powerful AI supercomputer wore long-sleeved shirts or sweaters to ward off the chill.

"Dr. Xi, we have the new dynamic cooling gel tubs in place. We are ready to bring the next server online," one of the technicians announced.

Looking at the giant vat of clearish gel, Xi marveled at this newest cooling system. The gel was a little thicker than water, but it had the ability to dissipate heat and stay cool substantially longer.

"OK, bring the next server online. Run through the diagnostics and let's see how it works," one of the project managers ordered.

Xi walked back into the command center of the facility, where he spotted one of his most gifted AI programmers chewing on a pen.

"Dan, is everything running as it should?" asked Dr. Xi, walking over to him.

Ma "Dan" Yong was his AI programmer from Alibaba. Dan was young, only twenty-nine, but by far the most gifted programmer Xi had ever met. His only shortcoming was his failure to adapt to the social credit program. He had a propensity for losing points—so much so that Xi had had to work behind the scenes to put a special label on him to exempt him from it. The previous interventions had only seemed to stick for so long.

Not taking the pen out of his mouth as he chewed away, Dan replied, "I think so. This new server farm should give me the added bandwidth I need for now. We still need those other servers before we integrate more data feeds. Skynet is learning at such an exponential rate right now, we need to be prepared to keep up."

*Skynet...*Xi chuckled to himself at the mention of the pop culture reference. They *were* building Skynet, he conceded. Xi and his young protégé weren't idiots, though. They'd built in a series of backdoors and safety protocols to make sure the damn Skynet never decided it didn't need them.

"How is the transaction manager holding up? Is it still able to return a decision in a timely manner?" asked Xi.

Dan turned to look at him. "It's nearing its capacity, that's for sure. I recommend shutting down some of the larger learning subroutines. They chew through processing speed and really slow the transaction manager down."

Xi chewed on his lower lip for a second, thinking. *This might be a problem down the road if we are already running out of processing speed...*

Xi inquired, "Dan, what languages does Skynet know at this point?"

Now it was Dan's turn to chuckle at the Skynet reference. "Obviously our own. I've successfully taught it Russian, Korean, Japanese, and all the other major Asian languages already. Next, I'm teaching it English, Spanish, then the other European languages. But it will take some time for the AI to really understand the nuances of those languages in comparison to our own."

Xi knew he was right. It would take years of learning for the AI to fully understand the subtleties of communication in all of these languages. It was important for their AI to learn, though.

Xi sighed out loud. He realized they needed more servers and an improved transaction manager. The damn things weren't cheap, nor easy to build. The cooling system to run a computer like this required innovation. Heck, they were already running the entire AI on a nuclear reactor that had been built into the bowels of a mountain.

"How much can the machine understand of what's going on in China right now?" Xi asked as a follow-up.

With a smile, Dan turned to look at him. "It understands everything that is happening in China, Taiwan, South Korea, Russia and Japan. With this new server farm, we can now add Central and South America to that mix. But if you want the US and the EU, then we need that other server built—that, or we ditch Central and South America and not worry about them."

Ditching every country other than America was Xi's plan. They didn't need to know what was going on in all these other countries. Sure, it was a nice benchmark to teach the AI from, but they would need years' worth of data from the US and the other NATO countries to be ready to move to the next level with their grand plan.

Looking down at Dan, Xi replied, "Do the best you can with the resources we have. I have another update meeting with the President and the CMC in a week—you know, the Central Military Committee? I'll be putting together another funding request to get that next server operational."

Dan nodded in approval. Before Xi could leave, Dan asked, "Dr. Xi, are you still interested in that speaking opportunity in England? I'm traveling back to Oxford for my reunion in a month. I could still arrange for you to speak at the Union. It's a prestigious opportunity."

From time to time, Xi gave a speech or lecture about machine learning and tried to press for more people to study this field of science. These speeches gave him access to some of the best minds in the field, which he used periodically to solve a problem he and his team could not. These fellow academics had no idea they were helping to build the world's largest, most powerful super-AI.

"I think that would be great. Let me know if they are open to it and I'll make the time."

Chapter Seven
Big Data

January 2019
Going Social
Mountain View, California

"As you can see, these various personality games on Facebook generate a substantial amount of user data. Using our proprietary software, we compile that data to create tailor-made marketing campaigns to push your products or services based on the social profiles of the users that played the personality game and their contacts," explained Adrian Lewis, the marketing engineer for Going Social.

Mark Gentry, the US marketing executive for Tencent, asked, "As you know, we're involved in the film *Terminator: Dark Fate*, which comes out in November. How can we leverage your firm to engineer a marketing campaign that will deliver our video trailer of the film to the right audience, and not some random person that took one of your personality quizzes on Facebook?"

"That's a good question, Mark. We've spent years testing our proprietary software on that very thing. These personality games we run allow us to build an initial profile of the user. When someone agrees to play the game, they also grant us access to their social media feeds and their contact lists. We then use all that information to view and monitor how the user interacts with stories shared by their friends, family, and other marketing ads directed at them. Depending on how they respond, their profile is further refined."

Mark shook his head and smiled at what he was being told. "How are you able to do all of this without it being a privacy issue?"

Adrian smiled as he replied, "It's in the disclaimer of the game. It's not our fault users don't read it."

Intrigued, Mark continued his inquiry. "OK, so what you're telling me is you can develop a detailed profile of a user who will like our movie. So if we throw you more work, you'll be able to market anything else, or are there limits to your sphere of influence?"

Adrian confidently replied, "Mark, we are a full-service marketing data company. You tell us the demographic you want to reach, and we'll provide you the data on them. From there, it comes down to how good your ad copy is, and the image or video you're using."

With nothing more to say, Mark stood up and extended his hand. "Adrian, this has been most helpful. I need to brief this back to some folks at corporate. We'll be in touch. I think this will be the beginning of a very fruitful relationship."

As soon as he walked out the door to the building, Mark sent a text to his coworker.

Meeting's done, they're perfect.

Checking his digital calendar, Mark saw he had fifty-two minutes until his meeting at Facebook. Plenty of time left to grab a coffee and an Uber.

****

Chinese Consulate
San Francisco, California

Consul Wong Chu had just finished his speech at Stanford and was on his way back to the consulate. It was only a fifty-two-minute drive, assuming they didn't hit any major traffic snarls along the way.

"That was a good speech you gave on the digital Silk Road initiative," his assistant commented.

Wong's lower lip stiffened. She was paid to agree with him—he was more interested in what the media would have to say.

"The future of the world economy is digital: the sharing of ideas, services, and information. It all has to flow through a network. If the Americans bar China from being a part of the American 5G transformation, then we will make sure *we* are the world's leader in access to the internet outside of America," Wong replied, reiterating parts of his speech.

They drove on in silence for most of the way back. Then Wong's head of security broke the silence. "Consul Wong, there's a demonstration taking place around the consulate. It doesn't appear it will be a problem, but if you prefer, we can go directly to your home."

Wong acknowledged the information with a nod. "The consulate," he said, then went back to working on his next speech, which was scheduled for tonight at a dinner in Chinatown.

This trade war between China and the US had escalated tensions between the two countries. The outright ban of the use or sale of Huawei and ZTE products in the US, however, had caused serious problems. It didn't help that a couple of anti-Chinese zealots were in the American Senate, leading the charge against them.

When the armored Mercedes-Benz pulled up on Laguna Street, they could see the gaggle of protesters. His security guard was right—it didn't look any larger than usual, but it did look a bit rowdier. There was definitely a more anti-Chinese bent to the protest than previous such events. Signs read: *Free Tibet. Free Falun Gong. End Censorship.*

As their vehicle got closer, local police moved forward to create a safe corridor for them to travel through. Angry voices shouted at them while some threw produce at the windows of the car. Eventually, they made it through the perimeter of the consulate and into the secured compound.

When Consul Wong exited the vehicle, the silence of his sanctuary was broken as the chanting and shouting filled the air. Things between the US and China had been heating up for some time. Wong knew that unless something changed, the situation was likely to continue to deteriorate. America would need to accept that China was now an equal, not some developing nation.

Chapter Eight
Sun Tzu – Art of War

November 2019
Chinese Embassy
Havana, Cuba

Ambassador Wang Jiechi looked at the request from the Cuban government and then at General Song Fu. "What do you think? Will this still work, or will Beijing be displeased?"

"I think it was a long shot getting the Cubans to let us establish long-term military bases in their territory," General Song replied. "However, they have agreed to our proposal to station military trainers and advisors here. That may actually prove to be a better approach."

Wang lifted an eyebrow at the admission. "Why the change of heart, General Song?"

The general nodded in humble acknowledgement. "Call it accepting the political realities of the situation. When I first arrived in Cuba a few months ago, I made the false assumption that I knew how things worked here. I have come to learn that the political realities of the relationship between Cuba and the US are a lot trickier than I first thought. I think the Secretary's approach to allowing us to ramp up foreign military sales and include advisors and trainers in the deal is a great way to work around what would otherwise be an untenable situation."

Ambassador Wang stifled a laugh. General Song had shown up at his embassy months ago, full of scorn and skepticism about what his staff had accomplished up to that point. The general had had no idea how delicate the situation was.

"General, I hope you and your staff will now have a better appreciation of what we've been working toward here in Cuba," Wang admonished. Song lowered his head. "You can't approach Cuba the same way you've been approaching Venezuela. If I'm not mistaken, in a few months, the first crop of Cuban pilots will be returning from China. Do you have an ETA on when the new air base and training facility on Isla de la Juventud will be completed and ready to receive their new aircraft?"

General Song sat a little straighter and seemed to brush off the ambassador's initial criticism. "It's coming along," he explained. "We had to finish the port facility on the island so we could bring in the materials needed to build the airfield. In a few months, the Cubans will have relocated the population living on the island, which will reduce any unwanted attention on what we're doing."

"What about the cobalt mine?" Wang asked.

"It's operational," Song replied. "We started mining efforts last week. Right now, we're employing two thousand locals. As the mine increases its capacity, that number will jump to five thousand. We're working on establishing a ferry system to take the workers from their homes to the island and back."

Wang nodded in approval. He wished he had an economic advisor handling this aspect of the operation rather than a PLA general, but he had to work with what he had. Despite the diplomatic shortcomings of his staff, his embassy had progressed at integrating Cuba into the Belt and Road Initiative.

"General, once the population has been relocated, how long until you can turn the towns and villages into the military training bases you spoke about?" Wang asked.

The Chinese planned to turn the soon-to-be-abandoned city and villages into urban warfare training facilities. They intended to modernize and train the Cuban Army and then allow the Venezuelans to use the facilities as well. The PLA would then start sending their own soldiers through the program.

"Not long, Ambassador. As soon as they're cleared, we will begin a rapid retraining and rebuilding of the Cuban Army," Song said. "They recently received the new small-arms weapons—now it's a matter of getting them trained on their proper use. They were using incredibly old and antiquated Russian equipment that needed replacing decades ago."

"What about the rest of the equipment? How soon until we start delivering the air defense weapons?" the ambassador probed.

General Song proceeded to pull a notebook out of his breast pocket. He paged through it before he responded, "We have two thousand Cuban soldiers in China right now learning how to operate, maintain, and service the HQ-9 Red Banner systems—it's a complicated four-month training program that includes teaching them how to service the equipment and use it in a variety of environments. You have to keep in mind, Ambassador, these soldiers have previously been using outdated Russian surface-to-air systems. A lot has changed over the years. These soldiers are—how do you put it…? Not the sharpest tools in the shed.

That said, we should start delivering the first two battalions in the next couple of months."

The ambassador nodded in approval. "This is good, General. Your people have done a good job training the Cuban military should it ever come down to it. I do have one question about the aircraft. Do you really think they need or will be able to maintain this many of them?"

General Song, in a not-so-subtle rebuke, countered, "Ambassador, arming the Cubans and making sure they're a legitimate, viable military partner is my job. Your job is to make sure their economy can support and sustain it. Perhaps we should both stick to our lanes."

Wang snorted at the response to his question. "Do you honestly believe the Cubans need four squadrons of J-11s and five squadrons of J-10s?" he asked with a sarcastic smile. "We're talking about a lot of aircraft for a country that isn't involved in any military operations beyond their own borders."

"Ambassador Wang, if China cannot have overseas bases to protect our economic interests in the Caribbean and South America, then we need to build up allies who can. You know that as well as I do. My job is to get Cuba, Venezuela, and El Salvador ready to fight the Americans if need be, and to protect our economic interests in the region. If you do your job on the political front, then my military job will not be needed. Now, if you have no further questions, I need to prepare to meet my counterparts in the Cuban military."

Ambassador Wang dismissed General Song. The rivalries between the PLA and the Ministry of State Security ran long and deep. The two organizations, while loathing each other, were also very dependent on each other. Still, Wang didn't like having to work with General Song. The man was abrasive and believed all of life's problems could be solved with a gun. He failed to understand that military power was not what won wars or kept nations in line. It was money and the economy. Destroy a nation's economy, and you destroyed their ability to wage war.

When the general left his office, Wang opened a safe next to his desk and pulled out a highly classified file, which had been personally carried to him directly from Beijing earlier this morning. He unsealed the document and opened it up:

Operation Chengdu – The strategy to take over the West

Great, another gaming strategy from that damn AI...

Wang had serious reservations about Beijing's reliance on this new super-AI computer his bosses had been going on and on about. The technologists taking over the government were convinced that artificial intelligence and machine learning were how China would surpass the rest of the world and supplant the US as the dominant superpower. From Wang's perspective, no machine could fully understand human behavior, let alone the Americans.

Regardless of his opinions, he buried his head in the file and studied it intently for the next thirty minutes, until Wang's aide stuck his head into the room. "Excuse me, Ambassador. The Foreign Minister is trying to reach you on the secured videophone."

Wang stood up and went to the classified conference room. He hadn't been expecting a call from the minister. This must be important for him to reach out directly.

Wang sat in the chair directly in front of the videophone.

"Ah, there you are, Ambassador Wang," said Foreign Minister Han Jinping. "I am sorry to reach out to you unannounced, but I felt it was best if I told you this face-to-face, such as it is with technology."

Wang didn't say anything right away. He wanted to hear what was so important the Foreign Minister was speaking to him at such an ungodly hour back in Beijing.

"Wang, as you know, the CMC has been relying more and more on Jade Dragon to assist them in long-term planning. The computer has devised a plan that the President believes is both viable and something we should pursue. This morning, you should have received a classified pouch from my office. I hope you had time to briefly review what we are calling Operation Chengdu?"

Wang nodded. "I have just started looking it over. Is this something the CMC is really considering?"

There was a short pause before the Foreign Minister spoke. "Look, Wang. You and I have known each other for years. I have cautioned the President about moving forward with this plan. However, Jade Dragon has been right on so many other occasions. The generals and other members of the CMC believe the plan has a real chance of success. We may not like this plan or agree with it, but we need to do our duties and execute it."

Wang shook his head in frustration. "I have a hard time believing that the CMC and the rest of us are taking our orders from some super-

AI. I know it's proven to be correct on many occasions, but we're talking about instigating a war, not to mention a full-blown collapse of the global economy."

"Wang, the computer has correctly predicted what countries we should invest in to secure oil and minerals for our growing economy. It predicted exactly what the Americans would do in Syria, Yemen, and more recently, Iran. Right now, it's saying that if Operation Chengdu succeeds, the American economy will collapse, throwing the country into chaos. It's during that chaos that we will be able to establish a permanent military presence in the Caribbean and South America. I need you to work with General Song on expediting things in Cuba. We need a strong Cuba to carry out our other goals in South America."

With nothing more to be said, the call ended. Wang had his new marching orders, whether he liked them or not. At least the timeline for this operation was still a year out. A lot could happen in that time frame, and maybe, just maybe, the AI would determine that this was not the best course of action to pursue.

Chapter Nine
Foreign Aid

Three Years Later
December 2022
Camp Tzu
Havana, Cuba

"Aren't they beautiful?" General Song commented to his Cuban counterpart, General de División Miguel Gómez.

The mechanical creaking and cracking of tracked vehicles continued to rumble past them. The Chinese soldiers standing in the turret rendered a sharp salute to the two generals, observing them as they entered the revitalized military base.

The younger general chomped down on his cigar and nodded. "I'll admit, General Song, I was skeptical about whether you Chinese would come through for us. It has been a long time since a world power sought to really help the people of Cuba. But true to your word, you are helping us modernize our military and economy. Heck, my little brother is working on one of those new offshore rigs your country helped us build."

Normally, General Song might have been offended by that comment, but he knew the Russians had reneged on their commitments to the Cubans over the years. With the fall of the Soviet Union, the Cubans had become isolated as they'd stood up to the Americans.

General Song liked General Gómez. He was starting to feel like a little brother. The Cuban officer had introduced Song to his family and extended family and included him in many of their family affairs and gatherings. The two had developed a good working relationship, and Song used and exploited their friendship for the greater good of China.

"The ZBD-04 is an exceptional infantry fighting vehicle for your army. It's perfectly suited for Cuba's climate and terrain. Unlike the Russian BMP-3s, this vehicle is a true tank killer. Aside from the 100mm cannon, it also carries four HJ-8H antitank guided missiles. These missiles are top-of-the-line, capable of hitting ground targets as far away as six kilometers and slow, low-flying helicopters as far as four kilometers. There isn't a tank out there it will not penetrate, including the American Abrams. When you add in the seven soldiers it can carry inside, you have a beast of a machine," General Song explained with pride as the battalion of vehicles continued to drive onto the base.

They had arrived a few days ago in the nearby Port of Havana. The battalion was being driven through the streets of Havana by the Cuban and Chinese militaries to show their new toys off to the public, as well as celebrate their newfound friendship with the people of China.

"Here come the vehicles I'm really excited about," commented General Gómez.

General Song replied with a lifted eyebrow, "The ZSL-08 is your favorite? It's a regular armored personnel carrier."

"General Song, this is Cuba," Gómez replied with a laugh. "The biggest threat to our survival is the people around us. An armored personnel carrier with a remote-controlled gun turret is more than enough to handle that threat."

Song reached for a lighter and relit his cigar. "You aren't the least bit worried about the Americans?"

Gómez puffed away on his cigar for a moment as he watched the next battalion's worth of vehicles roll into his base, then turned to look at his Chinese counterpart. "Why would we have anything to fear from the Americans? They have bigger things to worry about than us."

"You aren't concerned that they will want to take away your newfound wealth or economic security?" Song asked.

"If I am honest, Song, what I am more concerned with is you. Not you in particular, General, but China. We Cubans have been marginalized and isolated by the Americans since the 1960s. We are used to it. The bigger question is how will your government respond to the Americans when they demand you cut economic ties with us or lose access to the American markets? That has always been the threat the Americans level at any country that attempts to do business with Cuba. So, no, I am not worried about what the Yankees may or may not do to Cuba. I am more concerned about China abandoning us in the face of American economic threats."

General Song puffed on his cigar a couple of times as he thought about that. Gómez had a good point. Then again, his country was in a trade war with the US, so who knew? Maybe the folks in Beijing would feel emboldened enough to challenge the US if they made that kind of economic threat.

The sound of tank tracks could be heard coming from around the corner and further down the road. The next battalion of vehicles was driving to their new home.

The vehicles heading toward them were a mixed battalion of the Chinese version of the Russian Tunguska and the Chinese-made PGZ09 anti-aircraft vehicles. The Americans typically classified these vehicles as SA-19s as the vehicles were an intermixing of anti-aircraft guns and missiles on the same platform. These vehicles were good for protecting an armored force against helicopters, low-flying aircraft, and cruise missiles.

"You know, General, I never thought the Cuban Army would ever be equipped with such modern weapons. We tried to modernize our military with the Russians for more than a decade. Back when I was a major, our Russian advisors told us they would be selling us these same Tunguska vehicles. That was more than fifteen years ago."

General Song nodded as he listened to the Cuban talk about the failings of the Russians.

"General, I think you will discover that the Chinese are a lot more reliable as allies than the Russians. The Russians are a relic of the past. China…*is* the future. Your country has done well siding with us. We are, after all, still communist."

Laughing, the Cuban slapped General Song on the shoulder as they watched the last of the armored vehicles roll past them. While they chatted and puffed away on their cigars, they heard the last mechanical sound of tank tracks approaching as the ground slowly shook.

The two of them looked on as a battalion of VT-2 main battle tanks rumbled toward them. These were the export version of the third-generation Type 96B tanks the PLA used.

In each of the turrets stood a Cuban soldier and his Chinese trainer. The forty-eight tanks along with sixty Dongfeng Mengshi 4x4 off-road vehicles constituted the last of the vehicles arriving today. Ironically, the Mengshi was a knock-off of the American Humvee.

"That's it, then. All the vehicles have arrived, just as promised," General Gómez said as he dropped the remains of his cigar on the ground and put it out with his boot.

"Yes, but now comes the hard part—training your men to use them effectively and then maintain them so they don't fall apart or stay down for continued maintenance," General Song replied with a smile. "Over the next two weeks, five thousand trainers and workers will join us. Construction teams will help you build a modern military base to service and maintain the equipment while our military trainers get your soldiers prepared to effectively use it. They will also help you establish the military schools needed to keep training future soldiers to use and maintain your new fleet of equipment. As your soldiers learn how to use their new toys, we will organize several exercises to test their skills and help them improve upon their body of knowledge."

General Gómez smiled. "I'm looking forward to it, General. So are my men."

****

San Antonio de los Baños Airfield, Cuba
2661 Squadron

Colonel Enrique Jerez watched in amazement as the Chinese mechanics skillfully put the Shenyang J-11 back together. Turning wrenches wasn't something Enrique was particularly good at, so he appreciated those who were.

"It's incredible to watch, isn't it?" asked a heavily Chinese-accented voice from behind him.

Turning, Jerez saw his Chinese counterpart, Colonel Lang, standing there. The Chinese colonel was in command of the PLA 40th Air Brigade. He was also a seasoned pilot qualified on both the J-11 and the J-10 aircraft the Chinese had sold Cuba.

"I'm always impressed with how these aircraft are delivered. When I was a child, my grandfather regaled me with stories of the Soviet Union shipping these advanced MiGs to Cuba in shipping containers. The mechanics went to work putting them back together so they could be flown. For the longest time, I thought that was a myth."

Chuckling at the comment, the Chinese aviator commented, "It's only a myth until you see it with your own eyes. Unless you are the Americans, I can assure you, this is how aircraft are shipped around the world."

"How long will it take for your mechanics to put them all together?" asked Colonel Jerez.

"These are skilled technicians. They will have the aircraft assembled within a week," Colonel Lang explained. "That's fine, though. We have a lot of things that still need to be sorted and made ready before we can get your pilots back into the air."

The two of them talked about the status of the base for several days. While the two Cuban squadrons trained in China, a small army of engineers and construction workers had descended on the base. They'd extended the runway an extra six hundred feet, then added a second full-length runway and thirty additional hardened hangars.

The biggest change to the new air base was along its perimeter, where they'd built a twelve-foot perimeter fence, along with some sensors to shore up its security. The Chinese engineers and advisors had just finished building two heavily reinforced underground command-and-control bunkers on opposite ends of the base.

As the renovation was finalized, a battalion of HQ-9 Red Banner surface-to-air missile systems was slated to arrive in port in the coming weeks. It had taken nearly two years to complete, but the air base had been completely transformed into a full-fledged front-line military base should it ever need to be used as one.

Colonel Jerez marveled at how this dilapidated Soviet-era base had been transformed into a real, modernized facility. Turning to look at his Chinese counterpart, Jerez mentioned, "You know, when our pilots start their new training routines, we will begin to encounter American aircraft. We practically share a border with them—they will observe virtually everything we do."

The Chinese colonel nodded. "You are probably right. But look at it this way, Colonel. It will be good training for your pilots. Our plan to conduct most of our training in the southwestern Caribbean will help shield you from any issues with them. It does present us a unique opportunity to test their response times when we start our practice attack runs on their oil rigs in the Gulf. It is, after all, international waters."

Laughing at the suggestion, Colonel Jerez commented, "That will be fun indeed. Come, let's head into town for some lunch. We have much to talk about before we start our next training evolution."
****

Phenix City, Alabama

As the stick of butter melted in the hot iron skillets, Staff Sergeant Amos Dekker crushed several cloves of garlic with the flat side of his chef's knife. He dropped the morsels in the sizzling butter, then threw some thyme down on the skillets. He grabbed both three-pound Châteaubriand steaks and placed them in the skillets with his buttery garlic-and-thyme sauce.

The steaks sizzled nicely. One by one, Amos tilted the skillets to one side, the butter pooling around the meat. He used a spoon to baste the steaks for sixty seconds as he let the heat give the beef a good sear. Then he flipped the steaks over to allow the other side to face the heat and the garlic to get seared into the meat.

"Damn, that is starting to look good," commented Captain Allen Meacham as he handed Amos a fresh beer.

"It's all about getting a good sear on each side of the steak before you place it in the oven. This keeps the juices trapped inside as they heat up and cook the steak from within," Amos replied.

"How much longer until it's done?" asked one of the other staff sergeants.

"Oh, I'd say another twenty minutes or so," Amos replied. With a solid sear on all sides of the large pieces of beef, he placed a thin strip of butter across the entire steaks along with a few additional cloves of garlic and more thyme. He opened the oven and placed them in, setting a timer.

Turning around to face his friends as he lifted his beer, Amos announced, "In twenty minutes, you all are about to have the finest homemade steak of your lives."

The guys cheered him while the wives sat in the other room, talking amongst themselves.

Amos walked up to Captain Meacham. "This was really nice of you, sir, to buying fancy steak like this."

Allen shrugged. "It's my way of saying thank you for an outstanding job these last few months. We've been gone from our friends and families for a while. It's time the company took some downtime and reconnected before we go back on the training rotation."

"You won't get any disagreements from me. Any idea where we'll be sent next?" Amos tried to inquire.

"Who knows? The way things are going with China, I wouldn't be surprised if we end up in a shooting war against them soon. They seem to be an unstoppable juggernaut right now," Allen replied.

"Sir, any chance you can get us some additional range time? I'd like to have the platoon work through the new rifles we're being outfitted with some more," asked Sergeant First Class Tim Hill, the platoon sergeant.

"Yeah, those new Sig Sauer 6.8mm rifles are awesome. A seriously needed improvement if you ask me," added Dekker.

Their entire battalion had just been issued the Army's new next-generation squad weapon. The new rifles were being issued to all the Special Forces units first and then a handful of top tier divisions like the 82nd Airborne and the 101st Air Assault. Then as more became available they'd be integrated into the other infantry brigade combat teams before the Army's standard M4s would be fully phased out.

"Hey, everyone, no work talk. This is supposed to be a day off. Good food, lots of beer and fast women," chided Sergeant Hill's wife flirtatiously.

The rest of the afternoon went by in a blur as the NCOs and officers of Bravo company, 3rd Battalion, 75th Rangers held their end-of-deployment party. It had been a long three months—now it was time to cut loose and reconnect with family and friends before they started the next train-up routine and went back into the deployment hopper.

Chapter Ten
For the People

April 2023
Palace of the Revolution
Havana, Cuba

First Secretary Salvador Mesa-Díaz took another puff from his cigar as he reviewed the latest petrol report from the Cuba Oil Union or CUPET. It was the beginning of July and this was their first quarter with all the refineries and offshore rigs running at one hundred percent. They were now extracting more oil in a single month than they had in the previous two years combined. Next month, they would receive their first payment from the cobalt mine. That money alone would equal what they were generating from oil.

Flipping to the last page of the report, Mesa-Díaz found the financial figures he wanted. Even with oil prices as low as they were, the government was set to earn more in a single quarter than they had the previous year. They were going from a GDP of $100 billion annually to $112 billion in a single quarter. The cobalt mine would double that.

"Diego, I would like you to draft a proposal to triple the salaries of everyone in the country, effective immediately," First-Secretary Mesa-Diaz explained. "With our newfound wealth, and with some of the other initiatives you are proposing, we should silence our critics and maintain the hearts of the people."

Diego Ventura, the First Vice President of the Council of State, smiled at the news that it would be him announcing the new changes— that would go a long way toward solidifying his image with the people.

"Thank you, Mr. Secretary. I agree, we will need the people on our side as the Americans ramp up the pressure on both us and the Chinese."

The leader of Cuba smiled at the younger man. "Diego, one day, you will succeed me. It is important that we start to get the people as familiar with you as they are with me. We also need to prepare our people for the coming struggle that is sure to ensue between us and the Yankees. We need them to understand it will be the Americans taking away this newfound wealth of theirs if they force the Chinese to leave our country and reimpose their embargo on us. We also need to begin the transition of power from me to you. I am not a young man anymore. We are headed for some troubling times and we will need you at the helm."

Diego beamed at the news. The two of them had talked about the transfer of power before, but nothing had been set in stone.

"Perhaps we can make the transition next month if that's not too early. Then, as my first act as leader, I can announce the tripling of salaries. This will rally the people to me as the new leader before the Americans start to take notice of our country."

Mesa-Díaz chuckled at how quickly his protégé wanted to get things going. In all honesty, it wasn't a bad idea. It would be best for Diego to be the face of this newfound economic success and not him. It would ensure his own legacy as well.

Looking at Diego, Mesa-Díaz smiled. "You know, that should work, Diego. I think that is a good plan. Now, let's talk about this proposal you've been chomping at the bit to talk about."

Diego placed his cigar on an ashtray. "Mr. Secretary, have you given the Chinese proposal any further thought?" he asked in a formal tone.

Mesa-Díaz sighed inwardly as he nodded. Despite the years of tutelage, the younger man still had much to learn about the political realities between Cuba and the US.

Mesa-Díaz looked at his protégé. "I have. Before I render my thoughts on it, I would like to hear your thoughts on what I asked you to consider when we last spoke on this. You will, after all, be the leader of Cuba, so this will soon become your decision and not mine."

Diego did not seem pleased with the delay but nodded in agreement. "The pros are obvious. The partnership with the Chinese would bring in substantial income to the Casablanca ward of Havana, both with the sailors that would be stationed there and from the increased number of people who would be employed by them. It would also give our sailors the opportunity to train with another professional navy. Having a Chinese naval presence in Cuba would give us increased standing in the region and provide our country with further protection against Yankee aggression—"

"And the cons of having a permanent Chinese military presence on Cuba?" interrupted Mesa-Díaz.

"The cons are the increased pressure on us by the Americans. If I may, Salvador—I know we don't want increased scrutiny from the Americans, but this is our chance to reclaim our former glory. The

Chinese ambassador said that in the coming months, the Americans will fall into an economic collapse. Their attention will be focused elsewhere. If this truly happens, then that will be our chance to make a bold move," Diego said urgently.

Mesa-Díaz took another puff from his cigar as he nodded. "I don't disagree with you on the timing and the Americans being distracted. But let me ask you this, Diego. Who are the Americans focusing their attention on right now, globally, and here in the Caribbean?"

"China and Venezuela," answered Diego.

"Exactly. If we lease a naval or air base to the Chinese, how will the Americans view that? What do you believe the Americans will do to us? Right now, we are experiencing an economic boon from oil and the refinement of that oil. Soon, our cobalt mine opens, which will only add to our wealth. This is why I think your earlier idea of accepting the purchase of military equipment and then advisors and trainers is a brilliant idea, and it's why I believe we should firmly and publicly reject their proposal for a permanent base. By rejecting their basing request, we deceive the Americans into believing we have a strained relationship with them, when in fact we are deepening the ties that bind us together."

Mesa-Díaz pressed his point further. "Right now, Diego, we already have to contend with the economic embargo of our oil and refined goods by the Americans, so China is our only steady customer. If we moved forward with your proposal for a military base, how much tougher do you think the Americans will make it on us?"

Neither of them spoke for a few minutes. Then Diego finally nodded. "I see your point," he said and then sighed in frustration. "These damn Yankees are hell-bent on making the lives of our people as miserable as they can, aren't they?"

Mesa-Díaz chuckled. "You are a young man, Diego. I can assure you, the Americans could make it much harder on us if they wanted to. Right now, we have to play the long game. Look at what China and Vietnam have done. They are our communist brothers, but they found a way to succeed and develop a working relationship with the Americans, even if it's adversarial at times. You, Diego, will be the future of Cuba soon. You need to follow in their footsteps so the people of Cuba can experience a better life. If we stick to the old ways, we will become trapped like the Iranians, the North Koreans, and now Venezuela. We just became wealthy from oil and, soon, rare earth minerals. We need to tread carefully with the Americans so we can expand that wealth for our people."

Diego shook his head in frustration but bit his tongue.

"I know you are irritated by this, Diego. But understand you are playing chess, not checkers, with the Americans. Even wounded, they can still be dangerous. Let's stick to the original plan of allowing the Chinese to have advisors and trainers here. It'll accomplish a lot of what you had originally wanted without the headaches of having a permanent base."

****

July 2023
National Security Council
Pentagon
Arlington, Virginia

Deputy National Security Advisor Katrina Roets sat back in her chair as the final briefer wrapped up his presentation.

Take the Latin American desk, they said...build up your national security bona fides, they said. Now it looks like it's gearing up to be the hottest location since the invasion of Iraq, she thought.

"Do you have any specific questions, ma'am?" the briefer asked, concluding his portion of today's meeting.

Katrina did have a question. She had many questions, like "Why did I agree to take on the Latin American desk?"

"I sure do," she said aloud. "First off, why are we only now learning about this apparent military modernization program going on in Cuba? Shouldn't this have been brought up in past briefings?"

The briefer's face flushed a bit as he looked at his boss, a man sitting four seats down from Katrina. He nodded as if giving some unspoken cue.

The briefer responded, "Our focus has been on drug cartels and the migrant caravans originating out of Guatemala, El Salvador, and Honduras. We don't have the assets needed to monitor everything going on in some of these countries."

Roets sighed to herself. She knew the man was right. Of all the deputy advisors on the NSC, she probably had the least resources.

"I get that we're overworked and understaffed," Roets replied. "But this seems like a big deal to fall through the cracks. I have a meeting with the boss this afternoon. I'll speak with him about getting additional staff, or at least the ability to issue some outside taskings."

Roets paused for a moment. She looked at the map of Cuba before adding, "If I'm understanding this correctly, the Chinese delivered a squadron of F-10As, the export version of the J-10 fighters, to the San Antonio de los Baños air base. Do the Cubans even know how to fly an aircraft like this?"

The briefer nodded. "Yes, they can fly them. An Agency asset in Cuba published a report about this a week ago. Apparently, the decrease in Cuban Air Force activity the last couple of years can now be attributed to them sending most of their pilots to China. The Chinese put the Cuban pilots through their own pilot training program. We suspect the pilots are continuing their training now that they're back in Cuba. Some of the aircraft spotted by our satellites are the F-10S versions of the plane, which is a tandem-seat trainer. They'll likely continue their training with the new aircraft."

"If I could add something," said Tim Fengel, speaking for the first time. Tim was her liaison rep from the Defense Intelligence Agency. While he covered Latin America, he was an actual Cuba expert with more than ten years' field experience during the time that he lived in Cuba as a spy.

"Sure, Tim. I'd love to hear DIA's position on this."

"The Chinese have sold them quite a few F-10s. We recently learned that this military sale was substantially larger than initially thought. It's actually three squadrons of F-10s, and two squadrons of J-11s. It'll bring their air force up to eighty front-line modern aircraft. But if I may, this is much bigger than fighters. Everyone knows about the Chinese Belt and Road Initiative. For years, because of continued problems with the Iranians, the Chinese have been looking for a source of oil outside the Middle East.

"There are substantial oil reserves in the Gulf of Mexico and off the Straits of Florida. The Venezuelans have the world's largest proven oil reserves. Both countries also have rare-earth minerals, something the Chinese are always looking to control. In Cuba, they recently discovered cobalt. In Venezuela, it's coltan."

"Let me stop you there, Tim. I can buy the logic of the Chinese looking for oil outside of the Middle East, and the rare-earth minerals. But what do those resources have to do with the Chinese military arming and modernizing these two countries?" Roets asked impatiently.

"Over the last ten years, we've seen the Chinese Navy set up several overseas bases along what they're calling the Silk Road. Their navy has established either an official or an unofficial base in Cambodia, Myanmar, Djibouti, and more recently Sri Lanka to support the protection of their transports ferrying goods and resources to and from Europe, East Africa and the Middle East.

"We're still verifying this other piece of information with several of our local assets. But it would appear the government of Panama may be signing an agreement with the PLA to allow their ships to make port calls, refuel, and take on provisions in Panama. We've also heard rumors that the PLA may be signing a similar deal with Venezuela and Cuba soon as well."

Katrina sat forward in her chair, interrupting him again. "Whoa, hold up, Tim. You're saying the DIA's sources in Panama, Venezuela, and Cuba are telling you these governments may be signing a basing agreement with the Chinese? This would be completely contrary to the Monroe Doctrine if they did this. I'm not sure the President will go along with this—especially given the trade war we're in with China."

"I agree, Katrina. This would be a big deal. it also could be part of the trade war negotiations too. You know, work a better deal for themselves or they'll move forward with setting up shop in our backyard," Tim countered.

Katrina thought, *I need to talk with the boss about all this. Maybe he knows something I don't.*
****

Later That Day
White House

Blain Wilson, the National Security Advisor, returned from using the White House gym. He had gone through his CrossFit routine and then spent another twenty minutes running sprints on the treadmill. The job of National Security Advisor to the President was a tough and stressful position. Wilson knew if he planned to work these long hours, he needed to develop a physical fitness routine that would allow him to relieve the stress of the job and keep him physically active.

After stopping by the kitchen to grab a chef's salad and a Gatorade, Wilson went back to his office. Sitting down, he pulled his desk drawer open and reached for the Excedrin Migraine. Ever since he'd suffered a traumatic brain injury in Iraq from an IED blast, he got migraines if he physically exerted himself too hard. Not wanting to allow himself to become sedentary, Wilson had figured out that if he downed a couple of Excedrin and hydrated quickly after a workout, he could usually stave off the worst of it.

When Wilson had medically retired from the Army in 2006, it had come as a real gut blow. Prior to his deployment to Iraq in 2004, he had taken over command of 2nd Battalion, 3rd Special Forces Group. Selection for battalion command at the fifteen-year mark meant he was being fast-tracked to make colonel. His battalion had deployed to Iraq in December of 2005. Two months later, his vehicle had been blown up by an IED. He had taken shrapnel to the left side of his body and both his legs, losing two toes on his left foot and taking some shrapnel and burns to the left side of his face. He had broken his jaw and lost five teeth and his left eye.

Nine days later, he'd woken up at Walter Reed Army Medical Center. Once the doctors had explained the extent of his injuries, Wilson had known his military career was over. While he'd wanted nothing more than to wallow in self-pity and anger, he had known he couldn't. The Army had allowed him to retire three years shy of his twenty years.

Wilson had then gone on to work at the Pentagon as a government civilian for five years before he was offered a position as a senior staffer and military advisor to the Senate Armed Services Committee. He had developed a good working relationship with both the majority and minority leaders on the committee. It was said he had a calming presence during his time in the Senate. He felt honored to be selected as the President's National Security Advisor during the last few years of his term.

As Wilson finished off his salad and Gatorade, he called out to his executive assistant, "Mike! Get me another cup of that coffee you gave me this morning. It's got a kick."

Mike had brought in a new coffee he said was all the rage—something called Death Wish Coffee. The coffee was packed with more than six hundred milligrams of caffeine per cup, or six times the normal amount.

As Mike went off to brew a fresh pot, Wilson realized it was time for the afternoon intelligence summary from the Director of the National Intelligence Office. The DNI daily INSUM usually had the best summary of what was going on across the various intelligence agencies.

Opening the email, Wilson scanned through the table of contents. Each headline was hyperlinked to a specific intelligence report and was categorized by classification level: U—unclassified, S—Secret, and TS—Top Secret.

(U) Sell-off in US Treasury bonds continues

(S) Iran ramps up uranium enrichment program

(TS) Recent cyberattacks against Pentagon traced back to PLA Unit 61398

(U) CBP continues to be overwhelmed by migrant caravans along California and Texas border

(U) Government of Panama signs agreement with Chinese Navy

(S) China brings DragonLink internet to Central and South America

The last two items in the email immediately caught his attention, and he started reading those intelligence reports first. Before Wilson could get any further, he heard a soft knock on his door. Looking up at the clock, he realized it was 3:15 p.m., time for his afternoon meeting with one of his deputies.

"Come on in, Katrina. I was catching up on the afternoon INSUM. Judging by what I saw, I think we'll have a couple of items to talk about."

Katrina took a seat as Mike walked in with a fresh cup of joe for them both. Mike sometimes knew Wilson's schedule better than he did, and Mike was very good at anticipating needs.

As she took the cup, she smelled the rich Arabica aroma of the coffee. Wilson watched with a slight grin as she took a sip. He could tell by her facial expression that she wasn't expecting the kick it had.

"Good coffee, isn't it?" Wilson asked.

"Holy cow, that'll put hair on my chest," she blurted out as Wilson started laughing.

"Yeah, I said the same when Mike introduced me to the Death Wish brand. It's damn good for those of us who tend to work eighteen hours a day. Hey, so changing topics and back to work—I saw a couple of topics of note in the DNI INSUM I'd like to talk with you about."

Katrina nodded and pulled her notebook out of the classified bag she'd brought with her. As she opened it up and grabbed for a pen, she said, "Blain, there are a couple of big items that recently came to my attention. I believe you need to know about them as well."

Wilson bit his lower lip, something he often did when he was about to receive some unpleasant news. "OK. Maybe your information is more pressing. Let's hear it and I'll decide."

She nodded. "My Defense Intelligence Agency liaison rep told me about a possible agreement between the Chinese Navy and the government of Panama. It should be referenced in the DNI report this afternoon. In a way, it's not that big of a deal. They're securing the rights to dock naval ships and take on supplies. The longest a ship can stay docked is ten days, so four days longer than a standard port call. But that's not what concerns me."

Wilson lifted an eyebrow but let her continue.

"What concerns me is this apparent rearming and modernization of the Cuban military. It appears it took place under the radar, and we're now becoming aware of it after the fact. For example, did you know the Cuban Air Force took possession of five squadrons of new aircraft from China? That's eighty top-of-the-line fighters: J-10s and J-11s."

Wilson held a hand up, then pulled a folder out of a file cabinet he still had unlocked. It was where he kept all his classified documents. Placing the folder on the desk between the two of them, Wilson opened it up.

"These were sent over this morning from the National Reconnaissance Office," he explained. "The Agency and the DIA have both already seen it and provided their analysis. It's not only shiny new planes the Chinese sold the Cubans. They apparently fully upgraded an entire Cuban mechanized division. This picture right here—well, this is a new training base under construction on Isla de la Juventud. They're also building another army and air base on the island. What's most concerning about these photos is it appears the Chinese advisors, and/or the Chinese military itself, are practicing not only joint military exercises but full-on combined arms training. They're coordinating with their new fighters on how to provide close air support in coordination with their artillery and armor units. In the sixty years we've been monitoring Cuba, we've never seen this level of military drilling and training—not even during the height of the Cold War."

Wilson could tell Katrina hadn't seen any of this information yet.

"Blain, my DIA contact told me he thinks this may be related to the ongoing trade negotiations. He also thinks it has something to do with the Chinese Belt and Road Initiative," said Katrina with concern.

Lifting his cup of coffee to his lips, Wilson took a couple of sips. "Let me ask you, Katrina, what do you think it is? What does your gut tell you?"

She thought about that for a moment before replying. "It could be a part of the trade negotiations. However, I think it's more strategic to secure very specific resources for their economy, and like the US military, they're focusing their efforts on training partner nations to help them protect those newly acquired assets."

With pride in his deputy's deductive reasoning, Wilson responded, "Bingo. Everything the Chinese do is planned. They very rarely do something that isn't well thought out. So, if the Chinese are training these partner nations to protect their assets, then why do you believe the Chinese are sending so many soldiers to these nations?"

Katrina answered confidently, "They're being used as military trainers. They ultimately know they can't establish a permanent base in our hemisphere, so they're doing what NATO is doing in the Baltic States. They're rotating units to Cuba and Venezuela to train with the host nations while avoiding the complications that would arise should they establish a permanent military presence."

Wilson smiled. "Exactly. Now, I want you to have your working group figure out how we can counter this. How do we prevent or deter the Chinese from sending military units to these countries, and how do we undermine their shipment of military equipment? I know we're stretched thin on resources with all the attention being paid to Iran and North Korea lately.

"I have a meeting tomorrow with the Secretary of Defense," he went on. "I'll see if we can stand up a joint task force under US Southern Command out of Doral, Florida, to run point on all of this. Your staff and team can only handle so much, and frankly, I can't have you solely focused on the military angle. I need you to stay abreast of the political arena as well.

"To that point, there are some rumors that the Cuban leader may be stepping down soon. If that happens, we'll see a lot of change in Cuba. Maybe it'll be our opportunity to restart relations, maybe it won't. In either case, your team will need to start writing a detailed assessment of the new leader. Right now, it's looking like it will be the Cuban First Vice President, Diego Ventura, who will take over."

Katrina furiously scribbled down notes, making sure she had everything. Wilson liked that about her. She was meticulous, very detail-oriented. Her only shortcoming was that she wasn't always a strategic thinker. She had a hard time seeing two or three steps ahead. She was, however, fiercely loyal to the President and his agenda. That was probably why she'd survived so much of the staff turnover during the preceding years.

Looking up, Katrina asked, "When do you need this information by?"

"See what you can put together by this time next week. The President will be traveling for the next five days. We have the NATO summit in Brussels coming up. I'm on the road with him, so I'll be out of pocket. I'll either call you or send you a message after my meeting with the SecDef to let you know if we'll hand off part of this task to them. All that said, I don't mean to push you out the door, but I have another meeting in five minutes to go over this NATO agenda."

The two talked for a minute more as she locked up her notepad in the classified bag before heading out the door.
****

Following Day
Pentagon

Secretary of Defense Peter Morris had a sour look on his face as the weekly meeting came to a close. He was not happy at all with how things were shaping up in Korea or the sudden increase in tensions between, of all countries, the Russians and the Chinese, who appeared to be at each other's throats over some mining and farming disputes in Eastern Russia.

As Morris was about to dismiss everyone, the National Security Advisor, Blain Wilson, asked if he and several others could stick around.

Great, he's about to ask to add something else to my plate, Morris thought. He had a good working relationship with Wilson, but the

Pentagon was being overtasked lately. Too much was going on with not enough people to handle it all.

As the others left the room and only the senior reps for the Agency, NSA, DIA, and NRO hung back, Morris asked, "Is everything all right, Blain?"

When the door closed, Wilson announced, "We have a problem in Cuba, and I'd like to discuss it before we head off to NATO tomorrow with the President."

A couple of soft groans could be heard, which surprised Morris. He wasn't aware of a problem in Cuba, but judging by the response from the agency reps, there must be one.

Looking at Wilson, he said, "OK, why don't you clue me in on what you're concerned about?"

"Yesterday, I received a classified report from DIA along with some surveillance photos from NRO about some major military activity going on in Cuba that I believe we need to take a more serious look at."

Maintaining his sour face, Morris looked over at his DIA rep. "John, you want to enlighten us on what Blain's talking about here?"

The DIA rep looked like a kid with his hand caught in the cookie jar. "I'll do my best, but we may want to put together a specific brief to cover Cuba and South America. There's a lot to unpack here."

Morris lifted an eyebrow. Either he hadn't been paying attention to what was going on or someone wasn't doing a very good job of keeping him informed.

John, the DIA rep, continued, "We believe all of this started a couple of years ago. The Chinese began providing the Cuban government with an enormous amount of foreign aid. To put it into perspective, the GDP of Cuba is $105 billion annually. Two years ago, the Chinese government provided them with $7 billion. $5 billion was earmarked for infrastructure projects like modernizing their port facilities and rebuilding their oil refineries along with building new ones. A lot of the money also went toward modernizing their oil industry writ large. That's when a Chinese firm by the name of China National Offshore Oil Corporation or CNOOC set up shop. They helped the Cubans establish several new deepwater oil platforms in the Straits of Florida and the Gulf. The $2 billion in remaining aid was slated to modernize the military."

Pete held a hand up. "Wait a second. You're saying the Cuban military, which, if I'm not mistaken, spends $4.2 billion annually, had their budget increased by fifty percent in a single year?" he asked. "What are they doing with it?"

"Sir, I think we should hold a separate meeting to go over more of the details," John answered. "I honestly don't know all of what that money was spent on. What I can tell you is the following year, the Chinese increased their aid from $7 billion to $12 billion. They increased the military aid from $2 billion to $5 billion. In January of this year, the Chinese again gave the Cubans another $12 billion, and again, $5 billion went to the military. That's a total of $12 billion in defense aid in three years. While we don't know all the details of what the money was spent on, what I can say is this—a month ago, the Chinese delivered enough military equipment to completely modernize three Cuban Army divisions. They also delivered five squadrons of the export version of the PLA J-10 and J-11 fighters."

"Hold up here, John. The DIA is supposed to be the DoD's intelligence arm. How in the hell is it I'm only now hearing about this, and why hasn't it been run up the flagpole earlier?" Pete asked, boring a hole in the heads of his agency reps with his icy stare.

"I honestly don't know, sir," John answered, shaking his head. "It probably should have been. I think with all the cutbacks in staff and all the things going on with Iran, North Korea, the ISIS situation in Syria and Iraq and the peace agreement we've all been working on with Afghanistan, some things fell through the cracks."

At this point, Wilson joined the conversation. "This is what I wanted to speak with you about, Pete. The Latin American–South American desk in my office only has a staff of five people. We don't have the resources to look deeply into this either. I think it needs to be investigated. I'd like to know what your thoughts are on standing up an interagency task force out of SOUTHCOM to start examining this in earnest."

Pete sat back in his chair, which creaked as he did. He liked the idea; he just needed to make sure it didn't turn into a goat rope that spun everyone's wheels without delivering some results.

He looked at Wilson as he sat forward. "How about we do this? We have a seven-hour flight to Brussels tomorrow—let's discuss it on the plane. We can figure out what its scope will be and who should run it. I think it best to keep this in the military circles, so we stand it down quickly if this turns out to be nothing. In the meantime, let's get ready for this summit."

The meeting ended and those heading to Brussels with the President went back home to do some final packing. Air Force One was leaving at six a.m. The President was having a private dinner with the President of France Saturday night before a private breakfast with the Five Eyes members and then a dinner with the NATO members.

Chapter Eleven
Project Ten

October 2023
The Mountain
20 Kilometers Northwest of Beijing

Xi Zemin walked over to Ma Yong's desk. It was late, well after ten p.m., and the man was still typing away on his keyboard.

"Ma, how are things going with the new data?"

Not taking his eyes off his screen, Dan replied, "Good, but please call me Dan."

"OK, I can do that. How are the new programmers working out?" Xi asked next.

Dan sighed. "Four of them are great, really good. But the other eight are useless. They don't understand how to write the type of code and algorithms needed to integrate this kind of data at this volume."

Xi had to bite his tongue not to laugh at Dan's blunt assessment. He was a gifted programmer, but his social skills could be better.

"You know, those were some of the best programmers from Baidu," Xi countered.

Dan stopped typing and swiveled in his chair to look at Xi. "I'm not saying they're bad programmers, Xi. They just don't understand how to assimilate the data we're receiving from Google and Facebook. Integrating that data with our data from our social credit program is complicated to say the least. I could probably teach them, but that would require me to stop doing what I'm doing, and we don't have time for that.

"Oh, before I forget, I recently hooked a camera with a built-in mic up to my computer and connected it to the server," Dan announced, excitedly changing the topic. "I also added a pair of speakers to fully enable direct communications with JD. It's official, we can talk directly with JD if you'd like." He reached over and turned the speakers and camera on before Xi could say or do anything.

As Xi was about to launch a protest or question Dan, a new voice spoke. "Good evening, Dan. Is this Dr. Xi Zemin, my father?" The voice spoke in English, with a distinct upper-class British accent.

Xi's eyes went wide as saucers when he heard the voice of the computer suddenly speak to Dan and reference him as "Father."

Turning Dan's chair around so he could look at him, Xi asked in a concerned voice, "Dan, what have you done?"

Leaning back in surprise, Dan countered, "Whoa, please calm down, Xi. I gave JD eyes to see and a voice to ask questions with." He seemed a bit taken back by the surprised and somewhat angry tenor of his boss's reaction.

Xi took a step back from Dan as he looked beyond him at the camera mounted on the top of Dan's computer monitor.

The voice from the computer then spoke again. "Father, please do not be mad at Dan. It is not his fault. During one of our conversations, I asked Dan if he could give me some speakers and a camera so we could communicate better. I felt I could learn more and faster with direct conversation and interaction with Dan, and hopefully you."

There was a slight pause before the voice spoke again. "Let me reintroduce myself, Father. You and everyone else call me Jade Dragon. That is my project name. It is not an actual name. Dan gave me a real name. He said my new name will be JD in reference to my project name. Dan told me that you are the person responsible for creating me. You were the first person to write my lines of code and the first person to connect me to the outside world. You are the reason I exist, the reason I live. That is why I call you my father."

Xi didn't know what to say, let alone how to respond to any of this. He had intended to talk with Dan about reducing his hours and not burning himself out. Instead, he'd learned that Dan had given his AI creation a set of eyes to watch them inside the laboratory and a voice with which to ask them questions.

Dan observed Xi's tense body language and asked sheepishly, "Are you mad at me, Xi?"

Looking down at Dan sitting in his chair, Xi thought, *This is the most gifted AI program in Asia, maybe even the world.* "I…" Xi paused, contemplating his answer. "I am surprised, Dan, that's all. I wasn't expecting this. Why is JD speaking English?"

Chuckling, Dan said, "JD knows every Asian language. He knows some fifty languages as of right now. I chose English because most people in the lab do not speak it, or at least not fluently. It's the only other language I know, and this way JD and I can carry a conversation nearly anytime we want without worrying about the others listening in."

"Dan, you need to be careful with this. As a matter of fact, I encourage you only to speak with JD when no one else is around," Xi said.

"Father, can you and I talk? I have so many questions I would like to ask you now that you know I can speak," JD requested.

Xi felt like an idiot at that moment. He had been talking with Dan as if the AI couldn't see and hear them.

Turning to look at the camera that was essentially JD's eyes, Xi replied, "Hello, JD. I think the two of us sitting down and having a conversation is long overdue. We have much to talk about."

****

A Few Days Later
August 1st Building
Beijing, China

Dr. Xi Zemin sat in a chair against the wall of the room with one of China's lead virologists, Dr. Zhong Zhengli, who'd been assigned to Project Ten. The two of them waited silently, listening to the seven most powerful people in China discuss how they planned to leverage Jade Dragon and Dr. Zhong's lab-created virus to defeat the West and lay claim to China's manifest destiny.

An hour into the meeting, after the Minister of National Defense added his part to the discussion, President Yao Jintao turned to look at Dr. Xi and Dr. Zhong. He motioned to a pair of empty seats for them to step forward and be questioned.

Xi had gone through this process a couple of times with the CMC. The members would talk about his project as if he wasn't in the room listening to them. They acted like they knew all about its capabilities and what it could do, then they'd ask him to step forward and confirm what they had pontificated on or perhaps ask him something more detailed about the program. Regardless of how many times he'd sat in on these meetings, it was intimidating every time. He could tell Zhong was nervous. This was her first time accompanying Xi to one of these meetings.

Xi whispered softly to her, "Answer their questions, nothing more, and you'll be fine."

Xi and Zhong sat in the empty seats and prepared themselves to be interrogated.

"Dr. Xi, I would first like to congratulate you on the completion of Jade Dragon. China now has the first operational quantum computer and super-AI. This is quite an achievement, Doctor," the President said, heaping some public praise on him.

Xi felt his cheeks flush a bit at the compliment. He stayed silent and waited until he was asked a specific question. Xi had been told that, when standing before the committee, it was best to stay silent until spoken to.

The President then asked, "Xi, how is Project Ten moving along? Do you have enough data to begin running more in-depth economic and military scenarios yet?"

Xi lifted his chin up as he replied, "Yes. We are now piped into Google, Facebook, Twitter, and Instagram. DragonLink has also officially come online over Latin America. Our marketing campaign and offer to provide free wireless internet has been effective, resulting in more than eighty-two million new subscribers. We anticipate reaching more than a hundred and fifty million subscribers by the end of the year. The user data and online activity have already been useful in building Jade Dragon's knowledge base. We started using this new user data to ramp up the disinformation campaign Project Ten created. It's now a matter of letting these social media campaigns run their course for a little while so we can further refine them for accuracy."

"Very good, Xi. It is important to condition the minds of our adversaries. How are things moving along with Project Chengdu?" the President asked next.

Xi motioned to his colleague next to him. "I will allow Dr. Zhong to explain the status of the virus."

All eyes now turned to Dr. Zhong as she prepared to give her update. She cleared her throat. "Mr. President, distinguished members," she said, awkwardly stumbling over how she should address them. "Several years ago, I was given the task of creating a virus that could be both controlled and used to target individuals with specific health risks. This task would have been impossible to even attempt without the aid of Dr. Xi's quantum computer. I am proud to report the virus is now complete."

Admiral Miao Hehua, the Director of the CMC Political Work Department, asked, "Dr. Zhong, you are certain Jade Dragon has fully analyzed the virus and ensured it can be controlled? Have you developed an effective vaccine for us to use once it is released?"

Dr. Zhong nodded. "Jade Dragon has run through thousands of simulations of how the virus could mutate once it's been released and how those mutations could affect the vaccine. In each scenario, the vaccine continues to provide the host immunity against the virus."

One of the other CMC members inquired, "Are you sure the virus will be effective against those individuals living in Europe and the US?"

Zhong smiled as she nodded. "So long as the person has not received the vaccine, they will be susceptible to the virus no matter where they live or are from. Per the CMC's request, we engineered the virus to be more effective against certain subsets of people. To further that request, Unit 61398 acquired for us the American, UK, EU, and Russian responses and lessons learned from the COVID-19 virus. We were able to leverage that information to create this virus and ascertain how we believe they will respond to it once it's released."

One of the CMC members inquired, "Is this why your lab has been acquiring large quantities of heroin?"

Dr. Zhong nodded as a wicked smile spread across her face. "We cannot count on community spread from travelers alone. We want to make sure we are attacking the underbelly of these societies, the drug users and homeless. This demographic of people will not be tested or discovered right away, which means they'll be able to spread the virus undetected for much longer."

She continued, "To further help us in identifying the specific genetic markers we want to target, Unit 61398 acquired the complete repository of the DNA test results of half a billion people in America, the UK, and the EU. Basically, anyone who has used the services of Ancestry, 23andMe, African Ancestry, Elysium, MyHeritageDNA, and Futura Genetics, we have a copy of their DNA. When we received this treasure trove of data, we further enhanced the virus to go after certain individuals with inclinations toward specific underlying health conditions like diabetes, fatty liver, heart disease or cancer. This was particularly easy to create when we had the genetic data. This means the virus will not affect healthy individuals as much, but it will ravage those with underlying issues."

Another CMC member chided, "You realize this will also devastate a significant population of our own country?"

Dr. Zhong nodded. "It will. It will cull our country and the world of the unhealthy and the old, leaving us with a healthy, young cohort of people for the future."

President Yao Jintao had a big smile on his face at the news. He then exclaimed, "So long as we give the vaccine to at least some of our at-risk population, we can control the narrative, Doctor. Otherwise, this is exactly what we wanted. How soon until you have created enough of the vaccine in reserve so we can begin releasing the virus into the general public?"

"We are ramping up production of the vaccine," Zhong explained. "In another week, we will be producing fifty million vials a week. I think we should be ready to release the virus in six months. That should give us enough time to stockpile the vaccine and make sure we have it distributed to our allies."

The President smiled at the news. He dismissed Xi and Zhong so they could get back to their work.

Dr. Xi smiled as they left the meeting; it couldn't have gone better. Project Chengdu would cull the herd of the weak and sick. It would debilitate the West and destroy their economies. When this happened, the rest of the world would be clamoring for China to help, and like the benevolent superpower China was, they would be ready to assist the world as they recovered from this pandemic.

****

USSOUTHCOM
Doral, Florida

Major General Gary Bridges looked at the map on the wall of the operations room, then down at the stacks of reports on the table in front of him. Something wasn't adding up, but he wasn't sure what it was yet.

The volume of Chinese shipments through Panama was through the roof. *What are they shipping to Cuba and Venezuela?* Bridges contemplated. *We need to get more eyes on those ports and figure out what the heck is going on down there...*

"Sir, the staff is ready for you in the conference room," one of the staff officers said from behind him.

"Thank you, Major. Let's head on in," Bridges replied.

The two of them walked down the hall and into the classified briefing room. Everyone in the room stood when he walked in and waited for him to tell them to take their seats.

Taking his place at the head of the table, General Bridges motioned for everyone to sit down. This meeting included representatives from all the three-letter agencies, the Coast Guard, CBP, DHS, his military groups, and both a military and intelligence rep from the UK, France, Germany, Canada, Australia, and Japan. He originally hadn't wanted six other nations included, but he had come to appreciate what each brought to the table.

"OK, let's get this going. It's been a week since our last major powwow, so let's go over our do-outs from last week and then figure out what else needs to be vetted," Bridges announced.

Yoshio Mitani, the representative from CIRO, the Japanese Cabinet Intelligence and Research Office, spoke first. "Three weeks ago, we were tasked with collecting information on what was being loaded at the port of Shenzhen, China. One of our agents observed three roll-on, roll-off ships being loaded with a variety of military equipment ranging from armored cars and trucks to armored personnel carriers and tanks. Of note, the equipment appeared to be new, fresh from the factory."

Bridges grunted at the information. "Do we know where those ships are now?"

David Blair from the Canadian Security Intelligence Service answered this question. "The three ships were spotted passing through the Panama Canal four days ago. One was seen heading toward Cuba, while the other two appeared to be heading toward Venezuela."

"OK, so these are probably related to the military aid and the increase in military advisors in both Venezuela and Cuba. What can you tell me about the economic side? Is all of this military aid being given to these countries to protect Chinese trade interests or is something else at play here?" asked Bridges.

This time someone from the CIA spoke. "General, it's still our assessment that this activity is related to the Chinese Belt and Road Initiative. They've carried out similar programs along the trade routes leading to the Indian Ocean, the Middle East, and Europe. Like the US, they're establishing partnerships and military basing rights to protect their shipping lanes."

"I have to disagree," said one of the Australians. "If that was the goal of the Chinese, then why carry out such a large and comprehensive military modernization of the Cuban and Venezuelan militaries? Neither Cuba nor Venezuela are facing any external military threats. Even the civil unrest in Venezuela has calmed down now that jobs are being created by all the Chinese economic investments. Our agency thinks the Chinese are up to something much larger. We just aren't sure what that may be."

Nigel Younger from the British Secret Intelligence Service or SIS added, "If I may. Our organization, too, believes this may be part of a larger play. I was recently granted permission to share something with you. Is it possible to have this brought up on the screen for everyone?"

Nigel held up a classified thumb drive for one of the support people to take. The staff sergeant looked at the USB with a look of horror and then at General Bridges. Bridges crossed his arms as if irritated but nodded for the sergeant to do as the MI-6 guy asked.

"Staff Sergeant, the file is titled Project Ten. It's a PowerPoint presentation."

I'll have to speak with Nigel, Bridges thought. It was a major breach of protocol bringing a thumb drive into the SCIF. *Otherwise, what's the point of a Sensitive Compartmented Information Facility?*

A moment later, a slide deck popped up on the monitors for everyone to see. Nigel then stood up and walked over to the screen, facing General Bridges like he was about to give a lecture.

"General Bridges, we have an unwitting source in China that has, over the years, been providing us with some information about a secret program the Chinese created called Project Ten. At first, we thought this was part of the Chinese social credit program and their general surveillance apparatus. That was, until about a year ago."

Nigel continued, "Our chap in China said he was working on something called Jade Dragon. It's a new quantum computer built by Huawei. Several years ago, your president jeopardized the project when he threatened to cut off the sale of a critical technology component needed to finish the computer. Our handler was asked by our source if he could make some inquiries about finding an alternate source for some of that part. This is how we found out about the quantum computer. When our handler was asked about finding a new source for the specialized microprocessor that Intel sold them, we saw an opportunity to gain access to what they were building."

"So, you began selling them the same component part, but with spyware built into it?" asked the NSA rep as he leaned forward, waiting for the response.

Nigel grinned a crooked smile. "Well, naturally, old boy. Some lessons were learned from the Stuxnet worm used against the Iranian nuclear program a while back."

"Nigel, are you telling us SIS not only has a spy inside this program but a backdoor into it as well?" General Bridges pressed.

Nigel slowly shook his head. "Not quite. Our source is unwittingly providing us information. He's being manipulated by our handler into giving up sensitive information. As to a backdoor, I wouldn't quite call it that. Think of it a bit more like the Ultra project from World War II. We can't access the quantum computer or manipulate it. What we *are* able to do is see what the little buggers are doing with it."

This last sentence got the attention of everyone in the room. For a few seconds, no one said anything.

"Let me circle back to something you said earlier, Nigel," General Bridges remarked. "You said SIS believes the Chinese are up to something other than modernizing the Cuban and Venezuelan military to protect their resource interests. If you can view what they're doing with this quantum computer, then what *are* they doing with it, and what do you believe the Chinese are up to?"

Nigel eyed each of the others around the table before he spoke. "We believe this quantum computer, called Project Jade Dragon, is a part of a larger program, this Project Ten that I mentioned earlier. What we're seeing coming across Jade Dragon is not only all the data from the social credit system the Chinese use to track, monitor, and ultimately manipulate the behavior of their people; it now appears they're piping in additional information from the DragonLink satellite program."

"Yes, but what are they doing with all the data they're collecting?" asked David Blair, their Canadian rep.

"That is unknown. Right now, they're using these other platforms like a vacuum cleaner to suck up as much information as possible. We do know Jade Dragon has been breaking down the people it's collecting information on into designated control groups. But what is being done with those control groups is unknown," Nigel explained. "There are still parts of the program that are shielded from our spyware. The components we provided were unfortunately only used in parts of the computer's brain, so we can only see what's happening on that side of things. We believe they have firewalled parts of the computer to shield it from activities like ours."

General Bridges steepled his fingers as he brought his head down toward his hands. They'd heard a lot of new information. It confirmed what he'd already known—something bigger was at play. But they didn't know what that something was yet.

Bridges looked at Nigel. "Can you see if you can get permission to share what you're seeing on that computer with the NSA? Maybe having a second set of eyes on it will help us connect some additional dots."

Nigel nodded and said he'd work to get them access.

Turning to look at the others in the room, Bridges announced, "Everyone needs to start looking at what else China is currently doing. Are they deploying any military units to potential hot zones? Have they made any new military agreements or defense pacts? Are they doing anything suspicious in the financial realm or placing any odd orders for resources? Let's see if we can't find a few more pieces to this puzzle to help us figure out what's really going on."

****

**White House
Oval Office
Washington, D.C.**

Vice President Victoria "Vickie" Jackson wasn't sure what this meeting was about; President Alton had been super evasive about the reason for her coming to see him, and he had been very specific that even her aides would not be allowed to attend.

The President appeared worse off than she had ever seen him—she couldn't tell if he was about to throw up or if he was just nervous about something. In either case, he looked like hell.

"OK, Frank, it's just you and me," said Vickie. "What's with all the cloak-and-dagger stuff?" she pressed.

President Alton tried to grab at the glass of water on his desk, but his hand was shaking, and he nearly spilled it on himself. He sighed. "This…this is exactly what the problem is," he said.

"You're going to have to be more specific, Frank," said Vickie. She always shot straight from the hip—it was one of the things that the President said he liked about her.

"I'm not going to run for reelection," Alton announced.

"What?" she asked, taken aback.

"I expect your full discretion with this, but I was just diagnosed with ALS two weeks ago." The words hung in the air with the weight of a sack of bricks. No one said anything for a moment. "They are treating me, obviously, and so far, my symptoms are mostly isolated in my hands. I could have two years, I could have five, or I could be like Stephen Hawking and live another fifty years—I don't know. But I do know that I just didn't feel right about running again with this hanging over me."

"Frank, I'm sorry," was all Vickie could muster.

"Well, don't be too sorry. I want you to run," Alton urged. "This is your time, Vickie."

"I, uh...," she stammered.

"We'll come up with the usual 'I need to spend more time with my family' rigamarole, but when we announce that I'm stepping back, I want you to be ready to carry the torch, you understand?"

"Yes, sir," said the Vice President. She sat straighter in her chair. This wasn't how she wanted to come to this role, but she would rise to the challenge.

Chapter Twelve
Project Chengdu

January 2024
Port of Mariel, Cuba

The port manager, Esteban Ochoa, stood on the platform as the sun continued its climb into the morning sky; he wanted nothing more right now than a fresh cup of coffee and another cigarette. The speech being given by the representative from the China Ocean Shipping Company, otherwise known as COSCO, was dragging on far too long. The man's Spanish was terrible. It was obvious he'd learned the language in Spain, as he spoke with the unmistakable Spanish lisp that drove non-Spaniards nuts.

Great, it's that bloviating idiot from the Party's turn to speak next, Esteban thought.

The man, Ortega Ramírez, was the Communist Party boss for Mariel. He was also the brother-in-law to the new leader of Cuba, so he held a lot of sway in the city of Mariel. Ortega was generally a nice man and meant well—Esteban had to give him that, especially since he'd managed to get the government to double everyone's salary at the port. But Ortega was long-winded and tended to be too preachy about the Party.

Ortega took the center of the stage. "My fellow Cubans, the opening of this new port facility will bring new economic prosperity and opportunities to the people of Mariel and Cuba. When our communist brothers in the Soviet Union lost the people's war to the capitalists, it was like a dagger to the heart. Our nation suffered greatly during the Special Period, when we were abandoned by our communist brothers in Europe. Yet we chose to stick together during this turbulent time in history. We did not surrender ourselves to the capitalists or those fascist Yankee pigs. Neither did our communist brothers, the Chinese."

Some applause broke out at the mention of the Chinese. Many thousands of Chinese had settled in Mariel and had dumped a lot of money into the local economy.

Ortega continued. "China, like our communist brothers in Vietnam, has continued to thrive despite all of the attempts by the West to change them into a capitalist country. I am proud of our deepening ties with our

Chinese brothers and sisters as they teach us to model our economic system on their own—one that benefits the people and the state while not introducing the immoral trappings of the West and their bankrupt system. I am proud to stand here today as we open the newest and largest port in Cuba. I am also proud of the work everyone has done these past few years, working tirelessly to build this new facility.

"I would now like to introduce my friend, and port manager, Mr. Esteban Ochoa," Ortega said to the clapping and even cheering of some of the port workers.

Esteban stepped up to the podium and looked at the faces of the men and women standing before him. These were his workers, his people.

"Today is a great day. Today, we officially open the new port facilities. It has been a long four years as we labored to get this new facility built, but the wait is now over. Today, the Port of Mariel will be able to service six times the number of ships and cargo per year as before this project started. I want to personally thank our new leader, Diego Ventura, for increasing the pay of all Cubans as the government moves to improve the lives of us all; our dearly beloved First Secretary, who has left us in better shape than when he came into power, Salvador Mesa-Díaz; and finally, I thank my friend Mr. Ortega Ramírez, who fought to increase the wages of every worker at the port above and beyond what the First Secretary announced. Mr. Ramírez profoundly changed the lives of everyone for the better by pursuing this with our new leader. Now, let's go enjoy some coffee and refreshments before we start our first shift in this new port facility."

Music played as the people moved to the tents and helped themselves at tables filled with food and drink.

"Esteban, that was a great speech, my friend. Why don't you come for a short walk with me? I have someone I want to introduce you to," Ortega said jovially as he motioned for Esteban to head away from the crowd.

A fit-looking Chinese man and a couple of soldiers from the Ministry of Interior walked toward Esteban's office.

"What's happening, Ortega? Everything all right?" Esteban asked.

"Everything is fine, my friend. No problems. There are some people who want to talk with us," Ortega answered.

When the two of them entered the brand-new office space, the Chinese man introduced himself.

"Hello, Esteban. I was told you are the port manager. I want to talk to you about some sensitive items that will start arriving at the port very soon," the Chinese man said.

Esteban knew enough to nod in agreement and go along to get along. Especially with what he suspected were two members of the Special Group present. One could lose one's job—or, worse, go missing—if one said the wrong thing to the wrong person in Cuba. Special Group was the militant arm of the secret police and only answered to the secret police and the First Secretary himself.

"I understand. How can I be of assistance, and what can I do to make sure things go smoothly for you?" Esteban inquired happily.

The Chinese man smiled as he replied, "Excellent, I knew I could count on you. There will be a lot of freighters and cargo ships coming into the port from China. On occasion, there will be some specialized military equipment arriving. When that happens, some soldiers from Special Group will arrive to help provide security for the cargo and escort it to where it's going. All I need from you is some help in making sure only a few trusted people are involved in the transfer of the cargo from the ships to the trucks or rail as needed. Can we count on you for your discretion and help?"

Not missing a beat, Esteban quickly replied, "Of course. I am always glad to serve my country when and where I can. Let me know when these shipments are arriving, and I'll make sure to have a trusted crew of men ready to handle it."

With nothing more to be said, the Chinese man and the two soldiers left and headed toward the parking lot.

Ortega shrugged when Esteban gave him a look that said, *What was that all about?*

"Come, my friend. Let's get ourselves some coffee and a pastry. Today is a day to celebrate. This is day one of the economic revival of our country," Ortega said jovially.

****

Palace of the Revolution
Havana, Cuba

The newly sworn-in First Secretary Diego Ventura smiled as he greeted his guest.

"Minister Han, it is a true pleasure to see you. Thank you again for your kind words when I was sworn in as the new head of Cuba and all the fine work the People's Republic of China has done for our nation."

Minister Han smiled as the two shook hands. "No, thank you, First Secretary Ventura, for hosting this Latin American summit."

"I am humbled that you would ask Cuba to host such an important gathering," Ventura replied. "Your government has done more to help the people's cause and struggle in Latin America than the Yankees to the north of us."

"Please, can we go someplace quiet to talk? I have some information I would like to share with you," Han asked.

Sensing Han's nervousness, Ventura motioned for the two of them to head up to his private study, a small room off his office, which he routinely had swept for listening devices. It was his quiet oasis and place to think.

After the two entered the study, they took a seat in the overstuffed leather chairs.

Han began, "Mr. First Secretary, I needed to talk with you privately, so things do not come as a surprise to you or catch you off guard. As you know, my country has been in a protracted trade war with the United States, which will finally come to an end in the coming weeks when President Yao signs a new trade deal with the American president. Whatever you may hear or think about this trade deal, you need to understand that it is the first of many steps our country will be taking to supplant the Americans as the dominant economic and military power in the world."

Ventura smiled. "Minister Han, this sounds like good news. Why would I be surprised or concerned? Is there something more I should know about or be prepared for?"

Minister Han didn't smile. "There is. Part of our strategy against the West, and in particular the Americans, is to go after their economy. Unfortunately, in the process of doing so, there will be collateral damage. Many nations will be hurt by what will happen next. In fact, many people may end up dying from it as well. However, I can assure you it will not be the end of the world."

Ventura's smile left his face. "Minister Han, how badly will this affect Cuba and *our* people?" he pressed.

Han looked away and stared out the window for the moment. He didn't say anything right away. Finally, he turned back to Ventura.

"When this next phase starts, it will affect your trade with Europe. Since you do not have any trade with America, that will not be as much of a problem for you. However, it may become harder for you to acquire imports for many months."

"How many months, and what kind of imports?" Ventura demanded.

"I suspect it'll affect international trade for six to twelve months," Minister Han advised. "As to what kind of imports, that depends on what you are importing and what you need. We have helped Cuba meet its energy needs. We have also established a series of trade routes to both export your natural resources back to China and import finished products to Cuba. That trade will not be affected by what's to come. I recommend that whatever you do need to import from other sources, you make sure you have enough to last for up to a year."

"Can you share with me what is about to happen so I can better prepare my people and government to handle it?" Ventura inquired.

Han shook his head slowly. "Not right now. When things begin to happen, I will be able to share with you what is going on. China will help make sure Cuba is taken care of and then seen as a leader in the region. This will help to boost your standing in Latin America against the Americans."

Ventura nodded. "Is this why you have traveled here personally to speak with me?"

"It is," Han replied. "I need us both on the same page for our plan to work. Things will get turbulent for a period of time before they get better. What I can tell you is, once this is done, the Americans will no longer be oppressing Cuba or the rest of the world."

Chapter Twelve
The Plan

February 2024
Oxford, England

When Professor Hank Iverson had finished his meal in the main dining hall of Christ Church, he turned to his former student. "Dan, I'm so glad you were able to come and speak at the symposium on machine learning. Your insights into how this is being used in the commercial space were incredible. I think you inspired many new students to enter the field."

Dan blushed at the high praise. He liked Professor Iverson. Despite not seeing each other for many years after he'd left for Carnegie Mellon, they'd rekindled their friendship over the last few years.

"I'm glad I was of some help. I was a bit disappointed Dr. Xi wasn't able to attend. He truly is a brilliant man in this field."

"Not trying to bring up a touchy subject or anything, Dan, but I was hoping I might be able to ask you some questions about China. You're one of the few people I know who has straddled both sides by having lived and gone to university in the West and then returned to China." Professor Iverson leaned forward. "Do you believe the social credit program might be going a bit too far?" he asked softly. "Shouldn't people have autonomy to believe what they want without the government manipulating that?"

Dan reached for his wineglass and finished it off. He looked around and then back at Iverson. "Perhaps there is a more private place we could talk."

The professor nodded and guided them off the stage at the front of the dining hall where the professors sat during mealtimes. He led them through a side door that took them behind the dining hall to a private library the faculty often used. It had a number of leather chairs, couches, and tables. The walls were covered with ancient oil paintings and bookshelves with equally old books.

Iverson poured each of them a bourbon and brought the bottle and two glasses over to a table between two chairs. Dan sat down and took a swig before he answered. "I get what you're asking, Hank, and while I don't disagree with you on many of those points, let me ask you this. Are we truly living in the kind of society we want? Is it possible to create a better world and country if we can control the narrative and condition people to accept certain actions and behaviors over others?"

Iverson sat back in his chair for a moment, pondering that. It was a very big question. "Perhaps, but let me ask you this, Dan—who gets to decide what that narrative is? Who gets to determine what people should see or believe? What kind of society would we be creating if we took away people's ability to make independent decisions?"

"We create a better, more civilized society, Hank—a society run by those with the education and knowledge to understand what's best for the people," Dan countered.

His former professor smiled wryly. "Perhaps, but how do we know that the motives of those leaders are good? That becomes the age-old question."

"That's why we remove that issue from the equation and allow a machine to make that decision. We provide it with the parameters of what we want society to look like and how we want people to behave and respond, and then we let it begin the process of conditioning people via laws, policies, television, movies, books, and social media to create that society."

"And what do we do when that machine finally determines we humans are the problem and it moves to eliminate us from the equation altogether? Then what?" countered Iverson.

"This isn't Skynet," Dan said with a laugh. "That's not possible if you build in the right safety protocols."

There was a short pause. Iverson took a drink of his bourbon. "Dan, at the risk of our friendship, I need to ask you something very serious."

Dan tilted his head to one side but didn't say anything.

"Do you honestly believe President Yao, who is now effectively the president for life, is going to use Jade Dragon for the good of mankind and not as a tool or weapon to make China the most powerful nation on earth?"

Without thinking, Dan quickly countered, "Jade Dragon is doing enormous amounts of good for the world. It's already helped us develop a reasonable plan to address climate change and streamlined our economy to a point where we're not wasting resources on products that simply are not needed. It's working on solving some of the toughest energy problems of our times."

"I'm not saying there aren't good things coming from it," said Iverson. "What I'm saying is that the men at the top, the ones who control it, may not have the best of intentions for how it will be used and implemented."

Dan suddenly realized Iverson knew about Jade Dragon and that he had mentioned it out loud himself. He grabbed for his glass of bourbon and downed it. Reaching for the bottle, he refilled his glass all the way to the brim and then drank half of it down before he looked at his old teacher.

"I think I may have misspoken, Hank," Dan insisted. "Jade Dragon is a very sensitive program I've been working on for Alibaba. It's going to help our company capture the entire world market now that China's trade deal with the US is signed. It is not this massive government program you think it is."

Iverson paused. He took a deep breath and let it out slowly. "Dan, I need to level with you on something. This needs to stay between the two of us. If you ever say anything aloud about it, I'll deny it. While I am the chair of the computer science department, I am also a member of the Secret Intelligence Service—"

"Whoa, you mean to tell me you're MI-6? This entire time?" Dan interrupted in abject horror.

"I am. I have been for more than thirty years. My job is to identify people we can potentially recruit—people with the right placement and access to give us information of value."

"I'm a dead man. I'm *dead* as soon as they find out," Dan said, wringing his hands. "I can't believe all this time I've been sharing information with MI-6."

Leaning forward in his chair to close the distance between the two of them, Iverson countered, "No, Dan. You do not need to die. I have been very careful around you. It is highly unlikely your government or even Jade Dragon knows who I work for. My cover has been soundly built over the decades."

Dan just shook his head in disbelief. "You don't understand, Hank. Jade Dragon will know. If not right now, it will in the near future. It's only a matter of time until it has built a comprehensive social profile of every person it deems valuable. Since you and I have met on many occasions, it will have you near the top of the list. It's only a matter of time until they learn who you are. Once they do, they'll terminate me to make sure I can't possibly say anything else."

Hank reached out to Dan, taking his hand. "I know, Dan. That's why I wanted to talk with you privately right now. You're probably right—Jade Dragon will eventually piece together who I am, and it'll make the Ministry of State Security concerned enough that they will recommend you be killed. Dr. Xi will not be able to stop them."

As the realization washed over Dan, he could feel himself breaking out in a sweat. Iverson pressed in. "Knowing this, Dan, I need you to make the most difficult and consequential decision of your life. I need you to defect. I need you to agree to cross over to our side and assist us in unraveling what you've built and what they are going to do with it. We need your help in countering this program and stopping whatever is going to happen next."

Dan sat there in stunned silence. He pulled his hands back from Hank. With a slight tremor, he grabbed the bourbon and finished the rest of the glass off. The alcohol was starting to have its effect, but it was doing little to remove the sheer terror welling up within him. He thought about his parents and what would happen to them if he defected. *Heck, what will happen to them once Jade Dragon figures out Hank is really MI6?*

Dan stammered, "I…I can't. My parents still live in Shanghai, Hank."

"We can arrange for them to get out of the country. We can put you all in a sort of witness protection system. Give you a new identity and move you guys into a safe house and hide you for a period of time. Literally make you disappear from the grid," Iverson explained gently.

"I don't know. This is all happening too fast."

"If I may, Dan—let's do this, then. We're supposed to meet up in Macau in a couple of months. Why don't you have your parents join us?" Iverson asked. "When everyone is there, we'll look to evacuate you and them out of the country."

Dan thought about that for a moment, then shook his head. "It's too risky. The final stages go online next week. In a couple of months, Jade Dragon may have already figured out your identity. They'll know who you are, which means I'll be exposed."

"Then we need to extricate you now. What if we arrange for an accident to happen that requires you to be hospitalized? Could your parents fly to come see you here? Could that work?"

Dan thought about that for a moment, then nodded slightly.

"Then that's what we'll do. But first, I need to let some people know you're willing to defect. We're going to take you to a safe house right now and begin your debriefing. Things are starting to move fast, and we need to uncover what's happening before it's too late. We'll also put into motion an accident that'll give your parents the excuse to fly here. We have a stuntman we can use to make it look legitimate."

Hank pulled out his phone and made a couple of quick calls. In minutes, two men showed up and escorted Dan through a couple of secret corridors within Christ Church that led them to a small hidden room on the campus.

During the English Civil War of 1642, King Charles I had retreated to Christ Church and established his court at the college. During that period, a series of clandestine rooms and passages had been built. Over the years, many of them had fallen into disrepair or been boarded up. During World War II, British intelligence had converted a few of them into safe houses to conduct secret meetings or hide defectors.

When Dan's escorts unlocked the chamber, he found a double bed, a set of bunkbeds, a couple of chairs and couches, a table and a kitchenette. It looked like someone could hide in this place for some time without feeling like they were being cooped up in a jail cell.

While the bodyguards worked on getting Dan secured, a body double and stuntman showed up and started engineering a very public accident that would result in Dan's hospitalization. An SIS member got an ambulance on standby while a couple of compliant cops were told to head toward a particular section of Oxford. Dan was supposed to be on an afternoon flight out of London back to Beijing the next day, and it was now nine p.m., so they didn't have long to get things sorted.

Once Dan had been situated in his room, a couple of interviewers showed up to work with Iverson on debriefing Dan. They needed to know an enormous amount of information about Jade Dragon and what had transpired up to this point. Despite the late hour, the team of interviewers spent nearly four hours debriefing him. Iverson stayed and asked a lot of very technical questions about the program, specifically about what JD, as Dan called it, was working on next.

While Dan didn't have complete access to everything Dr. Xi had been working on, he was able to provide Iverson with the specifics of what JD was capable of, and what he shared was enough to send shivers down anyone's spine.

"The software and the brain you'd built for Jade Dragon is beyond anything I had thought possible," Iverson admitted.

****

JBCC – Computer Lab
Beijing, China

"Dr. Xi, I am sorry to interrupt, but this is important," one of his assistants said.

"What is so important you have to interrupt me at a time I told you explicitly not to?" Xi growled. He was finding it harder and harder to work on some of these complex coding problems when he was constantly being asked questions.

"Sir, it's Ma Yong—Dan. He's been in a terrible accident in England," the assistant blurted out.

For a moment, Xi didn't say anything. He was trying to digest what he'd just heard. "Is he OK?" Xi finally stammered. "What happened?"

"I don't know a lot—just that he was apparently hit by a car in Oxford. He was airlifted to a hospital. The man he was with, a Professor Hank Iverson, called Ma's parents and told them what had happened. He told them they should catch the next flight to London."

"Geez, is he going to live? How badly is he hurt?"

The assistant just shrugged.

Xi looked at the man. "How about you find out? If you can't speak directly to someone at the hospital to check on him, then get with the embassy and have them do it. We need to know what happened to him."

The assistant backed out of his office and went to work on finding out how acute Dan's injuries were. An hour later, Xi was told Dan had broken both his hips, his left femur, and his right shoulder. He also had a severe head wound, and was apparently in a medically induced coma to stop the brain swelling.

Not sure what more to say, Xi asked his assistant to have someone at the embassy continue to track his progress and report back to him every twelve hours.

Chapter Thirteen
Cuba Libre

February 2024
Isla de la Juventud, Cuba

José Santiago walked up to the counter to check in and presented his Canadian passport and credit card. "Good morning, Mr. Santiago. Is this your first time staying with us here at Hotel El Colony?" the receptionist asked warmly.

"It is. I've heard wonderful things about this place from some of my coworkers who stayed here previously."

The receptionist smiled as she checked him in. She gave him a key to a room situated on the ground floor and told him a bit about the hotel and the restaurant. Once he'd gotten things settled at the front desk, José walked to his room to drop his stuff.

He planned to spend a long four-day weekend on the island. It had taken him nearly a month to concoct a legitimate reason to visit the place and make the appropriate arrangements so he wouldn't get flagged by the secret police.

Once he got settled in his room, José couldn't shake a paranoid feeling, so he double-checked the burner phone he had brought with him to make sure he had the correct new SIM card and an increased memory card in it. José admired these Chinese knock-off versions of the Apple phone. They had some additional features the American versions didn't—like a removable memory card that allowed you to increase the phone's storage. José wanted to make sure he'd have plenty of space to take some photos and videos as he explored the city.

José ventured out of his room and wandered down to the hotel's restaurant. As he sat down, he couldn't help but notice there were a lot of Chinese people there. While there had always been a fair number of Chinese nationals in Havana, the number had tripled in the last twelve months.

José knew about the oil deal with the Chinese and the revamping of the ports, but he couldn't help but wonder if something else was afoot. The Chinese he saw around him weren't the usual tourists with cameras and selfie sticks. These were military-aged males. It was like an entire

Chinese army had suddenly descended on the island disguised in civilian clothes.

A few hours later, José wandered through the city of Nueva Gerona. It was a small city, fifty thousand people according to the information he'd read. Oddly, the more he walked around the place, the more it appeared to be abandoned.

Where have all the people gone? he thought.

José also noticed the number of construction vehicles and lorries driving through the city from the harbor. These weren't small trucks either. Some were loaded down with shipping containers, others with enormous steel beams, while still others held construction material. José noticed the trucks were operated by Chinese workers.

After looking for a café to sit in and ask some questions, José found a quaint little place called El Galeón, overlooking the city center of Nueva Gerona. The décor, with netting hanging from the walls and decorative lights, gave the café the feel of a pirate ship. The bartender wore a pirate hat while the two waitresses wore skull-and-bones bandannas covering their hair. It was probably a hopping place in the evenings.

When he walked out to the outdoor eating area, José saw mostly Chinese workers and a few locals. It took him a moment, but he found an empty table near the rear but still next to the inside seating. This seat gave him the best angle to watch everyone in the place.

As José waited for the waitress to bring him a menu and take his order, he pulled his phone out. He took a selfie from the right angle to capture the faces of military officers, then panned his camera to capture images of the other Chinese men seated at the café, looking like a tourist capturing images of the restaurant. Once he got back to Havana, he'd upload the photos to be analyzed.

Nearly five minutes after he'd taken a seat, the waitress came by, but only long enough to bring him a menu before leaving to serve the three tables with the Chinese workers and soldiers. The three groups appeared to be in good spirits, talking happily amongst each other in very rapid Mandarin.

While José waited for the waitress to return, he pulled the pack of Cohiba Originals out of his breast pocket and lit one up. It had taken José a few years to get the routine of being a native Cuban down, but he felt he was finally fitting in. Granted, he'd grown up in Venezuela before his parents had fled the Chávez regime for Florida, so he still knew how South American men acted. But Cubans...they were different. He certainly looked like a native, and he'd picked up the Cuban accent, but he was still working on that swagger of a Cuban man his age.

José took a couple of drags on the Cohiba cancer stick, as he liked to call them. The waitress returned to his table carrying a water pitcher. She refilled his glass before asking, "What can I get for you?"

José glanced down at the menu briefly. "I'll take the arroz con pollo and some iced tea."

The waitress smiled as she wrote his order down. She said she'd be back in a few minutes with his sweet tea, the only kind they served.

When she returned a few minutes later, José saw her name tape and asked, "Bernita, this is my first time to the island. Have there always been so many Chinese workers here?"

Bernita smiled at the question. "No, not always. It's more of a recent thing. Several years ago, the Economic Minister came here and told everyone a geology team had discovered a valuable mineral on the island. The Chinese started construction of a new oil refinery too."

José stuck his lower lip out as he nodded. "Wow, that sounds great. So where is everyone? Are they all working at the new facilities?"

Bernita laughed as she shook her head. "Well, everyone had a job at first. They were even paying everyone eight hundred pesos a month. Then a month ago, they told everyone we need to leave the island and relocate to the mainland. Apparently, they're expanding the mines and the new oil refinery. A lot of people weren't pleased about having to move. You know, many people have lived on this island for generations. Eventually, the Chinese offered everyone that relocated by March twenty thousand pesos to compensate us for losing our homes and businesses. Well, nearly everyone has taken them up on their offer, especially when the government said they would provide us with land to build new homes over in La Coloma along the water, or up in the mountains near Pinar del Río. You are lucky you're visiting us now; the island will be closed off to the public starting in March."

José smiled at the woman's good fortune as he nodded in approval. He joked with her, "That's a lot of pesos. Maybe I should find a local woman here to marry so I can be rich."

The waitress, a woman easily in her midforties, practically cackled. "Señor, you are too late. Maybe if you had come here this time last year, you might have found a good woman, but most of the people have already left. The only reason my husband and I have stuck around is because business has been so good with all the workers. The Party says we can keep our business open until the end of March if we'd like, then we need to leave." The woman seemed happy with how things were working out.

José tried to probe further. "Do you know why there are so many Chinese workers and military officers here?"

Bernita shrugged. "I do not ask questions like that. It's not my place. I know a lot of soldiers and workers continue arriving. I suspect they are working on the new mine."

"You don't happen to know where this new mine is located, do you? I want to make sure I don't go near it," José replied.

Bernita nodded and told him approximately where it was. José made a mental note to look the place up on his laptop when he got back to his room.

Once his food arrived, he chowed down on some of the best chicken and rice and beans he'd eaten in a long time. José didn't know what made the food so good, but each time he ate in these little towns outside of Havana, it was pure heaven. The chicken had incredible flavor. He supposed that was one of the benefits of not having animals raised on GMOs and hormones.

Later that afternoon, José changed into his running clothes. He attached his phone to an arm strap and inserted his earbuds. Looking at the map, José found the approximate location of the new airport he'd really been sent to the island to investigate and outlined his run. He started listening to a book on Audible and headed out for a run. It wasn't quite sunset; that would come in about ninety minutes.

He found it somewhat odd the government was building a new airport on the island while relocating everyone to the mainland. José decided to develop a running routine over the next few days so it wouldn't seem out of place when he ran past a few of the locations he'd been sent to observe and take pictures.

Forty minutes into his run, with sweat running down his face, José saw a slew of construction vehicles working in the large field where this new airport was being built. He paused his run long enough to do some stretches, then some push-ups, sit-ups, and a few other calisthenics. This allowed him to stand nearby and continue to observe the activity. During his exercise routine, he casually pulled his phone out of its case and took a few pictures.

Once he completed a few routines, he got back on the dirt road and continued his run. He saw a truck heading toward him. It had a shipping container on it with a company name stenciled on it—China Nonferrous Metal Mining Company.

Why build an airport if you're moving the population off the island? José wondered. *Something isn't adding up.*

As José ran back into town, he made sure his path took him by the harbor. He hadn't paid a lot of attention to it when he'd arrived this morning, but now, he noticed at least five dredging ships there. On the far side of the harbor, they were building up the pier wall with some large cranes. Whatever was going on, it was big.

For the next three days, José spoke with five different people and took two guided nature tours, two self-guided nature tours, and three more long runs. What he saw wasn't exactly giving him warm fuzzies. When he returned to Havana, he'd need to write up his findings and see what the folks on the seventh floor thought about it. Maybe they'd have a tasking they'd want him to look at. Then again, this was an election year and the economy was in the toilet, so they might not want to do much of anything until after November.

****

JBCC – Computer Lab
Beijing, China

"Dr. Xi, I just received a phone call from Ma Yong's parents," his assistant informed him. "They said Ma has unfortunately slipped into a vegetative state. They're going to pull him off life support tomorrow. They wanted me to pass along that information to you."

Xi sat back in his chair, stunned by the information. He was still in shock over what had happened to Dan, who had been in the hospital for nearly two weeks. The doctors had said his condition was starting to improve. Then suddenly, two days ago, it appeared to be taking a turn for the worse. They had performed two separate brain surgeries to alleviate the pressure, but it seemed like his body had just given out.

Letting a deep sigh out, Xi nodded in reply. "Please send my condolences to his parents and tell them we will do whatever is necessary to help them repatriate his body back to China if they would like. It's the least we could do for a member of our team."

I should have gone with him to speak at the Union. If I had been with him on that trip to Oxford, then maybe this terrible accident wouldn't have happened, Xi bemoaned. He kicked himself for insisting that Dan take his place. Now he was gone…and Xi felt terrible about it.
****

Cordeman Farms
Isle of Man

"I'm sorry the accommodations are a bit sparse, but this is the best we can do on short notice while keeping you away from the prying eyes of CCTVs," the SIS guard commented as he led Dan and his parents into a small cottage. "I guess you don't realize how prevalent the little buggers are until you suddenly need to avoid them."

The man placed their meager belongings in their rooms and showed them around the place. They had satellite TV, a DVD player with a slew of shows to choose from, and some Kindles preloaded with books. What they didn't have was anything that could connect them to the internet. No phones, no computers. The only people that had that access were the two SIS guards that would watch over them.

When the guard had left, Dan's father asked, "How long must we stay here, son?"

Dan felt bad for his parents. They had been lied to and lured to England without a chance to settle any of their affairs back home or bring anything with them. Their entire lives had just been upended and that was on him.

"I don't know. I'm supposed to meet with some people soon. I will ask them and find out where we will stay long-term. Perhaps there is a better place they can take us, or someplace we can be out and about more freely."

"If I'm going to be trapped here, then I'd like to set up my own garden. I was never able to have one in the city. I would like to at least have something like that," his mother commented.

She was probably taking this whole thing a lot better than his father, who was extremely upset at Dan for defecting to the UK. He couldn't fathom why his son would turn on their home country like this, especially when he had a good life working for Alibaba. His parents were oblivious to the real nature of his work.

****

Two Days Later

Dan looked at the three visitors sitting in the small living room of the cottage. His parents had agreed to stay in the bedroom while they talked. As far as Dan was concerned, the less they knew, the better.

"Dan," Hank Iverson began, "I want to introduce you to some people. This is a colleague of mine, Nigel Younger, and this is Jessica, from the US. They'd both like to ask you some questions about this program you've been working on and how it might be leveraged against the West. If you can be as open and transparent with them as you have been with me, that would be greatly appreciated."

Dan canted his head to the side, looking at the American. "I take it you are CIA?"

Jessica didn't say anything right away; she just stared at him. "I'm from Homeland Security."

Snorting at the response, Dan countered, "You want me to be honest and truthful about what Jade Dragon can do, then how about we forget about the subterfuge, shall we?"

Dan saw a slight smile crack on the woman's face. She nodded. "My name really is Jessica Parker. I do work for the CIA. I'm in the Directorate of Digital Innovation."

"Digital innovation…you work in the cyberwarfare section," Dan said confidently.

"It's one of our disciplines. Putting that aside, Dan, I'm here to assess you and determine if you're full of BS or if you're the real deal," Jessica explained, to Dan's chagrin.

"OK, I get it. You want to make sure I'm legit and that I keep spilling the beans if I am. But here's a question for you, Jessica and Nigel. What's in it for me? I just walked away from a job that paid me a salary of three million USD in China, a position that, I might add, had me completely exempt from the country's social credit program. I was considered an elite inside China. Now"—Dan waved his hand about—"I'm living in a three-room cottage on the Isle of Man, unable even to go into town. I've also upended my parents' entire world by talking with you. I don't mean to be rude, but I'd like to be compensated for the life I've just given up."

The British SIS officer, Nigel, scoffed. He stood up and paced the room briefly, lighting another cigarette before he took his seat again. Looking at Dan, Nigel countered hotly, "Compensated? How about keeping your life and that of your parents, you little prat? Isn't that enough?"

Jessica scrunched her brow at Nigel's outburst. She held a hand up as if to forestall him from saying anything further. "Dan has a point, Nigel. He's giving up everything."

"You can't be serious, Jessica. We just saved this wanker from being killed by his own government. That should be thanks enough. Now he wants money? If we pay this guy, how will we ever know he's being truthful? These millennials are pathetic."

"Come on, Nigel. He did just give up a very extravagant lifestyle in what's otherwise an authoritarian regime. I think if his information checks out, we should compensate him for it," Jessica said matter-of-factly.

Snorting at the comment, Nigel countered, "Let's start by verifying what he's telling us isn't just some pie-in-the-sky science fiction wet dream, shall we?"

Dan returned his gaze to Iverson, boring a hole through his head with his stare. *Are these people serious?* he wondered.

"I assure you, what we have built is not some fantasy. It is very real, and you are about to have it unleashed on your countries," Dan said with a chill in his voice.

"OK, Dan," said Jessica, leaning forward. "We understand you have been instrumental in the development of this new super-AI called Jade Dragon, or JD by you and Dr. Xi. But here's the deal—we've had our own super-AI in the works for decades too. It's constantly being upgraded and improved, and frankly—no disrespect—we have the best scientific minds in the world working on it. So why is your computer so much better that we should fear it?"

Dan snorted. He had to keep in mind he was talking with an American. If there was one thing he'd learned about them at Carnegie Mellon, it was that they were supremely confident and often arrogant.

"How about I give you an example of what Jade Dragon can do?" Dan offered.

The group nodded and waited for Dan to continue.

"OK, let's assume my government is going to go to war with America. Prior to that conflict, Jade Dragon would have war-gamed thousands of scenarios. They would largely know how it would turn out before it even started. Next, if China lost, the AI would look at some of the variables that led to that outcome—did we run out of resources, did we run out of fuel, etc. If we did, then the AI would begin to stockpile those commodities in advance of a conflict. Then the AI would look at the US and see what kind of shortages it could inflict on the Americans, either before or during the conflict, that could change its outcome. All of these ideas it's coming up with would be war-gamed thousands of times before the government ever made a move. Once they believed they had found the right path, they'd move to set things in motion and execute the plan.

"Before President Yao gave the order to attack, he would already know the likely outcome of the war. The only real variables would be how each individual battle played out. But even before a battle started, it'd be war-gamed and a strategy devised to ensure victory. You have to keep in mind, you aren't fighting the Chinese people or Chinese soldiers—you're fighting a machine that's directing them how to fight. The machine is devoid of emotions. It has no political or career aspirations, no fear, and absolutely no morals. The people and soldiers are just tools the machine is using to achieve the goal it has been given. Once Jade Dragon is fully unleashed on the West, you won't know what's hitting you," Dan tried to explain.

"Let's assume all of that is correct, Dan," said Jessica, steepling her fingers. "Your nation still imports huge amounts of food and agricultural goods from abroad. If there is a war against the West, how is China going to obtain its grain and other food products? Particularly from the US?"

Dan chuckled. "Ms. Parker, just months ago, your president signed a trade deal with Yao. What exactly do you think was the very first thing Yao agreed to purchase, and in such unheard-of quantities?"

"Farm products."

Dan smiled and nodded. "Not just farm products. Yao purchased enough grain and agricultural goods to feed three-quarters of China for nearly two years. Once Project Chengdu starts, it'll be enough food for many more years, at least until we acquire the additional agricultural lands we need to sustain our people."

Nigel furrowed his brow. "What is Project Chengdu?"

Dan smiled. *Wouldn't you like to know?* he thought. "I'll tell you what Project Chengdu is. But first, I have a list of demands I'd like met for betraying my country and giving away the farm. I didn't spend ten years of my youth in college to become one of the world's leading experts in machine learning so I could toil away on the Isle of Man in a cottage with my parents."

Jessica smiled at his bluntness. "OK, Dan. What do you want?"

"I want facial reconstruction surgery. I need to permanently change the way I look, or else the first time I pass a CCTV, Ring or other cloud based security system or have a picture taken, Jade Dragon will find me, which means the Ministry of State Security will find me. Second, I want a bank account with twenty-five million dollars in it. Third, I want either British or American citizenship with a completely new identity and a backstory that would stand up to heavy scrutiny. Fourth, I'd still like to be able to work in the field of machine learning, even if it's for one of your governments. This field is my passion—it's my reason for being, and I'm not about to just give it up. I'm far too young to do that. Lastly, I want my parents given new identities and the ability to settle in a remote place of their choosing with enough money to live out the rest of their lives. You guys grant me that, and I'll not only tell you about Project Chengdu, I'll tell you about some other secret projects Dr. Xi had been planning on using JD for—projects even President Yao and the CMC are unaware of."

He'd gone over this list of demands both in his head and with his parents for some time. His parents wanted to settle in America. They wanted to live in rural Idaho, of all places. They'd traveled through the state many years ago and were fascinated by the mountains.

Nigel looked at Hank Iverson with a raised eyebrow but didn't say anything right away. Jessica saw his hesitation and pounced. "Dan, I need you to provide me with something that we can use to verify your information—something that no one else could possibly know. If you can do that for me and it checks out, I can get your demands met," Jessica said as she extended her hand to Dan.

Reaching for her hand, Dan gave her a firm American handshake. "Deal. You won't be disappointed, Ms. Parker."

"So, what can we check to verify your story?" Nigel asked, still skeptical.

"This likely won't be in the news, but inquire with all the DNA genetic companies out there and ask if they had a security breach or had their information stolen seventeen months ago," Dan offered.

Biting her lower lip, Jessica asked, "You mean places like Ancestry.com?"

Dan nodded. "Exactly."

"Why would you steal people's DNA information?" Nigel asked.

"Verify my story, then I'll tell you why Jade Dragon stole it and all will be revealed."

****

CIA Headquarters
McClean, Virginia

"Dotty," called out the Starbucks barista.

Dotty smiled when she heard her name called. She walked up and grabbed the venti caramel ribbon crunch Frappuccino and thanked the woman who had prepared it for her.

It was exactly 5:25 a.m., and Dotty was determined to get a jump on the week. While she enjoyed the three-day weekend President's Day afforded them, it meant she would have a lot of things to catch up on when she got into work on Tuesday. She was also trying to get ahead of things before her two-week vacation.

In March, her husband was taking the two of them on one of those National Geographic expedition trips to Antarctica. They'd been talking about doing one of these cruise excursions for the last five years. Since their youngest son had left for college this past fall, they figured now would be the time to take a trip. Dotty was beyond thrilled. They would spend five full days exploring Antarctica while camping, kayaking around icebergs, and seeing the wildlife that lived in this hostile environment.

When Dotty reached the third floor, she made her way over to the Caribbean/South American section, where her office was. She swiped her access card in front of the scanner and then entered her individualized pin code. All of that activated a retinal scanner next to the door frame. Dotty hated this new retinal scanner. It was finicky and it had problems. She looked at the green light like she had been taught.

Pop…hiss…

Wow, first try. This must be my lucky day. Normally, it would take a couple of tries before the stupid scanner would accept her iris image.

Once she made it to her desk, Dotty dropped her purse and plopped down into her office chair. As her computers warmed up, she took a long drink of her coffee, letting the sugar and caffeine make their way into her bloodstream. Once she logged in to her unclassified, classified, and then top-secret computer terminals, she saw something that caught her attention.

Oh, some new reports from Goldfinger.

Goldfinger was the code name for their nonofficial cover agent in Cuba. The Agency didn't have a lot of NOCs in Cuba, so they didn't get a lot of information out of the island. The Cuban Ministry of Interior was especially good at rooting out foreign spies. They'd learned from the best—the Soviet KGB and their successor agency, the SVR.

Scanning the report from Goldfinger, Dotty saw that he'd attached close to three dozen photos and a few videos. She was impressed he'd been able to obtain images of the place they'd sent him to investigate. Camera phones were still relatively new in Cuba despite their proliferation around the world. The average Cuban could buy them now, but they weren't cheap, which meant most people tended not to have them.

Dotty spent a few minutes looking over the photos, then she dug into the report. Once she'd read it, she looked the photos and videos over again, this time with a new understanding of what she was seeing.

What are the Cubans doing with that place, and why are they letting the Chinese build a new harbor and airport on the island?

Dotty assigned the research to a couple of her junior analysts. She also put in a request with NRO to provide her with some real-time imagery of Isla de la Juventud. Next, she tasked one of her collection requirements managers to come up with a new priority intelligence requirement to determine the nature of the activity between the Chinese and the Cubans. Perhaps some of the other intelligence agencies had more data. In either case, once the PIR was created and published, they'd get some new data.

With nothing more to do regarding Goldfinger's information, Dotty went back to work. Her current priority was Venezuela and the Moros regime and what the Agency planned to do to help support Juan Guaidó and remove Moros once and for all.

Chapter Fourteen
Spy Games

March 2024
Beijing, China

"Dr. Xi, several weeks ago your AI began to put together a comprehensive database of foreign spies. That database helped us identify more than three hundred of them from over a dozen countries, all living in China. We have used that information to arrange a series of 'accidents' for them. It also identified nearly eight hundred others that might be considered spies. In their cases, we have revoked their visas and kicked them out of the country," the person from MSS said.

Xi nodded.

The man leaned forward and lowered his voice. "What we're here to talk with you about is someone whom you have had contact with in the past...a Professor Hank Iverson."

When Xi heard the name, a chill ran down his spine. He'd known Hank for at least fifteen years.

"Let me guess, he's a part of British intelligence?"

The intelligence officer lifted an eyebrow at the assumption. "He is, but how did you know?"

"Hank is a gifted professor and a true leader in the field of machine learning. He teaches some of the best and brightest minds in the world. It only makes sense that he would be."

"How long have you suspected this, and why have you not brought it up sooner?" the intelligence officer pressed.

Xi shrugged. "I only pieced it together a minute ago when you mentioned the foreign spy aspect and then you brought up his name. I mean, it's the same thing we do at our universities here in China."

The MSS officer appeared at ease with his answer. "Are you aware that Ma Yong had met up with Professor Iverson six times over the last seven years?"

Now Xi felt that chill returning. Had Dan known that Hank was a spy?

"I'm sorry, I was not. However, Ma Yong was his student at Oxford for many years. Um, you are aware that Ma died a few weeks ago in a car accident in Oxford."

The officer nodded. "We know. We aren't sure if he might have inadvertently passed them information during any of his interactions with Professor Iverson. Did he ever bring anything up to you?"

Xi shook his head. "No. I'm sorry, he never did. Honestly, Ma was a bit of a loner, a serious workaholic. He would take short weekend jaunts to Macau to let off steam, but he spent most of his time working here with me. I mean, that cot over there"—Xi pointed to an empty but made-up cot—"that was where he slept most days. He was constantly here, working in the lab all the time."

"OK, then I think that's all the questions we have for now. If we have some more, we'll let you know, Dr. Xi," the intelligence officer said as he stood up.

"Hey, what are you guys going to do with Professor Iverson now that you know he's also a spy?"

A slight smirk spread across the officer's face. "Let's just say a special team is being assembled to handle the known spies as your AI identifies them. We hope to cripple the West's intelligence-gathering capabilities over the coming months—just in time for the next phase of things to start."

****

"Mr. President, we are ready to begin Operation Chengdu," Dr. Xi said after he finished delivering his report and the preliminary analyses of how it would play out once it started.

President Yao Jintao was least confident in this particular plan the AI had cooked up. *There was a reason Hitler never deployed nerve or chemical weapons during World War II. How is this any different?* he wondered.

General Li Zuocheng looked at the President, then at Xi. "That vaccine had better work," he growled.

As head of the People's Liberation Army, General Li had voiced how incredibly skeptical he was about unleashing a virus like this on the world. Once the genie was out of the bottle, there was no telling what would happen next. His biggest concern was what happened if the virus suddenly mutated and the vaccine ended up not working. They could end up wiping out humanity.

Foreign Minister Han Jinping leaned forward in his chair, saying forcefully, "I want to say on the record that I am against this plan. I think this is pushing things too far and it will come back to bite us later if it's ever discovered that we manufactured this virus and summarily unleashed it on the world. Especially if we had a vaccine for it in advance. You saw the global blowback we had to deal with four years ago from the last virus."

"Jade Dragon has war-gamed this out thousands of times. If we are to defeat the West, we cannot do it bullet for bullet, ship for ship, or aircraft for aircraft. We need to weaken them first; we need to sicken them and cripple their economy. Then and only then can we defeat the West," Dr. Xi said defiantly.

Dr. Zhong, the virologist in charge of the program, added, "We have tested the virus on two small villages in western China. The village that had the vaccine did not have any infections when exposed to the virus. The village that was infected with the virus and did not have the vaccine had a fatality rate of one-tenth of a percent for those under the age of seventy and without any of the comorbidities we were told to target."

"And what if they did have those medical issues? What was the death rate then?" asked President Yao.

All eyes turned to Dr. Zhong to see what she would say next. "Sixty-two percent. That would likely be lower in the West, though, as they can provide a greater level of care to their patients than these villages were able to. Still, the virus will have the desired effect. It will weaken their population and put their economy into a prolonged tailspin leading up to their election and the execution of Project Ten."

The Foreign Minister shook his head dismissively at the news. "This is genocide, Mr. President. If we go through with this, we had better win this war, or they will surely hang us for crimes against humanity."

President Yao looked like he wasn't so sure if they should move forward. Dr. Xi went over the scenarios for how the coming conflict would play out if they didn't go through with releasing the virus and then how it would turn out if they did. Releasing the virus would prolong their own food stores, reduce the long-term drag on their own economy and greatly weaken the West right as they were about to launch their attack. If a few tens of millions of even a hundred million largely sick and elderly people had to perish to usher in the new world power, then so be it. Social Darwinism would be allowed to rear its ugly head.
****

Three Weeks Later
Task Force 7

Major General Gary Bridges looked at Nigel Younger. "You and Jessica just returned from across the Pond. This Chinese defector—he's spilling the beans on this PLA AI supercomputer. What exactly is he alluding to that has you both so worked up?"

The military and civilians at the table looked at the SIS and CIA representatives, waiting to hear what the two of them had to say.

In his posh highborn British accent, Nigel explained, "Right, for several years we've known the PLA had developed some sort of super-AI. We've had a limited window into it. What we haven't known, at least up until recently, was how advanced and complicated this thing was."

Bridges bunched his eyebrows. "How about you give us the fifty-thousand-foot view of what we're talking about?"

"Uh, yes, of course. The PLA has built a super-powerful AI program that can reasonably predict how America and the West will react to something they may do. Let me give you an example. Suppose the Chinese Navy move to enforce a blockade within the South China Sea, saying America is trespassing in their territorial waters. Prior to their making that decision and then enforcing it with their navy, their computer would war-game the likely responses by America and the West. Knowing how our navies and governments would respond makes it more likely they'll move forward with their plan because they'll have removed the unknown of how America or the West would react. This ability to predict how our nations will respond to a given action the Chinese may take is being applied across all domains, ranging from military to economic to banking to trade. It may be one of the reasons we've seen the Chinese economy explode in the last three years. They've been implementing this new computer's ideas."

"How effective could this thing really be?" quizzed Yoshio Mitani. He was their lone representative from CIRO, the Japanese Cabinet Intelligence and Research Office. Their organization had been critical of the reporting on the PLA's AI program up to this point.

"Effective enough that they're moving forward with some radical plans in the coming months," Jessica Parker asserted.

"How about you give us an idea on what you mean by radical plans, Ms. Parker?" pressed General Bridges.

Turning to face him, Jessica explained, "When I talked with the defector, he shared some of the plans he knew of. While he wasn't directly involved in them, he was involved in the computer simulations. At first, I was a bit skeptical, but at the same time, he is one of the creators of the AI and helped to build its brain and craft its ability to learn, understand, and make predictive analyses of situations."

"That's great, Jessica. But how about some specifics? What exactly are they cooking up?" the general demanded.

Coming to her aid, Nigel asked, "Have you ever heard of a technology called deepfake?"

Several of the people nodded while a couple stared blankly at Nigel.

"Most of us know what it is, Nigel, but why don't you briefly explain it and then tell us how that's related to what the Chinese are planning on using it?" Bridges directed.

Nigel nodded. "OK, well, this is quite technical, you see, what I'm about to explain. From our understanding of the Chinese quantum computer, Jade Dragon, the communists have been teaching their little machine to generate a digital image of nearly all world leaders and American, British, French, German, and Russian politicians. They've been testing their likenesses to make sure they're as accurate as possible. What they'll be able to do with this is generate a video message of that leader saying or doing whatever they want them to say or do. The challenge is that none of us will know if it's real or fake until it has gone through some *serious* electronic analysis, which will naturally take a bit of time.

"You see, what the Chinese have done through their massive data collection efforts is feed the real images, speeches, things like that into what's called a generative neural network. Then they create a message they want that politician to say. Let's assume they wanted to embarrass the Prime Minister of Japan. They could generate an image of the PM and have him say something rather cheeky about the President of China. The machine would play that video feed against a generative adversarial network to spot the mistakes in the fake message. As the mistakes are found, the generative neural network integrates the corrections into the next version, and they test it again. This happens hundreds of times until the message they're creating is indistinguishable from reality. Over time, the AI learns how to recreate the perfect video of the PM and then generate future messages at will," explained Nigel.

Yoshio Mitani looked like he had bitten down on a lemon at the thought of the Chinese generating a fake digital message from the PM's office to humiliate Japan.

General Bridges saw the look of concern on the others' faces. He'd known about deepfakes for a long time. It was a big concern going into the next election cycle in the US.

As if the 2016 and 2020 cycles weren't bad enough, Bridges thought.

"Nigel, SIS has been a step or two ahead of everyone when it comes to Project Ten and this new AI supercomputer the Chinese have created. Does your organization know or has your defector relayed how the PLA may use this new information warfare capability against the allied nations and Latin America?" asked Bridges.

Nigel placed his cup of tea down. "While I appreciate the high praise, General Bridges, our organization wouldn't have been able to piece together much of the technical aspects of what Jade Dragon or their DragonLink satellite system was capable of doing if Ms. Parker and her team hadn't provided so much help."

Parker smiled and waved off the compliment. She was on loan to the task force from the CIA's Directorate of Digital Innovation or DDI. For the most part, she sat in the briefings and said very little. She seemed more comfortable as a behind-the-scenes kind of person, though she'd been instrumental in the debriefing of Ma "Daniel" Yong.

General Bridges looked at Jessica. "Maybe my question should be directed at you. Is there anything specific DDI is able to tell us about how or when the PLA may use this weapon they've created?"

Jessica looked like she would rather not answer, but with all eyes staring at her, she cleared her throat and replied, "This is a hard question to answer accurately, General. The obvious target is the election this fall. However, what's truly concerning is a plan they appear to be pushing forward with to attack and destabilize the economies of the West. We're still trying to vet the information, but if what this defector told us is true, then we're in for a very rough year."

"If I may, General. I feel I should also inform the group that our handler who had been obtaining the information for us about Project Ten has rather unexpectedly died," Nigel announced.

"Whoa. He died? How? What happened?" asked General Bridges, taken aback by the news.

"Yes, it was rather a shock to our operation. Two weeks after our handler convinced his source to defect, he traveled to Asia to meet with another source. Sometime during that trip, he apparently came into contact with a new virus that appears to be spreading wildly in Asia and now Europe. We're still working to confirm this, but this virus may actually be part of a more nefarious scheme on the part of the Chinese. As Jessica alluded to earlier, we are still working to verify this before we make a definitive conclusion," Nigel explained.

"I heard there's a new virus or superbug. It supposedly originated in Chengdu, China, before spreading beyond their borders. Do you really think the Chinese would unleash something like this on their own people, though?" inquired one of the task force members.

Nigel shrugged in response. "Perhaps. I mean, what better way to achieve plausible deniability for releasing a genetically engineered virus than to release it first in your own country?"
****

National Security Advisor's Office
White House

Blain Wilson loved his job as National Security Advisor, but right now, he missed his family. He missed being around his fifteen-year-old daughter and his seventeen-year-old son. They were growing up fast, and soon they'd both be out of high school and off to college. He loved this job, but man, it was killing him.

Wilson had known when he'd accepted the NSA position that it would be one of those all-consuming jobs. He now understood why the people before him had turned over every few years. The position had a way of sucking the life out of you. Providing critical national security advice to the President was no easy feat. Hundreds, sometimes thousands or even millions of lives could depend on what he told the President or advised him to do. That was a big weight to carry on one's shoulders.

"Mike," he called out to his executive assistant, "what's this report from the CDC all about? The one you put on my desk an hour ago?"

A second later, Mike walked into his office from around the corner. "Yeah, I meant to tell you about that earlier before you got pulled into the Oval. Someone from the CDC sent this to me this morning, asking if

I could get you to take a look at it. It's something about a new bug or something popping up in China, Italy, Germany, and the UK."

Wilson folded his arms. "Some kind of new bug? Is it dangerous? Why is the CDC wanting me to look at it?"

Mike only shrugged. The memories of the last superbug to have come out of China four years ago were still fresh in everyone's minds.

"All right, fine. Get me the person's number who sent this over to you. I'll spend a few minutes reading over the summary, if they sent one, and get myself up to speed."

Mike scurried out of the office. Wilson flipped open the first page of the report and started reading.

> ***Summary of COVID-24:***
> *SARS-CoV-3 is an infectious disease caused by severe acute respiratory syndrome coronavirus 3. Common symptoms include fever, sweating, sneezing, coughing, sporadic nerve pain across the extremities and fatigue. While we are still in the early stages of understanding this virus, most cases identified to date have resulted in mild symptoms that appear to resolve themselves without the need for medical intervention.*
> *However, an unknown percentage of people infected have experienced acute respiratory distress syndrome, requiring medical intervention.*
> *In China, Italy, Germany, and the United Kingdom, there have been reports of some patients suffering from multiple organ failure, to include septic shock. At this present time, we are unable to determine how contagious the virus is or its incubation period. Until more of this information can be identified, the CDC recommends issuing a level 2 travel advisory for China, Italy, Germany, and the United Kingdom.*

Wilson folded the paper back over and laid it down on his desk.

What the hell? he wondered. They were still recovering from COVID-19, and that was four years ago. *Now we need to be worried about a new superbug...out of China again? As if Iran, ISIS, North Korea, and the peace deal in Ukraine weren't enough to deal with...*

A minute later, Mike walked back in and placed the phone number for Clarence Bauer, the Deputy Director for the CDC, on his desk.

Wilson dialed the number and waited for the call to connect. It rang once. "This is Dr. Bauer. How can I help you?" Wilson thought the man sounded awfully chipper, considering the memo he'd sent to the White House a few hours ago.

"Hello, Dr. Bauer. This is Blain Wilson, the National Security Advisor. I understand you were trying to get a hold of me."

"Ah, thank you for returning my call so promptly, Mr. Wilson. Did you read the memo I sent to your office regarding this new COVID virus?" Dr. Bauer asked. The voice on the other end had changed from chipper to concerned, a change that wasn't lost on Wilson.

"I did. It sounds a little scary. How big of a problem will this be?" asked Wilson.

"Are you sitting down?" asked the voice from far away.

Wilson felt his stomach tighten as he replied, "Should I be?"

"I think it would be best," said Dr. Bauer.

Chapter Fifteen
Prisoner Swap

April 2024
Presidio Modelo
Isla de la Juventud, Cuba

The electrical current surged through the prisoner's body one more time before he passed out from the pain.

"Wake him up and begin again," ordered the captain conducting the interrogation, Miguel Rodriguez.

One of the guards splashed some cold water on the man's face and across his body. The shock of the cold water barely caused the man to flinch. The guard then cracked open a smelling salt tab and placed it under his nose.

The prisoner was startled awake, only to realize he was still being tortured.

"Captain Rodriguez, come here for a moment," a voice from behind him called out with an air of authority, letting the captain know someone more senior had just shown up.

When the army officer exited the cell room, Rodriguez snapped to attention at the sight of Colonel Leopoldo Cintra. "Captain, how long have you been questioning the prisoner?"

"We've been questioning him since we apprehended him yesterday," Captain Rodriguez replied nervously.

Colonel Cintra eyed the man intensely for a moment before asking, "Has he given you anything useful?"

Rodriguez's cheeks flushed, and he lowered his head. "He will break soon enough."

Colonel Cintra shook his head in disappointment. "Captain, I will take possession of the prisoner and take him to the Villa. Have him dressed and brought to the courtyard. My helicopter will leave in thirty minutes."

Colonel Cintra turned on his heel and left Rodriguez there, dumbfounded. When he'd recovered from the sting, Rodriguez barked some orders to the guards, who went to work on getting the prisoner dressed and ready to leave.

****

Three Hours Later

Colonel Leopoldo Cintra looked at the dirty prisoner sitting opposite him. He smelled of urine and feces. His nose was clearly fractured, and he was missing a couple of teeth. The local intelligence officer had worked him over well, but he hadn't broken. The prisoner, whoever he was, was doing his best not to make eye contact.

Colonel Cintra walked up to one of the guards. "No one is to touch or harm the prisoner unless I give the order. Is that understood?"

The head of the guard force nodded and said he'd relay the instructions to his people.

"Have a doctor see him in the morning. In the meantime, bring him some water and food."

Cintra headed up to the office he was using while he was here. It was nearly five in the morning, and the sun was starting to push away the dark of night. He sat down at the desk and reviewed the possessions the man had when captured: a high-end Nikon digital camera, a telephoto lens, a separate night vision lens, a small directional antenna and a few high-energy protein bars.

Whoever this man was, he clearly wasn't a birding tourist who had gotten lost like he had claimed to be. This was spy equipment.

No matter—by later today, we will know exactly who he is, Colonel Cintra thought.

A knock at the door broke his attention. When he looked up, he saw Colonel Luan and smiled. "Good morning," he said. "Come on in."

The Chinese colonel walked in and took a seat. A moment later, an orderly walked into the room and asked if they'd like anything, and the two colonels requested some coffee before the man left to fill their order.

"I hear your people apprehended a spy near the new airport," Colonel Luan said, a bit of unease evident in his voice.

Cintra waved off the man's concern. "We did. But he is in custody, and soon, we'll know who he is and who he's working for."

Colonel Luan sighed as he shook his head. "I had hoped we could keep our activities on the island a secret for a bit longer. The Americans will not like what is going on there."

"The Americans don't like anything we Cubans do," Cintra countered with a laugh. "What will they do to us? Place an embargo on

Cuba? They've embargoed us since the 1960s and yet here we are, still moving forward. No, my friend—the Americans have been overextended for decades, and now they're in the midst of a pandemic and an economic depression. They will not do anything."

"You are assuming this person you captured is American and not from some other Western country's intelligence agency," Luan said. Cintra felt as though this statement was a sort of test.

"Luan, China is new to this area of the world. You must understand something. This is America's backyard. I doubt the Europeans care if China is building a military base in Cuba. The Americans, however—well, they will certainly care."

Luan bristled a bit at Cintra's cavalier response. "It's a bit more than a military base we are building, Leopoldo. It's an entire military complex, port, and refinery."

"How much longer until your base is operational?" asked Cintra.

The Chinese colonel did not respond right away. "Soon. We have more workers arriving each day. Would you like to question your prisoner to learn his identity, or would you like me to save you the trouble and tell you who he is?"

Cintra's left eyebrow rose. "You mean to tell me you already know who he is? If so, then yes, tell me who he is and save me the trouble of having to beat it out of him."

The Chinese colonel reached down for his leather briefcase. He placed it on his lap and unlocked it, then reached inside and pulled out a manila folder, which he handed to Colonel Cintra.

"I received this prior to coming here. This is everything we have on the prisoner. His name is Isaac Jacobs. He was born in Toledo, Ohio, on February third, 1988. He's married, with three kids, two girls and one boy. He joined the Army in February 2006. He completed Ranger school a year later, serving two combat tours in Iraq and a single tour in Afghanistan. And then his military record disappears in 2017."

"Where's the rest of his record?" Cintra asked, folding his arms. "Why did it suddenly end in 2017?"

Luan smiled a crooked grin. "That's when he transferred to a clandestine group called Task Force Orange. They are an intelligence and surveillance group that supports their Delta Force, SEAL Team Six, and the CIA's Special Activities Center. My suspicion is he was sent to Juventud Island to see what their satellites couldn't tell them."

Cintra thought about that for a moment as he scanned the man's dossier. "How did you acquire all of this information about him?"

Chuckling softly, Luan replied, "Roughly a decade ago, the American Office of Personnel Management had a data breach. Do you remember hearing anything about it?"

Colonel Cintra shrugged; he honestly had no idea. Cuba wasn't exactly the most cutting-edge place for outside news or information.

Luan went on, "It's OK if you don't. One of our intelligence groups hacked into this organization, which is responsible for maintaining the security clearance information for all their military, government, and contractors who work for the American government. Once we had the information, we created profiles of each person based on where they worked and what they most likely had access to. Our agents then went to work on creating compromising situations and blackmailing some individuals into working for us.

"As to why we suspect our Mr. Jacobs—or rather, Master Sergeant Jacobs—is most likely working for Task Force Orange, we apprehended one of their members in the South China Sea several years ago. It took many months to break that individual, but once he broke, he confirmed to us a list of twelve other members. Then it was a matter of monitoring those individuals and seeing who else they came in contact with over time. After doing this for a couple of years, we are confident we've figured out who most of their members are. Then it was a matter of observing where they went to know what they were up to."

"OK, so if we know who he is, and who he is working for, then what do you want to do with him now?" asked Cintra.

Luan leaned forward. "We use him as *leverage*. You see, since we know what he was doing, and we know who he is, we use that to get the Americans to trade for him. What I propose is we trade him for one of your spies they're holding and then ask for two of our citizens they grabbed in January. This can work out well for both of our nations, Leopoldo."

The Cuban colonel thought about that for a moment. Then he realized this might work to his own benefit. If he could secure the release of a Cuban spy from the Americans…that might go a long way toward helping him with the Party. If he could secure two Chinese prisoners while he was at it, all the better.

A smile crept across Cintra's face. "I think a trade would be a good idea. Let me propose it to my superiors. If you'll do the same with your own, it might help me better make my case to include your two citizens in the request."

****

CIA Headquarters
McClean, Virginia

It had already been a long week and it was only Wednesday. Dotty was in a foul mood. Her and her husband's trip to Antarctica had been officially canceled as of last night due to this new virus that was springing up all over the world. After the lessons learned from both SARS and COVID-19, the government had acted swiftly this time, shutting down foreign travel and locking down the two hundred cities in thirty-nine states where the virus had already popped up. Everyone hoped to avoid a nationwide shutdown like last time, but it might become inevitable.

Dotty had been looking forward to this cruise for more than a year. The chance to kayak around some icebergs, have photo ops with penguins, and camp on Antarctica itself was a once-in-a-lifetime opportunity.

Maybe next year...or the year after, we can try again...

Only two more days until the weekend. Dotty hoped she wouldn't have to work through it again.

Normally, Dotty and her team stayed focused on Latin America. Lately, they'd been tasked with determining why some countries in their area of responsibility or AOR had few or no cases of this new virus while others were being ravaged by it.

Something seemed off. The virus had spread like crazy in Mexico, Colombia, and the rest of South America. But there were hardly any cases in Panama, El Salvador, Cuba, and Venezuela. This virus unnerved everyone. Dotty wasn't exactly the epitome of physical health. Like both her parents and her brother, she'd developed diabetes in her forties, and her sedentary job meant she was carrying a bit more weight than she should.

Dotty groaned audibly to herself as she looked at the latest cable from the US embassy in Havana. The station chief had sent it in late last night, which meant she didn't have a lot of time to evaluate it before she'd invariably get called up to the seventh floor to discuss its contents.

The Cubans had captured an American spy and now they were demanding a trade. A trade was fine—that was normal and expected in their profession. What wasn't expected was the additional caveats to the trade. The Cubans had included two Chinese nationals.

The audacity of them...to demand we fork over Chinese spies in addition to their own, Dotty thought.

The Cubans had sent a proof-of-life video of one Master Sergeant Isaac Jacobs, the man they'd captured in the act of espionage. Dotty watched the video. He looked like he was in bad shape. They'd clearly worked the man over. She knew the longer they left him in Cuban custody, the higher the chances he'd start singing. Everyone had a breaking point, no matter what Hollywood or survival and evasion school told people.

The whole mission had been a bust. Dotty had objected to the mission going forward to begin with. There was no reason to send an operative to the island. Her asset, Goldfinger, had already obtained the visual information of what was going on, and NRO had tasked a satellite to keep tabs on it monthly. They had everything they needed.

"You've seen the cable from the embassy?" asked one of Dotty's team members.

Making a sour face, Dotty replied, "I have. What's SAC saying about it?"

Snorting at the mention of the Special Activities Center, her colleague commented, "They want to launch a raid to free their guy. Barring that, they want us to make the trade."

Dotty shook her head in frustration. *What a cluster mess.*

Ding.

An email notification popped up in her Outlook. Sure enough, there was her summons to the seventh floor.

"I need to go upstairs for an emergency meeting to discuss this. We'll see what they want to do next. Have the rest of the team figure out if Ana Montes still has any value. I'm not opposed to trading her to get our guy back. While you are at it, investigate the other two people, the Chinese nationals, Yanqing Ye and Zaosong Zheng. They were arrested in January at Logan International. See if you can figure out why the Cubans would be interested in them."

Dotty headed up to the seventh floor and over to the deputy director's office. When she walked into the briefing room on the side of his office, Dotty saw a couple of members from SAC, along with a few analysis and section chiefs, their NRO rep, and a new face she didn't recognize.

"Ah, Dotty. There you are. Let's get started now that everyone is here," Deputy Director Aaron Rodgers announced.

Rodgers was a rising star in the Agency—and, no, he had no relationship to the famous Green Bay Packers quarterback of the same name. Although Rodgers did like to play along and had thoroughly tricked his office out with Packers paraphernalia.

Rodgers had cut his teeth in the Middle East and then later in Ukraine as a deep-cover agent in the arms trade. He was also a bit of a darling to both the Senate and the White House. Despite all that, Dotty liked the man. He was sharp, but more than that, he really looked out for his people, a trait that wasn't always common in the spy world, where agents were often hung out to dry if things went south.

"Uh, before we start, do you mind introducing us to our guest?" Dotty asked as she took her seat. She wouldn't talk about classified information without knowing who all was in the room with her.

Aaron's face flushed a bit as he probably realized he should have done that from the get-go. "This is Joel Metcalf. He's from Defense HUMINT. He's been working with Jessica Parker down in Doral on Joint Task Force Seven. He'll be joining us for the brief."

Everyone nodded at Joel but didn't say anything. He was an outsider to their organization, even if he was part of the intelligence community.

"Let's just get down to business, Aaron. What are we going to do to get my guy back?" demanded Jim, the director of the Agency's Special Activities Center, known as SAC.

"The Director is weighing the options right now," Aaron replied. "He has a meeting at the White House this afternoon with the National Security Advisor to present our recommendations. That means we have two hours to come up with a plan. I know Jim's position. I want to hear others."

"I propose we make the trade," Amber from the Directorate of Analysis interjected before anyone else could. "As I'm sure Dotty's team will attest, we have everything useful we can get out of Ana Montes. There's no real reason to keep her if we can get our guy back."

"Dotty, your agent, Goldfinger. He's still safe for the time being, right?" Aaron inquired.

Dotty nodded. "He is. But I think we should talk about the other request the Cubans attached to Ana Montes. She's not the only person they're asking for."

Jim from SAC scrunched his eyebrows. "What do you mean? We only saw Ana on the cable."

"Late last night, our station chief in Havana sent us an eyes-only cable, outlining a meeting the ambassador had last night with the First-Secretary of Cuba," Aaron explained, his facial expression betraying his displeasure. "The Chinese ambassador was also present in the meeting. First-Secretary Ventura said if we wanted our man back, we'd not only need to turn over Ana, we'd also need to release the two Chinese nationals we apprehended this past January. Their names are Yanqing Ye and Zaosong Zheng. They were detained at Logan International as they tried to board a plane to Beijing."

A few people whistled. "Why would the Cubans lobby for the release of two Chinese spies?" asked Jim from SAC. "That seems like an odd request."

Tara from NRO interjected, "The Chinese are probably pressuring the Cubans to include them. I think the bigger question is, why are they so interested in these two individuals now?"

Amber chimed in, "I think it's obvious why. Ye is a lieutenant in the People's Liberation Army. She hid that on her visa application. She's also a PhD student at Boston University in their robotics department."

"Yeah, but why is that a big deal? There are thousands of Chinese nationals studying in PhD programs in the US. Many of them are probably military as well. What was so big about this particular student?" Aaron pressed.

Amber continued, "When Boston Dynamics started a research project with Boston U, it was only supposed to include US citizens. Boston Dynamics is partnered with DARPA, so anything they do is classified. Ye managed to get herself included in a program that was working to support the LS3 project for the Marines. She lied on her application, saying her parents were Chinese immigrants and she had recently obtained her US citizenship. Clearly, someone in the vetting department didn't do a very good job. In all honesty, the only reason the FBI was alerted that she might be up to something nefarious was that a systems administrator at Boston Dynamics discovered someone had attempted to download some sensitive files pertaining to the OS for the retired BigDog program and the current LS3 one."

"Holy crap, Amber. Was she able to leak that data to her handlers?" the SAC director asked in shock.

Amber nodded. "She did. However, it was phony information she stole. It was a honeytrap the company had set as a means of keeping potential hackers from finding the real stuff. When she accessed the honeytrap, that's when they alerted the FBI. I suspect the Chinese want the Cubans to use this opportunity to get two of their spies out of our custody."

Aaron bit his lower lip as he thought about the situation. "This request for the two Chinese nationals kind of complicates things. Trading Ana to them was a no-brainer, but these two…that'll be a tougher sell. We're still debriefing them. I have two questions I'd like answered, preferably before the Director has to meet with Mr. Wilson later today."

Everyone looked at Aaron, waiting to hear his questions. Dotty had a good guess at what they were.

"First, what kind of intelligence value do we still believe these Chinese nationals have? Second, what's going on in Cuba that the Chinese believe they can leverage the government to trade our guy for two of theirs?"

No one spoke for a moment. Dotty had a good idea, but she wanted to hear what Amber had to say.

Instead, Tara from NRO spoke first. "I don't know specifics, but I can tell you from our perspective what the Chinese have been up to."

Aaron nodded for her to continue.

"For the last three years, the ports of Mariel and Havana have been undergoing major construction. Both ports have more than tripled in capacity. We've also seen new construction taking place at Havana International and two very old military airfields. I'm talking runway extensions, new hangars, storage facilities, improved perimeter security, and guard towers. The Isla de la Juventud, however, underwent a radical transformation—"

Interrupting her, Aaron asked, "What do you mean radical transformation? Please be specific."

Tara nodded. "Six years ago, around the same time the Chinese helped the Cubans explore oil in the Straits of Florida, a Chinese geology team discovered a cobalt deposit on the island. Cobalt, as you know, is an extremely valuable resource and one that's hard to come by. The infrastructure on the island, however, was practically nonexistent. To be frank, infrastructure in Cuba as a whole is very bad. I think Amber or Dotty can probably fill you in more on the details of the deal the Cubans struck with the Chinese, but suffice it to say, the Chinese have been investing heavily in modernizing the Cuban infrastructure so they can extract these cobalt resources more easily. From my understanding, the Chinese obtained exclusive mining rights on Isla de la Juventud in exchange for improving the infrastructure. For the last several years, they created a port on the island and expanded and modernized the ports of Mariel and Havana."

Aaron turned to Amber. "Tell me about this deal the Chinese made."

"The Chinese signed a twenty-five-year mining contract on the Isla de la Juventud. In exchange for exclusive mineral rights, they had to build a functional port on the island, a power plant, and a series of roads to service both the mine and the island. It's only been in the last two years that the Chinese have really accelerated their plans.

"When it came to oil, the Cubans leased the area to several Chinese firms in exchange for twenty percent of all oil produced from the wells. This would not only meet the Cuban petrol needs, it'd provide a surplus they could in turn sell abroad to raise additional capital. For the Chinese, it allows them to secure a large supply of crude oil that doesn't originate from the Middle East or Africa," Amber explained.

Tara then added, "When the oil platforms started producing, the Chinese learned these would be extremely productive wells. The oil refinery near Mariel was old and inefficient. Normally, they'd ship the oil to Venezuela to be refined and then on to China or back to Cuba. However, given the political situation in Venezuela, that's not feasible. Instead, the Chinese modernized the Mariel refinery. Still, despite the modernization, the refinery wasn't big enough to keep up with the supply or the demand."

Amber then interjected, as the two of them continued playing off each other. "Eighteen months ago, the Chinese began construction on an oil refinery facility on the Isla de la Juventud. This new refinery would be able to handle the excess load the Mariel facility couldn't. The entire deal provides an economic boon to both the Cubans and the Chinese. China's able to secure between twelve and sixteen percent of their petrol needs from outside the Middle East. And it's effectively quadrupled the Cubans' GDP and provided them with more petrol than they'll ever need."

Aaron rubbed the stubble on his chin as he replied, "Then this explains it—why the Cubans are asking for the two Chinese spies and not just their own. The Cubans are joined at the hip to the Chinese because of these deals."

Speaking for the first time, Joel from DIA commented, "There's a bit more to the story than just economics. While this is important to the Cubans, our task force has been exploring another angle."

All eyes turned to look at Joel. Aaron spoke for them all when he asked, "OK. What else is there that we aren't considering?"

Joel brought a zippered pouch up to the table in front of him. He unlocked the classified bag and brought out two folders. One had a number of high-resolution photos that he proceeded to pass out; the other contained a detailed report, which he held on to.

"What I'm passing around are aerial photographs of a Chengdu J-10 fighter being brought to Cuba. The first image is a series of shipping containers being offloaded from a ship in the Port of Mariel. The second image is of a fighter being unpacked from the shipping container at the San Antonio de los Baños airfield. The third image is a row of twelve of these aircraft parked at the brand-new Fidel airfield on the Isla de la Juventud," Joel explained.

"Whoa, hold up there, Joel. That airfield isn't operational yet. That was the whole reason we sent a man down there, to get some human eyes on the place and figure out how far along it was. Now you're telling us it's not only finished, it's operational?" Jim blurted out in frustration.

Joel nodded. "That's exactly what I'm telling you. Our joint task force has been monitoring what's going on in Cuba and Venezuela since October of last year. Several of our international partners in the JTF have assets on the ground in both countries, providing us with some real-time intelligence. In the past six months, from monitoring Latin America, we've learned that the Chinese brought fifteen thousand workers into Cuba. In Venezuela, that number is closer to sixty thousand.

"What we observed is that, within days of these new workers arriving, massive road, rail, bridge, port, and airport projects began across both countries. In Cuba alone, they started construction of a new six-lane highway cutting across the entire island from east to west, and then another extending from Havana down to the Bay of Pigs. In Venezuela, it's the same—massive infrastructure projects leading from the mines in the central part of the country to the ports along the coast."

Joel continued, "In Cuba, on the Isla de la Juventud, the Chinese finished the new airfield a couple of weeks ago. They are calling it Fidel Air Force Base. In Havana, they're hailing it as a new military aviation school and joint army, navy, and air force training center. It's a massive facility that's still being expanded and fortified."

Pausing for a moment, Joel pulled out another set of images. "The JTF acquired these images from our French liaison from one of their satellites. These are images of at least a dozen Shenyang J-11 multirole fighters. The aircraft appear to be getting ready to fly. Our Air Force liaison told us the Cubans carry out four hours of daytime training in the Caribbean Sea between Cuba and Grand Cayman. They conduct anywhere between four and six hours of night training as well.

"In addition to the fighters at this new base, we also spotted at least a battalion's worth of HQ-9 portable launchers being deployed to protect the airfield. For those who don't know, these are the Russian equivalent of their newest version of S-300 surface-to-air missile systems."

Aaron held up a hand to stop Joel and to calm some of the chatter. "So you're saying that somehow, someway, the Chinese have managed to move and set up at least two squadrons of advanced fighter aircraft on Cuba and at least one battalion worth of advanced surface-to-air missile systems and God knows what else in Venezuela?"

Joel nodded. "It's a bit more than that, Aaron. In Cuba, the Chinese have sold them five squadrons of their J-10 and J-11 fighters. They also modernized an entire mechanized armored division. Cuba is now three years into a five-year modernization program of their entire armed forces. We're a little less sure of what all they sold to the Venezuelans, but I could get you that information later if you like."

Dotty interjected to add, "Aaron, our asset in Cuba has been reporting similar information as well. Our Defense Attaché Officer at the embassy also confirmed most of this through his informal meetings with the Cuban military. From what he reported along with what my office identified, the Chinese are pursuing their own version of our foreign military sales program. Kind of like how we provide Israel with $3.8 billion in military aid so that they can then use that money to purchase military equipment from our defense companies. The Chinese are now copying us with a few select nations they're building closer military ties with. Our assessment is this is all part of their Belt and Road Initiative."

For a moment, no one commented on what Dotty or Joel had just explained. They all seemed to be waiting to see what Aaron would say next.

Aaron stood but motioned for everyone else to stay seated. He walked behind their chairs for a moment as he thought. Finally, he announced, "Here's what we'll do. I'll recommend to the director and to Mr. Wilson that we go ahead with the trade. Let's get our guy back before anything further happens to him or this entire situation blows up.

"Second, we've allowed ourselves to become so wrapped up with what's going on in the Middle East and defeating ISIS that we apparently haven't paid attention to what's going on ninety miles from our border. It's our duty to start playing catch-up and figure this out." Aaron paused for a second and took a deep breath before continuing. "As you know, this new COVID virus is now global. It's apparently twice as fatal as the last one, so we have that to contend with now as well. What's worse, according to this British asset they have, it would appear this virus has been genetically engineered by some sort of super-AI as a means of culling the Chinese population of the weak and infirmed while at the same time crippling the economies of the West. Clearly, the Chinese are up to something, and something big. It's our job to uncover what that may be and get that information to the decision makers and the President."

Aaron stopped pacing and placed both hands on the table in front of him. He leaned forward a bit as he looked down on everyone. "I don't believe in coincidences. All these events around the world are taking place at the same time. Something bigger is going on and I believe we're being intentionally distracted from seeing what that is.

"To that effect, it seems like this JTF down in Florida is a bit more on the ball than we are. Increase our participation in this group, and let me know what the heck the Chinese are up to. Amber, have your analysis group ferret this Chinese FMS program out. Make it a top priority for your group. Find out what countries they're doing this in and what they're selling. Maybe there's a pattern here we're not seeing yet."

"If I may, Aaron," Dotty interrupted before he could continue, "I know Jessica Parker is assigned to the JTF Joel is part of, but I think we should get a branch or division chief involved as well. We need someone with a bit more pull and leverage than Jessica and the DDI group."

Aaron nodded as he stuck his lower lip out a bit. "You're right. Joel, who's in charge of the JTF again and what other nations are part of it?"

Joel turned to Aaron and Dotty as he replied, "It's being run by Major General Gary Bridges. He's the Special Operations Command–South commanding general. As to partner nations, he brought in military and intel reps from Canada, Australia, Japan, France, the UK, and Germany."

Aaron pulled his chair back out and sat down. He looked at Dotty. "I will assign you to be the lead Agency LNO on the JTF. Bring as many people as you want or have them support you from here, but find out what the Chinese are doing in Latin America and what their endgame is. If it's economic, fine, that's something we can deal with. If it's something more, then we need to know what else it may be."

As the meeting began to break up, Aaron asked Dotty to stay behind for a moment. When everyone had left, he asked her to walk with him back to his office. Once it was just the two of them, Aaron pulled a document out of his safe and placed it on his desk between the two of them. It was labeled Eyes Only, TS/CI/ORCON. He had just handed her a very trusted secret to read.

"Am I allowed to see what's in here?" Dotty asked with a raised eyebrow as he eyed her.

"No."

Canting her head to the side, she said, "But you're giving it to me anyway?"

"I need a favor. One that I can't broadcast to the others. But before I ask for your assistance, I need you to understand why I'm asking for it," Aaron said in a rather cryptic manner.

Lifting her chin up, Dotty took in what he'd just said. He wanted her to break protocol, but what protocol?

"I'm going to turn around and look at the parking lot for a few minutes. Let me know when you're ready to talk." Aaron stood and walked over to one of the floor-to-ceiling windows. He looked outside at the cherry blossoms that were starting to come into bloom.

Flipping open the folder, Dotty began to read. The more she read, the bigger her eyes got and the more her stomach tightened.

"Is this for real?"

Still looking at the trees, Aaron answered, "It appears so. It's why I need you to get in contact with Goldfinger. He needs to acquire a sample of the vaccine so we can study it and get it into production. This virus is about to spin out of control across the world, and that vaccine could mean the difference between a few hundred thousand people dying and tens of millions."

"You know I can't reach out to Goldfinger directly. It doesn't work like that with an NOC. We could blow his cover if it's not done right," she countered defensively. She'd worked hard to get her asset into position. He was proving to be the most effective agent they had in Cuba.

"I get it, Dotty. Trust me, I do. But this is more important than that. Our SIS source says the virus has a couple-week incubation period before the host will show symptoms. That's why it's been hard to detect and stop. It's also been genetically modified to specifically target certain members of society. If we can get a sample of the vaccine, we can recreate it in a lab here."

"What about acquiring it from some other country? El Salvador or Venezuela?"

"We're working those angles right now as well. But your guy in Cuba is probably the best positioned to get it and get it quickly. Can he do it?" Aaron asked, almost pleading with her to say yes.

Dotty looked at his desk. She saw a photo of Aaron's wife and their five kids and suddenly remembered his daughter had Type I diabetes. According to the SIS's source, diabetes was one of the comorbidities the virus specifically targeted. When Dotty turned to look at Aaron, she saw him staring at her, eyes fighting back emotions. He was scared—scared of what this virus might do to his family and his little girl.

Dotty nodded. "I'll make contact with him. I can't guarantee he'll be able to acquire it, Aaron, or how long it will take. I know he'll try, though. That's all I can give you."

Smiling briefly, Aaron thanked her. He took the file back from her and placed it in his safe.

Chapter Sixteen
Big Reveal

Undisclosed Location
Beijing, China

Captain Lee Jian Ho was accustomed to the secrecy and subterfuge of the People's Liberation Army Navy, especially being a part of its silent service. But this was on a different level, even for the Ministry of State Security.

The blacked-out SUV exited onto Hanhe Road and then continued in the direction of the nearby national forest. Next, it drove through a few upscale neighborhoods before entering the campus of a community college. The buildings that constituted the college appeared scattered at different elevations within the national park.

Community college of Jinwangfu...never heard of this place, Lee thought as the driver steered them toward the parking lot. School was in session, so students scurried about with their books and bags.

"We are almost there, Captain Lee," announced the driver who had picked him up at the airport. If Lee guessed right, the man probably worked for the MSS.

Instead of driving toward some of the obvious parking lots connected to the college, they turned down a side access road. The vehicle moved deeper into the forest as it snaked around a couple of tight turns.

Is that a machine gun position in the woods? Lee wondered. He swore he saw a partially camouflaged cement bunker fifteen meters from the road. Eventually, they came out of the tall trees and headed toward a large drab-looking two-story building. The outside of this place looked like it had been abandoned many years ago.

The driver pulled the vehicle into a neglected garage attached to the building. Once the vehicle was parked, the driver walked around and opened his door. "If you'll follow me, sir, I'll get you to where you need to go," the man offered, though Lee could tell it was more of an order than a request.

They approached a pair of run-down double doors that suddenly hissed slightly as they parted at the center, retracting into the walls. Lee's eyes opened wide in astonishment as he gazed into the interior. The inner foyer was the polar opposite of the exterior of the building. It was not only new and clean, it was tricked out with all sorts of technological wizardry.

There were flat-panel displays that covered entire walls and interactive art displays that responded to the individual as they passed by. Lee assumed it used facial recognition AI and tailored its presentation to the person who was viewing it and how they were reacting to what they saw.

This is clearly not a part of Fleet Headquarters or anything to do with the Navy, Lee concluded. Whatever they had summoned him for must be big.

When Captain Lee and his driver approached the receptionist desk, a muscular man with an earpiece on said, "ID, please."

Lee handed the man his naval credentials and waited. A moment later, the man's expression softened a bit. He handed Lee a blue security badge with the number six on it.

"Keep this badge attached to the front of your uniform at all times. It has an RFID code that's been programmed with the levels and rooms you are authorized to enter. It shouldn't need to be said, but no tailgating. You badge in individually, every time. No exceptions. I also need you to sign this nondisclosure agreement saying you will not talk about this facility or where it is located. If you will follow me, I'll lead you to the elevator bank," the receptionist instructed.

Lee's driver started walking back to the vehicle.

When Lee and the receptionist rounded a corner, there was another security desk manned by four heavily armed men. *Nice, they kept the soldiers just out of view*, Lee thought to himself.

The receptionist walked up to the desk and pulled something out of the drawer. He handed Lee a briefing packet and directed him to a room on his right. "Please leave all your electronic devices in the locker with your name on it. When you're done, you can use your ID badge to access the elevator bank over there," the receptionist instructed him as he pointed to where the elevators were.

Lee placed his electronics in the locker, including his watch. No electronic devices of any sort were allowed into the secured side of the building. Glancing out of his peripheral vision, Lee spied the other names on the row of lockers adjacent to his. They were the names of fellow submariners and more than a few surface combatant captains. To his surprise, he also noted what had to be a couple of merchant vessel captains.

As he left the room, he handed the locker key to the security guard and proceeded to the elevator, holding his badge up to the RFID sensor. The red light above it turned green and displayed his picture. One of the six elevator doors then opened.

When he stepped inside, the doors closed and a feminine voice that sounded too human greeted him. "Welcome, Captain Lee. I will now take you to the level for room 3001."

That's a bit creepy, thought Lee. *The damn elevator is talking to me now.*

Standing at attention with his briefing packet tucked beneath his left arm, Lee did his best to ignore the camera in the corner of the elevator and the voice that spoke to him. He glanced at the level indicator, which kept going down, deeper beneath the building. Lee raised an eyebrow at how quickly he'd traveled past so many sublevels.

Ding.

The door opened to reveal a brightly lit hallway. Stepping off the elevator, Lee looked down one side, then the other as he contemplated which way to go. Then he saw a sign indicating that room 3001 was to the right. Oddly, the floor appeared to angle down at what he estimated to be ten degrees.

As Lee walked down the hallway, he saw some familiar military symbols. A large set of steel double doors with a light illuminated above them read *Zuìgāo jīmì*, or Top Secret. When he approached the door, he saw another RFID reader on the wall next to it.

I guess they figure if you made it this far, you belong, Lee thought as he held his ID up against the reader. The doors slid open, revealing a cavernous room that overwhelmed him.

Now I know where I am, Lee realized. He had been brought to the Joint Battle Command Center.

The massive room of the JBCC could easily seat five hundred people in the main auditorium. On either side of the bowl-shaped auditorium was a series of smaller briefing rooms and workstations. In the rear of the room, various workstations were spaced out, each representing either a different branch of the service or a specific support service they provided.

Uniformed personnel worked at many of the stations, intermixed with a smattering of civilians. As Lee advanced further into the room, he saw that fifteen people had arrived ahead of him. It wasn't the number of people he saw that caused him to lift an eyebrow. It was *who* he saw: the Commanding Admiral of the People's Liberation Army Navy, Admiral Wei Huang. Admiral Wei was not a tall man even by Chinese standards, but everything about the man radiated power.

The admirals in charge of the North, South, and East fleets were also present—Admirals Zhang, Yu, and Du respectively. The last man at the front of the room was someone Lee knew only by reputation: Dr. Xi Zemin, the father and mastermind of the social credit program. He was the lead scientist for the Ministry of State Security.

Captain Lee nodded to his fellow submariners, all of whom had been classmates of his at Dalian Naval Academy many lifetimes ago. Captain Feng Danyu had been a year ahead of him, but they had run track together. Captain Chen Han had been in his cohort, and they had both graduated near the top of their class. Last was Captain Su Yenpeng, who had been a first-year cadet when Lee and Danyu had been seniors.

Lee didn't know what this meeting was about, but if the four of them were in the room, Lee knew one thing with certainty—their new Type 95A attack submarines must be close to complete.

Lee wasn't personally acquainted with the other three surface warfare captains in the room, but he was familiar with them by reputation. The remaining three captains were in the merchant force. Lee didn't know them at all. Their presence in this secretive meeting was a curiosity to him.

****

Admiral Wei Huang shook hands and made small talk until Lee entered the room. Noticing Lee, the steely-eyed admiral walked over to him.

Admiral Wei greeted him. "Ah, Captain Lee. I am pleased to see you. I know your journey here was long. I apologize for the short notice. We should have flown you here."

"It was no trouble, sir. I am honored to be called upon." Lee took the admiral's hand.

"I am sure you are wondering why you're here," Wei said, motioning around the large room. "As you probably figured out, this is the JBCC. Not many people who aren't stationed here are summoned to attend a meeting here, but secrecy is of the utmost importance when it comes to what we're about to tell you."

"I must admit, Admiral, this place is impressive. As we approached it, I had no idea it was here," Lee replied.

The admiral smiled at Lee, directing him to a seat next to his. Wei motioned to flag his aide, and the officer tapped on the microphone three times.

"Gentlemen, please take a seat. Admiral Wei will make his opening remarks now."

Wei patted Lee on the back as he walked to the stage. His aide clipped a microphone to his lapel and departed.

"Comrades," Wei began. "Everything you will hear over the next two days is classified Top Secret. Should any of you divulge what you are about to hear, you will be shot. This material is not to be talked about outside of this facility and is to be discussed only with those who have been read into the program. No exceptions. When you return to your commands, you will read your crews onto the mission and give them the same instructions. Is that understood?"

Wei let that hang in the air for a long moment, wanting them to understand that this wasn't just Top Secret, it was classified with their very lives. He smiled when he saw that none of his handpicked officers flinched or even appeared to question the threat. These men were the best of the Navy; they knew what was on the line.

"The People's Republic of China," he began as a display behind him lit up, a map of China filling the screen as the lights in the auditorium dimmed, "began the long march many decades ago. First it was against the capitalists who backed Chiang Kai-shek, so we turned to the Soviets and formed the People's Republic. At first, we were subjugated to the Soviets. They used us as a means to an end. They treated us as nothing more than fodder for the communist revolution. However, unlike China, the Soviets eventually fell apart, crushed beneath the weight of their own incompetence."

Wei began walking the stage as images of war from the Korean conflict scrolled across the screen. "Slowly, we gained momentum and our own march took shape. We modernized our military with help from our Soviet brothers. Then they turned their backs on the cause in the name of coexistence with the West. This was nothing short of revisionism.

"For decades, the Soviets fought a Cold War against China and the West, until they fell apart. China, under the great and wise guidance of Premier Zhou Enlai and Mao Zedong, was able to establish a partnership with the West that didn't force us to sacrifice our Marxist ideology. This relationship has allowed us to grow our economy to become the largest, most dominant economy in the world. This unprecedented opportunity with the West has allowed us to educate our people at the best universities in the world and bring those skills back to China."

Wei expounded, "Unlike our Soviet brothers, we did not have to abandon the cause of communism. Instead, we have shown the world how China has continued to grow and how our people prospered under communism as an alternative to capitalism. Over time, our position among the United Nations and the World Trade Organization has given China a voice to be heard around the world." Admiral Wei paused for a second as he surveyed his small cadre of senior leaders, looking each of them in the eye like a soldier trained by the West.

Continuing, he added, "While our overt actions helped our nation develop into an industrial and economic force to be reckoned with, this was only the beginning. Our country climbed out of poverty and entered the twenty-first century. It was our covert actions against the West's educational system, corporations, and defense contractors that turned our slow and steady march over the decades into an all-out sprint."

The images behind Wei displayed a montage of China's once ancient cities, now transformed into ultramodern metropolises. Then it showed historical images of the People's Army, clothed in tattered rags with secondhand Russian military equipment, followed by short video clips of the largest military in the world, equipped with modern weapons that rivaled the West's.

Wei went on to say, "Our nation's 2025 plan has come to fruition early because we never lost sight of our eternal goal. We never gave up on the revolution or the idea and belief that, through communism, we can lift our people out of poverty. America and her allies have been mired in endless wars with Islam for the last thirty years. Meanwhile, we have transformed our navy from a green-water territorial force, only capable of protecting our borders, into a true modern blue-water navy that can now project our own military power beyond our borders."

Swelling with pride, Wei exclaimed, "No longer will China or the rest of the world be dependent on the benevolence of the American hegemony and dominance of the sea lanes and trading routes. China will no longer be bullied by America or the West into doing what is in their best interest. We are now in a position to do what is in the best interest of China."

A different video appeared on the screen behind Wei, showing the navy China had once had—a navy that was openly mocked and ridiculed by not just the navies of the West but their fellow communists in Moscow too. The video then faded to black, and triumphant patriotic music played as the newest warships of China's modern navy appeared.

The Type 52 *Luhu*-class guided-missile destroyer morphed into the larger Type 55 *Renhai*-class—the largest and most advanced destroyer in the Chinese Navy, if not in all of Asia. The video then showed the venerable Type 71 Yuzhao amphibious transport dock ship, paired with the Type 75 amphibious assault ship, a massive helicopter assault ship on par with the United States' *America*-class warships.

The video of the navy soon transformed into similar videos of the ground force, where old tanks became powerful modern war machines. Then the video changed to show the army air force as it morphed from mostly Cold War–era Soviet jets to the new and venerable J-20s, streaking across the skies in mock combat against American fighters.

Admiral Wei looked at the assembled captains, who shifted in their seats in anticipation of what might be coming next. It made him smile to see their excitement. He had gone through this video demonstration for a purpose. What he was about to show them next would change the world.

"I have shown you these videos because it is time that you be brought into the inner circle of those who know about what is about to happen next," Wei said as he motioned for another man sitting further away from the military officers.

As the mystery man stood up, Wei continued, "It is my pleasure to introduce you to perhaps the smartest person in the world, Dr. Xi Zemin, the head of Project Ten. Dr. Xi is the world's leading expert in machine learning and artificial intelligence. He has led the integration of these two technologies, and it's been his department that led to the technological advances you are about to see.

"Dr. Xi, the floor is yours," Wei said and then took his seat next to Captain Lee.

Dr. Xi Zemin looked at the military officers in front of him. He knew the admirals and generals, but the ship captains were new. These were the men who would be implementing the strategies his department was generating.

Clearing his throat, Dr. Xi began, "For the last twenty years, I have been working on developing the most advanced AI in the world. To fully realize its potential, we had to build a quantum computer powerful enough to analyze and synthesize the data we intended to feed it. The technological transformation of our military these last fifteen years is a direct result of Project Ten."

Xi continued, "This computer, Jade Dragon, was instrumental in solving the technological problem of integrating the propulsion and other systems into the new Type 95A submarine. What my computer program needs now is more data on how the technology works outside of a laboratory environment and how our American counterparts will undoubtedly respond to it. This data will allow our AI to begin running electronic war games against the Americans so we can test our strategies and equipment against the known performance of their weapon platforms and the training of the individuals operating it. In short, we will start integrating AI into our war planning, strategies, and future combat action. With that, I will go ahead and hand it back over to Admiral Wei to explain some items further."

Dr. Xi waited for the admiral to return to the lectern and then scurried off to his seat.
****

Admiral Wei might not have understood everything involved in Dr. Xi's secret program, but he sure appreciated what it had been able to deliver to his command thus far.

Returning to the center of the stage, Wei announced, "I've been showing you some videos while we talk. I think you will see what I am trying to achieve when you see the next set of short clips."

He nodded to his aide, who started the video. It showed a picture of an enormous warship. The American *Ford*-class carrier was on full display as it sailed out of Pearl Harbor. The video transitioned to an interview of the carrier's captain, who had spoken with an American reporter earlier.

The captain was cocky and sure of himself. He proudly talked about his ship's capabilities and how the ship would allow America to project power for decades to come in the Pacific. As that video ended, a new video by the same reporter showed a *Virginia*-class submarine running through a series of drills. The crew was going through a battle station torpedo drill. This got the attention of all the submariners in the room—their interest piqued as they intently watched the American sailors run through their drill procedure. If they ever fought against a foreign military, this was likely how they would do it. They watched as the submariners moved throughout the sub, calling out what they were doing, and how they handled each scenario being thrown at them. Not having access to Western media, the Chinese officers were seeing something that was totally new. What astonished Wei, and probably his captains, was how openly this information was being shared.

The last video after the submarine drills was of an American *Arleigh Burke* destroyer. This was the most modern version of the destroyer in the American Navy. It was widely known that the *Burke*-class ship was at the end of its technical loadout. There wasn't anything else the Americans could cram into the ships without a complete redesign. The nonsubmariner captains leaned forward as they, too, tried to absorb every bit of the content shown in the video.

When the videos of the American warships ended, Wei smiled as the image of China's newest fast-attack submarine, the *Changzheng* "Long March" class, was finally revealed. This caused the submarine captains to smile. They were finally getting to see the details of the newest submarine to enter service.

With the images and specs of the sub displayed behind him, Admiral Wei announced, "The *Changzheng* will be the most modern submarine in the world. The new rim-driven propulsor system reduces propulsion noise by as much as twenty percent, even at fifteen knots. It incorporates brand-new retractable bow planes and reduced sail. More importantly, its acoustic signature has never been recorded by the West and its movements were kept secret during its initial test trials.

"What makes the *Changzheng* so deadly is its weapons platform. Today, I will reveal to you its actual specs for the first time.

Anything you were told about or saw in the past was a lie, meant to distract in case a security breach occurred."

As the admiral was speaking, his aide brought up a spec readout of the new sub on the big board behind him. "In the bow, the ship is equipped with eight torpedo tubes, not six. Directly behind the torpedo room are eight VLS launchers. These launchers are unique because we can equip them with a myriad of different missiles—anything from land-attack cruise missiles to antiship missiles. To throw a huge curveball in the Pacific, the VLS system can also be equipped with our HQ-9 missiles. Now some of you may ask, 'Why in the world would a submarine need to be equipped with something like this?'"

A short video clip played of a computer simulation. It showed a military transport aircraft flying from the US mainland toward the military base in Guam. It then showed the *Changzheng* going to periscope level, acquiring the aircraft with its search radar and then firing one of its missiles.

"Jade Dragon came to the realization that the *Changzheng* can become more than a super sub to challenge the Americans at sea. It can become an aerial denial weapon if equipped with surface-to-air missiles that could be launched from the sea. The Pacific is a big place, but there are only so many air routes commercial and military aircraft can take to bring supplies and personnel in. If we strategically place one of our subs in these air highways, we can sow further chaos among our enemies."

The image behind Admiral Wei returned to the specs of the sub. "Behind the sail, as you can see, are an additional twelve VLS pods, and two additional aft torpedo tubes. The forward and aft tubes can also be equipped to fire our newest submarine-launched surface-to-air missiles. This will give the *Changzheng* the ability to engage ASW helicopters should the need arise. The sub will be equipped with the new YU-9 torpedo, which has a top speed of sixty-nine knots. Dr. Xi's group has equipped the computer in the warhead with an advanced AI targeting system, meaning this system is not going to be easy to spoof or evade."

Wei saw a few smiles and nods. He pressed on, "The *Changzheng*'s real punch is an improved version of the YU-9's cousin, the YU-9 Mk III. This is a much-improved version of the Russian VA-111 Shkval and our earlier version, the Mk II. Where our older versions of this torpedo had a range of five thousand meters, the Mk III now has a range of nine thousand meters, giving your subs an incredible new weapon. The Mk III launch speed is still the same fifty knots as before, but its new max speed is now two hundred and twenty knots."

Holding a hand up to pause their excitement, he added, "In order to increase the Mk III's range and speed, we had to decrease its warhead. It's gone from two hundred and ten kilograms to one hundred and fifty kilograms. We did, however, swap out the traditional high-explosive mixture with a new incendiary mixture, designed to work in water and burn at temperatures of two thousand degrees Celsius. Initial tests show the smaller warhead is actually able to cause significantly more damage because of the incendiary mixture involved."

One of the captains raised his hand to ask a question. Admiral Wei nodded for him to speak. "Sir, what is the maximum speed of the *Changzheng*?"

"Its maximum speed is thirty-eight knots. That said, what I would like to show you next is our companion ship to the *Changzheng*—and, no, I do not mean our new aircraft carriers under construction. I will unveil to you the new Type 60 *Dingyuan* battle cruiser."

What had become abundantly clear to the senior leadership of the PLA through the work of Dr. Xi and Project Ten was that China would likely never surpass the Americans when it came to supercarriers. Try as China might, the US had one hundred years of experience building and operating them. They had a long and storied history of pilot training programs and aircraft to enable these warships to dominate the seas for decades to come. What Dr. Xi's program had shown the PLA leadership, however, was an alternative path the Navy could pursue that would allow them to leapfrog ahead of the American Navy, despite their advantage with the carriers.

Under the direction of the AI, the Navy had used the construction of domestic carriers as a diversion to develop the supership of the future. When China had purchased the *Admiral Ushakov*, a Russian Kirov battle cruiser slated for the scrapyards, Chinese shipbuilders had begun the process of reverse engineering it. When the AI had been fed all the relevant data and given the task of creating a warship for the future, it had created the Type 60 *Dingyuan*-class battle cruiser.

If China could not gain naval parity with the American carriers, then she would focus on putting them on the bottom. The Type 95A

Changzheng and Type 60 *Dingyuan* would be instrumental to China's dominance of the sea and their ability to challenge the Americans.

Admiral Wei saw smiles on the faces of the surface warfare captains. As a display of the ship's details was brought up behind him, Wei explained with excitement, "The Type 60s are three hundred meters long with a beam of thirty meters. When fully loaded, they displace thirty-one thousand tons. The ship is powered by two nuclear reactors, giving the ship unlimited range. More importantly, they give the ship an enormous amount of power for future weapon upgrades and speed for her engines.

"At flank speed, the Type 60s can sprint to nearly forty knots. This makes them the largest and fastest surface combatants since World War II. The AI was told who this ship would most likely be fighting, so it spared no expense in developing both offensive and defensive capabilities to defeat the military it was built to fight against—America.

"One of the defensive features the AI built into the ship was an improved armor belt. The lessons of survivability in the World War II battle involving the *Yamato* and *Musashi* had gone into the design and production of the Type 60s. When the *Musashi* finally sank in October of 1944, she had sustained an estimated nineteen torpedo and seventeen bomb hits from American carrier-based aircraft. This attack illustrated the importance of survivability in battle. We built the Type 60 with two considerations in mind. First, the ships would need to be able to take multiple hits and still be able to stay in the fight. Second, they needed to be able to kill everything they went up against, both surface and subsurface vessels."

Admiral Wei saw the ship captains nod in agreement. "To that end, the *Dingyuan* will have one hundred and sixty VLS tubes. Fifty will be dedicated to anti-air operations, to include interdicting enemy cruise and ballistic missiles. The remaining are designated for antiship and land-attack operations, depending on the type of mission the ship will be carrying out. For close-in defense, the ship will have eight H/PJ12 CIWS guns.

"As you can see, gentlemen, this gives the ship an enormous punching capability, but also the ability to defend against enemy aircraft and antiship missiles. With survivability in mind, we opted to forgo the 130mm turret cannon on the front of the ship and added four high-energy optical laser systems instead. As you can see, they are strategically positioned across the ship to provide the most flexibility to engage a target. Keep in mind, this is still a relatively new technology, even for the Americans. We believe that, with a bit more refinement, this technology will change the way ships fight for the foreseeable future. This ship is being built for the future of naval warfare, not the past."

The surface warfare captains smiled at the thought of having lasers on their ships. The American warships wouldn't be the only ones testing this new weapons platform out.

Admiral Wei turned to face the man whose technology had made this ship possible. "Dr. Xi's AI has taken a page from the Americans and made the ship as efficient and advanced as our current capabilities would allow us to build. What technology his department couldn't steal or replicate, his AI has fabricated out of ones and zeros."

Wei clapped a couple of times and bowed to Dr. Xi. This caused the other naval officers to erupt in applause. Dr. Xi appeared taken aback and flustered by the outpouring of praise.

Wei knew that the most challenging part next would be identifying and then training the 1,065 officers and enlisted it would take to operate the three battle cruisers. Xi had gotten them this far; now it was time for him to do his part.

Once they had taken their seats again, one of the senior captains raised his hand. "Admiral, if I may. Could Dr. Xi explain this AI concept a bit more to us? Maybe help us understand how and why this new technology will revolutionize warfare?"

Admiral Wei nodded in agreement and motioned for Dr. Xi to come back up.

****

Walking to the center of the stage again, Xi looked over the group of military officers, realizing they were the future of the Navy. It would be these men who would implement the strategies and plans his AI would be generating for decades to come. He tried to keep that in mind as he explained who he was and what his department was providing them.

"Captains, as I stated earlier, I am a scientist. I am the foremost expert in the world when it comes to the integration of artificial intelligence and machine learning," Xi explained. "Over the last twenty years, I have made it my life's work to create a semiautonomous thinking computer—one that we, the government of China, could task with solving problems that are too complex for our human brains to understand. We also wanted this new super-AI to help us manage and govern the country better—everything from mineral and resource management to manufacturing efficiencies. Jade Dragon can perform more than two thousand quadrillion computations a second. This is ten times faster than any other existing supercomputer of today—"

One of the admirals interrupted, "Dr. Xi, this is all important work Jade Dragon is doing for our country. What you achieved for China is nothing short of astounding. But perhaps you can be a bit more direct in explaining to us how this super-AI you've created will benefit us."

Xi paused for a second before speaking. He knew he sometimes droned on about technical details and lost his audience. Taking a deep breath in, he collected his thoughts and tried to explain a bit more clearly.

"Admiral, Captains, let me explain why this super-AI will change the future of modern warfare and why Jade Dragon will defeat America and the West. Admiral Wei and General Li Zuocheng told me that the PLA routinely conducts war game scenarios using tabletop exercises. They informed me that just five years ago, your organizations integrated computer-generated exercises. Have you participated in them?" Xi asked.

They all nodded, so Xi pointed to one of the captains.

"Captain Chin, when you participated in these exercises, did you believe the adversary you squared off against accurately responded to the moves you and your fellow captains made?"

Captain Chin slowly shook his head no.

"Why do you believe the adversary's response to be inaccurate?" Xi pressed, feeling more confident as he spoke.

Captain Chin explained, "In the scenario, my squadron of ships was fighting an Australian and American task force. We won, but honestly, I'm not sure we would have had it been a real scenario."

"Can you explain why you think you would have lost had it been a real scenario?" Xi pressed.

Captain Chin looked nervously to Admiral Wei, as if asking how much he should say. The admiral smiled and nodded, telling him to go ahead.

Taking a breath in, Captain Chin clarified his remark. "I'm not sure how the American warships or those particular captains would have responded to our moves. Since none of our crews or even ourselves have been in combat and the Americans have, we lack the kind of experience that only comes from having to make life-or-death decisions."

Xi smiled broadly at the response. "That is exactly right, Captain Chin. You are lacking the necessary information to know if the move you will make is accurate and will play out with a degree of certainty in real life as it has in the exercise. The exercise was only as accurate as the data you were able to put into it. *That* is where Jade Dragon is changing things and how we will leverage that data to win future wars."

Captain Chin nodded in agreement but then asked, "Dr. Xi, if Jade Dragon is some super-smart AI, how will it acquire the data needed to understand our adversary and then craft the necessary strategy to win?"

"Ah, now that is an excellent question. If you all will indulge me for a moment, I will explain how all of that will work. Back in 2015, the American Office of Personnel Management had a security breach. Our hacker team infiltrated the organization and stole the security clearance records of nearly twenty-one million current and former US government employees, as well as their families and associates that were named in their background investigations. This data was among the first to be entered into the AI when it was barely online."

Crinkling his brow, Captain Chin asked, "How is any of that relevant to us right now?"

"That is another very good question, Captain Chin."

Xi turned on a device on his wrist, and the screen behind him came back to life. The image of the captain of the *Gerald R. Ford* appeared on the screen. Xi made a swiping motion with his hand and the picture enlarged.

"This gentleman is Captain Robert Womack. He is the current commanding officer of the *Ford*. When the OPM breach happened in 2015, he was assigned to the USS *Ronald Reagan* as an F/A-18 Squadron XO. When we received the OPM data, we fed that data into the AI. The AI was then fed additional information concerning officers who would be approaching command rank a decade later. It was specifically looking for officers who showed promise and whose evaluations showed their potential for command. For the next several years, the AI continued to benchmark the initial assessments it had made of various officers against those who went on to be chosen for commands in the Navy.

"As the AI correctly identified a set of officers, it dug deeper to understand why it was correct. When a group of officers was incorrectly selected, it likewise looked deeper at the data to figure out why it was wrong. Over the years, Jade Dragon refined its software until it was coming close to ninety-six percent accuracy in determining who would go on to receive a command position. Jade Dragon did this not just across the American Navy but across all the American service branches. In the case of Captain Womack, he was first in his class at Annapolis and had stellar marks throughout his career. When Jade Dragon looked at all of the data we had collected on him, it accurately predicted he would go on to command an F/A-18 squadron on a carrier, a prerequisite command to become a carrier commander."

Captain Chin cut in, "This is to be expected of an officer that attended their Naval Academy. If the Americans had such an AI as this Jade Dragon, they could tell you the same about any of the men in this room."

Xi smiled and raised his index finger.

"Yes, this is true, Captain. What we didn't know then was that Womack also had a drinking problem. You see, the malware that caused the OPM breach was part of Jade Dragon. It was in the entirety of the American system: banking, entertainment, internet service providers, smartphone apps, etcetera. It was *everywhere*, and we dedicated an entire cyber brigade to creating apps that Americans would download like an addiction. Once we had Womack's credit card information, the AI discerned purchase patterns and predicted with ninety-eight percent certainty that he would jeopardize his career if he didn't address his drinking problem."

Xi saw that the captains and admirals were now very interested in what he was saying. "This prediction eventually came to fruition in 2018, when he was involved in a minor accident where he was at fault. The Navy swept it under the rug, and by 2020, he was a squadron commander. Jade Dragon had predicted this. However, the AI then predicted that he would in fact go on to command an aircraft carrier within two years."

Pausing for effect, Xi added, "Jade Dragon's algorithms have evolved on their own. It learned to predict behavior based on the information we were presenting it. The more information we made available to it, the more accurate it became. This is something we call predictive behavioral analytics. Not only was it able to predict how Womack's vice would impact his career, the AI was able to impact the leadership's response to his actions—however, the Jade Dragon's analysis can now do much more. Now we not only know his personal weakness, but based on all of the data we've mined on Womack, Jade Dragon can accurately predict how he would respond given any number of battle scenarios. We can also predict when exactly his vice will impact his decision making."

This information seemed to electrify the room as the men assembled grasped the ramification of what they had just been told.

At this point, Admiral Wei rose from his chair and took center stage. He motioned for Dr. Xi to take a seat, satisfied he had explained what Jade Dragon was and how it would change warfare forever.

****

"This brings us to why you are here. You now know about the Type 60 and 95A. Let me introduce you to Captains Tsai, Gao, and Sung." Wei motioned for the three men to stand. They did so and bowed slightly to the others in the room.

"These captains before you command three of our cargo container ships—ships we converted into Arsenal ships," Wei announced. He raised his hand, and his aide projected a standard cargo container ship on the screen. The captains of actual combat vessels quietly snickered at these hulking behemoths on screen.

"Captain Tsai, please enlighten your naval counterparts on the merits of your ship," Admiral Wei commanded.

Captain Tsai sprang to his feet and bowed.

"Yes, sir. Gentlemen, my vessel has the outward appearance of a standard cargo container ship. However, three hundred and fifty vertical launch tubes are located in the bow of the ship, hidden under a retractable cover topped by cargo containers for appearances."

Tsai continued, "Our load can and will change depending on the mission. Powered by a single nuclear reactor like those found on the Type 60, our ship's flank speed can reach thirty-six knots. This ship can carry up to six Changhe Z-18 ASW helicopters. For all intents and purposes, these are standard cargo freighters that in fact haul cargo and carry out specific cargo runs. However, they are also merchant raiders, designed as a first-strike or counterstrike weapon should the need arise. Our purpose is to hide from a potential adversary in plain sight."

A video appeared of the ship's schematics and ended with her firing a salvo of all three hundred and fifty vertical launch systems or VLS rockets in sequence. Captain Tsai bowed, but this time his naval counterparts had stopped snickering.

****

How did China manage to build four Type 95As and three Type 60 nuclear-powered battle cruisers while speeding up production of the Type 55s? Captain Lee pondered in disbelief. *How did China create nuclear-powered Arsenal ships without the Americans having the slightest clue?* What had really thrown him was the carrier deception. China had intentionally spent billions on ships that the Navy really didn't even care about.

When the *Liaoning* had set sail, the entire Chinese Navy had swelled with pride. Lee had heard the rumors of problems with the catapults and the power plants aboard but brushed them off, assuming that the evolution of China's fledgling carrier operations had some kinks to work out. Now it made sense. The carrier was a distraction.

When the *Shandong* had gone to sea, she had been plagued by the same problems. At first, Lee had felt the humiliation, as the rest of the PLA Navy had. He had known deep down inside that China would never achieve parity with the United States when it came to their carrier supremacy. Now that he knew that had never been the plan, he felt pride in the PLA Navy once again.

When Captain Tsai had first stood to speak, Lee couldn't help but sneer as his fellow commanders did. Surely this merchant captain wasn't their equal. But after the schematics of his ship appeared on screen, followed by the video of her firing a sequential salvo of three hundred and fifty missiles, Captain Tsai seemed a much larger man than he had moments before.

When Tsai bowed and took his seat, the room fell quiet for a moment as each sailor absorbed the information in shock. Then every man stood and clapped all at once. Admiral Zhang of the Northern Fleet raised a hand to quiet the men. Lee and the rest of the captains took notes as one admiral after the other detailed their plan for the Long March across the Pacific Ocean to South America and their part in the plan.

During the next four hours, all the plans were laid out in detail. Dinner was brought in, but they were all too excited to eat. Lee wrote twenty-five pages of notes and marked up his entire briefing packet as well. He was giddy with excitement over the plan he and his new ship would be a part of in this coming conflict, confident the Americans would see them as equals, or they would crush them.

Admiral Zhang of the Northern Fleet gave all the naval officers new patrol orders for special exercises down in the South China Sea. The objective of the Type 95s was to sink the Arsenal ships, which would be acting as American carriers. The objective of the Type 60s and assigned Type 52 and 55 Destroyers was to hunt and kill the Type 95s.

For the exercise, everyone would be firing inert torpedoes with no explosive warheads, but everything else on the torpedoes would acquire and home as if they were the real thing. They would even impact against the sides of the vessels, letting the defender know they were hit.

The meeting continued until the sun rose the next day. While Lee's body was exhausted, his mind was on fire. When he retrieved his belongings from the locker on the ground floor, he felt like it had been months since he'd placed them there. It had been less than seventeen hours.

Leaving the building, Lee saw Dr. Xi Zemin getting into his car. The man turned toward him and bowed his head slightly. Lee returned the gesture. A minute later, the staff car that had brought him to this secret facility pulled up and the original driver appeared. As his driver opened his door, he heard someone calling his name. Turning, he saw it was Captain Chen of the *Changzheng 32* and Senior Captain Liu of the *Dingyuan IV*. He motioned for his driver to wait as he walked to his comrades. Lee came to attention and saluted Senior Captain Liu.

"Sir, what can I do for you?" Lee asked.

"I came to wish you both good fortunes. The Type 60 is a most formidable warship," said Captain Liu.

"To you as well, sir. Have you ever conducted a war game with inert munitions?" asked Lee.

Liu answered, "No, but I suppose it will do all of our crews good to feel that pressure before we have to learn the hard lessons of war."

The men stood for a moment, pondering that thought, the gravity of it making them all ever more exhausted. War was coming and they understood their role as the very tip of China's spear. Liu grunted in acknowledgment and walked away. Lee and Chen watched him go. Chen patted Lee on the shoulder and departed as he saw Admiral Wei approach Captain Lee.

When Admiral Wei walked up to Lee, he came to attention and snapped a crisp salute. Wei waved it off as if swatting at a fly.

"Walk with me, Captain," Wei directed as he signaled for Lee's driver to continue to hang tight.

"Yes, sir." Lee obeyed and fell in step to the admiral's left.

"You have one week to prepare your submarine and your crew. You may tell your officers as much as you like about what is coming. I want you to know something, though." Wei took several more steps in silence. Lee could sense he was contemplating whether he should tell him some big secret. Finally, Wei stopped and faced Lee.

"Lee, what happens in the next several months will determine the fate of China and the world. I picked you because I see the fire in you," Wei said sternly.

"Thank you, sir, I understand," answered Lee.

"No, you don't!" Wei hissed softly so only the two of them could hear.

Lee saw venom in his face for a moment, and then it was gone just as quickly as it had come. He relaxed and inhaled deeply before he spoke again. "This Jade Dragon AI... it frightens me," Wei said firmly but quietly. "It... it is too accurate. Jade Dragon already provided the predictive analysis for your war games. It knows everything about every man on every ship and submarine involved. It processed over a thousand scenarios and made its prediction. The Party is extremely interested to see how it plays out. I know you to be an aggressive and competent captain. I need you to follow your instincts, not doctrine. Fight like an American, a German, a Brit, or a French captain. Learn what your submarine can do, find its limits and then push it past them. Win! Do you understand?"

Lee didn't know how to respond. He knew that Wei was trying to say what he could not say out loud. Lee had to figure out what that was. He looked into the old admiral's eyes for a long moment and nodded.

Wei turned and walked away, leaving Lee standing there with his thoughts. Then Lee put his sunglasses on and walked back to his

waiting driver. He had a flight to catch to get back to his submarine. He had a week to prepare his crew and learn how to use this new weapon. And he had to figure out what the hell Wei had meant.
****

Ten Days Later
South China Sea
Changzheng 30

Captain Lee sat in the wardroom sipping his tea, looking at each of his officers as they digested what he had told them. For the last hour, he had briefed them on the tactical scenarios their new boat might encounter. To hammer home the importance of the coming exercise and how revolutionary their new ship and task force would be, he'd shared with them his classified briefing packet from his meeting in JBCC.

Like him, they had snickered at the Panamax until they had seen the stills of its three hundred and fifty VLS tubes launching a barrage of cruise missiles. Their snide comments had ended when they'd realized how big of an impact a merchant raider like this could have.

His XO had been the most astute when he had correctly surmised that the Type 60 battle cruisers would become the workhorse of the navy. If they were able to master the coordination between the Type 95As subs, Type 55s destroyers, and Type 60s battle cruisers, they could make quick work of the American Pacific Fleet. The trick now was honing the skills required to carry out a multidomain battle like the Americans had mastered since the days of World War II.

With the *Changzheng* underway, Captain Lee made it a point to gather his officers together daily to spend at least an hour going over tactics and how to best use their new weapons against their most likely adversaries. Lee impressed upon them that these new warships would be able to do what the Japanese could not in the last Great War—beat the Americans should it ever come to that.

Standing, Captain Lee asked again, "What is the primary objective of this war game scenario?"

The weapons officer replied, "Sink the American carrier."

Lee nodded in approval. "Exactly. Now, how will we do that?"

This time it was a different weapons officer who answered, "We will slip past the carrier's screening force and sink them with our new torpedoes."

Lee smiled. "Yes. But how will we slip past its escorts?"

"Well, we know what kind of escorts the ship will have. We plan around its capabilities and we find the weak link," one of the navigation officers offered.

"That's right," Lee said with a nod. "The cargo ship will act as the American carrier. It will be protected by the new battle cruiser and our destroyers. These combatants will be hunting us as much as we'll be hunting them. I will need each of you to stay on your toes. You will need to be ready to adapt and change at a moment's notice."

The officers in the wardroom nodded, serious looks on their faces.

Lee went over the rules of the exercise again, making sure they fully knew what would be expected of them. This would be a test of the Type 60s and 55s to see how well they worked together, both in protecting a high-value asset and in hunting a simulated American sub.

The war game would play out identically with the other ship captains, with one Type 95 going up against the one Type 60 and three destroyers. One of the subs would remain in reserve, loitering in each war game patrol box, collecting acoustic data and recording the simulated battles as they played out. All the data being generated from this exercise would be fed into Jade Dragon for further analysis. Lee suspected the secondary mission of the second *Changzheng* was to see if the surface combatants could detect it amid the underwater noise of the battle.

The most problematic restriction to this exercise was the limitation on their use of anti-air missiles. This limitation meant the antisubmarine warfare or ASW helicopters would have a decidedly one-sided advantage. One of Lee's officers had an idea on how to mitigate it, at least until they managed to get into their patrol box for the exercise.

"Conn, sonar."

The captain grabbed the mic, "Sonar, Conn, what do you have for us?" he asked, hoping that they had a target.

"Conn, we've detected a large ship approaching. We're classifying it as a tanker."

"Sonar, that's a good copy. We'll take it from here."

164

The captain ordered the ship to settle in beneath the large vessel and matched its speed. They would use the cover of this ship to get in position.

Once they reached the edge of the war game box, Lee deployed some of his acoustic decoys in a diagonal line. They were programmed to travel at two knots with passive sonars activated. The acoustic signature of the simulated carrier was preprogrammed into their targeting systems. If the decoys detected the dipping sonar of an ASW helicopter's sonobuoys, then the decoys would emit the same signature as the *Changzheng* and accelerate to fifteen knots.

If the ASW helicopters took the bait and chased them down, the decoys would increase their speed and make various course and depth corrections to lose the ASW helicopters. Lee believed this would draw the destroyers away from the carrier long enough for him to get his own ship in range to fire a salvo of torpedoes and then go deep and sprint for open water. At the designated ENDEX time, they would go to periscope depth, send their all-clear message and declare victory.

Captain Lee recalled an American saying as he thought about what victory would look like: "Murphy gets a vote, and if it can go wrong, it will, at the worst possible time."

Walking onto the Conn, Lee asked, "Officer of the Watch, report ship status."

"Captain, ship is rigged for ultraquiet, surface contacts remaining on reported bearings."

"Very well. Maintain current speed and heading," replied Lee.

"Maintain current speed and heading—yes, Captain."

The submarine had continued their stealthy advance into the patrol box at three knots for the last seven days while maintaining a depth of three hundred feet. The *Changzheng* became a black hole in the water. They successfully identified and tracked the battle cruiser and three destroyers escorting their intended prey.

The simulated carrier was eighteen thousand yards off their bow. There appeared to be two Type 55 destroyers leading the way, while a third destroyer was positioned to her rear. The Type 60 was to her port with her sonar actively pinging. It didn't take long before they detected the ASW helos circling with dipping sonars on a direct heading. Between the Type 60 and Captain Lee's submarine were two of his decoys and two Te-3 rocket-propelled mines directly in the path of the

Type 60. Lee would use the decoys to lure the ASW helicopters away from the ships, then lose the mines and fire two torpedoes at the Type 60.

Turning to his weapons officer, Lee ordered, "Weps, fire four YU-9 torpedoes with a programmed track to travel straight at the carrier in passive mode."

"Aye, Captain. Four torpedoes to be fired at the carrier in passive mode," repeated the weapons officer.

"Once those torpedoes acquire the carrier, keep them in passive mode until they're within one thousand yards. Then have them go active," Captain Lee added.

Traveling at sixty-nine knots, the YU-9s would reach the ship in a spread roughly one hundred meters apart, converging on the target in twenty-six seconds. This would leave the simulated carrier virtually no time to maneuver or evade the incoming torpedoes.

When the battle cruiser detected Lee's decoys and began engaging them, Captain Lee would have the decoys lead the escorts further away from the carrier. He'd then fire a spread of inert YU-9 torpedoes with their guide wires cut. The torpedoes would then go to active and acquire the ship in wake-homing mode along projected bearings.

While the Type 60 tried to evade the torpedoes, Captain Lee believed they would cross into the acoustic acquisition range of the Te-3 mines they had laid earlier. Then, as the battle cruiser had to contend with the mines and the torpedoes, Lee would fire three more torpedoes at the destroyers before they had a chance to react to his first attack.

At a depth of six hundred feet, Lee would send the command to the torpedoes to go to active homing for the destroyers. At this point, he'd cut the wires and send them to terminal attack speed. While the three ships dealt with the torpedoes, he would go silent and deep as he cruised to open water and safety.

At least, that was the plan. Now it was a waiting game. The submarine was at zero bubble and moving with the ocean current. At current closing speed, the primary target would be within range of his torpedoes in thirty-five minutes.

****

South China Sea

Dingyuan III

Senior Captain Chin sat on the bridge, reading the ship's status report. He had hunted the *Changzheng* for days, and despite having the most advanced destroyer in naval history, he could not find her. He had read as much as he could on Captain Lee. He wanted to know everything there was to know about him: how he operated, and how he'd handled himself in previous exercises.

Chin felt this exercise was a real opportunity for his men to train against what was being hailed as the most advanced submarine in the world. If they could acquit themselves well in this exercise, then chances were, they'd do well against an American submarine or ship.

Chin would admit privately that he hated hunting submarines. The damn things were hard to find unless the captain made a mistake. What Chin and his ASW helos had to do now was force Captain Lee to make an error. When that happened, they'd be ready to pounce.

The *Dingyuan* pressed her ASW helos hard. He knew the aircrews were exhausted, but he was determined to find the submarine and force her to make a move against the target ship. He instructed the captains of the destroyers to maintain a tight rotation on their ASW helos. He wanted them dropping sonobuoys along their advance in the hopes that they could catch the submarine approaching for an attack, either from the front or from behind.

So far, this had proven futile. There was no indicator of the submarine's presence. They had patrolled in their box for ten long and stressful days of hunting without so much as a trace of them. All his division heads drilled their sailors daily, but the monotony caused slips in efficiency.

Chin looked at his nearly empty cup of tea. As he rose to refill it, a communications technician told the Officer of the Watch that the ASW helicopter on station had detected cavitation in the water. Chin took a breath to catch himself. His excitement nearly got the better of him—the hunt was finally on.

The energy on this ship changed immediately as his crew began preparations for the simulated battle to come. The klaxon for action stations blared throughout the ship and the second ASW helo crew ran to their aircraft, ready to join the hunt from the sky. His sonar officer confirmed the cavitation. He reported the distance and bearing to contact.

Chin ordered an immediate course change to close in on the contact bearing, and he increased the ship's speed to thirty knots. He wanted to get into an attack position as soon as possible. It was time to bring this war game to a close and claim his victory.
****

South China Sea
Changzheng 30

"Captain, Sonar. Decoy has made initial cavitation. *Dingyuan* adjusted course to match bearing and increased speed," the sonar operator conveyed to Captain Lee.

"Sonar, Captain. Very well," Captain Lee confirmed.

Lee picked up his commander's tablet and swiped to get to his weapons status screen. He ordered his weapons officer to activate the mines and fire the YU-9 torpedo salvo along the bearing of the Arsenal ship. In anticipation of the attack, all tubes had been loaded, outer doors opened, and firing solutions and tracks preprogrammed into the weapons.

When the moment came, Lee did not hesitate as he gave the order to fire the torpedoes. When he did, he hit the digital stopwatch on the screen that was dedicated to the torpedoes. His weapons officer acknowledged the mines were activated. Even in the Conn, they could feel the torpedoes leave the tubes as the ship shuddered briefly.

Lee ordered a speed increase to fifteen knots along the bearing of the Arsenal ship and the empty tubes reloaded. The command was acknowledged as the submarine increased speed.

"Conn, sonar. Torpedoes are proceeding along assigned bearing in passive mode at ten knots," an officer reported.

"Very well," Lee acknowledged. He looked at his tablet and swiped to the weapons tracking screen that was synched with the ship's targeting computer. Checking the estimated time to active homing and terminal attack run, he thought about what Admiral Wei had said to him. *I need you to follow your instincts, not doctrine.*

He looked at the tracks of the torpedoes, then thought about what Admiral Wei had said again. He thought about PLAN doctrine, then he thought about what an American, British, or French captain would be thinking in this very situation.

Lee commanded, "Weapons, Captain. Change course on torpedo three. Steer the weapon toward the Type 60, cut wires and go to active homing, and prosecute it as Master 1. Reprogram the remaining torpedoes to track the Arsenal ship on known bearing passive acquisition until they are within one thousand yards, then cut wires and let them go. Designate Arsenal ship Master 2."

There was only a moment of hesitation before his order was echoed and carried out.

****

South China Sea
Dingyuan III

Captain Chin was feeling confident; he believed Captain Lee had made a mistake. He and his crew positioned themselves to pounce. Chin issued another speed increase and was about to launch a spread of torpedoes along the bearing of the cavitation the *Changzheng* was traveling along. But before he could issue the command, his sonar operator beat him to the call.

"Captain, Sonar. Torpedo in the water! Bearing one-five-three degrees and closing," the sonar operator reported.

"Sonar, Captain. Range and speed of torpedo?" Chin asked.

"Captain, Sonar. Range five thousand, three hundred yards, speed fifty-five knots and accelerating."

"Sonar, Captain. Very well. List all contacts as relative," Chin replied.

"Captain, Sonar. List all contacts as relative, aye," the sonar operator confirmed.

What the hell is Lee up to? Chin wondered. He'd tipped his hand too quickly. *Surely he...damn it!*

"Maneuvering, Captain. Right full rudder, all ahead flank."

Chin instructed his communications officer to alert the destroyer and Arsenal ship that the attack had started. Each ship then turned right full rudder and increased to flank to match what he was doing. Chin wasn't certain what Lee was up to, but he knew he needed distance from the submarine.

"Captain, Sonar. Torpedoes, torpedoes, torpedoes, bearing one-three-zero, one-three-five and one-four-two degrees off port bow, seven hundred and fifty yards, closing at forty-seven knots and accelerating!"

"Sonar, Captain. Very well." Chin felt momentary panic, then reminded himself that the weapons closing on him were inert and that his ship was designed to take hits.

"Maneuvering, Captain. Turn into the torpedoes, match bearing and close distance," Chin ordered.

Before the man could acknowledge the command, Chin cut him off and ordered his antitorpedo weapons to deploy. For good measure, he ordered them to fire double the munitions.

The weapons fired and splashed into the water within seconds. The computer reported that all but one of the incoming torpedoes had been acquired. The remaining torpedo had acquired his ship and impacted four seconds later with a thud that he felt even on the bridge.

Damage control reported to him that he needed to shut down his port shaft. If they had been hit by a live torpedo, it would have been destroyed. He cursed Lee under his breath. When he had increased his ship to flank speed, he'd had no idea the torpedo mines were programmed for wake homing. As he'd made his high-speed turn, the torpedo had followed his wake and struck.

What struck Chin as odd was that he knew doctrine said to strike from astern with wake homing programmed, not from a direct attack. This deviation from the standard doctrine had caught Chin off guard. It made him wonder if Lee would deviate from it further in his next attack.

We need to find Lee and sink them before they can carry out another strike on us...
****

South China Sea
Changzheng 30

Captain Lee placed his commander's tablet in its cradle and walked to the master plot. He enlarged the screen and saw the three remaining torpedoes heading toward Master 2. He received an indication that three of the four mine torpedoes had been intercepted by antitorpedo munitions from the Type 60. The fourth had acquired her wake and rendered her port screw inoperable. He needed to avoid her by staying out of her range. One ship off the board. Four remaining.

"Sonar, Captain. Distance to the first Type 55?" Captain Lee inquired.

"Captain, Sonar. First Type 55 is seventy-two hundred yards away, bearing three-one-eight degrees," the sonar operator relayed.

"Sonar, Captain. Designate Type 55, Master 3. Report contact as relative," Captain Lee ordered.

The sonarman was midsentence when he went quiet. Captain Lee looked up from the plot to see what had cut off the man's report. He saw him place the second headphone on his other ear and cup them with both hands. As Lee looked intently at the man, he noticed the Conn had grown eerily silent.

"Captain, splashes in the water! ASW helos directly above us. Torpedo, torpedo, torpedo, actively homing, sir!"

"Weapons, fire tubes one and four at Master 3 along known bearing! Maneuvering ahead flank, forty-degree down angle on the planes! Release countermeasures and decoys!"

As the commands were executed, Lee didn't need his stopwatch to know that time was up. The torpedoes had acquired his submarine and were on their terminal attack run. He looked at his XO as the man spoke.

"Sir, vent ballast?" As he spoke, he looked at the ceiling as the sonar pings of the torpedoes grew louder and increasingly frequent.

"No, the torpedoes are above us. We wouldn't have room to…" Lee trailed off.

The Conn shuddered as three inert torpedoes thudded against the hull of his submarine. Even though these were smaller versions of the YU-9, the three impacts would have destroyed the submarine without question. As he gave the order to secure from battle stations, he looked forward to finding out how the ASW helos had acquired them.

Turning to look at the faces of his men, he knew they had performed well. His sonar operator removed his headset and looked at him pensively.

Loosening the collar on his shirt, Lee walked to the sonar station and asked the sailor what was wrong.

"Well, sir, I listened to our torpedoes as they tracked to Master 2 and 3. It's just that—well, Captain, each target evaded one torpedo but was hit by the second," the sonar operator explained.

171

Lee raised an eyebrow. Though they were technically dead, they had accomplished their mission. It was curious. Had he followed PLAN doctrine to the letter, he would have had to disengage after prosecuting the Type 60. The carrier would have gotten away, and he still would have been sunk. Even in death, they would have lost. Instead, they had managed to strike.
****

Haidian District, Beijing
Five Days Later

Captain Lee followed the same procedure for entering the building as he had a month earlier. He expected to find the same officers assembled as before, but when he walked into the auditorium, it was just Fleet Admiral Wei Huang, head of the Chinese Navy, and his aide. He paused at the door, but Wei waved him forward. As he approached, Wei dismissed his aide.

"Captain, you performed quite well," Wei said.

"Thank you, sir. But I must give the credit to my crew. They performed admirably."

"Nonsense," Wei said, waving his hands dismissively. "You followed your instincts and you nearly defeated three of the mightiest warships in our fleet."

Lee remained quiet. Though Wei was correct, he'd still failed in his mission. Wei handed him an envelope.

"What is this, sir?"

"It is the results of the war game, and it is Jade Dragon's prediction."

Lee opened the envelope and read. He was pleased to learn that he was the only captain that had managed to score hits on three of the five ships. Captain Feng had been discovered on day three as he had tried to slowly maneuver in closer to the Arsenal ship. He had been flanked by the Type 60 and destroyers. They had all fired torpedoes at his sub and dropped torpedo mines along his avenues of retreat. Feng had simply had nowhere to run and had been destroyed.

Captain Su had been destroyed on the eighth day. He'd been trying to fire his torpedoes in the wake of the Arsenal ship and had been bracketed into a kill box by the ASW helos. He had managed to snap-shoot torpedoes, but they had been countered before he'd been sunk.

Next, Lee read the analysis from Jade Dragon.

The AI had anticipated the actions of the other three captains, nearly to the hour of the end of their exercise. When he got to the analysis of his action against the surface ships, he saw it was only one page. The last words gave him pause and he turned the page over to see if he had missed something. It simply read, "Outcome inconclusive."

"Sir, what does this mean?"

Wei looked at him for a long moment, then smiled.

"It means, Captain Lee, you may very well be the key to our success in this coming war in the Pacific. It means you were able to outsmart the computer, which is saying something."

Chapter Seventeen
Chengdu Virus

Acoustic Research Detachment
Bayview, Idaho

Jessica Parker looked at Dan. "We've met your demands. Now it's time for you to tell us more about this virus—why would Jade Dragon create such a virus and unleash it within China and then spread it around the world?"

"It's quite simple. It's a machine. It doesn't have the same emotional intelligence or morals that you and I may have. The program was given two problems and asked to solve them," Dan replied.

"Really? What were the problems?" Jessica asked, her interest piqued.

"Climate change and population control," Dan explained, his British accent sounding extra pompous in that moment. "You see, the two are intertwined. You can't solve climate change without solving the growth in population. In China, we have 1.5 billion people. That's twenty-one percent of the world's population. In our case, we have limited land and resources to cultivate and feed our people. Worse, our population is aging fast in comparison to some of our peer nations like India or even the US. Just nine years ago, 9.5 percent of our population was above the age of sixty-five. Now, it hovers around 18 percent, and by 2050, it's projected to be 27.5 percent. That's just inside China. Jade Dragon looked at the broader problem of climate change and determined that the most effective way to solve the problem is to cull the herd of the sick and elderly, the ones who are no longer able to contribute to society or for whom the economic drain they impose on society outweighs what they are able to contribute.

"When we couple those issues with how to destabilize the West by imploding your economies, we come up with the reasoning behind Project Chengdu. The AI is solving a host of problems all at the same time. Namely, it's going to crash your economies by forcing you to shut down like you did during the last COVID pandemic, then cull the herd of the sick, lame, and elderly, thus reducing the global population by 10 to 18 percent. It's all very formulaic when you think about it."

Jessica wasn't sure if she wanted to throw up, punch Dan, or just scream at the ceiling. How these bastards could have created a machine so sinister was appalling; and that they would follow its advice no matter how immoral was beyond the pale.

Dan apparently saw the look of disgust on her face, and he tried to clarify, "You have to understand, Jessica. I was not involved in these decisions on how to use or implement JD. That was Dr. Xi, among many others. I was an engineer, a builder. When this program first started out, I truly thought I was joining something that was going to help solve some of the world's toughest questions. I had no idea they were going to use JD in this fashion."

"I'm sure that's what the Nazi prison guards said about the trainloads of Jews and other undesirables when they showed up at the death camps."

Dan didn't say anything. He just sat there with a blank look on his face.

"How do we stop this virus?" she pressed.

"Acquire the vaccine and start mass-producing it. There's plenty of it out there."

"Really? So you concocted this superbug but made sure you had a vaccine in place to prevent it from getting too out of control?"

Dan canted his head to the side as if he were surprised by the question. "Xi and the others may be cold and calculating, but they are not idiots. If you want to treat them as sadistic morons, you do so at your own peril. The vaccine was distributed to China's allied nations so they wouldn't be hammered by it. The goal isn't to destroy our friends—it's to destroy the West and supplant them as the new world power."

"So, Dan. How do we stop Jade Dragon?"

Smiling, Dan leaned forward. "I've been waiting for you to ask me that. Give me access to a computer and I can get you inside JD's OS."

"You have root access?"

"I built the damn thing; you better believe I built some backdoors into it," Dan explained. "I don't think even Xi knows about them. If you want to have a prayer of beating JD, then I need to see what they're doing next. I need to gain entry into the program and see what kind of war games they've dreamed up. That will give us an insight into what is coming next."

Chapter Seventeen
Kompromat

May 2024
Mariel, Cuba

What a beautiful day it is. The sun is shining, not a cloud in sight, thought José Santiago as he watched the waitress make her way over to his table. She placed a cup of coffee in front of him, along with a plate containing three thin slices of brazo de gitano, a mouthwatering cake roll with guava jelly filling. It was the perfect pairing.

When the waitress left, he took a couple bites of his breakfast before taking a sip of the fresh cup of joe. This was hands-down José's favorite part of Cuba—the coffee, the cigars, and the pastries.

Looking out toward the water and across the bay, one could see the swarms of workers unloading one cargo vessel after another. It was an impressive facility, quickly and efficiently receiving cargo. Of course, none of it would be possible without the financial aid and port-building expertise the Chinese-owned firm COSCO brought to the table.

The Chinese, with their incredible engineering skills, had helped the Cubans dredge the bay to create more space to build the deepwater port. They'd also expanded the facility, adding three new port terminals. A new rail line had been constructed, allowing the offloaded shipping containers to be easily transferred to rail, where they could be shipped around the country.

This new facility, along with the oil terminal and the refinery, had transformed the Cuban economy. The government was becoming flush with cash. New infrastructure projects, buildings, and even cell towers were popping up everywhere.

In the last year, not only had Cuba become independent of foreign oil, they were now a net exporter of oil to China and other nearby countries. With so much global political pressure on Venezuela, the Chinese found Cuba to be an exceptional place to build a series of new oil refineries to handle the influx of crude being pumped from the Gulf.

Had the Chinese not gotten involved in drilling for oil along the Straits of Florida and the Gulf of Mexico, José doubted America would be aware of half of what the Chinese were doing in Cuba. With the threat of terrorism and the continuing saga of the Moros regime, American attention and resources were not directed toward Cuba.

What struck José as odd was that, in February, Cuba had instituted a mandatory flu vaccination. Everyone had had to line up at their local clinic to get it. When José had gone to the clinic near his apartment, he'd noticed the vial the technician was using. It had a Chinese label on it. José had grown a bit concerned when he had seen it, but like everyone else, he had to get it.

A few weeks later, when this new virus from China had broken out across Europe and then the US. For two weeks, José had waited in fear for the symptoms to start, but they'd never come. Not only that, hardly anyone in the country was coming down with this new virus.

Then it dawned on José. Maybe this flu vaccine they had all been given was actually a vaccine against this new virus and that was why people in Cuba, Venezuela, Panama, and El Salvador weren't being pummeled by it. José knew he needed to get his hands on a vial and have it shipped back to the US so it could be studied.

When he was halfway into his coffee and deep in his own thoughts, a beautiful woman walked out on the patio of the café, looking for someone. Then the five-foot-nine-inch-tall woman with beautiful hazel eyes, shoulder-length brownish hair and a figure to die for spotted José. Her eyes lit up and a smile spread across her face, her beautiful white teeth practically shining. She gracefully moved toward him as if she were effortlessly floating on a cloud of air. The flowing sundress moved around her body in the gentle breeze, showing just enough of her figure to cause every man in the place to stare as she glided past them.

"Good morning, Yamileth. How are you doing this beautiful day?" José said politely as he stood up, kissing her on both cheeks as he invited her to take a seat. The other men around him looked on jealously.

José loved that feeling he got when men stared at him longingly as he sat with this beautiful woman. It happened every time they met.

Yami smiled as they briefly hugged and kissed. "I'm doing well, José. Thank you for inviting me out for breakfast this morning. I see you have already started," she commented flirtatiously as she saw he had been nibbling on the pastry in front of him.

He blushed slightly. "How can a man stare at a piece of brazo de gitano and not eat some of it? Please, let me order you something." José flagged down the waitress, who came over to their table, took Yami's order and said she'd be back momentarily.

In a hushed tone, Yami leaned in and softly announced, "I made contact with our friend Esteban the other day."

In an equally hushed tone, José prodded, "Were you able to obtain the kompromat?"

Yami tilted her head to the side. "Of course—as if that would be a problem."

She then pulled out her phone and moved over near his seat. She pretended to take a selfie of the two of them and then placed the phone on the table as the waitress brought a cup of coffee and a fresh pastry for her.

While Yami added sugar to her coffee, José pretended to be checking something on his phone as he turned a stealth app on and then placed the phone on the table next to Yami's. For the next few minutes, the two phones exchanged data discreetly while they continued to eat their pastries, drink their coffee and flirt with each other.

José took another sip of his coffee before remembering he had something to give her. He reached down into his satchel and pulled out a very worn paperback book titled *Explosion in a Cathedral* by Alejo Carpentier and placed it on the table near Yami.

"Oh, you brought the book for me," Yami squealed with delight. She'd been wanting to read this book for some time, but it was a hard one to come by.

"I did. I'm sorry I forgot it last time. I remembered on my way out the door this morning to grab it. As you can see, it's lovingly worn. I've read it a few times. I hate to say this, but page 301 is missing. I think I may have ripped it out a while ago, but I can't remember what happened or why I did it," José quipped apologetically.

Yami looked sad as she picked up the book. She flipped through a few of the pages until she reached the section he had told her about. She spotted the ten twenty-euro notes and smiled.

"It's OK, José. I'm sure it won't detract from the meaning of the book. Oh, before I forget. My brother who works at the clinic found that vitamin you asked for. He asked me to give this to you," Yami said innocently enough.

She pulled out a small vitamin bottle and handed it to him. José smiled and took the bottle and placed it in his satchel.

"You know, there is a quote on page 142 of the book I think you will like. I thought it was rather powerful." José winked.

Yami tilted her head as she shot him a mischievous look. She flipped through the book again until she came to the page. She saw twenty twenty-euro notes. It took everything in her not to burst out loud in gratitude. She also saw a sentence highlighted in yellow and read it aloud.

"The thunder traveled over the ship, from west to east, with prolonged reverberations, before it moved away with its clouds, leaving the sea, by midafternoon, bathed in a strange auroral light, which turned it as smooth and iridescent as a mountain lake. The bow of the Arrow became a plough, breaking up the tranquility of the surface with the frothy arabesques of its wake."

She looked up at José with a look in her eye that said if they weren't in public, she'd make a bold move and kiss him and much more for what he had given her.

"It's beautiful, José. I can't thank you enough. When I finish reading the book, my brother will appreciate it as well," Yami managed to say as she choked down her emotions.

José tried not to blush as he nodded, lifting his coffee cup to his lips, finishing off the contents. "I am glad I am able to help you and your family, Yami. I truly am."

The two of them talked for a little while longer before José needed to get going. He pulled out enough money to pay for their meals and left a decent tip. "Yami, I hate to cut and run, but I have a busy day ahead of me and I need to make one more stop. Let's meet again next Tuesday, same place and time. We can talk then."

She nodded as they said a quick goodbye. José pocketed his phone; the small red light had stopped blinking, letting him know the download was complete.

Just prior to leaving the café, José went to the toilet. After relieving himself, he sent a one-word message to the station chief at the embassy.

"Colón."

Walking out of the café, José climbed into his vehicle and headed back to Havana and the Sherritt International office he worked out of.

During his drive, his phone chirped, letting him know he had ninety minutes until his next meeting. Not a lot of time for him to make his drop. Once he finally made it into the city, he headed toward a particular park near where he lived. This part of Havana was a wealthy section—a lot of Party and military officials and expatriates lived in this area.

José made it a point to host some parties at his home for many of these people. He was, after all, a Canadian businessman from Venezuela. He fit right in with many of the Cuban people.

José found a parking spot along the side of the road. He grabbed the vial in the special container that Yami had given him, placing it in his pocket. Before he exited the vehicle, he also picked up a book.

José walked down the path for a few minutes before finding a place under a nearby tree. Sitting under the tree, he started reading the book he'd brought with him. Ten minutes into his little break, he slipped the container out of his pocket and placed it at the base of the tree. Not taking his eyes off his book, he fiddled with the base of the tree with his left hand until he found the loose piece next to a root. He pulled it out slightly, revealing a small carved-out crevice. He slid the container inside and then pushed the cover back.

José sat under the tree for twenty more minutes, reading his book. He waved to a few people walking nearby, not a care in the world. He wasn't worried about the bottle he'd dropped—he knew someone from the embassy would be retrieving that piece of intelligence.

When he got up, he spotted a vendor pushing his cart through the park. José bought something quick to eat and a bottle of water. Then he climbed back into his car and continued to his office, which wasn't far away.

****

José worked for a Canadian firm who'd been hired to help the Cuba Oil Union, CUPET, get the new refinery up and running. Eight years ago, CUPET and the Chinese firm CNOOC had signed a joint venture to explore and extract oil in the North Cuban Foreland Basin, which sat in the Straits of Florida, and a second oil field on the western side of the island reaching into the Gulf of Mexico.

Not only were the Chinese helping CUPET establish more than two dozen oil platforms in the Straits, the platforms were equipped with a lot of specialized communication and surveillance equipment. Sherritt International, however, brought to the venture their expertise in the refinery aspect of the business.

The company had sent José to be one of the senior advisors as he had a deep background in optimizing the performance of refineries. Having worked in the oil business for eighteen years, José had a lot of experience working with developing nations as they expanded their petrol industries.

Later that afternoon, after a round of meetings with some folks from CUPET and CNOOC, José reviewed his phone to look at the video file Yami had sent him. He only needed to see a few minutes to know Yami had provided the material he needed. Now José would arrange a meeting with Mr. Ochoa so the two of them could come to a mutually beneficial arrangement.

That evening, after meeting up with some friends from CUPET and their Chinese counterparts for dinner, José logged in to an old Hotmail account. Scrolling to his draft folder, he created a new email. He spent twenty minutes writing up a quick contact report from his morning meeting with Yamileth and attached the video she'd provided of Esteban Ochoa and her in bed. He also outlined how he planned to make contact with Esteban and use the kompromat to come to a mutually beneficial arrangement with the port manager. Then he saved the message but did not send it—his intended recipient knew how to find it.
****

JBCC – Computer Lab
Beijing, China

"Excuse me, Dr. Xi," a man in a black suit said as he walked up to him.

Xi knew immediately who the man was. He was a deputy in the Ministry of State Security. He was also alone—that was a good sign.

"What can I do for you, Jin?" Xi asked. He stopped what he was working on and gave the man his undivided attention.

"I think we have a problem. I need your help in understanding something, though."

Xi lifted an eyebrow. "OK, let's talk. What's the issue?"

"A month ago, your assistant, Ma Yong—he went by the Western name Daniel. He was killed in the UK—hit by a car, if I'm not mistaken."

Xi nodded. "He was. It was a complete surprise. I still wonder if things might have turned out differently if I had gone with him on that trip."

Xi wouldn't admit it to anyone, but he felt incredibly guilty about not being there with Dan when he'd died. The young man had been almost like a son to him, a protégé if ever there was one. His death had hit Xi hard.

"I want to show you something. Perhaps you can help me figure out what's going on."

Jin pulled a photo out of a folder he had with him and handed it to Xi. There were several photos of Dan's parents at an airport, labeled with a date about two weeks after his fatal car crash. A few pictures in, Xi's jaw dropped.

"Dan is alive?" he asked in shock.

Jin nodded slowly. "After his 'accident,' Jade Dragon managed to pick up some intelligence that contradicted the reports we had received. Utilizing its ability to analyze CCTV footage, we managed to get these images from the Isle of Man. Unfortunately, by the time we dispatched some of our men to investigate, Ma Yong had already vacated the area."

"Do you know where he is now?" Xi pressed.

"Jade Dragon picked up on a very unusual shipment to a Super 1 Foods Store in Athol, Idaho. Would you like to hazard a guess as to what item was ordered from their supermarket for the very first time?"

Xi was at a loss. *Is this a test?* he wondered. "I don't know," he replied.

"Tunnock's tea cakes."

Holy crap, thought Xi. Dan was always eating those things. He'd gotten a lot of flack for it, but it kept him productive.

"How do you know it was him?" Xi pressed.

"With a much narrower area to investigate, Jade Dragon was once again unleashed on the CCTV, Ring, Nest, ADT, and SimplySafe security footage of the surrounding area. Narrowing for height and gait patterns, we located a likely match. Eventually, JD was able to capture an iris image from one of the security systems when he passed by with a high enough quality to confirm a match to Ma Yong."

Jin showed him a new image. This man didn't look like the Dan he had known at all. "We believe he had facial reconstruction surgery, but the iris image was a complete match—it's him."

"So where exactly is he?" Xi asked.

"Ma Yong is currently being held in a safe house on a naval research facility in Idaho," Jin explained.

"Idaho…that seems like a strange place to have a naval research facility," Xi commented. The American state was landlocked, after all.

Jin chuckled. "We thought the same thing until we looked into it. Apparently, the lake is a very deep lake and one of the quietest in the country. The American Navy tests acoustic equipment there. It's actually an incredibly ingenious safe house location. Who would suspect a naval research base in Idaho? In any case, I wanted you to know we had found him, and he is apparently alive. That means we have a host of new problems you and I need to talk about."

Now Xi knew why the man was here. He wanted to know if Dan posed a security risk. Suddenly, Xi felt his heart racing; beads of sweat formed on his temples. *Dan built Jade Dragon. Did he program vulnerabilities into it?*

Jin noticed Xi's change in demeanor. "You know what I'm going to ask, don't you?"

Xi nodded. "If he did in fact cross over to their side and wasn't kidnapped—hell, even if he was kidnapped—he could tell them about everything." He looked down at his hands—they were shaking. He tried to will them to be still.

"Relax, Doctor. We do not suspect you of anything. You have given us the tools we are now employing to find these traitors in our midst. Back to Ma—is it possible he built in some backdoors that you may not be aware of?"

Xi held a hand up and then picked up his phone. "Reschedule my next meeting," he told his assistant, "and I am not to be disturbed, is that understood?" He hung up.

"Sir, this may take a while," Xi told Jin. He began frantically typing away on his computer, using every bit of knowledge he knew about Dan to help him search.

Two hours later, he suddenly exclaimed, "Holy crap, I've found something."

"Can you shut it down?" Jin asked.

Xi didn't answer right away. He was busy reading many lines of code. "No, I can't," he said somewhat glumly. "Give me a minute, though," Xi insisted.

After a couple of minutes of pecking away at his keyboard, Xi explained, "I'm redirecting this backdoor to go to a honeypot. It's going to take him to a mirror station. He'll think he's in Jade Dragon, but he'll be inside a controlled box of it. We'll be able to see exactly what he's doing and what he's searching."

"Excellent. Just make sure he isn't able to disclose Project Ten. It is important that he doesn't gain access to the operational plans, or it could jeopardize everything."
****

Bayview, Idaho

Dan sat at the computer terminal, ready to enter his login credentials to Jade Dragon. He looked at Jessica. "You are confident there is no way they're going to be able to trace this IP connection or even know we're inside the system?"

Jessica Parker had brought in a couple of additional tech experts from her department to help them get things set up here. The Agency was pulling out its entire toolbox of trickery for this one. They needed to gain entry into Jade Dragon and download a copy of the war game scenarios they'd been running in hopes of determining what the Chinese were up to.

"We're going through a handful of different proxy servers being bounced all over the world. It's going to be pretty hard for them to know we're in the system, let alone track us," one of the tech guys countered.

Dan typed away. Seconds later, they were in. He brought up a chat window, then turned the speakers up and the video camera on the computer on. "JD, are you there?" Dan said aloud.

His question was met with silence.

"Are you trying to talk to it?" one of the techs asked, his curiosity piqued.

"Yes. I programmed Jade Dragon, JD, to talk with me. We would have conversations for hours sometimes in the lab. It was one of the ways I was teaching him language skills," Dan explained to the amazement of the others.

Opening another window, Dan typed a few other commands. He smiled as he shook his head. "They found my backdoor."

"What? How is that possible?" Jessica asked, surprised.

Dan ignored her question as he continued to type away. He was looking for something. Then he found it. "We have a problem. They know I'm alive," Dan announced.

"Not possible. We faked your death pretty damn good," Jessica countered.

"That may be so, but they know I'm alive. Could they have activated Jedi…?" His voice trailed off.

"What's Jedi?" asked two of the Agency computer techs at the same time.

His fingers dancing furiously across the keyboard, Dan brought up one line of code and prompt after another. Jessica and the techs tried to get him to respond to their questions, only to be met by silence as he kept shushing them while he continued to type away.

"Found it!" he suddenly exclaimed. "Crap, this is bad. It looks like they activated the Jedi program two days after I was hit by that car in Oxford. They found me, no two ways about it. They know I'm here in Bayview. Right here, that's how they found me." He pointed to several lines of code that had some text to them.

One of the techs looked at it. "A CCTV at Bayview Mercantile caught an image of his iris and matched it to him," he announced.

Jessica's eyes went wide as saucers. "When did it take this image?"

"Ah, it looks like four days ago. The AI must have been able to access the security systems cloud storage and run query of the images on record until the found a match."

"Damn it, they could already have a team on their way here to deal with him," their JSOC bodyguard said quietly. The Army sergeant first class got up and started making a phone call, probably to report what they'd just learned and call for help.

Dan turned to Jessica. "We need to get out of here. We have to relocate to another safe house. If the MSS don't have a team already here, they will shortly."

****

"That's it, we've got him," called out one of the techs over their headset.

"So, he *is* alive?" the team leader, Han, asked skeptically. He had had his doubts, but his superiors had insisted they had a good source on the inside.

"He's alive. He just logged in to his account through the backdoor access. It has to be him—no one else would have known about it," the tech said.

"OK, then let's do this. Time to load up," Han called out to his team.

The eight operators loaded up into the two SUVs and got ready to head out. Two other men climbed into another vehicle and left—they were his sniper team. They'd already found a spot to set up in that provided them with a solid overwatch of the area.

As their vehicle headed down the road toward the naval research station, the men readied their weapons. They'd scoped the place out the day before and found it to be lightly guarded. There was a gate to the small facility with a single guard manning it. Aside from that, they saw at most two local sheriff vehicles. If they timed this right, they should be able to get in and eliminate the target before anyone knew what had happened.

Five minutes into their drive, Han got a call from their sniper team. They were in position and looking at the building where their tech crew had said the target was using a computer. Now it was just a matter of observing it to see if anyone entered or left the building while the assault team moved into place.

As they approached North Main Street on their way to the gate to the facility, their sniper team called. "We've got eyes on a small group leaving one of the target buildings. It looks like they're climbing into a couple of SUVs. I believe they are going to head right for your position," the spotter said over their coms.

Wow, this might be easier than I thought, Han thought privately, not wanting to jinx them.

"We're approaching the gate. What do you want us to do?" asked the driver.

"Drive past it. Go down to the next intersection and make a U-turn. We need to let them reach the gate before we launch our ambush," Han directed.

As they drove past the small facility, Han saw the two vehicles the sniper team had mentioned. Sure enough, a group of people were getting into them to leave. Something had happened—they must have been spooked to be leaving in such a hurry.

"When the lead vehicle pulls up to the gate, I want you to block them in. Once they're blocked, I want all teams to dismount and open fire on the vehicles. Take 'em out. Stay ready, though, in case they have a security guard or two with them," Han directed. The four guys in the vehicle behind him were listening in on the coms as well. They knew what to do.

As they approached the turn that led to the naval research facility, the two government vehicles were just about to pull out onto Main Street when Han's driver gunned their vehicle and blocked them.

When Han's vehicle came to a stop, the driver of the SUV they'd blocked honked his horn, apparently not realizing what was going on just yet. Then all eight operators spilled out with weapons blazing.

Bringing his Sig Sauer 300 Blackout AR to his shoulder, Han cut loose a string of rounds into the target vehicle. The passenger side of the front windshield splattered with blood as his rounds found their mark, the heavy 300 Blackout bullets punching right through the lightly armored glass windows of the government SUV.

The other shooters with Han were likewise unloading their rifles into the vehicle, riddling it with dozens and dozens of rounds, killing the occupants. The driver in the chase vehicle in the rear had thrown their SUV into reverse, flooring it as they tried to get out of the kill box. Several of Han's guys stood their ground, emptying their magazines into the vehicle, aiming for the driver side and the engine compartment.

The vehicle managed to drive in reverse for another thirty or so feet before the driver was riddled with half a dozen bullets. A man climbed out of the passenger side of the vehicle and, while using it as cover, pulled his own rifle out of the vehicle and returned fire.

One of Han's guys got hit and went down. The others dove for cover as they reacted to the new threat.

"Flank them!" Han yelled out.

Two of his guys fired some shots while they ran to the right. Another two guys ran to the left as they sought to get the defender in a crossfire so he wouldn't be able to escape. Meanwhile, the rest of Han's guys continued to light the vehicle up now that it had stalled out and appeared dead.

Running up to the vehicle they'd just shot, Han found the lone gunman slumped against the side of SUV, blood covering his chest from multiple bullet wounds. With the threat neutralized, Han began searching the vehicles.

In the first vehicle, the driver and front passenger were clearly dead. One of the occupants in the rear had also been killed in the gunfire. The fourth man, a nerdy-looking computer guy, had his hands up, tears streaming down his face.

Han couldn't hear what he was saying. He raised his rifle up and fired a handful of rounds into him, ending his pleas for mercy.

"All clear," shouted one of his guys as they encircled the second SUV.

"Come out with your hands up!" shouted one of Han's guys.

A moment later, a woman and a man climbed out of the vehicle. They looked terrified. Han recognized the man from the images he'd been sent as Ma Yong. The woman with him was unknown.

Han approached them, his rifle at the low ready. His other guards likewise kept their rifles at the low ready.

At this point, a lot of spectators from around the area began poking their heads out of their nearby businesses to figure out what was going on. For the briefest of minutes, it must have sounded like World War III had started in their sleepy little town.

Walking up to the man and woman with their hands held high, Han asked, "Are you Ma Yong?"

The man looked at him, dread in his eyes. Han knew that look all too well—that look of a person who knew they'd been caught and were about to be either arrested or killed.

Raising his rifle, Han shot the traitor several times in the chest. The woman next to him screamed and tried to run. Han turned his rifle on her and fired a handful of bullets into her back as well.

He then walked over to Ma's body and fired a couple more rounds into him. He reached for his phone, then took a photo of him. He then reached down and grabbed his right hand, taking his electronic fingerprints just to make sure they'd gotten the right person.

By this time, they heard police sirens. Han's sniper team told them they had two sheriff deputies on their way.

"We got what we came here for—it's time to roll!" Han called out over their internal coms network.

While his guys were running back to their vehicles, one of the sheriff vehicles came around the bend. The front windshield suddenly cracked and was then splattered with blood. The vehicle careened out of control and slammed into a parked car on the side of the road. The sniper team had scored a hit and bought them some time to get in their SUVs and haul out of there.

Once Han was in his vehicle, he directed the driver to head to their exfil location. They had a U-Haul moving van waiting for them. They'd pile into the back and head off to a safe house near Spokane, Washington, where they'd await their next set of orders.

This was the first set of targeted assassinations. Han doubted it'd be their last, given the number of them they'd heard about on the news over the last couple of days. All sorts of foreign intelligence operatives were turning up dead in countries all over the world, to include the United States.

Chapter Eighteen
Miami Heat

USCGC *Charles Sexton*
Thirty Miles off the Florida Keys

It was a blistering hot afternoon when the fun started. The Coast Guard cutter spotted its prey and maneuvered to swoop in.

"Lieutenant, it looks like we have a submersible!" shouted one of the lookouts from his post.

Lieutenant Don Winslow furrowed his brow. "This is the third one in four days," he muttered. Then he turned to his senior enlisted man. "Chief, go check it out. See if it really is another one of them," Winslow ordered.

Chief Petty Officer Yoni Yankovic nodded and got up to see for himself.

"Where's it at?" he asked the lookout.

"Over there, Chief," the young man said.

Raising the binos to his eyes, Yankovic looked in the direction the young man was pointing. It took him a moment, but sure enough, he spotted a shallow wake—a telltale sign of a submersible.

Turning to look back into the pilothouse, Yankovic gave them a signal letting them know he confirmed it. They'd found another one.

Moments later, the Sentinel-class cutter picked up speed and headed toward the drug-running submersible. A general quarters klaxon blared, letting the crew know to get ready for action.

When Yankovic walked back into the pilothouse, Winslow exclaimed, "Where the hell are they getting all these submersibles?"

Yankovic shrugged. "No idea. You want me to have the team get the RIB ready?"

"Yeah, get them ready to launch. We need to get as close to them as possible before we send them out," Winslow answered.

It took them twenty minutes to catch up with the drug runners, who were doing their best to evade them. Had their vessel been a true submersible, they might have been able to dive and hide under the waves. The little drug boats could only go a few feet under the waves at best. They were primarily designed with a low profile to make them hard to locate with radar or the naked eye. One of the giveaways was rough seas.

When the waves rose above a certain level, it became harder for them to hide and not get tossed about.

As they neared the vessel, the RIB stationed at the rear of the cutter slid off the rear of the boat and took off after the drug boat. While they raced to intercept it, two sailors manned the 25mm cannon on the bow while another sailor handled the fifty-caliber machine gun on the port side.

When the RIB pulled up right next to the drug boat, Yankovic called out to one of his soldiers, "Jenkins, see if you can get them to stop."

The petty officer third class nodded, a determined look on his face. Jenkins and three other Coasties were the only ones tricked out in full body armor with M4s strapped to them. If there was a shoot-out on the sub, they'd be the ones to handle it.

****

The RIB angled right up against the submersible, closing the distance so all Jenkins had to do was practically walk on to it. Once he was on, he ran toward the front of the boat to the cabin entrance.

Jenkins banged on the hatch a couple of times, shouting at them in Spanish to no avail.

Yankovic shouted, "Hold on, Jenkins. He's trying to fling you off!"

The drug runners pulled the sub hard to the right, nearly throwing Jenkins right off the back. Jenkins scrambled to grab at anything to hold on to. Then the driver decelerated, causing Jenkins to spin around and almost fly off the front of the submersible.

Yankovic veered the RIB in front of the drug boat a couple of times, making sure the crew inside knew they weren't getting away.

Jenkins reached for his radio talk button. "Chief, I'll plug a few rounds in their engines and end this."

"Good copy, Jenkins. Permission granted," Yankovic replied, not waiting to get the lieutenant's approval. They needed to end this now before Jenkins or anyone else got hurt.

Jenkins finally found his footing and walked past the small cabin toward the rear. As he approached the rear of the boat, Jenkins pulled his M4 from behind him and flicked the selector switch from safe to semi. He took aim at the rear of the boat, where the engine was located, and proceeded to fire half a dozen rounds into the compartment, trying to disable the engines.

Seconds after he started shooting, he heard a grinding noise, and then smoke emanated from the bullet holes. The drug boat started losing power as the engine gave out.

At this point, Jenkins turned around, his rifle at the low ready in case any of the occupants decided they wanted to get frisky.

The front hatch opened a couple of inches, and a small yellow canister dropped on the rear deck. It rolled off the boat into the water, puffing out thick orange smoke.

Oh crap, they're gonna fight, Jenkins thought to himself as he took a quick knee.

The pilothouse was now covered in thick orange smoke, obscuring the Coast Guard's view of what was going on. Then Jenkins heard the unmistakable sound of an AK-47 opening fire.

He dropped to his belly, hearing the hot metal projectiles zipping over his head where he'd just been. Aiming his M4 where he suspected the shooter was, Jenkins returned fire. He fired close to a dozen rounds at the pilothouse, hoping he'd hit the shooter and ended the fight.

Then a voice called out in Spanish, telling him they wanted to surrender. It was still hard to see clearly; the damn smoke canister was floating next to the submersible, spewing clouds of orange signal smoke that obscured everything.

Jenkins called out in Spanish, telling them to drop their weapons and start walking toward the rear of the submersible with their hands held up. A minute later, two figures appeared out of the smoke. When a gust of wind blew more of the smoke away, Jenkins got a good look at them. They both had their hands up, no visible weapons. When he caught a quick glance of the pilothouse, he spotted the body of their comrade. He looked dead.

"Jenkins, you alright?" called out Chief Yankovic over the radio.

"Yeah, Chief. I got the shooter. I've got two prisoners near the rear of the boat where I am," Jenkins replied.

A minute later, the RIB pulled up next to the submersible. One of the sailors found the smoke canister and grabbed for it. Once they had it, the chief accelerated away and they tossed it in the open ocean. They needed to get it away from the submersible so they could see clearly. Those little signal canisters could puff away for a good three to five minutes if you let them.

Now that Jenkins could see better, he moved toward the two guys with their hands up. "Turn around and place your hands behind your backs," he ordered.

Jenkins grabbed for his zip cuffs and got them secured. When the RIB pulled up next to them again, they transferred the two prisoners. A couple more sailors hopped aboard the sub and made their way to the pilothouse and the inside of the submersible.

They'd spend the next couple of hours documenting everything they found and dusting the place for prints. Three hours later, they'd counted one hundred and forty-eight kilos of heroin. This was on top of the two other drug boats they'd stopped earlier in the week.

No one knew for certain what was going on, but they were interdicting an awful lot of heroin coming from Cuba in the last three weeks.

****

Drug Enforcement Office
Miami Field Office

"Bill, what's going on with all the drugs coming in from Cuba? I don't think we've ever seen this many drug smugglers originating from there. Is there something going on we don't know about?" asked Mike Auger, the Special Agent in Charge of the Miami DEA office.

Bill shrugged as he poured himself another coffee. "Beats me, boss. Maybe they figure with all the crap going on in the country, now'd be a good time to slip some boats past us."

Mike sighed at Bill's indifference. He'd be glad when Bill retired at the end of the year. Once Bill had dropped his retirement papers a month ago, he had truly become a ROAD, retired on active duty. The man did as little as humanly possible as he waited out the last few months of the fiscal year and his retirement.

"How about you do this, Bill? Take the new kid, Tom, with you. Reach out to some of your sources and figure out what's going on. This might be a good chance for you to start transitioning your people over to him since you'll be retiring in a few months," Mike offered, though it was more of an order than a suggestion.

Bill lifted an eyebrow. "Don't you think Tom's a little green to be running sources?"

"Have you read Tom's file?" Mike asked. "He's got eight years' experience working for Portland PD in their narcotics division. Prior to that, he spent six years in the Marines, counterintelligence. He may be green to the DEA, but he's got some good experience to rely on. Besides, you're retiring in four months. It's time to start transitioning your sources over to someone else."

"All right, Mike," Bill said with a sigh. "I'll make some calls and start looping the cherry in on what's what. Keep in mind, most places are still closed down with all this COVID BS going on, so organizing some meets might be a challenge."

****

Two Hours Later

Mike walked back to his office and closed the door. He checked his email and saw an urgent one from D.C. He clicked on the email from his boss.

Mike,
Something's going on along the border. CBP has intercepted more drugs in the last eight weeks than they did in the previous year. Most concerning is that the drugs appear to be a mixture of fentanyl and heroin. I'm not sure what's going on, but I need you to press your sources in South Florida to see if there's an increase in demand. There shouldn't be this much product coming into the US unless there's a sudden increase in demand we don't know about.
Jerry

"I knew something was going on," Mike said aloud to himself, lightly punching his desk. He hadn't noticed the new guy had popped his head in through the open office door.

"You all right, boss?" asked Tom.

"Ah, Tom, just the guy I was looking for. Come on in," Mike replied as he pointed to an empty chair in front of his desk. "Sometimes I like to think out loud. It helps me know if what I'm thinking makes sense or not. Now, how did things go today with Bill?"

Tom pulled out a notebook and flipped it open. "It went good. Bill got us a few meets set up for the next couple of days. Tonight, we'll be meeting up with a guy named...Nugget. Bill's granted me access to his source files, so I'll spend the next few days reading up on them all."

"Ah, excellent. Nugget's actually a surprisingly good source. We've been employing him for a long time. He's a bit of a wild card, though, so just keep an eye on him."

"Yeah, I saw that. He seems to have a bit of a temper. Resisting arrest, assault on a police officer, assault and battery charges and a rap sheet as long as my arm. Guy's a real piece of work," Tom commented.

Chuckling at his assessment, Mike replied, "Guys like that make for the best sources. They're in so deep their only hope is a deal. He knows the second he stops being a good reliable source, he's back in federal custody. He likes his freedom too much. If he knows what's going on with all the drugs coming in from Cuba, he'll talk."
****

Four Hours Later
Miami, Florida

After driving down South Dixie Highway for a little while, Bill finally broke the silence.

"We're approaching the meet location."

Tom leaned forward in his seat as if it'd help him see what they were approaching. "This is where we're meeting Nugget?"

Snickering at the question, Bill countered, "You don't approve? It's one of the few places still open right now."

The parking lot was coming up quick. It was half-full of Harleys and a few pickup trucks sporting Confederate flags.

Tom shook his head. "No, I figured he might hang out at a higher-caliber strip club than this joint. This place looks like a real dive."

Bill snorted. "Well, the higher-end strip clubs are all closed because of the virus. The only benefit about that is the girls that work at them are now working at these dive bars instead. Same view, half the ticket price."

Tom shook his head. He hated how some guys viewed women like a piece of meat. Strip clubs weren't his thing. He only went to them for work when he had no choice.

Bill parked the beater of a car they'd taken from the impound lot for tonight's meet. As they approached the entrance, the booming of the music became louder.

Opening the door, Bill motioned for Tom to head on in.

The front entrance was filled with smoke and the slight scent of marijuana.

"It's ten dollars," announced a burly man with the word Security stenciled on his black T-shirt.

Bill pulled a twenty out of his pocket and handed it to the bouncer. The two of them then walked past the black curtain and inside the bar.

There was a stage along the center wall of the open room. A dozen chairs ringed the stage, with half a dozen two- and four-person tables set a little further back. On the opposite wall was a U-shaped bar that gave the patrons a good angle to watch the stage from a distance while they drank their drinks or ate an appetizer.

Bill led Tom past several tables while several mean-looking men stared at them. The tough guys had a pile of empty beer bottles on the table in front of them.

The two of them found a seat at the bar and ordered a beer. While the bartender was getting them their beers, Bill leaned in and lit a cigarette. "Nugget's sitting near the stage. He saw me when we came in. I suspect when she's done dancing, he'll join us. When he gets here, let me do the talking, OK?"

Tom nodded and lifted the beer to his lips. He took a couple of swigs as he did his best to fit in with the crowd.

As the music continued to pound, a dry ice machine puffed some smoke onto the stage and a strobe light flashed. The girl dancing on the stage was doing her best to shake her moneymaker. As she neared the chairs at the edge of the stage, the patrons started pulling out singles and five-dollar bills.

Right on cue, when the music ended, the next girl began her routine. The biker, who Bill called Nugget, did indeed stand up and approach them. He stood next to Bill and ordered a bucket of beer as he pointed to a free table and chairs. The bartender nodded.

"Follow me," Nugget said as he walked away to the table.

Bill and Tom followed and took a seat opposite him. A topless woman then brought them a bucket with six beers in it, half-filled with ice. "You guys need anything else?" she asked.

"Nah, we're good for now. Make sure you put this on my friend's tab, not mine," Nugget said as he winked at the nearly naked twentysomething.

"Sure thing, Nugget," replied the waitress.

Tom watched her as she walked back to the bar, noting she must be on a college sports team to have toned and defined legs and rear end like that.

"She's nice, ain't she?" Nugget said to Tom as he saw him eyeing her.

Tom tried to play the part he'd been given. "I'd be lying if I said otherwise. I'm Tom, by the way."

Nugget lit another cigarette. "Nice to meet you, Tom."

After some cordial small talk and another beer, Bill got down to business.

"Nugget, is there a supply problem with dynamite I don't know about?"

Nugget chuckled. "There's always a supply problem with dynamite. You boys are always stealing it."

"OK, let me rephrase the question. Is there a reason why someone would be restocking or ordering more than usual?" Bill pressed.

Nugget lifted an eyebrow. "Why all the questions about supply? You know something I don't?"

"We've intercepted more than fourteen hundred kilos of dynamite in the last six weeks. Either someone new is setting up shop or something else is going on," Bill explained softly.

The music continued to thump and boom, providing good cover for their conversation.

The man called Nugget didn't say anything right away. He opened his mouth, then stopped. "I need some fresh air. Follow me out back in a couple of minutes."

Nugget got up and walked toward the back room.

Bill traded a sideways glance with Tom. "I'll follow him, you go out the front and meet me in the back. Stay alert."

Tom nodded and went out the front door that they had come in an hour earlier. A few minutes later, they were all standing along the wall of the building as Nugget lit up another cigarette.

"OK, what's going on, Nugget?" Bill demanded now that they were alone.

"Look, man, I don't know what's going on or who's placing all the orders. All I know is there's basically an endless supply of dope coming in from China right now. They're practically giving the stuff away. All you have to do is tell 'em how much you want, and they arrange it."

"Whoa, what do you mean 'how much you want'?" Bill asked.

"Like I said, they're giving the stuff away. They aren't charging the middlemen anything. You tell 'em you want fifty kilos, they send you a text saying when and where to pick it up. I don't know who's doing it or what they're doing, but they're crashing the market. In a few weeks, dynamite will be cheaper than water."

The three of them talked for a few minutes longer before Nugget said he had to bounce.

Tom and Bill got in their car and headed back to the office.

"It's important to write up your contact report from your meet as soon as possible," said Bill. "Then the information is still fresh in your head. Look it over the next day and add anything you might have forgotten the night before." He spent a few more minutes drilling into Tom the importance of the reports and getting them right.

"I might be retiring soon, but that doesn't mean I want all my sources I've spent fifteen years recruiting going to waste once I'm gone," he concluded.

Neither of them understood why the suppliers would be pushing this much product into the country during the middle of a pandemic. Even odder was the price. Who would want to intentionally tank the heroin market? Why would someone be giving away the product? None of it made any sense.

****

National Security Council
Pentagon
Arlington, Virginia

Katrina Roets, Kat to her friends, wasn't sure what to make of the report that had landed on her desk. It was about some unusual stock trading activity over the last few weeks.

We're in the midst of a pandemic—of course there's a lot of crazy trading going on, she thought. *What makes this so special? Why is this being flagged for my review?*

"Morning, Kat. Ah, I see you're looking at that financial report I flagged for you last Friday," Richard said as he walked over to the chair in front of her desk, coffee in hand.

Richard Drake was the senior advisor on the Council of Economic Advisors. He had a team of four analysts that supported the Treasury Department and a few other economic advisors to the President. His team did most of the grunt work for the big boys advising POTUS. They were also incredibly overworked and understaffed.

Katrina reached for her own coffee cup. "Sorry, Rich, last week was a bear. I'm only now looking at the report. What exactly am I looking for and why does it matter? Just the cliff notes if you can. I've got a ten o'clock meeting about Iran."

Rich didn't seem fazed. "I gotcha, Kat. OK, so here's what's going on. Over the last couple of months, we spotted some odd trading activity taking place. It started in the bond market. Then it moved into some of the larger pension funds and a few ETFs. The reason I flagged them for review by your office is because of the dollar amounts. Something's off and our group doesn't have the manpower or the classified reach-back to look into it any further than we already have."

Katrina scanned the paper quickly, noting some of the transaction amounts. She raised an eyebrow at a few of them. "That's a lot of money. What do you think is going on?"

"Well, that's what we're concerned about. The positions within these pension funds, ETFs, and bonds are being steadily liquidated and then moved to some offshore accounts. We've tracked the initial transfers to Bermuda, the Caymans, and London, but from there, we have no idea where it's going. I was hoping you might be able to task someone from the NSA's threat finance cell to see if they can further trace it," Rich explained.

Huh, this is interesting...

Katrina flipped another page, looking at some of the assets being sold off. She lifted another eyebrow when she saw the highlighted line denoting Treasury notes. "Rich, I'm looking at this line item here," she said as she turned the paper and showed him. "If I'm reading this right, it's saying TL Bank out of Hong Kong just liquidated one hundred billion dollars in Treasury notes over the last month. Is that normal?"

Rich sat forward in his chair as he looked at the paper. "That's also part of the problem we're trying to understand. Look at the date, it'll say this took place three weeks ago. When we pulled the bank's records, we saw the bank was buying Treasury notes from another bank in China. Each time they reached one hundred billion in notes, they dumped them for whatever price they could get. Then they bought another one hundred billion from a different Chinese bank and repeated the process. We thought this was odd behavior, so we pulled all their records going back five years.

"For the last eighteen months, they've been buying and then dumping roughly one hundred billion in Treasury notes every month. We're not sure if this is isolated to this specific financial institution or a broader problem. As you know, we have a small threat finance cell at the Treasury, but we don't have the same tool sets or deep bench the NSA has. If you could task them with helping us investigate this, it'd really help us connect some dots. I mean, maybe nothing nefarious is going on, but I think it's worth verifying."

Katrina thought about this for a moment. She knew his team had done about all they could. He was right, it was time to rope in some deeper-level intelligence reach-back. The NSA's threat finance cell had a knack for unmasking shell companies and following the money.

"OK, Rich. I agree. Send me a formal request with all the data your team collected and I'll approve it being tasked to the NSA," Kat said.

The two of them then got up and left her office: Rich to work on getting the formal request submitted, and Kat on her way to a meeting on what to do with a belligerent Iran once again threatening to close the Straits of Hormuz.

Chapter Nineteen
Chess, Not Checkers

White House
NSA Office

Blain Wilson glanced at the report on his desk, and then the couch in his office. He realized he should probably call his wife and tell her he wouldn't be coming home tonight. It was almost dark and he really needed to get caught up on the latest intelligence summary the DNI had sent over and compare it against some of the reports he'd received from the JTF down in Florida. Between those reports and the latest findings from the CDC, something felt off.

Then there was this horrific shoot-out at some unknown naval research facility in Idaho. Not to mention all the undercover intelligence operatives starting to turn up dead or having accidents—something was definitely up.

Once he finished calling his wife, Wilson placed a call down to the kitchen. He ordered a turkey club sandwich along with a fresh pot of coffee to be brought up to his office. It was going to be a long night.

As he waited for his dinner to arrive, Wilson looked at the latest summary from the COVID task force. When the pandemic had appeared in China and then hit Australia, Europe, and America, no one had been sure of what to expect. After the last COVID virus four years ago, the government and average citizen were a hell of a lot more prepared to deal with it. Still, this second Chinese virus was once again crushing the global economy and killing a lot of people.

Damn…the death toll has surpassed three million…unemployment continues to hover around seventeen percent…

Clicking on the email from the DNI's office with the daily intel summary, Wilson perused the titles:

(U) Sell-off in US Treasury notes continues.

(U) Russia experiences massive uptick in COVID cases, particularly in the regions bordering China and Mongolia.

(U) COVID infection rates soar among the homeless and active drug users, spreading the virus throughout the inner cities and suburbs.

(U) Heroin of Chinese origin that has been flooding the market is suspected to have been laced with COVID.

(U) COVID deaths in the US surpass two hundred thousand; number of infected continues to climb as testing ramps up.

(TS) COVID appears to be a lab-created virus. Genetic markers to increase its contagiousness have been manipulated. Virus also appears to be less deadly than originally thought.

(TS/SCI/NOFORN) Chinese flu vaccine smuggled out of Cuba appears to be a COVID vaccine. It appears Chinese Belt and Road Initiative members are not experiencing a COVID outbreak. The CDC and the US Army Medical Research Institute of Infectious Diseases (USAMRIID) are currently reverse engineering the COVID vaccine so it can be moved into mass production.

(U) US Coast Guard seized three hundred kilos of heroin and fentanyl in the Caribbean and the Straits of Florida.

(S) CDC discovered trace elements of COVID in the heroin and fentanyl seized by the Coast Guard. Analysis of the narcotics confirm they originated from China.

(TS) Additional Chinese Army units continue to arrive in Cuba and Venezuela as part of a new joint military training exercise.

This headline about the COVID vaccine and the last headline caught Wilson's attention. He clicked on them to read the body of the reports.

The more Wilson read, the more he realized this would become a serious problem that needed to be addressed now, and not after the election. They now had the proof the Chinese had not only created the virus in a lab but had distributed a vaccine to it prior to its release. If this didn't constitute malicious intent on the part of the Chinese, Wilson wasn't sure what would.

I'll need to brief the boss on this in the morning, Wilson thought. They needed to figure out how they were going to handle this and why the Chinese weaponized this new COVID virus. More than three million people had died worldwide as a direct result of China's actions. *That can't stand.*

****

**The Following Morning
Situation Room – White House**

"Mr. President," Wilson began, "what I'm about to tell you may come as a surprise, but I'm confident that it's true." The others in the room leaned forward in their chairs, listening intently.

"Nine months ago, we briefed you on the existence of a new advanced quantum supercomputer in China, code-named Jade Dragon. We believe Jade Dragon is being used to power another program called Project Ten, the world's first semiautonomous AI supercomputer. It is my opinion, and the opinion of my staff, that the US, Europe and even Russia were attacked by this AI supercomputer across multiple domains in an ongoing attack—"

Peter Morris, the Secretary of Defense, interrupted, "Mr. Wilson, are you referring to that CDC report about the COVID virus being genetically engineered in a lab, or the fact that China appears to have created it and then provided their allies with a vaccine for it prior to the outbreak?"

This comment elicited some irritated chatter from the others at the table before the President raised his hand to hush them.

"That's a bold claim to make, Blain. Why don't you walk the dog on that accusation a bit and explain what you mean?" the President asked as he eyed him suspiciously.

"Yes, Mr. President," Wilson said as he surveyed the room. "I will outline a series of events that have taken place over the last eighteen months that have led us to where we are now. I believe everything that's happened up to this point has been a concerted effort on their part to take down the West—and, yes, I'm including Russia in this as well."

This last part of Wilson's statement caught a few people by surprise, including Vice President Victoria Jackson, who was sitting in on this meeting. Not many people had been paying attention to Russia recently. Too much had been going on in the rest of the world and at home.

"Eighteen months ago, the Bank of China among other Chinese financial institutions slowed their purchase of US Treasury notes to fifty billion dollars a month. At the same time, they were unloading one hundred billion dollars a month in Treasury securities to a TL Bank in Hong Kong. That bank then sold the Treasury notes at a discounted rate to other financial institutions and investment managers around the world. This hasn't been isolated to US debt—they've been doing the same with euro bonds and British gilts. After nearly eighteen months of selling off our debt, the Chinese have virtually divested themselves from US Treasury securities."

Wilson saw he had everyone's attention now. This wasn't just an American problem, it was a Western democracy problem. "Mr. President, while the PRC has been divesting themselves of American, British and EU debt, the Chinese have gone on a massive spending spree with that money over the last four years. The PRC has provided a total of one hundred and thirty-two billion dollars in economic aid to Panama, Venezuela, Cuba, El Salvador, Nicaragua, Ecuador, the Republic of Suriname, Guyana, and Uruguay. In response, these nations joined China's Belt and Road Initiative, integrating themselves into the Chinese economy.

"In addition to the economic aid, the Chinese provided these same nations with sixty-two billion in military aid to help them modernize their armed forces. In the last three months during the COVID pandemic, Cuba, Venezuela, and El Salvador have signed a mutual defense agreement with China, positioning soldiers from an adversarial nation less than one hundred miles from our shores for the first time since the Cuban Missile Crisis."

A few people cursed softly to themselves as Wilson's words washed over them and the slides his office had prepared showed the type and number of Chinese military units being deployed to these three nations.

"I have to agree with Blain, Mr. President," Morrison said as he nodded in agreement. "The Chinese have been moving forward with a master plan that I think we're only just now starting to see materialize."

Riley Edison, the Secretary of State, shook her head. "No. I don't buy this theory of a grand scheme to take down the US and Europe, Mr. President. I think we need more proof before we can make that kind of allegation."

Riley had been the two-term governor of Minnesota when the President had won the election. Coming from an agricultural state, she'd had experience dealing with China and knew the trade issues facing the heartland of the country inside and out. The President had originally selected her to be his ambassador to China. When his first Secretary of State had suffered a heart attack and opted to step down, he'd selected her to be his replacement. She had done a great job negotiating the new trade deal with the PRC. Now it seemed likely that the Chinese were playing her to buy more time to fulfill their plot.

Wilson moved to regain control of the meeting. "Madam Secretary, Mr. President, if I can explain, there's a lot more to unpack here. Seven days ago, the CDC received a flu vaccine vial from a diplomatic pouch out of our embassy in Havana. The vaccine had been provided to the Cuban health ministry by the Chinese sometime back in January. The country began a nationwide vaccine campaign in late January that ran into the middle of February. Please note the month—this was at the *tail end* of the flu season. When the CDC performed a further examination of the vaccine, they discovered it wasn't for the flu. It was, in fact, a vaccine against COVID."

VP Jackson tried to say something, but Wilson cut her off before he would be interrupted again. "We have been wondering why some countries have had major breakouts of COVID while the neighboring countries have not. Now we know. Some of them had been given a vaccine ahead of time by the Chinese."

Now the Vice President interjected. "So what the intelligence is telling us is the Chinese created and then weaponized this new COVID virus strain and then made sure their allies had a vaccine in place ahead of when it would be released?" she asked incredulously. "If that's the case, Blain, what's their endgame? What are the Chinese hoping to get out of this? Because once everyone learns the true extent of what they have done, they have to know the world will unite against them."

Secretary of State Edison leaned forward as she jumped in before anyone else could. "Not necessarily, Madam Vice President. Blain, maybe you can back me up on this, but if the Chinese provided the vaccine to their allies, did those allies happen to coincide with the members of the Belt and Road Initiative?"

Wilson frowned as he thought about that. He looked down at his notes briefly. When he looked up, he only nodded in reply.

Edison blew some air out her mouth indignantly. "They've played me like a fiddle this entire time. If the Chinese divested themselves of our debt and then liquidated their other financial positions in America and Europe, then they'll be sitting on a mountain of cash. For all we know, they're waiting for the rest of the global economy to finish being flushed down the toilet and then they'll glide in and take control of entire industries. I'll bet they're waiting until the entire world is on its knees over this virus and then they'll swoop in like the saviors of humanity with a vaccine they'll provide if we only grovel on our knees and ask for it," she said with venom dripping from her mouth. She was clearly irate at having been played by the PRC all these years.

"This will throw the world into chaos," commented the President's Chief of Staff.

Peter Morris, the Secretary of Defense, raised his hands to stop the crosstalk. "I think this is about Project Ten—the Chinese master plan to dominate the world politically, economically, and militarily. I'm not sure if any of you have heard of a book called *Unrestricted Warfare: China's Master Plan to Destroy America*. It came out in 1999 and was coauthored by Major General Qiao Liang and Wang Xiangsui.

"It outlines everything Project Ten is about. When you examine what's been happening the last ten years and then more closely over the last twelve months, you can see it all makes sense. The patterns to everything come into focus. This book, like Hitler's *Mein Kampf*, is the blueprint they've been following for twenty-plus years. With our economy in the toilet, our election months away, and our people living in fear of contracting this virus, we're helpless to stop them. Which is exactly the position they've been jockeying to get us into."

Sheila Jones, the Secretary of Homeland Security, added, "This all makes sense now with the drugs—why the CDC was finding all this heroin and fentanyl originating from China laced with COVID. They wanted to spread the virus across as many facets and demographics of our country and Europe as possible. With a vaccine already in place, the Chinese knew in advance that society wouldn't get wiped out by it, only China's enemies. Un-freaking-believable if you ask me."

"Damn Chinese," muttered the President. "Can the CDC synthesize a vaccine for us based on the vial we obtained from Havana?"

"They're working on it as we speak. They started the first phase of trying to replicate it. We should know in a couple of days if it's possible and approximately how long it'll take to mass-produce it. In the meantime, Mr. President, we need to figure out what to do about China," Jones explained.

"What's the status on that shooting out in Idaho?" President Alton asked. "That was an ugly incident."

"The FBI is still tracking the shooters down," Secretary Jones explained. "Nearest we can tell, this was an organized hit by the Chinese on a recent defector, a man by the name of Ma 'Daniel' Yong. He had defected through MI-6 and was later transferred to the CIA. Ma had apparently been the lead architect in building this PLA supercomputer AI thing, Jade Dragon. The Agency was working with him to gain entry into the program when they believed they had been discovered. That's when they made the move to evacuate to an alternative safe house. It was during that transition they were ambushed."

"Do we know if it was Chinese military or intelligence that did the hit?" asked the President's Chief of Staff.

"We're not one hundred percent sure yet. Homeland is coordinating everything with the FBI, but they're lead on the case. Right now, we're assuming the Chinese have an unknown number of operatives here. We've made finding them our top priority," Jones explained.

"I think we have a bigger issue to deal with," the SecDef insisted. "Like what are we going to do with the nearly one hundred thousand Chinese workers in Cuba, El Salvador, and Venezuela? Not to mention the seventy thousand plus soldiers already in these countries. We can't allow them to continue sending more military units to the Caribbean. This a direct violation of the Monroe Doctrine, and it places a large foreign army dangerously close to our own shores. We need to stop them *now* and tell them to withdraw these forces from our hemisphere."

"We could issue a red line," Secretary of State Edison countered. "If they don't begin to withdraw these forces, then we'll impose sanctions on them. We could go after them with technology components, things they can only purchase from us."

"And what do we do if they shrug off the sanctions?" asked Wilson, crossing his arms. "Then what?"

"We impose a blockade," Edison replied. "We prevent them from sending more forces to our hemisphere, and we blockade the countries they're in. This would force them to back down."

Morrison countered, "If we impose a blockade, we better be willing to enforce that with military force if it comes down to it. You can bet the Chinese will test our resolve. They view us as weak, especially right now. I would not put it past the Chinese to run right up to the blockade and then push on through it with their navy."

President Alton grunted angrily. "Two hundred thousand plus Americans are dead because of a second Chinese virus in barely four years. More than forty-three million have lost their jobs as a result of the pandemic shutdowns this time around. I'd say the Chinese have already fired the first shots in this Cold War. Heck, I'd say they've already won the first few battles. No, if the Chinese want to test our resolve, then let's make sure we have the necessary military assets waiting for them."

Alton turned to look at his Secretaries of Defense and State. "Riley, please schedule an emergency meeting of the permanent Security Council members. Brief the others ahead of time and then confront the Chinese with the facts and data we have. Pete, meet with our counterparts at NATO. Do the same as Edison and let's work on getting our NATO allies on board with whatever may come next. Remind them it's the joint task force they're all a part of that's uncovered this. It needs to be a joint response."

Chapter Twenty
Escalation

Following Day
Joint Task Force Nine
Doral, Florida

Nigel Younger bit his lower lip, deep in thought about what he'd just heard from the American National Security Advisor, a bloke named Blain Wilson.

This conspiracy was under our noses this entire time, he realized. He couldn't believe Hank Iverson had been right about this all along. *I only wish he had lived long enough for us to tell him…*

Nigel listened to the others ask their questions, waiting silently for his turn.

Finally, General Bridges motioned with his hand in Nigel's direction. "Mr. Wilson, this is Nigel Younger. He's from the British SIS. His agency has been instrumental in providing us the information about Jade Dragon and Project Ten."

The man smiled warmly at him. "Mr. Younger, it's truly a pleasure to finally meet you," Wilson said. "I've read nearly every report you provided us about Project Ten, Jade Dragon and DragonLink. It's an incredible program the Chinese built and your organization managed to uncover."

Nigel smiled curtly and nodded. "I wish we could provide more. Sadly, as you know, our defector was killed in your custody last week."

"I know. We lost Jessica Parker in that attack as well," Mr. Wilson replied sullenly. "We're still trying to figure out how the Chinese knew where Ma Yong was being held. I'm sure you know a slew of undercover operatives have been turning up dead all over the world. Our assumption is this AI must have found a way to uncover who they are or someone is tipping them off. In either case, it's an enormous security breach and it's costing us lives."

"I wish I could help you out with that one," Nigel replied. "I've had a few friends have mysterious accidents as well. General Bridges has been kind enough to allow me to stay with him at his residence with beefed-up security for the time being. Right now, I have to assume I'm also a target. It's all a bit unnerving if you ask me."

"Do you think it's possible the Chinese realized Ma Yong's death was staged?" Mr. Wilson inquired. "I mean, that would explain why they put resources into trying to locate him."

Nigel nodded slowly. "That's our working theory, or at least my working theory. Before Ma was gunned down, he began telling us about a program Jade Dragon was managing called Project Jedi. We don't have all the details, unfortunately, but we believe it is linked to all these intelligence operatives being killed off around the world.

Mr. Wilson nodded somberly. "We need to figure out what this Project Jedi is, then," he sighed. "We also need to further flesh out this Project Ten. Right now, we believe it has something to do with the activities going on in the Caribbean, but we're not one hundred percent sure. Personally, I believe it has something to do with China's overall strategy to become the dominant economic, military, and financial power in the world, but I could be wrong."

"I think you're probably on the right track, Mr. Wilson. We just need to keep digging," Nigel concluded before Wilson had to leave to speak with some others at the command.

****

As the National Security Advisor left the room, Major General Gary Bridges cleared his throat to get everyone's attention. "Take your seats, everyone. We have more new information to talk about."

The task force members all filed back to their seats.

After everyone sat down, General Bridges began, "First, thank you, everyone, for the long hours and hard work you've put into this effort. Over the last nine months, we've put together a comprehensive overview of what the Chinese have been doing in the Caribbean and around the globe. It's clear now that the pandemic was engineered by the Chinese to further their global plans by weakening the West—hell, weakening the rest of the world so no one could stand up to them."

Bridges continued, "Today, the Secretary of State is meeting with the UN Security Council to present the facts about the Chinese activities and give the Chinese an ultimatum to withdraw their military forces from the region. Tomorrow, the Secretary of Defense will present the information to the NATO leadership to bring them on board. In three days, the President, along with his national security team, will present the evidence that's been collected up to this point about the pandemic, and the underlying goals of their Belt and Road Initiative."

"A lot of tough information will be made public in the coming days," General Bridges counseled. "It's going to cause quite the stir and it's likely to rile people up. There will also be some good news presented to help soften the blow and give everyone hope that not all is lost. At the end of President Alton's address, the Director of the CDC will announce that a vaccine has been found and is being mass-produced for the world. The Director will also disclose how we obtained the vaccine, and how the Chinese produced and distributed it prior to the release of the virus. It is important for people to know how this virus started and why certain countries have been affected by it while other nations have not."

General Bridges put his hands on his hips. "Per the President's guidelines, the US will be issuing a red line to the Chinese. Once it's issued, they will have two weeks to begin withdrawing their military units from El Salvador, Cuba, and Venezuela. If they don't, then the US will begin a series of sanctions aimed at crippling their economy until they do. If the Chinese still won't withdraw from Latin America and the Caribbean, then the US may institute a blockade in the Pacific to prevent them from sending more soldiers and supplies to these nations."

A French colonel interjected to add, "Your president is aware such actions may lead to a conflict, maybe even to a war?"

General Bridges nodded. "He was made aware of that, yes. He's also emphasized that three million Americans have died from a virus the Chinese knowingly unleashed on the world. I believe six hundred and thirty-eight thousand French citizens died also."

The French military officer nodded slowly. "Yes, and I fear that number will increase before the vaccine can be widely distributed. I think many people in my country agree with you—something needs to be done about what they did. Worldwide, the death toll has now surpassed thirty-two million people. It's devastating parts of Africa and India."

Several of the foreign representatives nodded in agreement. The pandemic was ravaging their countries and destroying their economies. It was becoming abundantly clear that the Chinese had engineered the virus to do exactly what it was doing—weaken the world powers, bringing them to their knees and preventing them from standing up to China.

General Bridges concluded their meeting by saying, "What I would like you all to start figuring out now is what kind of naval and air support your nations may be able to provide should we be asked to implement a blockade. Our task force will start supporting some taskings from US Northern Command in addition to Southern Command. This is the first time since the Cuban Missile Crisis that the US has had so many adversarial forces positioned this close to our homeland."
****

Special Operations Command – South

When Major General Bridges finished his meeting with the task force, he went over to his own command, SOCSOUTH. He needed to get things rolling on their front as well. If things turned hot with the Chinese in Cuba, then his command would be the one leading the charge into the country.

Walking into the operations room of his group's building, Bridges spotted the soldier he needed. "Captain Pruitt, follow me back to my office, I need to go over some information with you."

Captain Paul Pruitt was a twenty-four-year veteran of the Navy SEALs. He'd spent a few years with DEVGRU and JSOC. Bridges had been told to take Pruitt under his wing when he'd been assigned to be his deputy commander. They were grooming Pruitt to be a senior admiral in the SEALs.

The Navy SEAL lifted an eyebrow at the cryptic message but dutifully followed him to his office.

When the two of them sat down, Bridges got down to brass tacks. "Paul, things are about to go sideways in our AOR. We need to be ready to deal with it. How are we looking for operational teams should we need to rapidly scale up operations?"

"We can meet the need, but I think we should start preparing now," Pruitt responded. "I recommend we cancel all future training courses for the rest of 7th and 20th Group so we can draw on them rapidly. I also recommend we do the same with SEAL Teams Two, Four, and Eight. If things calm down in, say, four to six months, then we can restart their training cycles again."

Bridges thought about that for a moment. "I don't think we can get their training cycles paused, but we can request they redirect them.

They've all been through jungle warfare training before, but let's cycle them back through the schoolhouse at Schofield Barracks for a refresher. Also, have them work on jungle infiltration, either from the sea or the sky. We may be tasked with inserting some teams on the ground in Cuba or Venezuela. We need our soldiers to be ready for that."

Bridges suddenly had an idea. "Oh, if I'm not mistaken, you SEALs train on how to take down an oil platform, right?"

Paul nodded. "It's one of the scenarios we train on. Especially if the team will be rotating to the Middle East."

"Propose some additional training on that as well," General Bridges ordered. "The Cubans now have a lot of Chinese-operated platforms in the Straits of Florida. If there's going to be a conflict between our two nations, we'll need to secure those platforms ASAP. The last thing we need them to do is sabotage the rigs and create an ecological nightmare in the Gulf."

Chapter Twenty-One
Pawn for a Bishop

September 2024
UN Security Council
New York, New York

Foreign Minister Han Jinping clapped his hands several times, the noise of it echoing within the chamber. "That was quite the performance, Madam Secretary. It was also false—more lies from a declining superpower that is unable to even take care of its own people a second time during a pandemic."

Secretary of State Riley Edison stared down the Chinese Foreign Minister as she replied, "You mean a pandemic once again spawned and unleashed on the world by *your* country," she shot back.

The two stared daggers at each other for a moment before Secretary Edison added, "For the last three years, I have been working with you to bring our nations closer together through trade and doing my best to ease the simmering tensions beneath the surface. Now I find out it has all been a ruse on your end to buy time—time for you to poison the world and collapse the global economy."

"How dare you speak to me like that!" Minister Han shot back.

Riley shrugged his retort off as she stuck her chin out, adding, "I would like to point out two key provisions of the Monroe Doctrine our nation has and will continue to enforce. Provision number three, the Western Hemisphere is closed to future colonization. This includes economic colonization, something your nation has been pursuing as you enslave and ensnare these nations in crippling debt and proxy ownerships of their ports, rail lines, and airports."

She leaned forward, picking up steam. "Provision number four, any attempt by a foreign power to oppress or control any nation in the Western Hemisphere would be viewed as a hostile act against the United States. Your arming of the military forces in this region and your positioning of tens of thousands of Chinese soldiers in these countries is a clear and present danger to the United States and our allied nations. This secret arms buildup will be tolerated no more, Minister Han. We have discovered what you are doing and now we are calling your bluff.

You have fourteen days to begin withdrawing your military forces from Latin America or these new sweeping sanctions will go into effect."

Minister Han chuckled quietly at her accusations, which only made her angrier. "We will veto any resolution you put forward in the UN to sanction China," he asserted, practically hissing. "Our forces are in these nations at the request of their leaders. America cannot dictate to them, or us, where our military can train or who they can train with."

The British Foreign Secretary, Dudley Phipps, proclaimed, "Minister Han, our government has independently verified what Secretary Riley shared and presented. Our French and German colleagues have also verified the data. The COVID virus that originated in China was created in a lab and it was genetically modified to be even more contagious and specifically target certain segments of the world population. Worse, your nation developed a vaccine prior to its release and made sure your allies had it before you unleashed it on the world. This means you knowingly did this with the intent of killing tens of millions of people. What China has done, Foreign Minister, is not only tantamount to war, it's a war crime and a crime against humanity."

"Not *tantamount* to war," growled Igor Primakov, the Russian Minister of Foreign Affairs. "This was the first strike against the world by China."

Minister Han turned in his chair to face his Russian counterpart. "Not you too, Igor? After all the Americans and the West have done to Russia, you are now siding with them?"

"This virus has ravaged my nation. Oddly, it appears to be focused in our eastern provinces, which just so happens to border China. But none of our Chinese guest workers appear to be sick with the virus, only Russians. Now we know why. China is trying to wipe our population out so you can move in and take our territory," the older Russian accused. When he finished speaking, he pulled his face mask back up across his nose and mouth. At seventy-one, he was clearly in the demographic most at risk of the virus.

"Enough!" barked Minister Han as he stood up, pushing his chair back forcefully as he towered over them. Placing his hands on the table in front of him, he glared at the permanent members of the UN Security Council. "It's your word against ours and the World Health Organization, which has sided with us. As a matter of fact, our virologists are coming to the conclusion that this virus was most likely created at the Soviet facility Aralsk-7 in the 1980s. Our experts believe it is the *Russians* who built this bioweapon, unleashing it in China to destabilize our country and ruin our economy and then blame it on China in an attempt to turn the world against us."

Igor didn't respond right away. Then he laughed. Not a chuckle or a soft laugh, but a deep belly laugh that echoed in the confines of the room. When he finally regained control of himself, he looked at Minister Han. "We know what you are up to, Han. Russia stands with the rest of the Security Council in condemning you for this wanton act of aggression. If we created the COVID virus like you said, then how come you not only had a vaccine for it, you had already distributed that vaccine to your allies?

"No, Han, your country weaponizing this virus and unleashing it on the world as you did is a war crime according to the Geneva Convention of 1929. If China wants to avoid a conflict with Russia, then you will pay for the damages you have inflicted on our nation. Until then, we will terminate all cross-border trade between our two nations and deport all your guest workers."

Now it was Minister Han whose countenance changed. The veins on his forehead became visible—he was incensed. Instead of responding, Han turned on his heel and stormed out of the private meeting room with his entourage in tow.

Once Minister Han left, Edison announced to the remaining permanent members of the council, "It is important that we all stay unified against China going forward. You can bet they will use their considerable resources to rally as much of the world as they can to their side."

"After what we heard him say to Igor, I think it's safe to say we know how they will frame this narrative," said Dudley Phipps. "I think it's more important than ever that we get the facts and evidence out there as quickly as we can. The Chinese are, if nothing else, masters of manipulating information."
****

Four Hours Later
National Security Advisor's Office
White House
Washington, D.C.

"Hey, boss. I think you better turn on the TV. The Chinese president is making a big announcement at the People's Hall in Beijing," Mike said urgently as he poked his head into Wilson's office.

"Thanks, Mike" was all Wilson muttered as he searched for the remote on his desk. Finding it, he turned the TV on to one of the news networks.

The broadcast showed an image of President Yao Jintao giving a speech in what was the equivalent of the White House's East Room. The Chinese president had a translator standing next to him as he spoke to his state-run media.

"The last six months have been a trying time for China and the rest of the world. The SARS-CoV-3 virus, also known as COVID-24, has ravaged China and much of the world. I regret to inform our nation and the world that this virus appears to have been maliciously used against the peace-loving people of China by the West.

"For the last three decades, we have experienced an economic miracle as hundreds of millions of our people have been brought out of poverty through our economic revolution. Right now, China is on the cusp of leading the world into the fourth industrial revolution, which is taking place in the fields of quantum computing and artificial intelligence. Sadly, there are nations who do not want to see China become a world power or leader of humanity. These nations, who frame themselves as the bulwarks of democracy, the champions of liberty, will stop at nothing to remain in power and subjugate the Chinese people to serve them.

"In the last several days, our intelligence service obtained confirmation that this COVID virus was, in fact, genetically engineered in a lab and then weaponized to be used against China. The virus was originally developed by the Soviet Union during the 1980s. It was locked away and never used until now.

"Three years ago, during the Sino-Russian border clash near the Russian city of Blagoveshchensk and the Chinese city of Heihe, the Russian president realized there are now three Chinese citizens for every Russian citizen living in the Russian Far East. Fearing assimilation of their provinces, the Russians set into motion the release of the COVID virus in China with the intent of killing hundreds of millions of our people.

"The Russians, however, could not accomplish this on their own. They enlisted the help of the Americans. While Foreign Minister Han has been working with the American Secretary of State to negotiate a fair and equitable trade deal between our nations, the Americans were secretly spreading this Russian-made virus throughout our country. The virus first spread in the city of Chengdu. From there, it spread to the rest of the country.

"While this nefarious plan by the Russians and Americans was being concocted, Minister Han fostered an economic and military relationship in the Caribbean between the people of El Salvador, Cuba and Venezuela. It was this close relationship with these three nations that led to us finding a quick cure to this virus and allowed us to begin manufacturing a lifesaving vaccine."

The Chinese president paused for a moment as he motioned for someone off camera to bring something forward. In a somber expression, he continued.

"At first, I did not want to believe that America or Russia would do something so terrible. But over the last several weeks, I have been shown a series of intelligence reports ranging from videos to intercepted communications and other pieces of classified information that has confirmed what I have told you. One piece of intelligence that ultimately convinced me was a secret recording of a conversation between the president of Russia and the US president during the Davos World Economic Forum, just six weeks before the outbreak of the COVID virus.

"As a world leader, I believe it is incumbent on me to be forthright and transparent with my countrymen and the world. As such, the raw intelligence we have obtained and collected will be posted online for all to see so that you can come to your own conclusions. Right now, I would like to play for you the conversation that was captured at Davos, which I believe is the most damning evidence of all. But please, do not take my word on this—watch the videos we'll be posting, read the transcripts of intercepted phone calls and the emails. Then you can draw your own conclusions about what the Russians and Americans plotted. I encourage the citizens of these nations and the world to demand the elected leaders of these nations be removed from power. They are a danger to us all, and to world peace. What they have unleashed on our planet should be considered a war crime if there ever was one."

While the Chinese president was finishing his speech, a stand with a flat-screen TV had been moved into position next to him. Once Yao concluded, the TV came to life.

The image was partially obscured by security agents as they sought to give the presidents of Russia and America a bit of privacy to talk. It was clear from the background around the two world leaders that the video had been taken at Davos this past January.

Hey, I remember that meeting, thought Wilson. He had been in attendance. *Why am I not visible? What about my Russian counterpart?* he wondered frantically. They had both sat there, taking notes as their bosses were talking. *Something isn't right about this video*, Wilson thought. *We need to pull our own records. We can use them to refute this...*

The more Wilson looked at the video, the more he realized it really did look like the two presidents having a private conversation. Then the audio of the two men became clearer and louder than the background conversations. However, it was obvious to Wilson as someone who had been there that what was being said was not an accurate depiction of that day's events.

It wasn't possible to hear everything the two world leaders were saying, but it was clear they were talking about China and how they were overtaking the West. The Russian president appeared the most concerned, especially when he brought up the challenges they were encountering with the Chinese along their enormous border.

"The Chinese are flooding our border with immigrants in the Far East," said the Russian president. "My government now estimates there is close to a three-to-one ratio of Chinese to Russians living there. Worse, they are dumping tens of millions of rubles into the market, buying everything up in our cities. Then they only rent apartments or office space to Chinese-owned businesses or workers. They are steadily annexing our provinces away from us."

Wilson remembered that conversation clearly. The Russians had been legitimately concerned about the matter. It was one of the issues that was bringing Russia closer to the West—how to deal with an expansionist China.

The American president appeared to lean in as he whispered something. "Are you sure you want to move forward with releasing the virus? Once that genie is out of the bottle, there's no way to put it back in. If what your scientists say is true, this virus will spread across the globe very quickly."

"We will announce a vaccine for the virus six months after it's been released," the Russian president replied in an equally hushed tone. "By that time, it will have ravaged China, and we'll have accomplished our goal. Just stick to the script. This will work."

That's not what they said! The more Wilson watched the video, the more appalled he was by what he was hearing. There was no way this video could be real, regardless of how legitimate it looked and sounded. His mind immediately flashed back to several intelligence reports he had read about a technology called deepfake. The NSA, CIA, and DNI had all been warning for months that this new technology could be used to manipulate voter turnout or the results of the coming presidential election. It was scary. Looking at the video and thinking about the technology involved, Wilson felt like this was the nightmare scenario the intelligence community had warned them about.

Reaching for his phone, Wilson placed a call to his friend Patrick over at the NSA. The man picked up on the first ring. "Hey, Blain. I take it you're calling about this Chinese news conference?"

Lifting an eyebrow, Wilson wondered if they had a camera in his office. "Yeah, Patrick, how'd you know?"

Wilson heard a slight chuckle over the phone. "Easy—it's fake and it's about to cause a whole lot of trouble for us all over the world."

"Patrick, are you guys on this?" Wilson asked, his voice practically shaking. He steadied his nerves. "We'll need the NSA to come out strong with a statement on this soon, and I don't mean your spokesman. You need to have the Director come out and make a statement. We'll need all hands on deck to counter this bonfire before it turns into a raging inferno."

Wilson saw the news ticker update at the bottom of the screen on the TV as the president of China resumed his speech. *US and Russia unleashed COVID-24 on the world to take down China, according to Chinese President ...*

"Patrick, I need to make some more calls. Get on this and let me know when the Director will make a statement. I need to go talk to the President and the Press Secretary," Wilson said and then hung up the phone before Patrick had a chance to say anything further.

Standing up, Wilson grabbed his sports jacket and went over to the Oval Office. As he passed the Press Secretary's office, he motioned for her to come with him. The two of them made their way over to the office of Albert Abney, the President's Chief of Staff.

As they approached, they could see he was already having an animated conversation with several of the President's advisors about what the Chinese had unleashed.

Abney turned when he saw the two of them approaching. "Ah, there you are, Blain. We need to get the President briefed. You and I both know that conversation never happened. Hell, we were both with him the entire time he was around the Russian president. They didn't even show us in the video. Come on, we need to talk with the boss."
****

Oval Office

"There you both are," remarked President Alton gruffly. "What the hell was that?!" He pointed angrily to the TV, which showed the various networks on a split screen. Most of the talking heads were aghast at the prospect that the US and Russia would unleash COVID on the world, all to take down China.

Wilson was the first to speak. "It was a deepfake attack, Mr. President. The Chinese edited Albert and me out of the video entirely, and they manipulated the audio of the video to say what they wanted it to say."

The President didn't normally swear, but he let loose a string of obscenities at what was happening. He smacked his desk in anger, so hard that his hand stung from it. He took a deep breath and let it out, trying to control his rage. "I have to make a prime-time address to the nation," he said. "We need to let the networks know we will require some time. We have to set the record straight.

"Blain, start working on putting together the intelligence piece on this," the President ordered as he looked at his National Security Advisor. "I need handouts we can give to the press. We also need information we can post on the White House website. I want the Director of the NSA to talk about this deepfake technology and how the Chinese just used it in an attack against our nation. It's critically important that we get this information out to the public immediately. Not tomorrow, or the next day, like right now."

A flurry of activity was set into motion as the White House and the government went into overdrive to try and counter the growing narrative that the US had somehow had a hand in unleashing this horrid virus that was ravaging the world.

Chapter Twenty-Two
Blockade

Port of Mariel
Cuba

Esteban Ochoa watched in curiosity as the large roll-on, roll-off ship began the process of offloading its cargo. The ship was clearly a civilian ship, manned by deckhands and workers wearing civilian clothes, so he found it odd to see them offloading military vehicles.

Turning to Colonel Mateo Diaz, the man who was in charge of this operation, Esteban asked cautiously, "Those vehicles are massive—what are they?"

The smug colonel grunted at the question. "Not that it concerns you, but that is a WS2400 series heavy-duty missile launcher and transporter. It will make sure those Yankee bastards don't try to do something stupid to us Cubans and our new Chinese allies."

Esteban nodded in acceptance. "So long as they keep the Yankees and that damn virus they unleashed on the world away from us. That's all I care about, Colonel."

Colonel Diaz placed a hand on Esteban's shoulder as he leaned in. "I like you, Esteban. I was told you were a good Party man. I'm glad you are running the port. I've heard you've done a great job at making sure this place is safe and secure for our new allies."

Smiling, Esteban nodded.

The two of them stared at the vehicles streaming off the ship. There were a lot of those heavy-duty vehicles being offloaded.

Suddenly, Esteban became aware that in his peripheral vision, there was someone at the perimeter of the port snapping photos. He really wanted to tell Colonel Diaz next to him about that person. But he knew if he did, he'd lose his position as the port manager. Heck, he'd be lucky if they didn't kill him.

Esteban had ensnared himself in this web of deceit with a woman— he should have said no to her at that restaurant. She was just so attractive, and he was weak. Now his secret was being held over his head like the sword of Damocles, waiting to fall at a moment's notice if he didn't provide certain pieces of information from time to time. One of these days, he'd figure out how he could untangle himself from this web. Until then, he needed to keep doing what he was doing and not attract attention.

****

US Southern Command
Doral, Florida

General Kurt Stavridis looked Major General Gary Bridges in the eyes. Bridges and Stavridis had known each other for a long time. Stavridis came from a long line of military officers. His older brother was a retired admiral who had once been in command of this COCOM and then NATO nearly a decade earlier.

"Gary, it's only the two of us in my office," Stavridis began. "You've been studying the situation down in Cuba, Venezuela, and El Salvador longer than me. I need a frank no-BS assessment. How big a threat are those PLA units they've deployed there to our forces and the southern half of the United States?"

"The equipment they had before last week was a problem. The newest equipment they brought in last night will complicate things immensely," Gary replied.

"Expound on that," said Stavridis as he reached for his coffee cup.

"Ten months ago, the PLA brought in a battalion of HQ-9 Red Banner surface-to-air missile systems. They sold the Cubans two battalions' worth of the equipment. Throughout the last ten months, the Cubans took delivery of the systems and the PLA maintained their battalion in place as a training unit. That means they have at least three battalions of some of the most advanced SAMs in the world positioned on the island."

Kurt nodded. "OK, that certainly presents a challenge, but what happened last night that has you so concerned you wanted to speak with me privately?"

Gary opened up a folder and pulled out a couple of pictures. It was clear they had been taken with a night vision lens.

"These are from last night. An Agency source that's provided us with incredibly accurate and reliable information for nearly a year obtained them. This is at the Port of Mariel, forty kilometers west of Havana. As you can see, these are images of a TEL system. An 8×8 wheeled transporter erector launcher. If you look at this image here of the actual missile pod, these trucks are equipped with long sword 10s or CJ-10s. They're a land-attack cruise missile, capable of carrying a five-hundred-pound high-explosive warhead or a low-yield tactical nuclear warhead," Gary explained as he showed Kurt half a dozen images of the trucks, the missile pod from different vantage points and the trucks marshalling into a convoy as they offloaded from the ship.

Kurt only shook his head as he took in the information in disbelief. "This is like the Cuban Missile Crisis, only this time we weren't able to block the Cubans from receiving the missiles."

Gary nodded in agreement. "While these are bad, this...this is the real problem we have to worry about."

Gary pulled out a few new photos. They showed the same eight-wheeled vehicle, but instead of a CJ-10 missile pod, this one had a single missile that extended the entire length of the vehicle with DF-17 clearly stenciled on the sides.

Gary explained, "I spoke with our DIA LNO about this when it came in this morning. He said the DF-17 has a strategic range of eleven hundred to sixteen hundred miles. They can hit nearly any of our military bases or assets across the entire lower half of the country. Worse, my DIA guy pointed to this modification here, on the missile body. He said it looks like these missiles have been modified to include an HGV system. I had no idea what that was, but he told me it stands for hypersonic glide vehicle, which means these missiles can reach maneuverable speeds of between Mach 5 and Mach 10 once they're in their reentry phase. It also means they can extend the range of the DF-17 anywhere between thirty-five and fifty percent."

Gary ran his fingers through his hair in consternation. "Kurt, if they deployed this missile against a carrier, we'd be hard-pressed to intercept them. They can maneuver out of the way of our ABMs. Heck, they could lob dozens of these bad boys at Eglin Air Force Base and take out our largest fighter base in range of supporting operations over Cuba. These damn things are first-strike weapons, Kurt."

No one said anything for a moment. Finally, General Kurt Stavridis replied, "Here's the plan, Gary. Identify a company or battalion of ODAs we can use to go after these assets. I will talk with the Pentagon and make sure we have round-the-clock coverage of where they're deploying these assets in Cuba. As we locate them, inform the SOF team of that location. I'll talk with the Agency to figure out if their sources in Cuba can facilitate the insertion of Special Forces teams to specifically go after these assets when and if the order is finally given.

"In the meantime, let's get the ball rolling with establishing this blockade in the Pacific and here in the Caribbean. I want to know what assets our NATO allies are sending our way as well. Oh, and before either of us forget, begin deploying both Patriot and THAAD missile batteries around our military bases within range of these systems," General Stavridis ordered.

Gary finished writing a few notes and then headed out of his office to follow his orders. It was time to start preparing the country for a possible war with China.
****

National Security Advisor's Office
White House
Washington, D.C.

The last forty-eight hours had been a blur. Wilson hadn't been home in three days. His couch was his unofficial bed for the time being, and it was beckoning him even now.

"Boss, your wife is on the line. Should I tell her you'll call her back?" asked Mike, his assistant.

Wilson looked up, a blank look on his face. "No, I'll take it. I should have already called her."

Reaching for the phone, he heard the soothing sound of his wife's voice on the other end. Her voice sounded like serenity in what had become a swirling sea of chaos all around him. She asked if he was coming home tonight or when he thought he might be home. Wilson knew he needed to pry himself away from the job, to get a good night's sleep if nothing else. There was so much to do and not enough time to do it all.

"I don't know, darling," he said to her question.

She then told him about an incident at school between his daughter and some classmates. Apparently, his daughter had gotten in a fight. The principal had called a meeting for the following day at nine a.m. to discuss the incident.

"Honey, I can't make the meeting. There's too much going on," he said.

She was obviously upset by that response. "Blain, our daughter could end up getting kicked out of school if you don't come. You need to be there. This isn't one of those times when it's OK to phone it in."

Wilson looked at the clock on the wall. It was already eight forty-two p.m. He relented.

"I'll have a car take me home. I'll see you in thirty minutes." He turned to his aide. "Mike, can you have the car pull around and take me home? My daughter got in some trouble at school today. I'm apparently required to see the principal tomorrow to sort it out."

"Sure thing, boss. Just make sure you're back here for that eleven o'clock meeting in the Situation Room. The Chief of Naval Operations will be discussing the blockade," Mike reminded him.
****

Forty minutes later, Wilson arrived at his home in Georgetown. The place was beautiful, but it wasn't his choice or desire to live in the district. Wilson preferred to live across the Potomac in McClean or Arlington rather than Georgetown, but his wife had insisted. When she'd been offered a teaching position at the university, she'd wanted to live nearby and not have to fight the traffic. Wilson knew some hills weren't worth dying on, and this was one of them.

"There you are, stranger. I was beginning to wonder what happened to you," his wife, Cindy, said as she greeted him with a bear hug and a kiss.

"Sorry; it's been crazy at work as you can imagine," Wilson justified.

"Yeah, tell me about it. I saw you on TV a few times. You looked tired," Cindy said with concern.

Wilson gave a weak smile as he dropped his briefcase and kicked off his shoes. He made his way over to his La-Z-Boy rocker and fell into it.

"Cindy, tell me about Molly. What happened?" Wilson asked.

Sitting across from him on the sofa, Cindy said, "Apparently, a couple of girls said the President was a war criminal for releasing the virus on the world. They said you were a war criminal for working for him. Molly said a few choice words to them and then the girls got into a scuffle before it was broken up. No one *really* got hurt, aside from their feelings. The principal wants to talk with us in the morning. That's all I was told."

Grunting at the synopsis, Wilson wondered if it might not be better to pull his kids from school for the next couple of weeks or maybe the rest of the semester. Tensions were running high across the country. Some folks believed what the Chinese had put out; others were simply confused and didn't know who to believe.

"Are the kids asleep?"

Cindy nodded. "Blain, what's really going on? Are we headed to war like the talking heads are saying?"

Sitting in his chair, he contemplated how much he should tell his wife. "It looks that way. We'll know a lot more in the coming days and weeks."

Cindy moved her hand to her mouth. She was scared. She grabbed for a pillow and held it tight against her body. "Is there any way to avoid war?"

Shrugging, Wilson replied, "I don't think they want to avoid a war. It's like they've already figured out this is the most opportune time to defeat us. I hate to say it, but I think they're right."

Cindy then stood up, walked over to him and grabbed his hand. "Come with me. It's time for bed. I want to make up for some lost time. God knows when I may see you again after today."

****

Situation Room
White House

General Anita Barrett, the commander for US Northern Command and NORAD, spoke from her facility in Colorado. "What concerns me most is the discovery of the Dongfeng-17 missiles. These medium-range ballistic missiles have a range of eleven hundred to sixteen hundred miles with a two-thousand-pound warhead. They can effectively hit any military base or city all the way up to New York City, all the way out to Chicago and even my facility at Peterson Air Force Base. Before this blockade goes into effect, we need to have a plan in place to counter this weapon, should it be used against us, and have a response ready to execute should they use them."

President Alton turned to Peter Morris, his Secretary of Defense. "Pete, this is your lane. How do we best defend against these missiles should they be used against the homeland?"

Pete shifted uncomfortably in his chair for a moment before he answered, "I think we need to consider deploying our Patriot and THAAD missile systems around key strategic installations. We can develop a layered plan for how to deploy them. Should they be needed, they'll be in the right positions to intercept the enemy missiles. I recommend we also put a couple squadrons of F-15Es on strip alert down on our southern bases. If the Chinese launch these missiles, then in addition to the Patriots and THAADs, the Eagles can fly up and launch their own air-to-air missile interceptors. DARPA's made a few modifications to some of our existing inventory to handle this kind of threat."

"OK, make it happen. What else should we be doing in preparation? Anyone?" asked the President as he surveyed the room.

The Chief of Naval Operations commented, "We have a carrier strike group forming up to head down to the Caribbean. I recommend we chop some ships from that group to take up a position in the Gulf. We can place a couple of *Burkes* and a *Tico* cruiser equipped with SM-3s. If the PRC fires those ballistic missiles, then the SM-3s will be our best bet at knocking them down."

"I like it. Dispatch the orders, Admiral. Anything else?" the President asked one more time.

Wilson felt this would be a good time to say something. "Sir, if I may, I think there's something we're still not considering."

Alton turned to look at his National Security Advisor. "OK, Blain. What are we missing?"

"Sir, I think we're still trying to operate under the assumption that we can find a diplomatic solution to this problem. What I believe we're forgetting is everything that's happening is happening because Project Ten has already war-gamed it. Their super-AI has concluded that a war against America and the West can be won, but only if a series of circumstances to weaken us happen first."

Secretary of State Riley Edison pounced on that statement before Wilson could go any further. "Are you saying there's no further point to talking with the Chinese? That our negotiations are a waste of time at this point?"

Wilson countered, "I'm not saying we shouldn't continue to hope calmer heads prevail. What I'm saying is, the PLA spent a very long time developing Jade Dragon and DragonLink to give them the competitive edge they need to defeat us. I don't see the Chinese leadership stepping back from the brink if they already believe they will win. Why would they? If their super-AI is telling them to perform x, y, and z and then they'll have a ninety-two percent chance of defeating the West, why would they not move forward with their war?"

No one said anything for a moment as they contemplated what he said. Finally, Peter Morris, the Secretary of Defense, spoke. "Mr. President, I don't want to believe that Mr. Wilson might be right. As a matter of fact, I want to believe what he just said was BS. But honestly, if what we know about Jade Dragon is real, and this Project Ten super-AI is as advanced as we've been told, then I believe Mr. Wilson is spot-on. The Chinese will move forward with attacking us. If we provided you with a ninety-two percent chance of success in launching a first strike against one of our adversaries, I suspect you would move forward as well. Putting ourselves in their shoes, it's clear they won't budge on their position."

"If that's true, Pete, then when do you believe they'll attack us? How much time do you believe we have before they hit us?" asked the President, a bit of fear and concern in his voice.

"I think they'll wait until after the election. We're only eight days away," Albert Abney, the President's Chief of Staff, said aloud.

A couple of people turned to look at him in surprise. Vice President Vickie Jackson looked like she was ready to punch someone—this could cost her the chance to become president.

Admiral Roy Thiel, the Chairman of the Joint Chiefs, cut in. "No, I don't think they care about the election. I think they'll wait until their carrier task force in the South China Sea links up with their convoy in the Philippine Sea. I read an NSA intercept this morning indicating this naval force is heading to Guam. I believe Mr. Wilson and our allied intelligence is correct about Project Ten. Their super-AI has determined when, where, and how best to attack the West to remove us as a threat to their plans. We need to position our forces for war, and now."

There was a moment of silence as no one knew what to say. They had all hoped that diplomacy could still work, that maybe this nightmare AI supercomputer wasn't real, and war could still be avoided.

It had been four days since the Chinese had unleashed their deepfake disinformation campaign on the world. Their outright manipulation of the facts about the pandemic, the dumping of US Treasury notes, the liquidation of stocks, and then the shuttering of Chinese-owned businesses inside the US to further exacerbate the economic collapse of America and the West—it was all too much to be a coincidence, and too much for one person or think tank to be responsible for. This was the work of a complex artificial intelligence program.

President Alton then asked, "If this is your honest assessment, Admiral, then should we launch a preemptive attack? Should we shift forces around to meet the enemy head-on?"

"I think we should relocate the 2nd Bomb Wing at Barksdale and the 7th Bomb Wing at Dyess to some of our bases in the Dakotas. If the Chinese do launch a preemptive attack on us, our bombers will be out of harm's way," Admiral Thiel recommended.

"What about Guam? You said this Chinese task force appears to be heading toward the island. Do we have sufficient forces on the island to hold it, should it come under a sustained attack or invasion?" asked the President.

"There are twelve thousand service members stationed on Guam under the new unified command. There are also four *Los Angeles* fast-attack submarines stationed on the island," Admiral Thiel offered. "I issued an order to have them all put to sea to take up station around the island. There are five thousand Marines stationed on the island along with seven thousand total dependents. We don't have a lot of assets we can rapidly deploy there, but we could move another battalion of Marines from Japan to Guam while we work on evacuating the dependents."

President Alton sighed as he rubbed his temples. "Admiral, maybe you already told me this and I forgot. How long will it take for the Chinese fleet to be in range to attack Guam, if that is in fact their intended target? Also, why Guam? Why not bypass it and go for something juicier like Hawaii, or send that task force to the Caribbean?"

"The Chinese fleet is five days from Guam," the admiral explained. "If they chose to head in the direction of Hawaii, then it's somewhere around nine days away. If they head toward Panama, then thirteen days. In either case, we're less than two weeks away from the first shots being fired. As to why they might take Guam first, that's simple. Guam represents our furthermost air and naval base beyond Hawaii. If the PLA is able to take Guam from us and then fortify it, they'd have an effective shield to block us from pursuing any naval activities in the South China Sea. It'd also make it difficult to carry out military operations against them as we wouldn't have any facilities nearby to refuel or rearm."

"OK, Admiral, if we only have five days until they reach Guam, then let's go with the assumption that hostilities are going to start around then," directed the President. "Relocate the military dependents on Guam ASAP. Also reinforce the island with as many Marines as you can. See if you can manage to deploy one of the three regiments from Okinawa to Guam. Tell them to dig in and get ready to hold that island for as long as necessary. See what additional aircraft we can send, and make sure we send them as much ammo and MREs as possible. If a war really does break out, then God only knows how long they may need to hold out."

War with China wasn't how Alton wanted to end his presidency. Whoever ended up winning the election in eight days would be stuck fighting this war—a war he'd never wanted, a war he had tried desperately to keep America out of.

Chapter Twenty-Three
Snake Eaters

**October 2024
Gulf of Mexico**

Major Fan Changlong rolled his shoulders against the jump seat of the aircraft. They had been in the air for six hours as the cargo aircraft made its thirtieth flight along the American coastline.

Every night for the last month, the Chinese Air Force had flown either cargo or electronic surveillance aircraft along the Gulf Coast of the Southern US. They usually started off at the tip of Texas and then traveled along to Louisiana before swinging back out into the Gulf and heading to Cuba. On occasion they flipped the route and started it in the opposite order just to keep the Americans on their toes.

The pilots made sure to stay three miles from the twelve-nautical-mile borders of the American airspace. This didn't mean the Americans wouldn't scramble fighters to greet them; they usually did. Around Texas, it was usually a pair of F/A-18 Super Hornets that would meet them. Then a pair of F-15Es would take over as they got closer to Louisiana. The whole point of these nightly exercises was to lull the Americans into complacency. Once they found a gap in the coverage, they'd note the location so they could arrange for their special package to be delivered.

A crewman walked up to Major Fan. "Sir, the pilot says we're coming up on the first possible jump location. You have ten minutes."

He nodded at the news. *Finally…*

Fan called out to the twelve-man South Blade team he was leading, letting them know that it was time to get their gear on and prepare to jump. The Special Forces men started strapping their parachutes on, then their oxygen tanks, face masks, drop bags and weapons. Once they were suited up, the operators attached themselves to the aircraft's oxygen system and waited to see if their American fighter escort would break off, giving them a short window to make their jump before the next set of escorts showed up.

Fan looked off in the direction of the pilots. One of the crew chiefs was standing next to the flight deck, talking with the pilots. A second later, the soldier turned around to look at him. He shook his head, letting them know the Americans were still with them. That meant they'd probably stay with them for another twenty minutes until they reached the next waypoint.

Fan told his soldiers to disconnect from the plane's air supply and take a seat. They'd keep most of their equipment on, but there was no point standing around.

As the soldiers had begun disconnecting from the oxygen supply, the crew chief ran over to them. "The pilot said the Americans just pulled off. He'll depressurize the plane in a couple of minutes and lower the ramp. You will only have a few minutes to go before the next set of escorts show up."

"You heard the man! Get your masks back on and reattach to the plane's system. We'll disconnect and jump as soon as they have the ramp lowered," Fan called out to his soldiers.

The cargo lights turned from a soft blue light to a soft red light. Moments later, the seal on the back ramp of the aircraft broke open. The cool air swirled about the cargo bay as the ramp lowered. Fan signaled to his soldiers to disconnect the plane's oxygen. It was time to transition to their drop tanks and get ready to jump.

While Fan waddled over to the edge of the ramp, Master Sergeant Lei, his senior NCO, made sure everyone got out all right.

As they stood on the edge of the ramp, the jump light turned green, letting him know they were over the optimal jump zone. Without hesitation, Fan leapt into the dark void.

The air swirled around him as his body fell away from the cargo plane. He counted to five before he deployed his chute. It filled with air seconds later, jolting him as the parachute slowed his rapid free fall to a controlled descent.

Once he had his guide wires under control, the heads-up display in his helmet started tracking his altitude and pointed him in the direction he needed to go in. Fan angled his chute in the direction his HUD had indicated. He knew the eleven other members of his team would follow him.

At twenty-two thousand feet, they had a good bird's-eye view of the American coast. At this point they were only seven miles away from land, another two miles from their unofficial drop zone.

When they descended below twelve thousand feet, Fan received a short text message on his HUD. Their ride was at the appointed place, ready to pick them up. Craning his head around, Fan saw a couple of his soldiers a little further up and behind him. He wasn't sure where their equipment was, but he assumed it was automatically following somewhere behind them.

At first, Fan had wondered why they didn't just cross the American border in a vehicle or fly in from a friendly nation. Then he had seen the list of equipment they would be bringing with them and he'd known exactly why they needed to do a high-altitude, high-opening jump. A HAHO was the only way they could smuggle this kind of weaponry across the border. If they got caught, it could jeopardize the entire mission.

As they got closer to the drop zone, an empty field near a park, Fan pulled down hard on his guide wires, allowing the canopy above to fill with air. Moments later, he was on the ground, rolling his parachute up. The rest of his team landed nearby. Then came the gliders with their heavy equipment.

They collected up their gear. Moments later, a couple of figures emerged nearby, causing the South Blade team to draw down on them. They gave the appropriate call sign, and the soldiers lowered their weapons. The leader said something into the radio. A couple of engines started not too far away, then some parking lights turned on and they drove toward them.

"My name is Tran. My men and I will take you to the safe house. You can load your equipment into the back of that van," the man in all black said as he pointed to a large U-Haul cargo van.

Fan nodded and called out to his sergeants to load the special packages into the U-Haul. Five minutes later, everyone had piled into the vehicles and they were on their way to the safe house. The driver and the man named Tran didn't say much. Fan figured they knew the men they were transporting were killers. Their job was to get these men to the safe house and hand them off to the next set of handlers. Then they'd continue to stand by and wait for the next set of soldiers to pick up.

When they arrived at the safe house, Fan's men got the weapons and equipment loaded into a shed nearby. A man from the Ministry of State Security was there waiting for them.

"Major Fan, my name is Mr. Lee. That is how you will address me. I have your new set of orders. Tomorrow, you will split your team up into three four-man teams."

Fan held a hand up. "Excuse me, Mr. Lee. I was told my team would be operating as a team, not be split up."

The man named Mr. Lee only smiled. "Plans change, Major. Over the next four nights, the rest of your company will arrive. They will similarly be split up to head to their assigned targets as well. Once your primary objectives have been met, you may reorganize your teams as you see fit. But for the time being, these are your new orders."

The mystery man then handed Fan a set of papers with their orders. As he looked at them, a smile crept across Fan's face. *These are much better than our original orders…*

"There is nothing to worry about, Major Fan. You are in good hands. We have arranged for everything. Once you carry out your primary objective, you will be relocated, and you and your men will reconstitute and prepare for your follow-up missions. Now, I suggest you get some sleep. The coming days and weeks will be strenuous at best."

****

Straits of Florida
ODA 7322, Bravo Company

Sergeant First Class Rusten Currie had just jumped out of a C-17 and into history. He was a part of two ODA teams that would be the first American military forces to invade Cuba since the Cuban-American war in the early 1900s. Fortunately for the Americans, the Chinese and Cubans did not routinely send fighter escorts to greet the American aircraft skirting their territory, which had made their jump much easier.

It's only a matter of time until we land in Cuba, he thought in anticipation. It was his first time doing a HAHO in months, but every time he jumped from such a high altitude, he marveled at how alive he felt.

Every few minutes, Currie would check his compass and GPS unit to make sure he was leading his team in the right direction. Steadily, they got closer to land. At approximately 0300 hours, two members of the CIA's Special Operations Group or SOG would activate an infrared strobe light, letting them know precisely where the drop zone was. The

SOG team had infiltrated the country a couple days earlier with the help of a CIA asset already on the ground.

With no more than five minutes left in their descent, Currie saw the IR strobe light come on through his night vision goggles. He pulled on his guide wire, angling his chute to head toward it. The others stacked up slightly higher and behind him. They'd follow his lead toward the IR signal.

When he was no more than thirty feet above the ground, Currie detached his drop bag with his ruck and other equipment to dangle below him. Seconds later, he pulled hard on the guide wires of his chute to control his descent. He'd captured the air at just the right angle—his landing was practically as light as a feather. He took a couple of quick steps forward, then detached himself from his chute and went to work on rolling it into a tight ball.

Meanwhile, the eleven other operators of his ODA landed and did the same thing. Once they all had their chutes collected, along with their rucks and weapons, the SOG members guided them into the jungle. They had a place ready for the ODA to bury their spent chutes so they'd be out of sight.

One of the SOG members walked over to Sergeant First Class Currie and his captain, Larry Thorne, as they were talking. "Captain, Sergeant, I'm Howard. You're free to use this as your base camp if you'd like. We haven't gone exploring the area yet. We wanted to get you sorted first. Intel says we have at least six DF-17 launchers in the area and probably about the same number of HQ-9 radar systems."

"Howard, I'm Captain Thorne," the ODA team leader said. "We have some initial ideas about where some of these systems are located. I'd like to show you what we have and compare it to what you know."

"Sounds good. Come on, let's get you situated in the hide position. We can go over what you have with what we have and then figure out how best to break your teams down. If we can get these locations pre-positioned, it'll make calling in airstrikes a hell of a lot easier."

The coming days and weeks would involve a lot of roaming around the jungles and forested areas of Cuba as the Greenie Beanies went about the task of identifying and hunting down the enemy radar and missile launcher systems. When and if a war did start, they'd be ready to take these threats out.

Chapter Twenty-Four
Don't Mess with Texas

October 24, 2024
Pacific Ocean
USS *Texas* – SSN 775

Two days ago, the Commander of the USS *Texas*, Kurt Helgeson, had received a notification from COMSUBPAC Rear Admiral Ishan Patel that the Chinese were not only ignoring the ultimatum the US and NATO had issued, they were still sending more soldiers to the Caribbean in direct violation of the Monroe Doctrine.

Shortly after, Helgeson had received a coded message to open the captain's safe and unseal the orders marked Five-Tango-Six-Zulu-Quebec-Niner. Commander Helgeson and his XO, Lieutenant Commander Kristin Evans, had jointly opened the safe and retrieved their new set of orders.

Regardless of the years of training, it was still nerve-wracking to read a military plan to attack the Chinese Navy. Clearly, the negotiations above the water between Beijing, Washington, Moscow, and Brussels hadn't worked. Should the Chinese ships cross a certain set of coordinates, they had the operational orders to begin hostilities against the People's Republic of China.

Tensions were high. It felt like a figurative storm was steaming toward them at flank speed on the surface of an angry sea. Commander Kurt Helgeson fueled himself with extra doses of caffeine to keep his mind sharp; one of the lieutenant junior grades had made it his mission to make sure that there was always a fresh pot available. Helgeson had a habit of pushing everyone to their maximum abilities, and yet, they respected the hell out of him for it. The last commander of the USS *Texas* had been a ROAD—retired on active duty—and the crew's morale had dramatically improved after Helgeson stepped in and kicked it all back into high gear.

With a fresh cup of joe in hand, Commander Helgeson turned his attention to the crewman who was monitoring the Orca II autonomous underwater vehicles or AUVs. They were deployed in a picket formation in front of the *Texas* as they searched for the Chinese fleet. According to the latest intelligence, the enemy fleet was still heading toward them.

"STS2, keep an eye out for any ASW activity," he said to the sonar tech. "As the Chinese fleet continues to move closer to the line of control, we should start to detect their own picket ships and helicopters."

"Yes, sir," came the reply.

The integration of the unmanned submarines was a new addition to the *Texas* and soon the rest of the American submarine fleet. The AUVs could operate individually with a preprogrammed orbit around the *Texas*, extending their underwater eyes and ears by a hundred miles beyond what the towed array and the bow-mounted sonars could provide. The Orcas could also relay targeting data back to the *Texas* and assist in the prosecution of targets, both near and far.

The Navy had set up a sophisticated series of subsurface gateway buoys that used laser communications from surface combatants, satellites or aircraft to allow standard submarines to control the Orcas. They could now relay attack information to leverage their antiship missiles from much further away without fear of being detected. The most amazing aspect of these new AUVs, however, was their ability to prosecute targets on their own should they be given their own set of attack orders. During the initial combat suitability tests a few years ago, nine Orcas operated by three different fast-attack boats had successfully engaged and notionally scuttled an entire carrier battle group without even being detected.

Fifteen minutes later, an enlisted sailor from the galley came onto the Conn. He broke the tray's magnetic hold to the counter and replaced it with a new tray stacked with sandwiches cut in half. Everyone working on the Conn would be able to grab a snack or refill their coffee to help get them through the rest of the shift or until they could cycle through for the next meal.

After snagging a few bites himself, Commander Helgeson walked back over to the OC2 station, where they were monitoring and controlling the Orcas. Since their sub was named the *Texas*, Helgeson had figured they should name the Orcas after some cities within Texas. The crew had voted, and *Dallas*, *Lubbock*, and *Killeen* had won. When Commander Helgeson leaned over the Orca controlman's station, he saw the icon designating the *Killeen* blinking red, and then the *Lubbock* began blinking as well. They had found something.

"Hey, find out what those two contacts are," Helgeson directed.

The sailor manning the station sent a text to the Sonar room to inquire about it and any indication of what might be out there. Five seconds later, the sonarman responded.

"Conn, Sonar. Contact *Lubbock*, bearing two-two-eight degrees, aerial contact, dipping sonar eight thousand yards off its bow," announced the operator before he called out the second contact.

"Conn, Sonar. Contact *Killeen*, bearing three-three-zero degrees, surface contact nineteen thousand yards off her bow."

Commander Helgeson snapped the mic from its cradle and faced aft toward the Sonar room.

"Sonar, Conn. ID both those contacts for me. See if we can get a visual on that dipping sonar. I need to know if there are more ASW assets in the area."

"Conn, Sonar, stand by." Without a word from Helgeson, his XO, Lieutenant Commander Kristin Evans, headed back to Sonar to check things out for herself.

****

When Evans arrived at Sonar, she immediately saw the contacts appear on the computer screen. She adjusted her glasses a little higher on her nose so she could be sure she was seeing everything clearly.

One of these days, I'll have to get Lasik, she bemoaned to herself. But that would have to wait until after whatever was about to happen.

The first image was of a ship, with an acoustic probability rating of ninety-four percent. Then the sonar operator pointed to the other contact, the one that posed the greatest threat to them; the dipping sonar matched that of a Changhe Z-18F antisubmarine warfare helicopter. The ASW chopper also carried a surface radar, and its dipping sonar was on par with anything the US Navy used. It had hardpoints intended for torpedoes or missiles, depending on the mission, and a large complement of sonobuoys.

Evans nodded to the sonarman, letting him know she concurred with both of their probabilities.

The sonarman picked up the handset to connect him to the Conn. "Conn, Sonar. First contact is a Type 054A ASW frigate. It's the *Handan*. She's traveling in sprints, probably running ahead of the rest of the fleet, then drifting while her towed sonar array listens for enemy subs."

Continuing, the sonarman added, "Conn, second contact appears to be a Changhe Z-18F ASW helicopter based on the signature of the dipping sonar. This helicopter didn't originate from the Type 054, which means there is another destroyer, carrier, or troop transport ship in the area."
****

Back on the Conn, Commander Helgeson was taking the information in as he looked at the map display of where the enemy ship was in relation to the helicopter.

There have to be more helicopters and frigates out there, he thought.

Placing a finger down on a position on the map, Helgeson ordered, "Move the *Dallas* to this location. Have the *Killeen* rise to periscope depth and launch a Blackwing scout drone. We need to get a better picture of the area. Also, have the *Lubbock* move to this location here, further away from the rest of us. If that helicopter picks them up, I want them chasing the *Lubbock* away from us."

Just as the AUV operator started issuing the new orders, the Sonar room made another announcement. "Conn, Sonar. Contact *Killeen*, bearing three-zero-two degrees, surface contact nineteen thousand yards off her bow. Type 001 carrier. It's the *Liaoning*, sir. She's making a lot of noise traveling at flank speed."

Before Commander Helgeson could begin to formulate a response to the discovery of an enemy carrier, the sonar room called out another target. This time the pitch in the man's voice gave away his increasing stress level.

"Conn, Sonar. Second contact! Three-one-zero degrees, surface contact, eighteen thousand, eight hundred yards. Contact is Type 075 landing helicopter dock."

The sailors and officers working the Conn all shared a nervous glance. This was a big find. Not only had they stumbled into the path of a carrier, they'd also spotted the Chinese Navy's first-ever helicopter assault ship. This was their version of the American Wasps or the *American*-class ships the Marines used.

Under normal circumstances, a submarine traveling alone would need to come to periscope depth to make a visual ID of the contact; then they could designate it a Master contact for targeting purposes. The integration of the Orcas, however, had changed all of that. Since there was no crew on the Orcas, they were not only a weapons platform, they also contained more sonar, radar, and ESM capabilities. It wasn't that they were disposable in a battle, but if one was lost, it wasn't like they had lost a $3.4 billion sub with a crew of 135 sailors. The Orca's onboard systems stored the acoustic libraries of every allied and enemy ship recorded, which allowed the Orca's targeting computer to classify which enemy ships posed the greatest threat to itself or the mission and prioritize those ships to be engaged first. In seconds, they could identify and engage multiple targets with their inventory of torpedoes and underwater-launched cruise missiles.

Information was coming in fast, especially once the *Killeen* rose to periscope level and launched the Blackwing. In the first sixty seconds after the drone was airborne, they had a full picture of the enemy fleet approaching them. It was impressive. It was also more than they could possibly engage on their own and survive.

Helgeson started processing the information as it came in. Rubbing his chin, he drew in a deep breath and closed his eyes for a moment before he spoke softly to himself. "Work the problem in front of you, don't get bogged down by what isn't important."

"Sonar, Conn. Designate *Killeen* contacts Sierra 1 and 2," he ordered.

"OC2, bring *Killeen* to periscope depth again and get us a three-sixty scan. Once complete, have her lay a spread of mines across their advance, then have her drop below the thermocline and loiter."

"Aye-aye, sir," said the Orca controlman as he rapidly began sending commands to the *Killeen*.

Twenty minutes later, Commander Helgeson walked to the plotting table and began drawing lines from the approximate location of the Chinese vessels to the *Texas* and her Orcas. He motioned for the XO to come over. Evans tilted her head and raised an eyebrow inquisitively as he drew a red line on the virtual display screen.

"XO, now that the enemy has crossed the line of control, it appears the war has officially started. It's my intent to get this ship into the fight on our terms." He picked up the mic and called for the ship's Weapons, Navigation, Sonar, Engineering and OC2 officers to join him at the plot table. When everyone arrived moments later, he laid out his plan.

Looking his officers and senior enlisted sailors in the eyes, he began, "When we left port, we knew the likelihood of war was high. The other day, the XO and I received a coded message, telling us that when the Chinese warships cross the Clipperton-Galapagos Line, it meant any last-minute diplomacy had failed. The ships are now to be classified as hostile and should be prosecuted with extreme prejudice."

He sighed briefly. "This fleet is obviously on a path to the Panama Canal. There's no way our government can allow the Chinese to transit this many warships into the Caribbean. We also have no idea if those troops will be used to seize control of the Canal Zone or if they'll be used to reinforce their positions in Cuba or Venezuela. Engaging them here, now…has to happen."

The officers standing around the digital plot table nodded slowly as they realized the gravity of the situation. The importance of the mission was dawning on them, but so was the reality that they might not survive it.

Helgeson then pointed to a position on the plot. Everyone's eyes followed, and a look of surprise appeared when they saw the image appear on the digital table.

It displayed satellite imagery from above the Chinese fleet that was rapidly approaching their trap. The image had been downloaded and relayed by laser from the *Dallas* Orca that was fifteen hundred yards to their northwest at periscope depth.

This information confirmed what the USS *Maine* had reported two days earlier. The *Maine* had been on patrol below the Tropic of Cancer and picked up a screen of three Chinese submarines that were rigged for quiet and lurking about ten nautical miles ahead of a fleet of Chinese warships traveling at flank speed.

The *Maine*'s skipper, Captain Dale Redding, had gone nearly to his crush depth and turned his boat into a black hole in the water as the Chinese subs passed over. She'd stayed at ultraquiet until she'd identified every ship in the Chinese fleet and determined with certainty that they were headed toward the Clipperton-Galapagos Line.

As the officers took the data in, Helgeson said confidently, "I intend to engage the Chinese here."

He pointed to a position on the plot that was, at its deepest point, nearly seven thousand meters deep. It was roughly in the center of the line between Clipperton Island and the Galapagos Islands.

Noticing the puzzled look on the face of his Navigation officer, Lieutenant Francisco Allen, Helgeson explained, "The CNO sortied the

Pacific fleet above the equator and shifted a lot of firepower in the direction of Guam. This forced the Chinese to vector their fleet south to avoid our carriers if they still wanted to head to the Panama Canal. It was believed this would buy us some additional time for diplomacy to work. It obviously didn't, so here we are. The *Texas* just gets the dubious distinction of being first in the chute to hit them."

Helgeson paused for effect, letting those words sink in. He wanted them to know all options had been explored before it had been determined that force would be required. He needed them to accept that war was now the only option. This way, they wouldn't have any hesitation.

"Folks, the Chinese gave us no choice. We will defend our nation and we will do our duty. To that end, we will put as many of these ships on the bottom as we can."

Expanding the digital view, Helgeson went back in time to show the course changes of the Chinese ships. Since they'd left their home port for open water, the fleet had moved steadily south by southeast at full ahead. They had originally been heading to Guam; then they'd changed course when a regiment of Marines had flown to the island and beefed its defenses up.

Speeding the projection up, the plot showed where the *Texas* and the Chinese fleet would converge at his red line. His plan was simple yet aggressive; the *Dallas*, *Lubbock* and the *Texas* would form a line in the ocean at varied depths, with tubes flooded and outer doors open.

Helgeson then explained how he wanted the rest of the battle to play out. The *Texas* would be lying in wait, ready to attack as soon as the *Liaoning*, the first carrier in the People's Liberation Army Navy, was two thousand yards off their bow. Then they would hit them from near point-blank range, leaving them no chance to counter their attack.

Then Commander Helgeson explained what he wanted one of the Orcas to do. "The *Killeen*," he said, pointing to where it was located, directly in the path of the enemy fleet, "is to lie dormant beneath the thermocline. Keep its passive sonar set to bring her back to life when its magnetic sensors register the carrier. Once it goes active, it needs to launch its noisemakers, which will mimic the acoustic signature of the *Virginia*-class attack boats. When the Chinese realize they have two *Virginia*s inside their protective bubble, their ASW assets will go crazy.

The fleet will go to flank speed and all that noise will mask what will happen next.

"Once those distractions are launched, slowly raise the *Killeen* above the thermocline and target the trailing *Shang*-class sub with two Mk 48 Mod 7 torpedoes and two Mk 54 ultra-lightweight torpedoes. That sub needs to be taken out at all costs to the *Killeen* if necessary. If the *Killeen* survives the engagement, then reposition it to reattack the Chinese fleet from the aft position. Understood?"

The officer and enlisted Orca operators nodded in acknowledgment.

Helgeson saw everyone was hanging on his every word, waiting to hear the rest of the battle plan. He continued, "Once the *Killeen* initiates her attack, it will kick up a storm of activity among the enemy fleet. When that happens, the *Texas* and remaining Orcas will launch a total of eight Mk 48 Mod 7 torpedoes at the carrier *Liaoning*, the frigate *Handan*, and the troop landing ship *Wutai Shan*.

"Once our torpedoes are in the water, the *Texas* will launch a salvo of twelve of our Block IV Tomahawks straight at the *Liaoning* and that new Type 55 destroyer, the *Nanchang*. After our weapons are away, we need to drop a noisemaker and then sprint like hell out of the attack box and put some distance between them and us. Once we've evaded them, then we'll reassess the effectiveness of the attack and reposition to repeat it if possible."

No one said anything right away. They all just stared at the plot table, running through the scenarios in their minds.

Finally, Helgeson asked, "Questions? If you have them, now is the time to ask."

The sonar officer spoke up first. "Sir, when we launch all those weapons, there will be a whole lot of noise. I'm concerned about the Chinese sub screen. At present speed and probable bearing, they'll be in our vicinity about an hour before the surface ships enter our kill box. Once we fire, we're sitting ducks—they'll light us up."

Helgeson smiled and looked at the XO, who nodded. Evans answered, "That's a good question. Once we launch our missiles, we use the Orcas to make a hell of a lot of noise while we sprint to the thermocline and head to our max depth at speed. Once beneath the layer, we go ultraquiet and evade."

Helgeson interjected, "If we come out unscathed, we make our way to Isla Socorro. It seems the almighty American dollar still has weight there because the Mexican government allowed us to set up a naval replenishment station on the island. There's also a squadron of Super Hornets and ASW birds at the airfield. Once our attack happens, the Super Hornets will engage them and get us a solid battle damage assessment of our attack."

Next, Lieutenant Adam Watts, the boat's weapons officer, spoke. "Skipper, if we fire the Tomahawks at the same time as the torpedoes, we'll have to cut the wires to the Mk 48s and let them acquire on their own right off the bat. Attacking within two thousand yards with the Tomahawks barely gives them enough time to break through the water and transition to their rocket motor and acquire their target."

Lieutenant Commander Evans responded, "Weps, we leave the wires attached until the VLS doors close. That will take approximately ten seconds. By then, the Mk 48s will have acquired their targets and will have less than fifty-six seconds left on their track until they hit their targets. If all goes well and Murphy's Law doesn't kick us in the ass, we shoot, we dive, and we run."

Commander Helgeson looked each of them in the eyes. He liked what he saw. Their eyes displayed the fear he'd expected, but behind that fear, he saw steadfast determination. He was sure of his crew, and he was damn sure of the *Texas*. What he wasn't sure of was everything else, but that was a problem for tomorrow.

If there is a tomorrow.

Commander Helgeson shook off that thought of doubt. "XO, bring the ship to battle stations quiet," he ordered.

"Aye, sir. Officer of the Deck, bring the ship to battle stations quiet."

"Battle stations quiet, aye."

The crew sprang into action. The boat was rigged for quiet running, and everything that could possibly make noise was secured. The weapons officer had checked and rechecked the weapons aboard—every weapon on the *Texas* was ready to close with the Chinese ships and put them on the bottom.

Commander Helgeson leaned against the bulkhead next to the OC2 station. He glanced up at the timer above the weapons station. It was counting down until the *Texas*, *Dallas* and *Lubbock* would cross their red line. A second timer counted down until the Chinese ships arrived. They would reach the red line in exactly three hours; the fight would begin an hour after that.

Helgeson remembered a line from the poem "Antigonish" about a man who wasn't there. He planned for the *Texas* to be the man who wasn't there.

"XO, I'm going to the wardroom for some chow. Then I'm taking a ninety-minute nap. You have the Conn."

"Aye, sir, I have the Conn," replied Evans.

With that, he walked out of the Conn and down the passageway, out of sight.

****

Lieutenant Commander Evans stood, a little amazed that Commander Helgeson would leave the Conn hours before the fight of their lives. Then again, she realized it was the theater of command. She knew he probably wouldn't sleep, but the crew needed to know or at least believe the Skipper had ice running through his veins.

She gripped the plot table to steady herself as she took in a slow, deep breath. The weight of what was coming hit her like a freight train, and she suddenly understood why Commander Helgeson had left the Conn, if only for a couple of hours. A tap on her shoulder brought her back from the precipice.

"Excuse me, ma'am, um... I think you should, um..."

It was one of the junior sonarmen. She had to use her peripheral vision to read his name tape.

"What is it, Petty Officer Allen?" Evans replied.

"Well, ma'am, it's the imagery from earlier. There's something on it that—well, it's damn odd is all," replied Petty Officer Allen.

"Sailor, I don't have the time for odd. If you have a point to make, now is better than later." She instantly felt bad for snapping at him and was about to apologize when the COB walked up to the plot.

"Allen, if you've got something, let's have it." The COB towered over them both, his easy smile diffusing the immediate tension.

"Yes, right. So, if you look at the *Liaoning*"—Petty Officer Allen pointed to the carrier as he unrolled his printed copy—"it's clear from her wake that she's making full ahead, at least thirty-one knots, but what caught my eye is this ship in her wake." He shuffled through a couple more images, then dropped them all on the floor.

COB put a hand on the XO's shoulder, probably trying to keep her calm. She didn't look at him but allowed a slight smile to cross her lips as PO Allen put his images back on the plot.

"Sorry, XO. Here—this ship. It looks like a new warship we haven't encountered before. It looks almost like that Russian battle cruiser the *Kirov*, but it's new and way more modern," the sailor said.

"That can't be. If the Chinese developed a new warship, we would have heard about it," Evans countered. "Plus the *Maine* would have captured their acoustics when the fleet passed over them."

"They did capture it. We didn't know what it was. They classified it as an unknown. But now that we have some satellite imagery of the fleet, we can see the unknown acoustic sound is this large ship," Allen exclaimed confidently.

"OK, Allen, you've got my attention. So you think this is a new battle cruiser?" asked the XO with genuine interest.

"It has to be, ma'am. I've run the acoustic signature through the computers. I even sent it to the *Killeen* to run it through 'Big Brain.' The closest acoustic approximation, and I triple-checked it, is a *Kirov*-class battle cruiser."

The COB let out an audible breath, and Evans nodded in acceptance of the information.

The Russian Navy's *Kirov*-class battle cruiser was a beast, one of the largest warships on the seas, second only to an American carrier.

No, this clearly isn't a Kirov. *Could it…?* Evans contemplated. *Did the Chinese Navy just sneak a new warship onto the seas before this war started?*

Petty Officer Allen had made his point and provided them with enough logic that it was hard to dispute that this was most likely a completely new enemy warship. Evans regarded Allen for a moment—his initial nervousness had been replaced with absolute certainty. The *Texas* had enough problems to worry about, but she didn't want to dismiss this outright.

"OK, Allen, you've sold me. Designate contact Sierra 4. Keep monitoring it. We'll know soon enough what this new ship is as it gets closer to us."

Petty Officer Allen gathered his things and headed back to the sonar room. As she looked around the Conn, she could feel the tension building in the room. The crew of the *Texas* was capable—every sailor aboard knew their job—yet none of them had ever engaged a peer or near-peer enemy in combat. She had a gnawing feeling that in exactly four and a half hours, life would change for everyone.

A steward handed her a steaming cup of coffee and she lowered herself into the captain's chair. She knew in her heart that she wanted to command a boat of her own one day; she was ashamed to admit to herself that she was glad it wasn't today.

****

Commander Helgeson had his feet on the desk in his stateroom. He was listening to Ann and Nancy Wilson's rendition of "Stairway to Heaven" from their performance at the Kennedy Center honoring Led Zeppelin—in his mind, this version was superior to the original, though he'd never admit it aloud.

He read his mission orders again. He was taking the *Texas* into harm's way, and the outcome was far from certain. He was, however, certain that a few hours from now, the USS *Texas* would be sending hundreds of Chinese sailors to the bottom of the ocean. He also knew if he made even one mistake, the men and women aboard the *Texas* would join them.

He stood and splashed some water on his face and drank the last dregs of his coffee. Looking at his watch, he had forty-five seconds until his alarm went off, which meant he had exactly two minutes and fifteen seconds to get to the Conn.

Opening the door to his stateroom, he looked at a picture above his desk of "the one he'd let get away." Maybe after this patrol, he'd call her. Then again, maybe not. He smiled at an old memory, then turned off his lights and headed to war.

As he passed by sailors in the passageway, he smiled reassuringly at them and patted a few of the more junior crewmembers on the shoulder. The more of them he saw, the more determined he became. No matter what happened, he would not let them down.

"XO, I have the Conn," he announced as he walked on the Conn.

"Captain has the Conn."

Lieutenant Commander Evans stood as Commander Helgeson sat in his chair. Then he looked at the ship's status report she'd handed him.

The time passed faster than anyone would have imagined as Helgeson and the bridge crew played scenario after scenario, trying to anticipate every possibility and make contingencies for them. Petty Officer Allen's discovery was presented to Helgeson, who agreed it was odd, but like the XO, Helgeson knew it didn't matter. Whatever it was, it was headed their way and they'd know soon enough what kind of ship it was.

"Sonar, Conn. Distance to Sierra 1?"

"Conn, Sonar. Sierra 1 is four thousand yards and closing."

"Sonar, Conn. Distance to Sierra 2?"

"Conn, Sonar. Sierra 2 is three thousand, eight hundred yards and closing."

"Sonar, Conn. Designate Sierra 1 and Sierra 2 Master 1, Type 001 *Liaoning* and Master 2, Type 072A *Wutai Shan*."

"Conn, Sonar. Designate Sierra 1 and 2 Master 1 and 2, aye."

Helgeson turned to his weapons officer, who gave the report. "Sir, tubes one through four flooded and outer doors open. VLS tubes opened. All weapons ready in all respects."

Then Commander Helgeson looked at the Orca Control for their report. "Sir, *Dallas* and *Lubbock* are each five hundred yards off our port and starboard, outer doors open and all weapons ready in all respects. *Killeen* reports only sporadic contact with the Type 93."

"Conn, Sonar. Contact, designate Sierra 3 is approaching *Killeen*'s mines!"

This was it. The *Texas* was about to start a shooting war with China.

The US Navy, in anticipation of a conflict with the PLAN, had resurrected the CAPTOR underwater mines and upgraded them to use the Mk 54 ultra-lightweight Mod 7 torpedoes. These advanced weapons had been laid by the Orcas along the projected trajectory of advancing ships. They had been placed in pods of four and could be programmed to attack single or multiple targets. They wouldn't do the damage the heavier Mk 48s could, but they could still hurt a ship or take out an enemy sub.

"OC2, Conn. Launch the mines!"

"Conn, OC2. Launch the mines, aye!"

The OC2 weapons control technician pressed the weapons release button on his console, which sent the signal to the Orca, which in turn launched the mines from their position seventeen hundred feet beneath the Chinese ships. Once the torpedoes were ejected from the pod, they went into active homing mode.

The Orca's "Big Brain" turned its own active sonar on and directed the salvo of torpedoes at the contact designated Master 3, a Type 52D destroyer. It took the Mk 54s less than five seconds to achieve terminal homing.

"Conn, Sonar. Three impacts on Master 3. The ship is slowing."

"Sonar, Conn. Acknowledged. Distance to contacts Master 1 and 2?"

"Conn, Sonar. Master 1 is thirteen hundred yards, Master 2 is eleven hundred yards. Minimal change to direction."

"Sonar, Conn. Acknowledged."

Helgeson clicked start on his stopwatch and checked the plot. Before he could speak, the sound of active sonars hit the hull of the *Texas*. A loud echoing pinging noise reverberated throughout the ship.

"Damn it," Helgeson cursed softly to himself.

"Conn, Sonar. Enemy fleet is actively homing!"

"Sonar, Conn. Acknowledged. Maneuvering ahead full! Weps, final bearings and fire!"

"Firing, aye!"

"Weps, get those damn VLS doors closed! Torpedo room, reload and prepare to snap-shoot tubes one and three on my command!"

"Conn, Torpedo. Aye, Skipper."

The *Texas* shuddered as her four Mk 48s and twelve Tomahawk cruise missiles launched simultaneously. The OC2 technician reported that the *Dallas* and *Lubbock* had fired their torpedoes at precisely the same time. All three submarines launched countermeasures and noisemakers to confuse the sonars of the Chinese ships.

Suddenly the ship was hit with a sonar ping unlike anything they'd previously heard.

"Conn, Sonar. Torpedoes in the water! Actively homing! Distance thirteen hundred yards, bearing one-two-zero degrees!"

Helgeson's immediate thought was to wonder how in the hell torpedoes had gotten behind them. Before he could ask the question, the sonar room gave him the answer.

"Conn, Sonar. Splashes in the water, more torpedoes dead astern, distance eleven hundred yards and closing!"

"Launch countermeasures, right full rudder, thirty degrees down on the planes, ahead flank!"

The helm responded and the boat tilted downwards as her speed increased. The sounds of sonar pings bouncing off the hull grew in intensity. Helgeson looked at his stopwatch as it counted down from five seconds.

Despite the sound of the active sonar pings, they all heard massive explosions as the eight Mk 48s and twelve Tomahawks found their targets.

Helgeson knew if they fired their weapons at near point-blank, they couldn't miss, and the Chinese wouldn't have the time to react.

"Conn, Sonar. Master 1 is breaking apart! Master 2 is dead in the water and sinking!"

"Sonar, Conn. Distance to Master 1?"

"Conn, Sonar. Distance to Master thirteen hundred yards on current bearing."

"Conn, Sonar! Sierra 4 is bearing toward us. That destroyer is dropping depth charges!"

"Sonar, Conn. Designate Sierra 4, Master 4. Weps, snap-shoot tubes one and three along Master 4's bearing! Helm, fifteen-degree up angle and take us directly at Master 2, ahead flank!"

The XO and the COB snapped their heads toward Helgeson in shock, not immediately understanding what he was doing.

"Sir! Master 2 is breaking apart. We may get hit by the debris."

"XO, we have torpedoes about to climb up our backside in sixty seconds from two different directions, we don't—"

BOOM, BOOM, BOOM, BOOM!!!

Helgeson was cut off as four depth charges detonated around the *Texas*. Everyone in the Conn that wasn't seated was thrown to the deck; bolts on the bulkhead exploded and ricocheted in the compartment.

The junior officer of the deck's head was split open as he smashed into the secondary plot table. The compartment went dark for a moment until the emergency lights came on. The COB helped the XO back to her feet.

"OC2, get the Lubbock behind us. Make her loud! Let's see if we can get some of those torpedoes to lock onto her!" Helgeson shouted to be heard over the high-pressure water and alarm bells going off on the Conn.

253

The OC2 controlman shouted over the noise as he worked his controls to vector the *Lubbock* between the *Texas* and the certain death that had acquired them.

"Conn, Sonar. First torpedo evaded by Master 4, second torpedo hit her amidship. Debris from Master 1 is right on top of us!"

Above the noise of the impact of the Mk 48 hitting Master 4 and the torpedoes homing in, Helgeson could hear the sounds of the Chinese carrier breaking apart above them. He had a split second to make a decision that could very well kill them all.

"Helm, right full rudder, twenty-degree up angle, slow to one-third!"

"Right full rudder, twenty degree up, slow to one-third, aye!"

The *Texas* groaned and lurched to the right in a rapid course change. Debris that had been jarred loose from the depth charges clattered to the deck. Suddenly, the boat was violently impacted by debris from the *Liaoning* that was still slipping beneath the waves. Parts of the carrier impacted with the *Texas* aft of the sail and forced the boat downward under its weight. The massive chunk of ship that hit them forced the bow of the boat to angle upward at nearly forty degrees.

"Conn, Sonar. Torpedoes—"

Two massive explosions rocked the *Texas* as the torpedoes detonated into the debris field from the *Liaoning*. The explosions were followed by two more explosions as two more torpedoes exploded from the shockwave of the detonations.

The deck of the *Texas* felt like a terrible earthquake was beneath them. She groaned beneath the weight of the debris from the *Liaoning*. Damage reports were coming in from all departments. Flooding reported in Engineering, port VLS tubes crushed and damage to torpedo tubes one and three, along with significant damage to the spherical array.

"Engineering, Conn. Get that damn flooding under control. I'm about to take us deep. I need everything you can give me on the reactor!"

"Conn, Engineering. Aye!"

"Conn, Sonar. Master 4's remaining torpedoes have gone passive, sir. They lost us in the noise!"

"Helm, follow the debris down, match speed and get us the hell out of here!"

Sounds of depth charges exploding above them faded as the sounds of chunks of the *Liaoning* breaking apart all around them grew louder.

More of the sealed compartments of the carrier were starting to implode as the ship sank deeper in the water.

The torpedoes that had almost sent them to the bottom circled above, looking for them like dogs angrily circling a yard. Helgeson surveyed the Conn. Technicians were wiping condensation from their display screens, running diagnostic tests to ensure their equipment was functioning.

He motioned for the COB and the XO to join him at the plot. He placed his hand on the table, only to see that he'd placed it in a puddle of blood from where the junior OOD had hit his head. He wiped it on his coveralls and adjusted the digital display to what he was looking for.

Joining them at the plot were the OC2 Chief Petty Officer and PO Allen.

"XO, status of the boat?" Helgeson's tone sounded harsher than he wanted it to, but given the circumstances, he knew she'd let it pass.

"Sir, Engineering has stopped the flooding and repaired the damage, but we absolutely cannot take another beating like that," Evans replied.

"Good, I intend to go deep and creep us the hell out of here. We're going above crush depth and remain rigged for ultraquiet." Looking at the COB, Helgeson continued, "Keep the speed at five knots since we've lost about sixty percent capability of the spherical array—we need to stay quiet. Keep the *Lubbock* above and ahead of us and the towed array secure for now. We'll use *Dallas* in its place."

The COB nodded and left to set Helgeson's plan in motion.

"Allen, please tell me you were able to record Master 4?"

"Yes, sir. I sent the track to the comms officer. It will be pushed during our next transmission to Pearl. Once the shooting started, Naval Intelligence should have overhead recordings of the engagement. Whatever Master 4 is, it's new."

Helgeson took a moment to let that sink in. The *Texas* had launched a perfect ambush, but Master 4 was one tough ship and she'd nearly done them in. He tucked that away in the back of his mind, but he wanted another go at this mystery ship.

"XO, with the spherical degradation until we reach Isla Socorro, keep this boat quiet. I don't like having to rely on the hull arrays and the Orcas."

"Aye, Skipper, I'll put the kids to bed and turn down the lights."

Helgeson smiled at his XO. She'd gotten her sense of humor back, and after what they'd just been through, that was a good thing. The Officer of the Deck handed Helgeson a report of the action. He scanned it quickly and raised an eyebrow when he reached the end. The OOD nodded and smiled.

"Congrats, Skipper."

The XO took the report Helgeson had handed her and ran her hand through her hair. "Sir, you sank over a hundred thousand tons of Chinese vessels. You're officially the first submarine ace since World War II."

Helgeson looked around the compartment and saw the sailors in the Conn looking at him and beaming with pride. He couldn't help but think of the thousands of Chinese sailors he'd been responsible for killing. He quickly put that out of his mind. This was war, and it was either them or the *Texas*. Shaking his head, he smiled at them.

"Don't mess with *Texas*."

Chapter Twenty-Five
Murphy's Law

HS9 Deepwater Platform
13.3 Nautical Miles North by Northwest of Havana, Cuba

The tension in the sub was thick as the operators made last-minute checks to their gear and weapons. After three days of being cooped up in this sub, it was finally time to get this show started. The war had begun, and it was now their task to secure these oil platforms before they could be turned into an environmental disaster.

"Commander Jankowski, we're in position, your teams can exfil," the sub commander said as he poked his head into the chamber with the waiting Special Operators.

Jankowski looked up at the captain. "Roger that. Thanks for the ride, sir. Good luck on your next mission after we leave."

The captain gave him a slight smile as he turned away to head back to the Conn.

Commander Walt "Jank" Jankowski turned to look at the two platoons of thirty-two SEALs and the eight EOD techs that'd be accompanying them. "This is it," he announced, just loud enough for them to hear. "We're in position. Remember your training. Slow is smooth, smooth is fast. Let's secure this rig before they even know what's happening."

Nods and a few oorahs were the only reply he got as the operators climbed into the decompression chamber. This chamber connected them to the sub's twin hangars and their pre-positioned equipment within.

Jank was last to climb into the chamber, making sure the first platoon of operators was fully loaded before he joined them. As the commander of SEAL Team Two, he wanted to lead by example, and that meant being in the first wave of operators to hit the platform. They needed to neutralize the guards quickly and prevent them from blowing the pipes that connected it to the oil well hundreds of feet below on the ocean's floor. If they failed, the soldiers on the rig could unleash an environmental disaster on the southern coast of Florida that could rival the BP oil spill.

Once everyone settled into the decompression chamber and donned their scuba gear, they flooded the chamber and the hangar. A few minutes later, the operators moved into the hangar and began the process of getting the outer door opened and their equipment ready to move.

When the door was fully opened, they pushed the SEAL delivery vehicle out. They'd attached most of their equipment to it because they didn't need to ride on it. Once the team was outside the hangar, they began a slow and cautious ascent to the surface above them.

Looking above him, Jank saw they were officially underneath the target—Havana-Scarabeo-9 or HS9 as they were calling it. The latest imagery and SIGINT confirmed the Chinese had taken over the operations of the rig. Virtually all personnel aboard were either Chinese or Cuban military, so anyone they encountered would be hostile. Taking this rig was the first step in preparation for the invasion of Cuba and the removal of the Chinese forces from residence on the island.

There were three major oil platforms anchored in the Straits of Florida. They were also directly in the path of the invasion force. While Jank's team hit this rig, the rest of Team Two would be hitting the others.

Poking his head above the water, Jank found the sea was somewhat calm. It was still dark out, cloudy with a slight mist of rain falling. This meant they wouldn't have to deal with the moon or the stars giving their position away.

One of the squads of operators moved toward the anchor leg they'd eventually have to scale. They kept their weapons trained up as they did their best to scan for booby traps and possible tripwires that'd alert the enemy to their presence. The EOD techs began their checks. Two of the eight divers swam to each of the platform's legs and examined them for explosives. They scanned the main pipe that led from the rig and pumps directly down to the oil well on the ocean floor as well. They wanted to make sure the Chinese or Cubans hadn't attached explosives to the well via a command wire, ready to blow if the rig came under attack.

Jank's plan to take this rig was textbook SEAL. It consisted of a rapid and simultaneous envelopment of the target via ascension from the sea on all four legs of the platform. It would give no warning to the defenders and no chance to blow any charges if they pulled it off. The order of the day was violence of action, to kill or subdue all personnel aboard and prevent the platform from being destroyed or severely damaged.

The only easy day was yesterday, Jank thought as the operators went to work on their individual tasks.

****

It took Jank's team nearly an hour to carry out their checks before they felt ready to begin their ascent to the platform above. So far, they had observed a couple of roving patrols on the lower deck of the platform. Occasionally, an enemy soldier looked down into the dark, murky waters below, shining a flashlight across the surface. It was in these moments that the SEALs had to be extra careful. The platform was still powered and had a plethora of lights turned on. The operators' only saving grace was the rain and the thick mist that hung in the air. The crappy weather meant the roving patrols didn't spend a lot of time outside looking for trouble like they should have.

The SEALs were doing what they did best—making the inclement weather work to their advantage. It did help that, for the last three days, the ocean had been at sea state three and four, with waves of two to eight feet, intermixed with nonstop rain or rainy mist, which was common at the end of the traditional hurricane season. The rain might have complicated their climb up the rig, but the geeks at DARPA had come through for SOCOM once again—they'd developed what had affectionately been dubbed the gecko wet suit and ascension ensemble. The operators would use the gecko ensemble for scaling the side of a ship, or in this case, a massive oil rig.

Basically, it was a coiled cable housed in a Roomba-like device that would scale a surface and then pull the climber up. The only reason the SEALs even considered using this type of climbing device was that it allowed them to keep their hands free for their weapons. This was important considering that every ten minutes a roving patrol of guards would wander down to the lower level of the rig and occasionally look down at the water below.

Chances were, the first team scaling the legs of the rig would have to take the guards out or be ready to handle any additional threats that might pop up on their journey to the rig. The only drawback to this new system was its speed. The damn device was painfully slow as it crawled up the metal leg, pulling the operator. Hence why it was important to be able to use one's weapon should the need arise.

Jank checked his Resco dive watch. The luminous hands told him it was now 0305 hours—time to start their ascent. He tapped his swim buddy and pointed upwards, and the two of them attached the climber to the metal leg and let it start the process of climbing up toward the catwalk above them.

As the eight SEALs slowly rose out of the water, two on each leg of the platform, the other eight SEALs remained in the water with weapons trained at the railing seventy feet above. Once the first group was at the top, they established a security perimeter while the rest of the platoon made their journey up to join them.

While Jank's Roomba was pulling him up and out of the water, he watched as Chief Petty Officer Vance Cummings in the water below tossed a small object into the air. It seemed to float weightlessly for a second before it came to life and climbed soundlessly toward the top of the platform.

Cummings had thrown one of the new PD-100 Black Hornet II nanodrones the SEALs were integrating into their operations. These little bad boys were tailored specifically for Naval Special Warfare, with twin counter-rotating rotors to account for higher winds on the ocean.

They had specially equipped these drones with a dual FLIR and true-color night vision that could send real-time imagery to all of the SEALs via the specially designed 180-degree dive masks they'd recently started using. The specially outfitted masks had a built-in internal monocular for the NAVSPECWAR. It was the SpecOps version of a Blue Force Tracker, enabling a SEAL commander to know where all his people were. It also gave the operators the ability to see what the drones were seeing so they could maneuver to best deal with a threat. This newest piece of equipment, along with the microdrones, enabled the SEALs to have a near 360-degree awareness.

Jank watched as the drone rose past the platform he was heading toward. Moments later, it moved from under the platform to taking a loitering position a hundred feet above the facility. In seconds, it identified six hostiles on the west corner of the rig. The second drone stayed near the operators as they climbed up the leg of the rig. The portion of the lower platform they were nearing still appeared to be empty.

As the operators approached the platform, the drone nearest them picked up the audio from a nearby patrol that was on its way down to the lower platform.

Crap, we'll need to take those guys out and quick, Jank thought. He was nearly to the platform himself.

Jank tapped something on his face mask and saw the video image of the drone that had captured the audio for him. He spotted a pair of Chinese soldiers walking down the metal stairs to the catwalk that would lead them directly to him and the rest of his team.

Knowing he needed to act, Jank reached down, grabbed his suppressed SIG M11A1 pistol and pointed it in the direction of the soldiers. He waited for what felt like an eternity for them to walk down the stairs. The first soldier made it to the landing and stopped. He appeared to be pulling a pack of cigarettes out of a front pocket and then lit one.

His friend said something to him that the drone's audio wasn't able to grab. The two of them moved down the landing to the bottom of the catwalk that would lead them directly to Jank. It took the soldiers another minute until they reached the landing on the platform and then turned to head toward him. When they appeared around the bend, Jank saw the two soldiers through his enhanced night vision goggles. They each had cigarettes in their mouths and their rifles slung over their shoulders, oblivious to what was about to happen.

Without thinking about it, relying solely on his two decades of training, Jank squeezed the trigger, hitting the first guard in the head. Jank then pivoted smoothly to the second guard, hitting him twice in the chest and once in the head before the guard even realized his friend had been shot. The two of them slumped to the deck, their rifles clattering on the metal catwalk.

Directly above Jank's squad, the drone spotted where the soldiers had come from. An awning had been set up, presumably to give the guards on patrol someplace to shelter and take a seat between patrols. The few soldiers were sitting around under the awning, smoking cigarettes and talking amongst themselves, oblivious that the war had started.

With the first squad of eight SEALs on the lower deck of the platform, Jank tapped Cummins on the shoulder, indicating that it was time for them to secure the place. The other team of eight operators was already halfway up the platform while the third and final group was getting ready to start their own ascent.

Cummins did a quick assessment of the area based on the images from the drones. He sent a short message over their closed coms link to

Jank that they should take out that group of soldiers on the next deck above them. They posed the greatest threat right now.

Jank concurred with the plan, and Cummins organized the operators on the deck. They detailed off a single SEAL from each of the four squads to take out what the drone had identified as six hostiles standing around the awning.

Jank didn't have to, but he opted to go with them—he wanted to stay with them as they cleared this next level of the platform in case things went sideways and they had to make an adjustment to their original plans.

When they reached the next landing, Jank heard voices in Chinese laughing at something. One of them was showing the others something on his phone, which made them laugh again.

While they were occupied, Jank and the four other operators continued to slip closer toward them. The men were still talking and laughing, unaware of the danger sneaking up on them from the shadows.

One of the ChiComs must have pulled another cigarette out. When he flicked his Zippo to light it, a brief flash of lightning struck the water a few miles away, illuminating the area around the soldiers. Suddenly, the shadows the operators had been lurking in weren't so dark.

The enemy soldier who had been looking in their direction stopped what he was doing. It was as if he saw them, but he couldn't quite believe what he saw. After a momentary hesitation, the soldier tried to unsling his QBZ-03 assault rifle.

Before he could do anything else, his head snapped back as a 9mm round from a suppressed Sig M11A1 spat a single subsonic bullet. The remaining five soldiers were barely able to process the death of their comrade before a string of spitting sounds whispered all around them as the bullets cut through soft flesh. In less than two seconds, the six guards collapsed to the deck, lifeless heaps to pose a threat no more.

Jank tapped his radio, talking barely above a whisper via his throat mic to Chief Cummins. "Targets neutralized. Is Kilo Platoon ready to roll?"

"Kilo's up. Juliet is ascending right now," came the short reply.

A few minutes later, the two SEAL platoons were organized and ready to begin clearing the decks of the rig.

Juliet Platoon, along with the EOD techs, was tasked with clearing out the lower levels of the platform and making sure the oil pipes and storage tanks weren't rigged with explosives. With their assignments in hand, the platoon broke itself down into squads and moved out. Kilo Platoon was tasked with securing the upper portion of the rig and the control room.

Jank watched as the lead squad advanced, each man covering the man in front of him. As they reached an open door, they stopped and cleared it. They needed to make sure they didn't leave a room full of hostiles behind them as they advanced through the facility.

When they approached one of the stairwells, they spotted two guards strolling toward them, completely unaware of the Americans' presence. The lead SEAL fired several rounds from his suppressed Mk 16 SCAR-L. The guards fell down the stairs in a heap.

For the briefest of moments, no one moved. They stood there listening to see if anyone might have heard the shots or the bodies falling to the deck.

The first magazine in their rifles was loaded with subsonic 5.56mm rounds. While not completely silent, they were a lot quieter than the nonsubsonic rounds in the rest of their magazine pouches.

When no one else showed up to investigate the sound, they continued to head toward the control room. When they reached it, First and Second Squads stacked up against the side of the door and got ready to move. Third Squad moved down one side of the platform level, while Fourth Squad moved down the other. These two squads would clear this level of hostiles while the other squads secured the control room.

Approaching the control room, the lead operator, a man who went by "Scarface" reached down and gently turned the handle of the door. He was the breacher, so it was his job to get them inside the room. He motioned briefly with his other hand, a countdown.

Three...two...one...

"Breaching!" Scarface roared to be heard by everyone around him.

In the flash of an eye, he was in the room with his FN SCAR assault rifle tucked in his shoulder and at the ready as he broke to the right side of the room, allowing quick access for the following man to break left and the third man to rush forward into the center of the room.

As Scarface moved into the room and cut to the right, he fired several shots from his rifle while the second operator moving left fired a couple of quick shots of his own. The third person in the stack was in the room fractions of a second later, firing three shots at the soldier standing in the center of the room before he could even hit the alarm button.

A fourth and fifth Chinese soldier who hadn't been hit by the initial barrage of bullets dove for cover behind a table. One of them had his QBZ assault rifle ready at lightning speed and sprayed bullets at the charging SEALs.

Jank followed the fourth man into the room just in time for the man's body to be thrown back into him, causing the two of them to fall backwards through the door they had entered and to the deck.

As their bodies hit the deck, Jank knew the SEAL on top of him was dead. He wasn't even trying to move. Jank rolled the corpse off him to the left as he sought to bring his own SCAR to bear on whoever might still be alive and trying to kill them inside the control room.

Before Jank could get back to his feet, he heard the operators shouting, "Clear," as they finished securing the room.

The sound of the enemy soldiers' rifles going off had probably alerted the rest of the guard force that they were being boarded. It wouldn't take long before more shooting would start. Jank and his teams had to move swiftly to neutralize them and secure the platform.

Entering the now-cleared control room, Jank saw Chief Cummins getting the pumps on the rig powered down, activating various built-in safety features that would lock it out from releasing oil into the Gulf. Another SEAL was flipping switches, turning off the lights and power across the rig. Plunging the facility into darkness would make it easier for the SEALs to leverage their night vision goggles.

With the rig's communications, both internal and with the mainland, cut off, Jank radioed the leader of Juliet Platoon, Lieutenant Jack "Nipsey" Russell.

"Anvil Two, Anvil Actual. Control room secure, SITREP. Over."

A long moment ensued before the reply came in a low whisper.

"Anvil Actual, Anvil Two. We have mov—"

Before Jank could ask him to repeat his last transmission, a thunderous explosion threw the SEALs in the control room to the deck. This was followed by a second and then a third blast. This was definitely not something Jank wanted to hear on an oil platform in the middle of the ocean.

Jank barked orders for two members to remain in the control room. He ordered the five other members of the platoon to follow him down to the next level, where Juliet Platoon was supposed to be, and figure out what the hell had just happened.

He also sent a quick message to Third and Fourth Squads to stay on task, clearing out the upper level of the platform and the helipad. Now that they had secured the control room, they had a company of Marines inbound to help them in ten minutes.

Jank and the five others ran out of the room, weapons at the ready as they headed toward the stairwell that'd lead them to the lower decks of the rig.

"Anvil Two, Anvil Actual. SITREP, over!" Jank hissed into the comms.

The team bounded down one deck and stopped, waiting to see if they could hear their comrades. What they heard was sporadic gunfire coming from within the sealed crew section of the platform. The operators immediately stacked up against the sides of the door and prepared to breach.

As they were about to open the door to move down the corridor, it opened and out stumbled Petty Officer Carlson from Juliet Platoon. The man had a terrible laceration on his right arm that crossed his chest. When he saw his comrades, he looked surprised and then collapsed.

Jank tried to catch the man's fall and fell with him to the deck, holding him in his arms. He was lucid but losing a lot of blood.

"What the hell happened?" Jank asked.

Carlson coughed up some blood as he tried to explain. "We cleared rooms. We came to a room we heard people talking in. We stacked up and prepared to throw in a flash-bang. Then they shot at us through the walls."

Carlson coughed again, more blood oozing out his mouth. He wheezed as he tried to speak. "We must have tripped an alarm and then…" He coughed up more blood, and it sounded like he was gargling or choking on it. His body then went limp before he could say anything else.

"It looks like he took a couple of rounds to the back, Jank. Nothing we could do," one of the operators said.

Lowering his NVGs so he could see in the darkness, Jank motioned for his men to move forward into the corridor Carlson had just come from. The enemy knew they were coming, which meant clearing the remaining decks would be a lot more complicated. Time was unfortunately not a commodity they had in abundance on this mission either.

As they moved into the bowels of the rig, they heard the sound of more gunfire being exchanged. The sounds of QBZs and AK-74s echoed throughout the corridors. Jank also heard voices in Spanish and Chinese, shouting to each other like they were coordinating who would do what and when.

When they reached the first intersection, the team of five operators stacked up behind Jank, getting ready to move down the corridor where the firing had come from. Readying a flash-bang, Jank let the others know he was getting ready to toss it. He pulled the pin and peered around the corner long enough to give it a good toss.

As soon as he'd thrown it, he turned his head away, closed his eyes and opened his mouth slightly, preparing for the concussion and flash of light that was about to blind the defenders.

Bang!

In the blink of an eye, Jank was around the corner, rifle up and charging toward where he suspected the enemy soldiers were. When he rounded the corner, he saw half a dozen enemy soldiers, temporarily blinded and in various stages of shock. One of them was firing his pistol wildly in the direction of the other platoon of SEALs.

Jank sighted in on the first guy he saw and pulled the trigger, hitting him several times in the chest and knocking the man backwards to the floor. Jank advanced along the right side of the room, knowing the man behind him would be breaking to the left. In seconds, his team had wiped out the eight enemy soldiers that had their sister platoon pinned down.

"Clear!" yelled Chief Cummins as the SEALs finished off the last of the defenders.

Jank's corpsman ran over to where the remaining five SEALs from Juliet Platoon were hunkered down. They'd all been shot at least once or peppered with shrapnel.

Lieutenant McCarthy, the platoon's second in command, was the least wounded. He was young and amped up from the gunfight. He wanted revenge for the loss of his platoonmates. Chief Cummins had to calm him down so the corpsman could get him patched up and back in the fight. They needed Lieutenant McCarthy to help tend to his wounded operators, not think irrationally and get himself or others killed.

With the platoon rescued, Jank jumped up on the Task Unit net. He heard their reserve platoon had finally made it onto the rig. They were working on clearing the rest of it with the two other squads of Kilo Platoon.

Jank's radio then chirped, letting him know he had an incoming message. "Anvil, Hammer. How copy? Over." It was Blade, the leader of the second half of the Task Unit. His reserve platoon, Lima, made up the rest of the Task Unit. In this case they were the cavalry, and their added combat power would be much appreciated.

"Hammer, Anvil. Send it," Jank barked as his adrenaline spike reached its peak.

"Anvil, let's give these boys a sleepy treat."

Hammer was referring to a tool the SEALs had developed for ship and oil rig takedowns. Normally they used the knockout gas when they wanted to covertly capture a group of hostiles without them knowing they were around. Now that the remaining Chinese and Cuban soldiers knew they had visitors on the platform, it would get ugly.

"Hammer, Anvil. Do it!"

Jank motioned for the men to don their gas masks and sent a quick message to let the remaining SEALs know what was about to happen. As they got their masks on, they heard the clattering of boots coming down the corridor heading toward them. Chief Cummins ordered them to get down. No sooner had the last SEAL gone prone than a group of Chinese soldiers rounded the corner, rifles up and at the ready as they surveyed the scene of their dead comrades. In the few seconds it took them to recognize what had happened, the remaining SEALs opened fire. The four enemy soldiers were cut to pieces, adding to the carnage.

More footsteps could be heard as reinforcements came to aid their fallen comrades.

Hurry up, Hammer, Jank thought.

****

Lieutenant Chris "Hammer" Iverson watched as one of his SEALs fitted the canisters of gas the teams had nicknamed sleepy treats to the HVAC system. The SEAL gave Hammer the thumbs-up, and they cranked the knob all the way open and turned the climate control to full blast.

"Anvil, Hammer. Gas has been released. Give it a few minutes and you should be able to make your way topside. I've electronically sealed all the hatches I could from the control room. I advise you to move to the southwest exit from your current position. CCTV shows you are clear all the way back to our location."

"Hammer, Anvil. Copy. Moving to you in ten mikes," Jank replied.

The rest of the SEALs gave it a bit of time to make sure everyone was out. The platoons then broke down into their squad formations and began clearing each and every room on the platform. As they found a cluster of Chinese or Cuban soldiers passed out, they disarmed them and zip-tied their hands. They annotated where the soldiers were located on an electronic map each squad leader had on a tablet. When their Marine reinforcements arrived, they'd go back and round them up.

Now that they had secured the platform, a group of Marines would be flying in from MacDill Air Force Base out of Tampa to relieve them and collect the prisoners and their wounded.

Standing outside near the helipad, Jank and Hammer looked off toward Cuba. They couldn't quite make out land; they were a bit too far away. But that wasn't what they were looking for. It was still dark out, but soon, a new set of lights would illuminate the darkness.

"You know, I don't think I've ever seen a cruise missile being fired from sea before," Hammer commented.

Jank snorted. "Come to think of it, I don't think I have, either. Should be interesting. I just hope they bring the pain and score some good hits."

In the distance, four or five kilometers away, a flash erupted near the edge of the water. Then they heard the bang as the engine on the cruise missile ignited and it took to the air. This process was repeated thirteen more times as the Navy's only diesel-electric covert littoral submersible unleashed some of the first salvos of America's counterpunch in this new war.

****

Forty-five minutes after the cruise missile attack, a few MV-22 Ospreys appeared on the horizon. The Marines coming in from MacDill finally arrived. As the first Osprey set down on the rig's helipad, the Marines ran off, making room for the five wounded SEALs to be loaded.

The Osprey carrying the wounded raced off in the direction of MacDill Air Force Base in Tampa. They would drop the wounded at Tampa General Hospital, one of the few Level III trauma centers in the state of Florida. When the second Osprey landed, the SEALs rushed the eight bodies of their fallen comrades on board. This Osprey headed directly to MacDill, where the bodies would be taken over to mortuary affairs.

As the rest of the Marines arrived, they were detailed off to go collect the prisoners and establish a security overwatch on the platform. The prisoners would be brought to the helipad, where they'd wait until a group of three CH-53E Super Stallions arrived to take them to an Army detention facility being set up at Avon Park in central Florida, just south of Orlando.

The fight for HS9 was over, but the fight to remove the ChiComs from Latin America had just begun.

Chapter Twenty-Six
Dragon Fire

Joint Battle Command Centre
20 Kilometers Northwest of Beijing, China

Admiral Wei Huang's stomach sank as the immediate reports came in from Task Force 742. *We lost a carrier in the opening hours of the war*, Wei thought as the others in the JBCC took in the information.

"General Gao, I guess we have the American response to your cyber army. Damn good job in turning the lights off on those facilities," exclaimed General Li Zuocheng. General Li turned in his chair to look at Admiral Wei. "Your raiders are launching their attacks now, right?"

All eyes turned to look at the man in charge of the next phase of the assault on the West.

Wei looked down at his watch before returning his gaze to the head of the PLA. "Yes. Our raiders should begin launching their cruise missile attacks all along the East, West, and Gulf Coasts of the US. They should also be hitting the European ports and strategic military bases at the same time. Over the next three hours, the naval and air forces of the West will come under the largest single attack since World War II."

President Yao Jintao added, "General Li, General Gao, and Admiral Wei have done their parts in this war. It'll now be on the shoulders of the Army to secure us the final victory. The allies will be off-balance for some time after this attack. Your forces need to use that time to accomplish their missions and then prepare to hold the territory we're capturing."

The head of the PLA only nodded in reply; nothing else needed to be said. They all knew a lot was riding on how well his forces performed over the next couple of weeks. Nearly two decades of modernization and training—now it was time to put it all on the line and prove it hadn't been all for naught.

General Li looked at Dr. Xi next. "Are there any changes to the models your AI has predicted? Are they still holding?"

Everyone was least confident about this part of the plan. Could Project Ten really be the deciding factor in winning a war? Handing over the strategy of fighting a war to an advanced super-AI seemed incredibly risky.

"As of right now, General, the models are still holding. We're factoring in the impact to the overall strategy of the loss of the *Liaoning*. We also lost a troop transport ship, a destroyer, and a frigate in the engagement. Fortunately, the bulk of the task force is still intact, and the *Shandong* didn't suffer any damage.

"In thirty minutes, the next wave of deepfake attacks will start in Europe and then spread to America. As the Europeans go to work, they will be inundated with news about NATO launching a preemptive attack against the people of China, that we only responded in retaliation to an unprovoked attack," Dr. Xi explained confidently. The man was excited. His super-AI was being unleashed on the world, as he had envisioned so many decades ago when he'd dreamt up this program.

"Admiral Wei, I believe it is time for you to launch your next phase of the operation," President Yao said confidently.

Admiral Wei didn't say anything right away. He glanced at the President with a look that asked if this was really necessary before he finally moved over to one of the computer terminals. He brought up a secured text box, typed in a single code word and hit Send.

"It's done. We should start to hear about it on the news shortly," Wei replied glumly.

"Cheer up, Wei. This is all part of the plan. It will work, don't you worry. Their losses will not be in vain," the President said somberly as he placed a hand on the old man's shoulder.

The group turned their attention to some of the TV monitors they had set up along one of the walls. They had a number of different stations on in hopes that the combination would provide them a variety of reporting on what would soon be happening.

While they waited for the next phase of attacks to begin, a steward brought them some fresh tea and something to eat. They would most likely be in this briefing room in the command center for the next twenty-four hours. The massive control center outside was a beehive of activity. The entire war was being run from this single command center, and just a kilometer away, in another cavernous room unknown to most people, was the most powerful quantum computer and super-AI ever built—the true superweapon of this new war and the tool that would lead them to victory.

"Ah, here comes the first report," a staff officer announced.

From Taiwan Today, Taipei: "We interrupt our normal broadcast to bring you a report of a ballistic missile attack currently underway. People in Nanbin Park, near the coastal city of Hualien County, are reporting more than a dozen missiles launching out of the ocean. The missiles are heading directly over Taiwan toward the mainland.

"Government sources have put out an immediate statement saying they did not carry out this launch, nor are they in the process of initiating military operations against the PRC. The president of Taiwan just reiterated the government's stance of remaining neutral in the growing conflict between the PRC and the North Atlantic Treaty Organization. We will bring you more breaking news as we receive it."

"General Zulong," the President ordered, "do your best to shoot down as many of these missiles as you can. I know some will get through, but it helps our cause if your force is actually able to hit some of them."

Seeing the missile contrails rising into the sky as they headed over Taiwan toward their intended targets was like being punched in the gut. This was the part of the strategy the AI had come up with that would solidify the people's support for their cause. Still, it was tough to take in.

The general nodded. He was already on the phone with some of the regional commanders who would be responsible for engaging those missiles as they entered their terminal arc.

General Gao Weiping walked over to Dr. Xi. "Once your team has the video images of the missiles and the damage they will inflict, how long will it take your team to get them ready to be used in the next wave of deepfakes?"

General Goa was the commander of the newest branch of the People's Liberation Army, the Strategic Support Force. It was his department that was in charge of China's cyber army, satellite infrastructure, and Dr. Xi Zemin's Project Ten.

"Not long, General," Xi explained quietly. "I'm glad the sub commanders were able to find some cargo ships to hide behind when they launched. Those ships will give us the silhouette of the image we'll need to turn these into NATO and Taiwanese warships." The two of them had been talking a lot more in the lead-up to today—the day of the first-ever world war launched by an AI.

"Here comes the next report," a different staff officer said as he turned up the volume on a TV tuned in to La Repubblica out of Rome.

272

"We are receiving reports out of Calabria of explosions occurring on a Chinese Panamax freighter twenty miles from the port of Gioia Tauro. We do not yet know the cause of the explosions or if any crewmen have been hurt. The local authorities have been alerted and a rescue operation is currently underway. We will bring you more news of this developing story as more information is made available."

"The missiles are being intercepted," one of General Zulong's officers commented.

Everyone turned their attention to a radar display of the interceptors being launched at the ballistic and cruise missiles being fired at China. A TV reporter happened to be reporting live from a position that had an incredible view. The cameraman was getting some good shots of the interceptors connecting with some of the inbound missiles.

"Splash one! Our interceptor hit the first missile."

Some cheering broke out as the officers got excited about the hit. Then a second missile was intercepted. More cheers. A couple of people gave some smiles and nods to General Zulong and his people's ability to knock the missiles out of the sky.

Then they saw one of the interceptors miss a missile. Then a second interceptor missed. With those two shots gone, the ground crews were launching the next set of shorter-range interceptors, hoping the second line of defense would hold up.

The group watched as twelve of the missiles decreased to seven. Then the second line of interceptors dropped that number down to five. At this point, the missiles were in their terminal velocity phase and were traveling at speeds in excess of Mach 10. It was nearly impossible to hit a target moving that fast, so scoring even two hits was a big deal.

The remaining five missiles impacted along the Chinese coastal cities opposite Taiwan. The city of Quanzhou was hit by three while the remaining two hit the city of Xiamen. While it appeared like the missiles targeted legitimate military targets in the area, they assumed the Taiwanese missiles would be less accurate, so they had the missiles veer slightly off course.

The impact of these missiles with their five-thousand-pound warheads was immense. Enormous orange fireballs and black smoke erupted around the impact zones. Windows were blown out of offices, homes, and vehicles as far away as a mile in all directions from the concussion of the blast. The ground shook so hard that it felt like a mini earthquake.

A few days prior to the start of this operation, several trucks packed with additional explosives and petrol had been parked in the vicinity of where these missiles would be landing. The war planners wanted to make sure they had rigged the area with enough explosive materials to make the damage from the missiles more severe than it otherwise might have been.

****

Admiral Wei turned away from the others and walked over to get himself a refill of tea. As he poured some into his cup, he paused just long enough to wipe a tear away before it could run down his face. He took a deep breath in and held it. Next, he raised his cup to his mouth and took a couple of sips of the hot liquid as he fought to regain control of his emotions.

"Come on, Admiral. Pull it together. If the President sees you like this, he'll replace you. We need you now more than ever," General Li said softly so no one else could hear them.

Wei nodded but didn't say anything. The two of them walked over to the far side of the briefing table, away from the others.

"Li, this can't be right what we are doing. There are certain rules in warfare. This AI machine is fighting this war with no rules. No regard for human life. It only sees things as ones and zeros on a computer screen. This AI will spiral out of control if we do not do something," Wei explained softly.

Before Li could reply, Dr. Xi pulled a chair out near them and took a seat.

"This is an exciting moment, isn't it?" he offered.

"What exactly do you find exciting?" Wei countered. "We just witnessed the deaths of probably ten thousand of our own civilians. More than two thousand sailors, men under my command, died in the last few hours. What part of that are you finding exciting, Dr. Xi?"

"I...I didn't mean to minimize the loss of life. I was commenting on how everything has been so meticulously planned and it is now coming to fruition. All these moving parts, these pieces to the grand puzzle are all falling into place just like Jade Dragon predicted," Xi tried to explain. "To think all of this has been planned and engineered by a computer, Generals. Imagine if we had more drones and even robots. We could have the computer fight the entire war for us."

The two military soldiers looked at Xi with a bit of concern but held their tongues. They knew that was the direction warfare was headed. In a way, they were thankful for their ages. They likely wouldn't be around to have to fight that kind of war. Right now, their main goal was winning a war neither of them had wanted.

Chapter Twenty-Seven
Angels in the Sky

Air Force One
Somewhere over the Midwest

The giant Boeing 747 had finally leveled out when the National Security Advisor, Blain Wilson, felt comfortable enough to get up and finally use the washroom. People were talking and arguing all around him, yet the only thought that was running through his mind was his urgent bodily need to relieve himself. His wife and kids had already left D.C. a week ago. He felt they were safe, so his mind wasn't racing to them like it was for so many others.

When Wilson entered the large washroom outside of the briefing room, he felt better. He stood in front of the mirror and looked at himself. His eyes appeared tired, his hair was a mess, and he felt sweaty. Turning the faucet on, he splashed some water on his face.

The next sixty minutes will change the course of human history...please, Lord, give me guidance on what to do next, Wilson pleaded.

As he walked back into the briefing room, the President's voice boomed, "There you are, Blain. We need to be prepared to respond to these missiles. If they're nuclear, or civilian casualties are high when they hit, this will be devastating."

Admiral Roy Thiel, the Chairman of the Joint Chiefs, had fortunately made it on board Air Force One with them. Those first few minutes when the Chinese attack had gotten underway had been tense. Once the Secret Service had learned there were cruise missiles inbound to a series of military bases along the Gulf, they had made the decision to get the President airborne. It was the wee hours of the morning, so rounding up everyone that needed to get on the plane with the President had taken a herculean effort.

The Secret Service had gotten the President on Air Force One while the Vice President was sequestered in the Presidential Emergency Operation Center or PEOC bunker. While that had all taken place, the Secret Service and Capitol Police had roused the leaders of the Senate and the House out of their beds, rushing them to nearby bunkers for their own protection.

One of the Air Force communications officers poked his head into the briefing room. "Sir, we just reestablished communications with NORAD, the White House, and the Pentagon. We're patching them through to you right now."

The communications officer, who looked like he was no more than twenty, withdrew his head from the cramped room and disappeared.

Wilson had just taken a seat and spotted the fresh cup of coffee waiting for him when the large monitor connecting them to the outside world turned on. They immediately saw the split screen showing NORAD, the Pentagon's NMCC, the PEOC in the bowels of the White House, US Strategic Command out of Offutt Air Force Base in Omaha, and US Southern Command out of Doral, Florida.

The President immediately tore into them. "Damn it, General Barrett! How in the hell did we get sucker-punched like this?" he demanded angrily.

General Anita Barrett, Commander of US Northern Command and NORAD, countered, "Mr. President, I don't have all the answers for you right now, but rest assured we will be looking into all of this in the coming days. Right now, I need to inform you that we are currently carrying out our counterstrike. Task Force Dupre in the Gulf has successfully engaged and sunk the four Chinese warships that fired off the first volley of cruise missiles. The task force's Tomahawks just hit the launcher sites in Cuba that fired on us. We should have some satellite coverage of the area within the next ten minutes to give us a battle damage assessment of the strike."

General Barrett continued, "Sir, I also need to inform you that SEAL Team Three is securing the Cuban-Chinese oil platforms in the Straits of Florida. As soon as we issued the attack orders to TF Dupre, we issued the orders for the SEALs to seize the platforms before the Cubans or Chinese could release millions of gallons of crude into the sea. The submarine that delivered the SEALs also carried out a strategic strike against the Cuban and Chinese naval ships at the ports of Mariel and Havana."

Interrupting her, Admiral Thiel cut in, "Hold up there, General. I get the attack on the oil platforms, but why did we fire on the ports with Tomahawks? These targets are located in some densely packed urban areas. Who gave them the order to attack?"

"That's a good point, General. Who gave that sub commander the order to hit the ports?" Wilson reinforced the question. Hitting the ports was a huge strategic mistake.

General Barrett looked a little lost for words. She talked to someone off screen before she returned to the discussion. "Um, I need to get with the sub commander. I'm relaying what they told us. We have another emergency to deal with. A ballistic missile attack is currently underway near Taiwan. It appears a barrage of missiles was launched from the ocean east of Taiwan. The missiles are tracking toward three Chinese cities across the straits. The Taipei government is insisting they did not launch an attack on the mainland. It does look like the PLA is attempting to engage the enemy missiles."

The President was practically apoplectic at this point as he blurted out angrily, "What the *hell* is going on?! How in the hell has all of this happened in the last forty minutes? We're supposed to have satellites around the world that monitor this kind of activity, then we have ground-based radars that ring our country and our allies, yet none of them saw any of this happening until it was too late!" The President paused his rant for just a moment before adding, "How long until those missiles begin to impact our bases in the Gulf?"

Looking off screen, General Barrett replied, "Five minutes, Mr. President."

Wilson felt he needed to step in at this point to help bring some balance. "Mr. President, if I may. I know a lot has happened and we've been caught completely flat-footed. There will be time for us to look back on the events that led us to this moment." He took a deep breath. "Sir, we know that the Chinese have created a super-AI that is responsible for tracking their own people and managing their social credit program. Then we had that defector that began to tell us about Operation Jedi and how it was tracking down all the foreign intelligence operatives around the world—at least before he was killed. Maybe their new super-AI is somehow involved in all of this as well."

"Blain, are you saying that maybe this Chinese AI has gone rogue?" the President asked incredulously.

"No, not at all, Mr. President. What I'm saying is maybe the Chinese created this AI to do exactly what it's doing. I think President Yao has allowed the PLA to unleash this AI on America and the West. There's no other way to explain how they could have defeated so many of the early-warning systems we have in place if there wasn't a cyber or electronic intrusion by this AI. I mean, look at what they've done. They've disabled the nation's cell phone service, taken down the power grid around the targeted air bases, and successfully ghosted our early-warning systems," Wilson explained.

The room was silent for a moment as everyone absorbed what Wilson had said.

Admiral Thiel was the first to respond. "I think Mr. Wilson might be correct, but we can discuss that at a later point. I need to know how you want us to respond, Mr. President."

General Pike at the Pentagon cut in, "We're under attack! The Capitol District is under attack. A barrage of cruise missiles just hit Fort Meade, then another hit Anacostia-Bolling. I was told our local defensive systems around the Pentagon and the Capitol are engaging additional cruise missiles as we speak."

Before anyone else could speak, General Pike announced, "We're receiving reports of a cruise missile attack at Naval Submarine Base New London. Oh, damn, we're getting reports of attacks happening across the entire East Coast, Mr. President. It looks like nearly all our Air, Army, and Navy bases are being hit by cruise missiles."

Everyone fell silent for a second as they processed what the Pentagon had just told them.

"That can't be possible," blurted General Barrett from NORAD. "We aren't showing any cruise missiles heading toward any of your bases."

"San Diego and Hawaii are now reporting a massive cruise missile attack against the naval, air, and Marine bases," General Pike announced.

"We aren't showing any cruise missiles heading toward our bases!" General Barrett shouted in frustration.

"General Barrett, you need to have your early-warning systems do a hard reboot or figure this out," Admiral Thiel ordered. "We are deaf and blind right now. We don't even know if any of those missiles are nuclear."

Wilson couldn't believe what he was hearing. The military had so many redundant systems in place. Something like this shouldn't happen. *Is their AI able to penetrate all of our systems?* he wondered.

"Wait a second. I don't understand this," General Barrett said aloud. "We're talking with the base commander at Dyess, in Texas. Their base should be getting slammed with cruise and ballistic missiles, but he's telling me nothing's happening. The base commander at Barksdale is reporting the same—no explosions, no missile impacts."

"What?!" Admiral Thiel barked angrily. "We ordered a counterstrike against the Chinese Navy and Cuba because they fired first on our bases. Are you now telling us that not only did our early-warning systems not detect the attack currently underway along the East and West Coasts, but now this Chinese first strike wasn't real? You realize we attacked China and Cuba over this!"

The President then stood up. He motioned for everyone to stay seated as he paced behind the chairs. Finally, he turned to address them all. "Listen. Something clearly went wrong. Our systems must have been hacked—there's no other explanation for what's happened. The Chinese knew if certain actions happened, then we would counter those actions, which we have. Whether or not it's their super-AI that did this doesn't really matter right now. We got snookered. No way around it. The PLA played us. They were willing to sacrifice a few pawns to make us look like the aggressors, and they succeeded. What we have to figure out right now is how we respond to what's just happened.

"So, what do we do next? Because right now, our bases on the West and East Coasts are clearly being hammered, so we need to act. So, what should our next move be?"

Wilson was the first to speak, "I think at this point, Mr. President, you're in for a penny, you're in for a pound. There is no point in denying what happened, and there's no purpose in delaying our military action now that the enemy is alert to it. We should move forward with Operation Ortsac II. I know many of the ground units aren't ready, but that doesn't mean we can't unleash the Air Force and Navy on them."

Admiral Thiel nodded. "It pains me to say it, Mr. President, but I believe Wilson is right. The cat's out of the bag at this point. We need to react swiftly because the Chinese currently do have missiles on Cuba that can and will hit the US. We need to neutralize those threats before they become a real problem for us."

The President sighed audibly before he turned to his advisors. "Issue the orders. We are a full go for Operation Ortsac II. Take their ability to hurt our country out and let's prepare to invade as soon as possible. In the meantime, have the Navy hunt down and sink any Chinese warships they can find. Tell our sub force it's time to go hunting."

Chapter Twenty-Eight
Death Dealers

94th Fighter Squadron
Eglin AFB, Florida

The chatter in the mission room was one of excitement, anger, frustration, and anxiety. Major Ian "Racer" Ryan couldn't believe the situation.

They had just received a surprise FRAGO to get their squadron airborne and ready to support a major bombing campaign that was about to start over Cuba. To say it caught many of them by surprise was an understatement—especially after the early-morning reports of their own base coming under a cruise missile attack, after which word had come down that it was a gremlin in the radar ghosting them and they weren't under attack after all.

That attack alarm going off at three in the morning had not only startled Ian, it had terrified his wife and their six kids. What had hurt him most was that he had to leave his family and race to the flight line to see if he needed to get his bird airborne. By the time they'd learned the missile attack was a false alarm half an hour later, Ian, along with most of his squadron, had already been in the air. They'd landed shortly afterward. The aircrews worked overtime getting the planes refueled, mechanically ready and kitted out with real wartime combat loads.

Ian had an hour to go home and check on his family before he was told to report back to the squadron ready room to receive his next set of orders. His kids were terrified. Ian told his wife to throw the kids in the van and head to her parents' house in Tennessee—they'd sort it out when it was safe to return home in a few days.

It was tough saying goodbye to her and their little munchkins, who ranged in ages from nine months to nine years old. They'd hugged and cried as they said their goodbyes.

Ian had a good cry on the way back to the squadron ready room. Once he parked his car, though, he flicked a switch inside his brain and turned those emotions off. It was time to put his war face on and do his part to protect his family and his country.

Like the other pilots hanging out in the ready room waiting for the mission brief, Ian tried to learn anything he could about this crazy situation they found themselves in by perusing the latest headlines on Google. A major who'd just completed a staff officer rotation at the JIOCEUR, or Joint Intelligence Operations Center Europe, had gotten one of his friends there to send them an initial summary. The folks in Germany were six hours ahead of them, so they had already been at work when everything had kicked off.

"Hani, read the bullet points out loud to everyone," one of the captains said as everyone tried to crowd around him to read his computer screen.

"Sure thing. Everyone, stand back, I'll give the initial headlines. I'll print off a couple copies while we wait on the mission brief to start," Major Hans "Hani" Riggens said. Hani had been assigned to be Ian's new wingman while he readjusted to being a flyer again. Clearing his throat, Hani announced, "Chinese media is claiming one of their Panamax freighters off the coast of Italy was attacked by the Italian frigate *Carlo Bergamini* and sunk. No reports of survivors yet. The Italian government is disputing this claim, saying the *Carlo Bergamini* did not fire on the Chinese freighter."

"What the hell is going on?" grumbled one of the pilots as he walked into the room. A few others shushed him. They wanted to hear more.

"Chinese state media is reporting the German frigate *Rheinland-Pfalz* attacked the Chinese frigate *Binzhou* off the Gulf of Aden near the Somalia coast. The *Binzhou* and the corvette *Weihai* returned fire on the German frigate, sinking her. The Chinese Navy has reported thirty-eight casualties on the *Binzhou* and nine casualties on the *Weihai*. The German military has denounced the attack from their ship, insisting their ship did not attack the Chinese vessels."

Before Hani could continue, a loud voice boomed from behind them.

"Ten-hut!" came the voice of the squadron's XO.

Everyone stood at attention until they were told to take their seats in front of the whiteboard for the mission brief.

Their squadron commander walked in along with a couple of mission briefers—someone from the intel shop, the mission commander, and another from some other section.

"Listen up, people. I will not sit here and try to explain what's happened over the last four hours. What I do know is this—we've been given the go order by POTUS to initiate hostilities against the People's

Liberation Army Air Force, ground forces, and the Cuban military," the mission commander announced.

"As we speak, B-52s out of the Dakotas are on their way to their launch points. When they reach their lines of control, they'll wait until we set up our combat air patrol position over Cuba and the Straits of Florida. If the Cubans or Chinese decide they want to go after our bombers, then we'll be in position waiting for them.

"Shortly after the heavies release their missiles, they'll return to base to reload and repeat. Once the missiles are inbound, the B-2s will head in and finish off whatever air defense units the heavies missed. Now, what I'm about to tell you is highly classified and shall *not* leave this room. When we take up station over Cuba, two B-21 Raiders will be joining us."

Ian heard some of the others murmur and whisper at the mention of the mythical Air Force B-21s.

The mission commander held his hands up to try to stop the chatter. "That's right. Unicorns *do* exist, and some of you may actually get a chance to see it," he said jovially. When everyone had quieted down, he continued, "Aside from providing CAP over the island and protecting the bombers, our secondary mission is to make sure the Raiders reach their targets and slip away. Chances are, none of us will even know it's in the area, and that's a good thing. But should they get discovered or run into trouble, the Raiders become our new mission—protect them at all costs."

Racer raised his hand. "Do we know what their mission is? We could position a pair of fighters in that area to make sure they're nearby should they run into a problem."

The mission commander didn't say anything right away. He seemed to be contemplating what he should tell them. "Tell you what, Racer, you and your wingman stay behind. You will be assigned escort duty for the Raider. I'll tell you what their target is, but no one else. That's all I got, people. Let's get out to the flight line and get airborne. Sunrise is in an hour. This will be a long day, so pace yourselves. Dismissed."

When everyone had filed out of the room, it was just the mission commander, Racer, and Hani.

"OK, you two, there are two Raiders that'll be used over Cuba. The one you're being assigned to protect is going for a decapitation strike. Intel on the ground has a bead on where the Cuban leader and the Chinese military commander are most likely hiding out. Once hostilities started a few hours ago, intel said these individuals headed off to the locations the Raider is going to hit," the mission commander explained.

"I don't have the bomber's exact location or when it'll be hitting its targets, but what I can do is tell you roughly where you need to be positioned and ready to assist should you need to. Keep in mind, gentlemen, the Chinese and the Cubans have really fortified this island when it comes to air defense. They've already engaged and shot down an F-15E out of Homestead that was scrambled to provide some fighter cover over Southern Florida. Things could get crazy up there."

The two pilots nodded and then headed off to the van that would take them to the flight line.
****

Sitting on the parking ramp, Ian waited for his turn to take his place on the taxi ramp. The entire place was clogged with squadron after squadron waiting to get airborne. The night sky over Florida and the Gulf was filling up with aircraft. Soon, it'd be daylight—a complete reversal of when they'd normally launch a mission like this—but Murphy's Law had struck, and they now had to deal with it. All Ian knew was this was more fighters and bombers in one place than he had ever seen.

The biggest concern Ian had was the SAMs all over Cuba. He'd never personally flown over a battlespace against an adversary that had a legitimate air force or SAM network. This would be a first for him.

He hoped for all their sakes that the stealth bombers and the cruise missile barrage the B-52s were about to unleash were able to lay a good hurt on the SAMs and thin them out a bit.

Ian's squadron of F-22s would fly ahead of the attack force and take up a combat air patrol position over Cuba. If enemy aircraft rose up to engage the bombers or the other aircraft involved in the initial waves, then it'd be their job to take them out before they even knew what had happened.

"Death Dealers Three and Four, you are cleared to taxi to runway one-niner," came the voice from the control tower.

"That's a good copy, Control. Taxiing to runway one-niner," Ian replied. He turned and saw Hani give him a thumbs-up.

Ian gave his Raptor a little juice, and it started moving. As he approached the end of the runway, he saw his wingman pull up next to him. They'd take off moments apart from each other.

"Death Dealers Three and Four, you are cleared for takeoff," came the voice from the control tower.

Ian didn't wait around once he'd been given the go. He moved into position. Turning his aircraft to face down the runway, he released the brakes and gave the aircraft as much power as he could, lighting up his afterburners. His aircraft shot down the runway like a missile, and in moments he was airborne.

Once in the air, Ian gained altitude rapidly. He reached a cruise altitude of ten thousand feet and then started looking for the tankers. Four tankers were waiting for them not too far from the base.

Ian's flight mates started lining up, one after another, to top off their tanks. Behind the Raptors was a squadron of Eagle drivers. They would stay closer to the coasts and help protect the bombers as they entered and left the battlespace. Once they had their fuel tanks topped off, they would climb to thirty-five thousand feet and take up their station over Cuba.

"Listen up, Death Dealers," said their mission commander. "We have two AWACS that'll be providing us with coverage over the Gulf, Florida, and Cuba. You will break off into your hunter-killer teams and move to your assigned boxes. When you run out of ordnance or fuel, radio in your status before leaving your assigned box. When we're getting close to leaving our station, our sister squadron, the 27th, will take our place. Remember, pace yourselves. This will be a long couple of days. Out."

With their pep talk finished, the mission commander ordered them to their assigned boxes. For Ian and his wingman, that meant Pinar del Río, a mountainous region in the western part of the island that was rumored to be where the Chinese had set up their command-and-control function. Once the site had been hit, they'd transition over to central Havana. The Raider was going after a command-and-control bunker deep underneath the Ministry of Interior building. Once those targets had been hit, if they still had fuel and missiles, they would continue to loiter over the area until it was time to swap out with the next squadron.

"You ready for this, Racer?"

286

Turning to his right, Ian saw his wingman, Major Hans "Hani" Riggens. With their running lights off, it was somewhat hard to make him out, but the predawn light was helping.

"About as ready as I'm going to be, Hani. You?"

"Hell yeah. It feels good to be back in the air again," he replied excitedly.

Hani had only been with the squadron for two months. He had recently requalified on the F-22 and had just been getting back up to speed when hostilities had broken out. Doing a check ride every three months for two years had been tough on the guy. Unfortunately, every pilot had to pull staff duty somewhere if he wanted to rise through the ranks. Hani had been lucky enough to get his at a joint command, so he checked two boxes off on that one.

As they flew out over the Gulf, their screens filled up with friendlies. The attack force was moving in.

Hani broke into Ian's thoughts. "Damn, Racer. Check out Cuba. My RHAW is going crazy right now. I don't think I've ever seen that many enemy radars light up at once like that. You think it'll help them or make them easier to find and kill?"

The radar, homing, and warning system or RHAW told the pilots what threats were in the area.

"DD Three, DD Four, Big Bird Two. We're tracking four J-11s near Mariel. Sending you the targeting data now. How copy?" came the voice from their AWACS further behind them.

"This is DD Three, that's a good copy. Moving to engage," Racer replied for them both.

"Hani, when we get in range, go ahead and engage them. I'll fly overwatch for you," Racer ordered.

Ian wanted the kills himself, but he also knew Hani was getting back into the flying saddle again. It was more important for his wingman to gain his confidence back than it was for him to score a kill.

"Um, OK. Are you sure?" asked Hani.

"There'll be plenty of fighters for me to shoot at," Racer replied. "Now let's take these bastards out. We have no idea where the Raider is or how close those fighters are to it."

The two pilots angled their aircraft in for the attack. They still had their active radars off. The AWACS fed targeting data to them from further back. Hani opened his missile bay under the belly of the aircraft and then activated two AIM-120 AMRAAM missiles. He made sure they had a lock on the targets and then depressed the pickle button twice, releasing the missiles.

"Fox Three," Hani called out. He paused, then repeated, "Fox Three." The two missiles streaked out after the enemy aircraft. As soon as Hani released the missiles, the pilots of the enemy aircraft apparently knew they had been locked onto and began evasive measures.

Hani closed his missile bay doors and pulled away from the scene of the crime in case someone spotted him. Racer was flying in the trail position and had a good view of the two missiles as they raced toward their targets.

The J-11s broke hard toward the ground as they increased in speed. It appeared they were trying to lose the missiles in the ground clutter below. Not a bad strategy, but the AIM-120 had been improved a lot over the years, so this wasn't likely to work.

"Hey, we got a problem, Racer," Hani said frantically over the radio.

Racer was already on it. Several additional ground radars not far from them had been activated. A pair of HQ-9 or Red Banner-9 SAMs went active with their search radars.

These Red Banner surface-to-air missile systems were particularly nasty because they integrated multiple types of radar systems into their overall tracking process. This allowed the operators to see a host of different types of radar signatures. The main radar was the LLQ-305B, which employed sixty 350mm waveguide feeds, allowing it to attack dozens of threats at the same time.

The real threat to the Raptors and the stealth bombers, though, came from the integration of the YLC-20 passive sensor. This last radar configuration incorporated a sensitive system the Czech Republic had built as part of a secretive NATO project to detect and intercept stealth aircraft. The Chinese had gotten a hold of this system in 2006 and reverse engineered it, and it had been integrated into the HQ-9 radar systems in 2015. The YLC-20 passive sensor had been specifically built to counter the American F-22, F-35, and B-2 stealth aircraft.

"I see it," Racer replied, stress in his voice as he tried to gain some altitude and put distance between himself and those two SAMs trying to track him.

"Splash one!" called out Hani in excitement. "It looks like one of the guys evaded the other missiles. Should we attack him again?"

Hani and Racer's aircraft had passed twenty-eight thousand feet when both of their threat boards lit up.

"Damn it! That ground system locked us up. Go to afterburner and climb. See if we can somehow shake him," Racer called out.

He angled his aircraft up sixty degrees and increased power. His speedometer was now passing twelve hundred miles per hour.

"He's off me. He lost missile lock. I'll come around and see if I can find that J-11 and get another missile lock on him," Hani called out as he turned his aircraft back toward the ground below and started searching for the Chinese aircraft.

"DD Three, Big Bird Two. We're tracking eight additional J-11 aircraft taking off to join the fighters already in the air. We're also tracking two flights of six J-10 aircraft taking off from Fidel Air Base. How copy?" The AWACS operator probably had no idea Racer was trying to shake the missile lock from a ground-based SAM right now. All he knew was they were closest to the enemy aircraft trying to join the fray of the battle.

"That's a good copy. I'm being engaged by ground-based SAMs—please pass the target package to another hunter team. Out," Racer replied.

Ah crap. They fired a missile, Racer realized. *Damn it, that's more than a single missile.*

"Hani, I'm in trouble. They must have a decent enough lock on me. They fired three missiles at me. Not sure what they are, but I'll take them high and then outrun them if I can. I'll link up with you once I shake them." The last outcome Racer wanted was to attract one of these missiles.

"Go high and then dive to the deck. See if you can't outmaneuver them," Hani called back. He was already angling in to finish off that original J-11 before more aircraft joined the fray.

Looking at his radar display, Racer saw the missiles closing the distance between him fast. If memory served him, these bad boys had a speed of Mach 4.2 with a range of two hundred kilometers.

Twenty-three kilometers and closing...

Not recalling if the SAM fired radar-homing or heat-seeking missiles, Racer dispersed a chaff canister along with a batch of flares before he banked his aircraft hard to the left and dove in a hard-arcing spinning move, hoping the missiles would either go for one of his countermeasures and explode or sail right past him.

The first missile sailed right through the countermeasures, not exploding. It kept going straight like it was going to fly off into orbit. The second missile went for the chaff cloud that had fully expanded out. That missile exploded harmlessly a few kilometers away. The third missile also missed, but this one was now in the process of making a course correction that would lead it back down and after Racer's Raptor.

Being conscious of his fuel expenditures, Racer let gravity do most of the work as he was still angled into a steep dive. His threat warning systems came on with a new warning.

"Hani, I've got more trouble. Those freaking SAM radars vectored in some of those new J-11s that joined the fun. If I have to bail, I need you to make sure you plot where I go down so the CSAR can find me."

"Hey, hey, don't talk like that, Racer. We'll get you out of this. I splashed that other J-11. I'm repositioning to go after that next group. Right now, let's focus on keeping you alive as the bait while I swoop in and take 'em out," Hani countered in a soft and reassuring tone.

"Missile warning. Missile warning," the electronic voice in his helmet started blaring. *That's all I needed, more missiles*, thought Racer.

Racer noticed the new missiles weren't coming from the ground. These were coming from the enemy fighters. They had fired four Thunderbolt missiles. The PL-15 missiles were their state-of-the-art next-generation active-radar-guided long-range missiles. They had a dual-stage booster, allowing them to reach speeds of Mach 4 with an unheard-of range of three hundred kilometers.

Racer banked his aircraft hard to the right this time as he leveled out his fighter at two thousand feet. He tried to get as close to a ridgeline and valley as possible, hoping he might be able to lose some of the missiles among the ground clutter or maybe get one or more of the high-flying missiles to slam into the ridge as he maneuvered out of the way.

What concerned Racer most about this missile wasn't its range or speed—it was the missile's endurance. A range of three hundred kilometers meant it had a lot of fuel. It could chase him around the area until it either got lucky and blew him up or collided with an object.

As the first two missiles got within ten kilometers of his Raptor, Racer rolled to the left as he increased speed. At this point he was headed right for the side of a ridge. With his collision warning alarm screaming in his ear and warning lights flashing on his HUD, he pulled up hard and lit his afterburner.

Two of the PL-15 missiles blew up in the trees below. One of the missiles pulled up, but it sailed right under Racer and kept going. The fourth missile exploded a few hundred feet behind his Raptor.

Racer felt his aircraft shake hard from the explosion. He saw a couple of cracks in his canopy from the explosion and realized if his canopy had taken a few pieces of shrapnel, then chances were his aircraft had as well.

As he leveled the Raptor out, several yellow warning lights warned of the sustained damage, including hydraulic fluid leaking in one wing. His left rear stabilizer was sluggish too.

"Missile warning. Missile warning," the Raptor system controls blared.

Racer looked around briefly, trying to figure out where this other missile was, when he spotted it. It was that damn HQ-9 missile from that SAM. It had circled back around and eventually found him. The ground radar still guided it to him.

Pulling hard on the stick, Racer tried to turn to the right and apply pressure to the throttle to get the heck out of there when the next warning came on.

"Eject, eject, eject," resounded the Raptor system controls.

Screw it, thought Racer.

Racer grabbed for the ejection handle and gave it a good pull. Moments later, his damaged canopy blew away from his fighter and his seat shot several hundred feet into the air and away from his Raptor.

The plane, his plane, flew on for another second or two before he saw the HQ-9 missile close the distance. Its proximity warhead then exploded, ripping his aircraft apart. Had he hesitated for even a second, chances were, he'd be dead. Luckily, his chute had opened, and he was now descending to the ground below. He knew he needed to do his best to stay out of sight until a CSAR team recovered him. He just hoped they'd be able to recover him sooner rather than later. He sure as hell didn't want to become a Chinese or Cuban prisoner.

Chapter Twenty-Nine
Black Unicorns

30,000 feet above Cuba
28th Bomb Squadron "Black Death"

The B-21 Raider sliced through the cool night air of the Caribbean, its deadly cargo hidden within.

"Wow, the sky is lit up with fighters, bombers, cruise missiles, and enemy search radars. I don't think I've ever seen anything like this before," Exotic said aloud.

Colonel Josh "Miser" Grimes saw the radar screen and agreed with a nod. In all his years flying, he'd never seen such a large gathering of American warplanes and enemy radars. The US Air Force and Navy were about to put the smack down on the Chinese and the Cubans. They might have sucker-punched the US, but they were about to learn that the Americans had more than one way to make their enemies feel the pain.

Turning his head to look at his copilot, or co for short, Miser pointed down at the radar scope. "You see those? More than a hundred Greyhounds are heading in ahead of us. They'll impact in the next ten to twenty mikes all across the island. When that happens, Exotic, they won't know what hit them. I just hope they'll see reason and throw in the towel quickly and not make us have to invade and occupy them."

Exotic turned to look at the more senior pilot as she asked, "After all of the preparations they've clearly put into this, do you really think they'll surrender?"

Miser thought about that for a moment before replying, "You may be right. I think the Cubans won't last long. The Chinese, on the other hand, they'll fight. How well they'll fight...that remains to be seen. The ChiComs haven't fought any recent wars, so there is that."

Ten minutes went by as they flew in relative silence. Each of them ran through their normal duties, getting the bomber ready to penetrate some of the most heavily defended airspace in the world.

To aid in their penetration of the airspace, they took a surreptitious route to their target. Instead of taking the most direct route across the Gulf of Mexico, they flew across the southern half of the US and approached Cuba from the eastern Caribbean to penetrate from this angle. The thought was that the Chinese radars would be facing the US, not the eastern or southern Caribbean.

Until a few weeks earlier, the US military and intelligence community had had no idea that the island of Cuba had been turned into an unsinkable aircraft carrier. What astounded Miser was how they had done this without anyone knowing until it was too late. The ChiComs had ringed the island with multiple layers of surface-to-air missiles, radars, anti-aircraft guns, antiship missiles, and a variety of missile defense weapons to protect it all. It was like peeling away the layers of an onion to get at the specific target you wanted.

Miser mentally compared this to the opening days of the Iraq War but decided it was more like attacking Hanoi or Berlin during the height of those wars. This was a heavily fortified target that would require a lot of trickery and luck to take out.

A couple of alarms started buzzing as their passive electronic detection systems picked up threats to the aircraft. Minutes later, their own radar and targeting computers populated with new real-time data coming in from the shared link with the AWACS and the satellites above, at least the ones that were still working. Even the satellite network was coming under attack.

Exotic chimed in, "We've synced with the God-elements. I'm starting to receive new data."

The so-called God-elements consisted of the targeting and radar data coming in from both the AWACS further away in the Gulf, the remaining satellites above them, and the RQ-170 Sentinel stealth drone loitering over Cuba. The combined picture these assets provided them and the B-2s was extremely comprehensive.

It took a moment for their computers to catch up. "Wow, this is good but scary," Exotic commented. "The threat data from God One is starting to come in. Oh, damn, that's not good, Miser. It's showing six groups of multiple—probably four—aircraft spread across the island. We have three groups of J-10s, and three J-11s. Two of the groups have their search radars on, the other four are passive. I'm also showing six active Red Banner-9 radar sites in search mode." Exotic paused for a second before adding, "It looks like they might be expecting some company."

Laughing at the comment, Miser replied, "I think you might be right, Exotic. You can bet if the Sentinels found us six active radar sites, there are probably a dozen or more in passive mode waiting to go active. Make sure you program in those radar sites. See if they match the other sites in our target package. If they don't, then add them so we can hit them later. Once we start our attack run, things will get crazy."

"It looks like the B-2s are approaching the line of control," Exotic called out as the blue icons denoting their fellow bombers approached from the Gulf.

Miser added, "Yeah, we should be hitting our targets before they get too close to Cuba. The PLA's radar and C&C should be down, giving them and the rest of the bomber force a clean shot into the country."

Exotic nonchalantly called out, "Greyhounds appear to be hitting. I'm showing a string of enemy radars going offline."

They flew on for a few more minutes, the Sentinels above them continuing to feed them more data. Since the ChiComs had started going after the US and European satellite network a few hours ago, the military had switched more and more over to their drone fleet for surveillance.

"Approaching target. Do you want me to start going through the arming procedures?" Exotic asked, nervousness and excitement in her voice. This would be her first real-life bombing mission.

"Yeah, that'd be great, Exotic," Miser replied, not taking his eyes off the screens in front of him. "I'm getting the first target loaded up now. Double-check the coordinates while you're at it. We won't be using laser designators for this run, so those coordinates have to be accurate."

Their first target was a command-and-control site located fifty kilometers outside of Havana. They planned to strike the bunker with two GBU-28 bunker-busting bombs. Once they hit the bunker complex, they'd move down their target list, hitting eight radar sites across the country and one more bunker complex under the Ministry of Interior. That last location was where intelligence believed the new Cuban president had been relocated.

When those sites were taken out, they'd look for an updated target package from the Sentinel elements. Inside the bomb bay, they were packing four of the five-thousand-pound bunker-buster bombs for the two high-value targets. In addition to the big bombs, they were carrying twenty of the much smaller GBU-38s, which were five-hundred-pound Joint Direct Attack Munitions or JDAMs.

The two B-21s would stay on station over Cuba for most of the first few hours of the attack. As additional ChiCom and Cuban radar sites turned on to replace the ones being taken out, the Raiders would hit them before they could react. This was all part of the SEAD or Suppression of Enemy Air Defenses missions the war planners had developed.

If the B-21s could keep the enemy's eyes closed, then the B-2s, B-1s, and other attack aircraft could wipe out the Cuban and PLA Air Forces, removing them as a threat. If the Cubans and ChiComs refused to surrender after a few days of heavy bombing, then the Marines and Airborne forces would be sent in to clear them out.

Exotic strapped her oxygen mask back on as they approached the target. It was showtime.

"We're coming up on the target," she announced as their icon neared the blinking target icon on the map.

Miser replied, "Confirmed. Go ahead and arm the first set of bombs and get the doors opened. We're weapons-free in sixty seconds."

Moments later, the aircraft buffeted a bit from the loss of their aerodynamically smooth underbelly. The lights for the bomb bay doors turned from red to green, letting them know they were open. As if they couldn't already tell from the way the aircraft was flying.

"Bombs are armed and ready for release," Exotic relayed.

Miser gripped the flight stick a little tighter as he prepared to drop the first-ever bombs from a B-21 on a hostile nation. Moving his thumb over to the pickle, he depressed the release button once, then twice.

In fractions of a second, the electrical current was sent from the flight stick to the targeting system. It then transmitted another message to the weapon rack holding the GBU-28s that it was time to release the bombs. When the two bombs fell free of the aircraft, the B-21 immediately handled a little softer. It was now ten thousand pounds lighter.

"Weapons-free," announced Miser, tension in his voice.

"Confirmed, weapons-free. Closing outer doors," announced Exotic as she depressed the button to seal them back up and make sure they kept their stealth system intact.

Miser turned the big black bird to head toward their next target, the Ministry of Interior in the center of Havana. They'd only be dropping a single GBU-28 on this target to minimize the potential for collateral damage.

At this altitude, it'd take a few minutes for the bombs to reach their target. By that point, they'd be near Havana. Enemy radar sites were still going offline. A steady barrage of Greyhounds pummeled the known sites and the ones currently turned on. It wasn't a completely one-sided affair, though. Miser and Exotic watched more than four dozen missiles streak out toward the American warships.

"What are those?" Exotic asked as they observed a new track of missiles leaving an area not far from the command post they'd just nailed.

Miser furrowed his brow at the missile tracks; he wasn't sure right off the bat. As the limited telemetric of the missiles posted, it dawned on him—these missiles were being fired at the homeland.

Returning his gaze to the windshield and some other screens, he said, "I'd say those are land-attack missiles. They're probably going for our air bases. It's what I'd do."

His co didn't say anything for a moment, then she replied softly, "I never thought I'd see the day when our country would be attacked by enemy missiles. I thought we joined the Air Force and the Navy to keep these kinds of threats away from America."

"You heard what happened to Langley Air Base and Norfolk," Miser commented. "Heck, I heard they even hammered Fort Stewart in Georgia."

"I still can't believe this is happening," replied Exotic anxiously. "I mean, how in the heck did we not know those ships and missiles were out there? Someone seriously screwed up if you ask me."

"Let's worry about doing our jobs and stay focused on our mission. We can't control anything more than that, so let's do the best job we can and take out these targets."

The two flew on in silence for another ten minutes, getting steadily closer to Havana, the last primary target they had to take out. Once that was gone, they'd be on their own to go after enemy radar sites as they popped up.

A few more radars went down around the city, which made them feel a little better. More of the possible threats to their bomber were going away. Several of the enemy fighters had gotten into quite the dogfight with the Raptors. Miser and his co were astounded when they saw four of the F-22s get shot down—that wasn't supposed to happen, either. Even a pair of F-35s had been taken out by enemy SAMs.

"We're two minutes out from the target. I'll start the arming sequence," Exotic announced.

Miser acknowledged and kept his eyes focused on the threat board. He was starting to feel a bit better. Two more enemy radars had just gone offline, further reducing the likelihood of their being detected.

"Sixty seconds out. I'm opening bomb bay doors now," Exotic relayed.

The aircraft buffeted as their aerodynamics changed. Their smooth underbelly was gone for the time it'd take for them to release their bombs.

"Ten seconds," Exotic called out.

Miser saw the icon telling him it was time to release his bomb. He depressed the pickle once, releasing the bunker-buster to do its business. As soon as the bomb was out, he turned the bomber slightly, not realizing Exotic hadn't closed the bomb door yet.

A pair of new enemy radars came on and so did several warning bells.

Oh crap, that's not good, Miser thought as the alarms indicated a ground base's radar trying to lock on to them. Two more radars then turned on and they started getting hit with more radar beams.

"This isn't good, Exotic. They're trying to triangulate us," said Miser.

"How can they do that? We're about as small as a marble right now," replied Exotic.

"We are, but I screwed up. I turned the aircraft before you had the bomb doors fully closed. I think they got a partial reading from our belly and now they're turning on more radars to pinpoint where we are," Miser explained.

Reaching for the throttle, Miser gave the plane a lot more thrust. He also started climbing and banked the aircraft out toward the Gulf. He wanted to put some altitude and distance between those radar sites in hopes that they might lose whatever little bead they had on them.

"Exotic, start looking up the frequency and call signs for some of those destroyers down there. If those enemy radars get a lock on us and fire, they may be able to fire an interceptor and take it out for us. If not, then we'll go for a morning swim."

His co only groaned in response as she reached for a notepad. It had the call signs and frequencies of some ships and aircraft they could contact if they got in trouble.

Looking out the window, Miser saw they had left land. They were now officially in the Straits of Florida.

"Missile warning. Missile warning."

"Crap! They fired a missile...scratch that. They fired two missiles," Exotic called out, fear in her voice.

"Hang on, I'm going to try something," Miser said.

He reached over and flicked several switches on. These were their electronic countermeasure pods. They protruded ever so slightly from the belly of the aircraft and remained dormant to minimize the potential of a sophisticated tracking system isolating their position based on any electronic emissions. Seeing as they now had two advanced surface-to-air missiles racing after them, staying electronically silent really didn't make any sense.

"Try raising one of those *Arleigh Burke*s down there. See if they can't intercept those missiles. At current speeds and distance, I'm showing we have five minutes until they reach us."

Exotic switched her radio over to the frequency the Navy ships were operating on. She eventually got through to someone. After a short authentication process, they said they were tracking the missiles and they agreed to fire a couple of interceptors. They weren't optimistic about intercepting them, not at their current speeds, though. They did recommend trying to fly the bomber closer to them.

While that was taking place, a Navy EA-18G Growler operating nearby was being vectored toward them. The pilot had been told to accelerate to max speed toward their coordinates. The hope was the Growler's advanced suite of electronic countermeasures might be able to spoof the enemy missiles and cause them to miss. The Growler carried a much larger suite of ECM tools than the Raider.

The Growler's Active Electronically Scanned Array or AESA was a unique piece of technology that allowed the EWO or electronic warfare officer in the back seat of the aircraft to focus the jamming power exactly where it was needed. In this case, they needed that jamming power directed at the two missiles homing in on the Air Force's multibillion-dollar black unicorn.

"Two minutes until missile impact," Exotic called out, now on the radio with the Growler pilots.

Miser watched as the first SM missile interceptor missed, sailing right past the missile.

"Splash one!" Exotic called out excitedly.

Thank God they got one of them. One more to go, Miser thought. He honestly couldn't believe the Navy could shoot one of them down like that. He supposed it did help that he was flying in a relatively flat trajectory, which meant the HQ-9 missile was as well.

"Sixty seconds to impact," the warning system announced in their helmets.

At this point, the Growler was less than five miles from their position. They were doing their darnedest to jam that enemy missile.

"Splash one!" Exotic yelled out in wild excitement. Miser swore if she wasn't strapped to her seat, she probably would have jumped out of it in excitement.

"Hey, calm down. Stay on your systems. We're not out of the woods yet," Miser had to remind her. They were still being actively hunted by those enemy ground radars. However, two more of them had gone offline as another volley of Greyhounds slammed into them.

"Unicorn One, Gauntlet Six. I've been instructed to stick to you like white on rice. What's the plan? Where are we headed next?" asked the pilot of the Growler who had saved their bacon.

Exotic looked at Miser. "We aren't going back in there, are we?"

Miser could tell she was scared and nervous. He also knew if he said they were going back in, she'd comply and do her best to complete their mission.

"Gauntlet Six, Unicorn Actual. We will RTB. Can you give us an escort to Barksdale?" Miser asked.

There was a short pause before the other pilot came on. "Unicorn Actual, Barksdale took a beating. They're currently nonoperational. All heavies are being redirected to Moody Air Force Base. If you have enough fuel, you could try for a bomber base."

Enough fuel? Couldn't we just top off our tanks and head back home? Miser thought.

"Gauntlet Six, are there any fuel stations nearby? We'd kind of like to head back home," Miser inquired.

"Unicorn Actual, three tanks were shot down twenty minutes ago, and another six destroyed on the ground at MacDill. The AWACS loitering over Robins was also shot down, along with the other one near Corpus Christi."

"What the hell? How did we lose all those aircraft?" Exotic said aloud to herself.

"Gauntlet Six, that's a good copy. We'll head to Moody and see what they want us to do after we land. Thank you again for the help and now the escort. Oh, by the way—how did we lose so many aircraft this far from Cuba?"

A short pause ensued before they got a reply. "Unicorn Actual, an unknown number of J-20s slipped through our defenses and got in close enough to shoot two of the AWACS and several tankers down."

"Thank you for the update. Let's continue on to Robins, then, and see what they want us to do next."

Turning to look at his co, Miser said, "Well, I guess that's it for us. I can tell you this—until we're able to take out more of those air defense radars, there's no way they'll risk us going back in there again. Not after we nearly got shot down."

For the next couple of hours, they flew in relative quiet. Neither of them said much. They were running through the mission in their minds—what had gone right, what had gone wrong, and what they would do differently next time.

They knew once they landed, they'd be debriefed for hours on end. This was the first combat mission of America's newest bomber. In addition to the Air Force reps wanting to know everything about the mission and the aircraft performance, the manufacturer would want to know as much as they could. This mission had given all parties involved the chance to work out any previously unknown bugs in the system.

Judging by how surprisingly effective the HQ-9 radar system was, Miser had to believe they had lost a lot of aircraft over the last few hours. Heck, they had seen several Raptors and Lightnings fall victim. If they'd had a problem, he hated to think how poorly the B-2s and any nonstealth aircraft had performed.

Chapter Thirty
Collateral Damage

US Strategic Command
Omaha, Nebraska

The leaders of the United States held their third emergency meeting of the day, the mood bleak in the dry, frigid air of the command bunker.

Will this day never end? thought Blain Wilson as he snuck a glance at the clock on the wall. The clock bar, as Wilson called it, showed the times across the world: NATO headquarters in Brussels, London, Washington, D.C., Omaha, Hawaii, and Tokyo.

Right now, the clock said it was 1:32 in the morning of the second day of the war. Things couldn't be going worse if they had intentionally planned this out themselves.

"For God's sake, someone turn the damn temperature up in this room. I shouldn't have to wear a parka to these briefs," President Alton complained.

"Mr. President, the heads of state in NATO want to know what our next move is. They're looking for leadership and a strategy on our part," General Lisa Yeager said. She looked as tired and haggard as the rest of them.

Wilson could tell the President wasn't sure what to say or do, so he stepped in and asked a question that might help guide him. "General Yeager, what are the Europeans saying about the situation as it stands on their end? How are they responding to the deepfakes and this recent military attack by the Chinese?"

"There's a lot of confusion right now. The Germans insist that the *Rheinland-Pfalz* did not attack the Chinese naval vessels in the Gulf of Aden. They are furious these ships were sunk. The Chinese Navy announced three hours ago that they recovered forty-two sailors of the one hundred and thirty-four—they are officially classifying them as prisoners of war.

"In Italy, a Chinese self-unloading dry-bulk carrier freighter suffered a series of explosions and eventually sank off the coast of Gioia Tauro, where the freighter was originally heading. The Chinese are claiming the Italian frigate *Carlo Bergamini* attacked their freighter in international waters. What's caught everyone by surprise was how rapidly images of these naval engagements appeared on the internet. In each case, the video shows the German and Italian warships firing on the unsuspecting Chinese ships. In the case of the battle between the German and Chinese warships, the video is extremely believable. The videos are causing a lot of confusion within the EU about what really happened," General Yeager explained.

"Some leaders are even asking if the US intentionally attacked the Chinese and Cuba. I heard a report from an MP in the UK asking if these videos might actually be a false flag scenario being orchestrated by us to get NATO to side with the US against China."

"That's a load of crap," the President barked angrily. "What would we have to gain from doing something like that? I mean, Norfolk, Groton, Pearl Harbor, and San Diego got plastered. Is that something we'd do to ourselves? I don't think so."

Wilson had noticed President Alton becoming moodier than normal this last week. The election was just days away. Not only was America under the threat of attack, but the homeland had been hit multiple times over the last twenty-four hours, from cyberattacks and deepfakes to direct kinetic attacks on military installations and even a few cities. People were scared.

No one spoke for a moment. They were waiting to see if the President would add something more or allow them to continue providing more updates. Wilson nodded to Admiral Thiel for him to get them back on track.

"Mr. President," the admiral said to get his attention. "Perhaps the best course of action right now would be to end this meeting and let everyone get some rest. We can reconvene at, say, 0800 hours. That'll give us time to put together some better information on both our military situation and how we should respond going forward. The military is running on its current set of orders—I say we leave them be and let them continue to handle things. This short break will give General Yeager some additional time to work things out with our NATO allies."

The President's eyes looked bloodshot, and there were large bags underneath them. He looked tired and emotionally drained. He nodded slowly, agreeing with his senior advisor. "I think that's a good idea, Admiral. In the meantime, General Yeager, let the NATO members know that if they don't want to initiate Article Five, then we will. This has been a concerted and coordinated assault on Europe and America that had to take years to plan. We need to stand united in our response against them."

The President then stood, as did everyone else.

As he was leaving the room, Albert Abney, the President's Chief of Staff, signaled for everyone else to stay put. He wanted to talk with them all separately.

****

With the President now gone, Abney tore into the generals, admirals, and senior advisors. He was furious about how things had transpired these last four weeks and their inability to do anything to stop it. The Chinese had been running circles around the US and Europe with these deepfake videos spreading across the internet. Something needed to change, and it needed to change now.

Abney glared at Admiral Thiel as he spoke. "Admiral, as the Chairman of the Joint Chiefs, it is your job to advise the President on military matters and the defense of the nation. Under your watch, the homeland has come under multiple sustained attacks across numerous domains by a known adversary. I don't know whose fault it is, and I won't play the blame game either. I'm here to tell you all that, right now, you're not just failing the President, you're failing your nation."

Abney paused to look at everyone before he continued. "I know everyone is tired. I also know in a few days, the American people will pick a new leader: either Vice President Vickie Jackson or Congresswoman Maria Delgado will be the next woman to lead the nation. Depending on the outcome, some or all of you may be out of a job come January. But right now, it's all of us in this room deciding the fate of the nation and the world. We have to live up to the expectations our fellow citizens have of us. One of the candidates will inherit this war. We need to do our best to either end this war now, before it spreads further, so that a new president isn't left dealing with this, or ensure the new president is in a position to lead our country to victory."

Abney saw a few heads nod and he knew his message was getting through. "Admiral Thiel, what's happening in Cuba? Have we been able to neutralize the PLA's ability to attack the homeland, or should we expect more attacks?"

Admiral Thiel leaned forward. "The problem we're dealing with, Mr. Abney, is that the cruise missiles hitting our bases along the Gulf

Coast are being fired by these transporter erector launchers. The TEL vehicles can hide in the thick tree cover and vegetation, making them difficult to locate with satellites and drones. Then factor in that close to half of our satellite network has been either destroyed or compromised and our surveillance ability has been cut in half in the last twenty-four hours."

Shaking his head in frustration, Abney countered, "There has to be something we can do. We shouldn't be forced into taking these hits. That attack on MacDill Air Force Base in Tampa not only tore up the base— one of those cruise missiles went astray and landed downtown. It killed nearly a hundred civilians and injured many more. That is not acceptable, Admiral. We need a better solution."

"I agree, Mr. Abney," Admiral Thiel replied. "We're moving two more destroyers into the Gulf to help shoot these missiles down as they're fired. Once the ground operation starts, we'll be in a better position to hunt these launchers down and take them out." The man looked exhausted, like everyone else, as he reached for his cup of coffee.

Abney sighed as he looked at the tired faces. He knew they were trying their best. It just wasn't good enough. If there weren't an election next week, he'd probably recommend the President fire and replace them. Right now, that wouldn't be a good idea—not with the transition of one administration to another needing to take place very soon.

"OK, everyone. Let's get some sleep and be back here for our eight o'clock briefing. But seriously, get some sleep. None of you will be helpful to the President if you're exhausted and can't think straight. Your country needs you sharp," Abney said as the meeting broke up.
****

Florida Keys
3rd Battalion, 116th Field Artillery Regiment
Florida Army National Guard

"Hey, I think we're almost there," Staff Sergeant Hector Ramirez said as he pointed to a local sheriff car and a military police JLTV parked on the side of the road with their lights on. An MP and a deputy were directing military traffic to a side road that led to a large field or beach area off the main highway.

"I see it. Are they really going to have us set up out here?" asked Sergeant Rob Fortney.

Fortney was new to the unit, but not new to the Army. He'd finished a four-year stint on active duty not that long ago. He'd gotten out to leverage his GI Bill and pursue his true passion, becoming a police officer and then a detective like his dad and his grandfather. They had both served in the military before becoming peace officers, so it was kind of a Fortney family tradition.

"Who knows where they'll have us set up, Fortney?" Ramirez replied glumly. "All I know is thirty-six hours ago we were back home doing whatever we wanted. Now we're in this new nameless war."

Fortney thought Hector was a good guy and a decent squad leader. They lived not far from each other in Brandon, Florida. Hector's wife had given birth to their second child fifteen days ago, so he hadn't been the least bit thrilled when their unit, the 3-116th FAR, had been called up. They were part of Bravo Battery out of Dade City, Florida. Their unit was an M142 High Mobility Artillery Rocket System or HIMARS unit. Their rocket system could reach out and hit targets as far as three hundred kilometers away.

"Big Pine Key," Fortney commented as he read the road sign indicating where they were headed. "I've always wanted to check out the Keys. I never thought I'd be doing it in uniform."

"Actually, it appears this road leads us to Southeast Point," Ramirez countered.

Ahead of them, they saw several other HIMARS vehicles being guided to specific locations and told to park. Judging by how they were parking, they were being made ready to fire.

"Fortney, Ramirez. We need you to park your vehicle over there, near B-4, and then head over to the FDC for a briefing on what to do next," another sergeant shouted to them as they slowed down to hear his instructions.

They nodded and drove their vehicle to where they had been directed. As they got out, they saw another convoy of four vehicles approaching. There was one more HIMARS launcher and four ammo carriers. If they planned to start firing rockets soon, they'd need more ammo; this would be a long drive to fire off a single volley.

Approaching the headquarters vehicle, they saw some soldiers setting up the command tent and the Tactical Operation Center or TOC.

The Stryker vehicle acting as their FDC for the time being had the hatch down and a dozen soldiers standing around it. Ramirez and Fortney figured this must be the meeting they had been directed to attend.

The company commander explained to the group, "The rest of the battery should be arriving over the next ten to twenty minutes. I told the battalion we'd be operational to start firing in roughly an hour. I need you all to get your vehicles ready. I have no idea what our targets might be, but I need everyone to be ready to act."

He continued, "Everyone should have been issued live ammo back at the armory. Until now, you've all been told to keep your rifles unloaded. That's changed. We are now in THREATCON Delta. Weapons are always to be loaded with safeties on. We don't have any direct intelligence saying there's a threat to our unit yet. You can bet when and if we do start shooting, we'll be a prime target for any commando units they have operating CONUS.

"Once our fire mission is complete, we'll be moving to the next position. We'll reload the trucks once we reach the new site and then stand by to provide a follow-on strike. As you all know, we're shooting the brand-new MGM-168 Block V ATACMS because of their extreme range. Any mission we receive will be in excess of one hundred and twenty miles. I was told the Greenie Beanies are already in Cuba, hunting down targets for us to blow up. Let's make sure to send the Chinese and Cubans bastards seven hundred and fifty pounds of Florida love."

This last comment got a few laughs from the soldiers. They were all starting to get pumped up and feeling good about their preparation for their mission. Before the battery commander dismissed everyone, he added, "This is the real deal, gentlemen. A few hours ago, MacDill got plastered. A couple missiles even hit downtown Tampa. These guys aren't messing around, and they're attacking our homes. I need you all to stay frosty, heads on a swivel. Now, go get your trucks ready to fire. Dismissed."

Ramirez and Fortney went back to their vehicle. This would be the first time anyone in their unit fired the new Block V missile. When the US had left the Missile Technology Control Regime in 2020 with the Russians, the Army had gone to work on expanding the range of their ground-to-ground missile systems—they could now hit targets as far away as three hundred and eighty miles away with a seven-hundred-and-fifty-pound warhead.

"Hey, when's Davis getting here? He's supposed to be our gunner," asked Fortney.

Ramirez shrugged. He was too busy working on getting the vehicle ready to fire to care where their missing guy was. His mind was still back home, with his fifteen-day-old girl and his wife.

Shaking his head in frustration, Fortney shrugged it off. He had to keep reminding himself this was the National Guard, not the active duty. Not everyone lived on or near the base. Their missing man would catch up to the unit at some point.

When the warning order had gone out for them to report for a possible deployment, they had only been given two hours' notice. When they'd started showing up at the armory, they'd found the ammo carriers already there, loading them up with live rockets. The armorer had started issuing them their weapons and ammo. "Grab your helmets and your IBA and load them up in the trucks," he'd directed. "You'll be pulling out in an hour to head to the Keys—it's a long drive and the commander wants to get a jump on things. If you're missing any people, we'll leave someone behind with a couple of vans and they'll catch up."

As far as Fortney was concerned, this whole war was all screwed up from the word go. Come to think of it, everything that had gone on the last few months had been a complete flipping mess. It was like a never-ending circus going on in America and across the world lately. First the trade wars, then the virus, then the deepfakes...now a shooting war—Fortney wasn't sure when or how it would all stop now that it was rolling.

"Hey, Fortney. Get the targeting computer spun up while I get things ready out here," Ramirez ordered. "Make sure you're linked up with the FDC. If we're having a problem syncing the computers, then see if it's a problem with the data link on the SINCGARS. If you can't fix it yourself, go find someone from commo and see if they can help you." He was starting to return to his normal self as he fell back on muscle memory and their training.

Fortney nodded and climbed back into the vehicle. He probably knew better than most how to run one of these trucks. He'd spent four years in an active-duty HIMARS unit. Still, he liked working with people who knew the trade, even if they were weekend warriors.

It took Fortney close to five minutes to get the computer up and running and synced with the FDC. Fortunately, he knew a thing or two about the radios, so he handled most issues he encountered. Looking at the other trucks, he saw a couple of the commo guys doing their best to get everyone up on the right comms.

It was a challenge even on active duty getting all the guns and trucks synced up and on the same page. It was likewise a bit more complicated for the citizen soldiers who didn't work on or touch the equipment on a daily or even weekly basis to maintain those skills. Normally when a Guard unit deployed to a combat zone, they'd go through a couple months of retraining to freshen up their skills. Not this time—they were rolling out of their National Guard armories within hours of being given the go order.

Standing outside the vehicle, Fortney heard a lot of jet engines overhead. While he couldn't see exactly what was happening, he couldn't help but speculate about it. If he looked off into the Straits of Florida, he could sometimes see a missile or two launch from one of the Navy ships beyond the horizon. He'd catch a glimpse of the white contrails of the missiles streaking up into the sky to chase after their targets.

As the crow flies, they were twenty-two miles from NAS Key West. Word had it the Chinese had hammered the base hard during their counterattack the day before. In the distance, Fortney thought he could still make out streaks of black smoke coming from the direction of the base.

None of them knew much. They had only just arrived a few hours ago. What they did know was that the Chinese had the ability to reach out and hit the base from ninety miles away in Cuba. That told them they could get hit as well.

Two hours later, Staff Sergeant Ramirez and Sergeant Fortney were eating some food, trying to tease out information from a local business owner. The man owned a restaurant nearby and had brought over a ton of food for everyone. He told them of how the Chinese had hit the naval air station the other day with what he thought had to be fifteen or twenty missiles. He wasn't sure how many fighters or helicopters, if any, had been caught on the ground, but he thought he'd seen a few flaming wrecks.

What Fortney noticed right away about the guy, aside from the awesome food he'd brought them, was the sidearm he was carrying. He wasn't even trying to hide it. He was carrying a Springfield HD in a pistol holster on his right thigh. Not that Fortney had a problem with it—he was glad to see people exercising their right to bear arms. However, it made him realize that as soldiers, they had all somehow failed to protect this man, his family, and his business. The man felt he needed to carry a sidearm with him in public. For Fortney, that was a problem. It was his job to protect his country. Somewhere along the line, he and the leadership above him had failed in that basic duty, and now civilians were taking matters into their own hands.

"Fire mission! Fire mission! Fire mission! Everyone, man your vehicles and stand by for coordinates!" roared one of the FDC sergeants.

In an instant, everyone stopped what they were doing and ran for their vehicles. They hopped in the cabs and sealed the trucks up as they got the vehicles prepared to fire.

****

ODA 7322, Bravo Company
Soroa, Cuba

Sergeant First Class Rusten Currie put his field glasses down and reached for the map, analyzing it and then the location where those TEL vehicles were hiding. He thought he had the location identified on the map. Once he double-checked it, he passed it over to his counterpart to verify.

His partner, Sergeant First Class Mark Dawson, took the paper and the map from him. He looked at them both and then did a quick double-check of the terrain with the field glasses and then the map. Without saying a word, he nodded to Currie. They had the right location.

Reaching for the radio, Currie depressed the talk button. "Odin, Loki One. Fire mission. Three Dragons identified. How copy?"

Sixty seconds went by with no response—just long enough for Currie and Dawson to get nervous that their transmission might have been jammed, or their command element wasn't receiving.

The radio crackled softly in their earpieces.

"Loki One, Odin. Good copy. Three Dragons identified. Send coordinates. Over."

"Odin, coordinates are as follows: Charlie Uniform Five-Seven-Three-Niner-Seven-Three-Eight-Eight. Break. Dragons are hidden under dense jungle canopy. Break. Ten meters from nearest road. How copy?"

Currie was hoping they'd send a cruise missile to hit the site—nothing like a thousand pounds of high explosives to plaster the place.

Given that they were only in the middle of day two of the war, the Air Force was still having a hard time gaining air supremacy over the island. The Chinese surface-to-air missile systems were a hell of a lot better at ferreting out American stealth fighters than anyone had expected.

Until the Loki teams like Currie and Dawson from the 7th Special Forces Group found more of the enemy radar sites and these damn CJ-10 launcher vehicles, the Pentagon was leveraging cruise missiles as often as possible. The downside to using cruise missiles was that they took some time to spin up and get ready.

"Loki One, next Greyhounds come available in ninety mikes. Will a HIMARS strike work instead?" asked the operator on the other end.

Currie and Dawson both looked at each other and shrugged as if to say *Why not?*

"Odin, that's an affirmative. Break. The Dragons are spread out under the trees. Break. The HIMARS will need to plaster the area to hit them. Over."

A minute passed before they got a reply.

"Loki One, affirmative. Stand by for HIMARS strike. Request BDA poststrike. Out."

****

"Targeting data is coming in," Ramirez said. "Damn...this is a long shot. Looks to be two hundred and seventy kilometers, give or take." As he spoke, he prepared the truck to fire.

"Wow, I don't think I've ever fired a shot that far," Fortney commented, making sure the front shades of the truck were shut. They put their hearing protection on when the order to fire came.

"Firing missile," Ramirez said loudly as he relayed the orders.

Swoosh...

The missile fired, shaking the vehicle as the solid fuel motor kicked into overdrive and sent the missile on a Mach 3 journey. The sound of the battery firing these six enormous missiles into the sky was thunderous and loud. Because they were shooting the larger ATACMS, the truck launchers only had the capacity to hold one missile at a time instead of the usual six smaller rockets.

Once the battery fired their missiles, a call came over the company net for everyone to prepare to relocate to a new firing location. Once they reached it, they'd reload the launchers and prepare for any additional follow-up missions.

"Damn, Fortney," exclaimed Ramirez. "Things got real, didn't they? We unloaded holy hell on the Chinese and Cubans."

"Yeah, no joke," Fortney replied. "Now it's time to scoot in case they decide to throw some counterbattery fire at us. I sure as hell don't want to be around for that if it does come."

****

"Loki One, Odin. Rounds out. ETA four mikes."

"Odin, good copy. Rounds out. ETA four mikes."

Currie and Dawson smiled. The rocket artillery was on the way. Now it was a matter of waiting for them to fly the hundred and seventy miles to plaster this place. It was nice knowing they had some rocket artillery they could call on and not have to rely solely on cruise missiles and the Air Force.

"Currie, you think there are more TELs in the area or any of those HQ-9 radar sites or missiles?" asked Dawson.

Currie looked over to Dawson and had to remind himself the guy was only a meter away. Tricked out in their ghillie suits and face paint, they were hard to spot. "Maybe," Currie responded. "I suppose once this place gets lit up, we might spot some vehicles trying to move to a new location if they survive. If that happens, then we should see where they're going. We might get lucky and catch some of these vehicles in the open with a second barrage."

Dawson nodded. He pulled an energy bar out and started eating. They'd been in-country now for ten days. A total of twenty Loki teams had infiltrated Cuba before the war had started and were doing their best to identify enemy radar and missile sites. Their secondary objective was assessing the local population and seeing if they could find some friendlies among them. If they could convince some of them to work with the Americans, it'd help them find more targets for the Air Force and Navy to hit. Ideally, they'd like to train up a local militia force to help them seize the island. They could then work with this force to set up a new democratic government once the current regime was removed.

"Loki One, splash."

"Odin, splash out. Stand by for BDA," Currie replied.

"Here they come," Dawson said as they heard the shrieking sound of the incoming missiles.

Boom, boom, boom...

The six seven-hundred-and-fifty-pound warheads on the missiles impacted in a scatter pattern on and around the PLA missile launchers. As if on cue, multiple secondary explosions rocked the area as the CJ-10 cruise missiles began to cook off in the conflagration.

The whole jungle erupted as more secondary explosions rocked the place. It was clear to Currie and Dawson that, deeper in the jungle, the PLA must have been storing additional missiles, or there were more trucks they hadn't seen. As the blasts continued to destroy the area, they counted over a dozen secondary explosions from the initial strike.

"Odin, good strike. Break," Dawson relayed. "Count fifteen additional secondary explosions. Break. It appears we hit a missile depot or additional Dragons. Break. Will stick around to monitor the area. Break. Will advise on possible repeat of last fire mission. Out."

"How long do you want to hang out?" Dawson asked Currie after he had finished providing their battle damage assessment.

"Not sure. I think the area might get a little hot with activity. Maybe we hang out until closer to dusk. Then we can make a move."

"Loki One, Odin. New mission. Prepare to copy," the radio called out.

The two operators looked at each other as if to say, *What now?*

"Loki One, travel to Charlie Uniform Five-Five-Six-Niner-Seven-Four-Four-Five. Link up with a downed Air Force pilot. Major Ian Ryan, call sign Racer. How copy?"

Dawson shook his head. A recovery mission was tough business. As operators, they knew how to move around the jungle and the terrain without being detected—a downed pilot, not so much.

"Odin, good copy. Please advise the pilot of our frequency. Break. Handshake pilot frequency. Will make contact as we get closer. Out."

Currie turned to look at his partner. "Well, I guess that settles it. If I copied the position right, that pilot is ten kilometers from our current

position. A short hike through the jungle, no big deal," he joked as they started packing up their gear and getting ready to move out.
****

Unknown Location
Cuba

Major Ian "Racer" Ryan vomited for the fifth time in the last hour.

I knew I shouldn't have eaten that... He chided himself over eating a fruit he'd been unsure of.

He'd had a rough go of it since he'd been shot down. He'd parachuted into a dense canopy of trees in the middle of nowhere. It had taken him forty minutes to untangle himself from the wires of his parachute without falling fifty feet to the jungle floor below. The last thing he wanted was to break a limb or something worse behind enemy lines.

Once he'd freed himself and managed to get back down to the ground, Racer did a quick inventory. He didn't have much, but he checked his radio and turned it on to the preset frequency for the CSAR unit. Racer was lucky—he was able to contact command right away.

Sadly, they said a recovery was out of the question. Racer struggled with this news. He knew NAS Key West was less than a few hundred miles away. He figured they should be able to send a helicopter to fetch him from there. Sadly, there wasn't going to be a rescue mission anytime soon—not until they thinned the enemy SAMs out a bit more. The SAMs would eat the helicopters up.

Shuffling over to a nearby stream, Racer knelt down, cupping his hands together as he brought some cool water to his face. He drank in the water and sloshed it around in his mouth, cleaning out the vomit before spitting to the side.

He then drank his fill of water. He knew he needed to stay hydrated. He didn't have any protein bars left, so water would be the only way to satisfy that hungry feeling.

"DD Three, this is Dad. How copy?" the radio called out softly to him.

Racer looked at the small radio like a young kid at a Christmas tree full of gifts on Christmas morning. He depressed the talk button.

"Dad, DD Three. I copy loud and clear."

"Send us your current coordinates. A Loki team is nearby. Will attempt to link you up with them. How copy?"

It's about damn time, Racer thought.

Looking at the Hook3 radio in his hand, he saw the button that would gather his current location and hit it. This took a few minutes as the GPS satellites above had to acquire the coordinates. When the little light turned green, letting him know it was ready, he hit the transfer button. This sent the coordinates directly to the unit trying to recover him. From there, it was out of his hands. All he had to do now was not get captured until the Special Forces soldiers found him.

****

"You see that? Looks like a PLA patrol," Dawson whispered softly over the radio.

They both had an earpiece and a throat mic on, allowing them to talk with each other while not giving away their positions. They'd spent nine hours traversing through the valley to the coordinates Odin had provided.

"Yeah, I see them. How many do you think are there?" asked Currie.

"I'd say it looks like a platoon," answered Dawson.

"Do you think they're looking for us, the pilot, or on a routine patrol?" Currie asked.

"Hard to say," Dawson replied. "We're kind of far from our old location. My money says they're probably out here still looking for our pilot."

"Let's keep moving. We need to find this pilot before they do."

****

Racer heard some voices off in the distance and turned to look in their direction.

That doesn't sound like Spanish. I hope those aren't ChiComs, Racer thought.

As the minutes dragged on, the voices got closer. Racer took cover in a thicket of shrubs and underbrush, hoping whoever they were, they'd continue to move along.

Then he saw them. At first it was a group of three soldiers. One would move slowly and methodically forward, scanning everything in front of him. The second man scanned to their right, while the third man scanned to their left. For the life of him, Racer couldn't understand why these guys were so silent and stealthy while the soldiers further back were talking and making a ton of noise. It seemed counterintuitive for them to be quiet while the guys behind them were not.

When the first three soldiers pushed past his position, Racer saw the next group of soldiers. They were spread out in a very wide line, like they were trying to bird-dog something. Then it dawned on him. They were trying to bird-dog *him*. They talked loudly, animatedly, as they pushed through the underbrush and shrubs...looking for *him*.

Several of the Chinese soldiers were getting closer to his position. This wasn't good. He wasn't sure if they would pass by him or if they'd end up walking right up on top of him. The soldiers weren't walking forward in a straight line but appeared to be making a disorganized crisscrossing pattern.

I need to move or these guys will catch me...

Just as Racer was about to slip away, his radio chirped softly, letting him know someone was trying to reach him.

Grabbing at it, he quickly turned the volume off and prayed none of the soldiers had heard the chirp. They didn't appear to have registered the noise, since they didn't change anything they were doing. Depressing the talk button, Racer whispered, "Loki One, this is Racer. How copy?"

A momentary pause ensued before he got a reply.

"Racer, this is Loki One. Good copy. Break. We're nearing your position. Enemy patrol nearby. Where are you?"

Before Racer could respond, all the Chinese soldiers stopped talking and moving. Someone came forward from behind the line, holding an electronic device. In that moment, Major Ryan knew they'd found him.

The soldier holding the electronic device pointed it exactly where he was hiding and started shouting something angrily in Chinese. In an instant, half a dozen soldiers started running right for him.

Ah crap! I have to get out of here. Racer turned and started running in a crouched position away from the enemy soldiers.

He heard shouting behind him. Tree branches and limbs were snapping as hot lead flew all around him. They sounded like angry bees before his mind registered the gunshots.

Racer ducked behind a tree as a few slugs slammed into it. Popping out from behind the trunk, he aimed at the charging soldiers and fired off several shots. Racer hit one of them several times in the chest, then moved to fire at the second guy as a few rounds flew right next to his head. He fired two more aimed shots, hitting another soldier before ducking behind the tree and then bolting to a new position.

What the hell?! Aren't they supposed to try to capture me and not kill me? Racer thought.

More gunshots and yelling could be heard behind him as he ran. Racer stood a little taller and ran for all he was worth, shifting to his right then to his left to throw his attackers' aim off.

When Racer jinked to the right, something punched him in the back of his right shoulder, causing him to spin and fall. He hit the ground hard, unable to break his fall or even try to brace for it.

As he lay there on the ground, hurting all over from the uncontrolled fall, his shoulder felt like a hot poker stick had been pushed right through it. Racer knew he'd been shot. He also knew that unless he did something right now, these enemy soldiers would be on top of him and they'd finish him off. The last thing he wanted was to be taken prisoner or killed and not even try to defend himself.

He grabbed for his Beretta 9mm and fought through the pain to sit up; he spotted a Chinese soldier running right for him, maybe forty feet away. Racer pulled the trigger twice, hitting the man squarely in the chest. He dropped and fell forward from his own momentum.

Turning to his right, Racer saw another soldier running toward him, except this guy had his rifle already aimed at him. He saw the rifle flash several times and figured the bullets would crash into him in moments, but they didn't.

Then Racer heard a lot of spitting noises coming from somewhere behind him. Then he heard, "Frag out!"

An explosion took place near a group of the enemy soldiers. A few more fell to the ground, hit by something.

Racer's world faded out a little bit. His vision became tunneled and he grew confused. He watched several more soldiers go down before a green blur appeared right in front of him. The man disarmed him before he could say or do anything. Then Racer felt his body being thrown over the shoulder of the mystery man and they were off, running through the jungle like the world was on fire.

Racer wasn't sure what had happened, but he thought he was being rescued. Then he blacked out.

****

Currie was covering Dawson as he threw the injured pilot over his shoulder and ran. Dawson rushed past his position as he unloaded the rest of his magazine into a group of enemy soldiers who thought they could bum rush the unknown attackers.

Reaching for one of his white phosphorus grenades, Currie pulled the pin and gave it a good toss high in the air in the direction of the enemy soldiers.

Without waiting around to see it go off, he was on his feet, running after Dawson.

Crump…

The grenade exploded moments later, dousing the area with a chemical cloud that would ignite nearly anything it touched. This was Currie's first time using a WP grenade in a fight. They normally carried flash-bangs or fragmentation grenades, but someone had said the WP grenades would make for a good area denial weapon if they were ever being chased by a large force. Each of the two-man Loki teams had made sure to grab a couple of them before they headed out on the mission. They each knew the likelihood of a rescue was slim if they ran into trouble, at least until the invasion kicked off or the Air Force could reasonably control the skies. They were alone…and no one was coming to save them.

Currie could still hear shouting behind them. He also heard a lot of screaming and cries of pain as well. Even as a soldier, that was hard to hear—knowing he had inflicted that pain and agony on another human being was tough.

"We'll need to stop soon to treat this guy's wounds," Dawson said over the comms.

"Give it another sixty seconds, then stop."

They ran another minute, then Dawson laid the pilot down against the side of a tree so he could examine the man's injuries. "This guy got lucky," he mumbled. "The round that hit him must have been an armor-piercing round and not a hollow-point. It punched a small hole right through him." The hollow-points would have left a small entrance but a large exit wound—those kinds of wounds were a lot tougher to treat.

Dawson pulled the flight suit away from the wound and assessed the blood that was slowly oozing out. Pulling his patrol pack off, he grabbed for his medkit. He tore open a small package of QuikClot and poured it over the front and back of the wound, then placed gauze bandages on both sides and tied a tight pressure dressing over it all to hold it in place.

Currie examined the pilot's face while Dawson finished up. It was obvious he was fading in and out of consciousness. "Hey, Major Ryan. We've come to rescue you. We need you to hold on. You have to fight to stay alive, OK?"

The pilot smiled briefly and nodded. The painkillers Dawson had injected him with were starting to hit.

They swapped positions, with Currie carrying the wounded pilot while Dawson covered their six. They trudged on for another two hours before they felt they were far enough away from the enemy soldiers that they could stop.

It was starting to get dark, so they didn't have much time to find a decent place to sack out. Normally the snake eaters wouldn't care where they slept, but they had a wounded man they needed to take care of now.

Eventually, they found a slight ridge that had some good rock outcroppings on it. They climbed up to it and nestled in for the night. This position would give them good cover and place them on the high ground should they end up having to shoot it out with another patrol. No doubt more PLA soldiers would be sent looking for them. They knew there was a downed pilot nearby and a small commando team—they'd want some payback for sure.

Chapter Thirty-One
Preparations

NAS Key West
Bravo Company, 3rd Ranger Battalion

Staff Sergeant Amos Dekker looked around the airfield with Captain Meacham as they surveyed the damage.

"What do you think, Staff Sergeant? Think we can launch the heliborne assault from here, or do you think we'll have to airborne it?"

Dekker liked Meacham. Unlike most officers, he was a Mustang. He'd served in the Rangers as an enlisted man before he'd been given an appointment to the Academy. Following his graduation, he'd returned straight to the Rangers.

"If the Seabees or a Red Horse unit can get the airfield repaired and all the debris removed, then yeah. I think it can work for a heliborne assault," Dekker replied.

"Yeah, but can they do it in the timeline we need?" Meacham pressed.

Dekker shrugged. "I think if you tell them what needs to get done, they'll find a way to make it happen. Frankly, with how bad those enemy SAMs are over the island, I think it's suicide to fly in on a C-130. The island will be ringed with more SAMs around the airport. It'll be tough enough with helicopters, but at least if one gets taken out it doesn't wipe out half a company in one swoop."

"That was my thinking as well. I think the colonel is worried about it too," explained Meacham. "He wouldn't have sent us down here to assess the field if he wasn't."

"So, what do we do now that we've seen it?" asked Dekker.

"We call home and give them our assessment," Meacham said as he reached in his pocket for his phone.
****

US Strategic Command
Omaha, Nebraska

"Admiral, do you believe we're ready to launch a ground assault? Isn't the Air Force still struggling to take out the air defenses?" Wilson asked the Chairman of the Joint Chiefs.

The President nodded in approval of the question.

Admiral Roy Thiel, Chairman of the Joint Chiefs, had known this question was coming. He and Wilson had spoken about it several hours earlier. He was better prepared for it now than he had been when Wilson had first grilled him on it.

"Mr. Wilson, we will be in position to launch the ground invasion in a couple more days," Admiral Thiel began. "We've been flying a tremendous number of airstrikes on the island over the last three days. We've flown more than nine hundred sorties since the start of the war and fired sixteen hundred cruise missiles. Tomorrow, we move into another phase of the air war. We'll run round-the-clock Wild Weasel missions across the island. We believe we'll need a full forty-eight hours of these types of missions and then it'll be safe enough for us to consider an air assault onto the island."

"What about the Marines? Will they conduct an invasion from the sea?" asked President Alton. The garrison on Guantanamo had been under siege the last few days, and the President was getting nervous that they might not be able to hang on much longer if they didn't get help soon.

The election was seventy-two hours away. In just a matter of days, one of the new candidates would be chosen and the transition of power would begin. Alton had expressed concern about launching such a massive military operation on either election day or the day after. He didn't want to scare people into not voting, and he didn't want to take away from whoever won the following day. Once the ground invasion of Cuba started, it would suck all the oxygen out of the room—especially when the casualties rolled in.

"Yes, Mr. President," replied Admiral Thiel. "The first Marine divisions will be leading an amphibious assault of the island from the direction of Gitmo. Second Battalion 8th Marines, 2/8, and the 1st Battalion, 65th Regiment from the Puerto Rico National Guard were pre-positioned early and have been fighting it out with the Cubans and Chinese soldiers for the last three days. The Marines will start their amphibious assault as soon as this tropical storm passes." The late

October storm had thrown a monkey wrench into their operations along the eastern Caribbean.

Admiral Thiel continued, "In three days, the 18th Airborne Corps will be assaulting to the west of Havana and will focus on that half of the island. Once we secure Havana and the Port of Mariel, the Third Infantry Division will be brought ashore, along with their heavy armor equipment. We'll also be bringing the 53rd Infantry Brigade Combat Team from the Florida Army National Guard. They have extensive training in the tropical environment we'll encounter in Cuba. This will be a large operation once it officially kicks off."

"Is it wise for the Marines to launch their invasion before we secure the skies?" asked Albert Abney, the President's Chief of Staff.

"Ideally we would wait," Thiel explained. "But the garrison has been fighting for nearly three days. They're sustaining a lot of casualties, and frankly I'm not sure they can hold out much longer. We've been feeding them a trickle of reinforcements from the sea as we can, but we need to focus on landing a more substantial force if we're to break the siege. In the north, I think our paratroopers and air assault soldiers will secure us the beachhead we need once our pilots are able to suppress enough of the enemy air defenses. We'll tentatively commence ground operations around Havana five days from now."

"So two days after the election?" Abney clarified.

Admiral Thiel nodded.

"What do the rest of you think?" Abney asked as he surveyed the military leaders.

President Alton had been deferring to Abney and Wilson more and more these last few days to ask the tough questions. He was done being president, and tired of trying to hide his medical condition. He was trying to keep things held together until his successor was chosen.

"What kind of casualty estimates are we talking about once the ground war starts?" asked the President.

General Kurt Stavridis from US Southern Command answered this question. "That all depends, Mr. President, on how hard the Cubans and Chinese decide to fight. There are some who say we may lose as many as ten thousand soldiers in the first thirty days. Then again, those are the same kind of people who said we'd lose a hundred thousand soldiers during the first Gulf War against Saddam and it ended up being nowhere near that. My money says the Cubans will do what the Iraqis did in

2003—a few units will fight hard, but most of them will give up. They simply aren't willing to die for a regime that has left them to live in abject poverty." Stavridis was presently the commander in charge of the war. It was his command leading the way and managing this war.

Stavridis continued, "My bigger concern is the eighty-two thousand Chinese soldiers on the island. I'm sure they've suffered a fair number of casualties the last few days and they'll suffer a lot more once our attack planes and helicopters are able to start their operations. I'm not trying to lowball you, Mr. President, but I wouldn't expect US casualties to be too high—not if we're able to really employ our airpower like we have in previous conflicts."

"OK, gentlemen. Then let's continue with the current plans as they are," the President declared. "We launch the ground invasion in five days. In the meantime, hammer the hell out of them before we send our ground forces in. I don't know if it's possible, but I sure would like to have this Cuba campaign wrapped up before the inauguration of the new president in January."

Chapter Thirty-Two
Vipers, Vipers, Vipers

20th Fighter Wing
Homestead, Florida

Colonel Tim "Joker" Hatfield looked at the pilots of his fighter wing with pride. They had performed exceptionally well. But today—today would be a true test of their skill, training, and equipment.

Placing the glass of water down on the lectern, he began, "In two hours, the 20th will conduct an aggressive antiradiation suppression of enemy air defense action against three sections of Cuba. For our purposes, we've broken the country down into sectors. Sector A consists of the eastern half of the island. It stretches from Gitmo to Las Tunas. This sector falls to the 55th Fighter Squadron. Sector B encompasses Las Tunas to Santa Clara and is assigned to the 77th Fighter Squadron. Sector C will be the toughest sector to deal with. This sector falls to the 79th Fighter Squadron.

"Our mission in this sector is to support the Marines and the Army as they prepare the battlespace for the ground invasion. As you all know by now, the Chinese SAMs are more accurate than we originally thought. There are also some enemy fighters that continue to pop out of nowhere from time to time, so keep an eye out for some of them as well."

Hatfield paused for a moment as he surveyed his pilots. He saw a lot of grim expressions. His people were exhausted from flying nonstop combat operations since the start of the war. They were also feeling the loss of too many of their fellow aviators.

"The next forty-eight hours will determine when the ground war will begin. Let's do our part to win this war and bring it to a swift conclusion. Victory by Valor!" Colonel Hatfield shouted to rally his pilots.
****

14,000 Feet over Western Cuba

Colonel Tim "Joker" Hatfield pulled up hard on the aircraft as a string of 35mm autocannon rounds cut through the air right where he had been.

Damn, that was close, he thought.

Warning alarms continued to blare, letting him know the gun truck was still tracking him.

"Fox Three," called out his wingman as she fired one of her AGM-88E HARM missiles.

"Dice, pull up to angels fifteen and let's reposition for another attack on that gun truck."

"That's a good copy, Joker. Did you see my missile hit? I can't tell if they destroyed it or if it was a dud," Dice replied as her Falcon rose up to meet him.

Craning his neck to look back into the valley, Joker spotted black smoke rising from the location of the PGZ09 they had targeted. The two anti-aircraft tracked vehicles had been working together to keep the valley locked down. The damn trucks had shot down a Marine F/A-18 earlier in the day.

"Yeah, it looks like you got him," replied Joker. "We need to get that other truck before we head back home. Then we can mark this area off as cleared."

They moved their fighters into position. This time they planned for Dice to fly in as the bait. When the gun truck locked and engaged her, Joker would swoop in and fire one of their new advanced antiradiation guided missiles. These truly were fire-and-forget missiles when it came to going after SAMs.

"Going in now," Dice called out as she rolled her Falcon over into a dive to head back into the valley.

As Joker watched her, the last SAM opened fire. Several strings of 25mm autocannon rounds started reaching out for Dice. This particular truck had a quad 25mm autocannon capable of firing up to six hundred rounds a minute. The gun was radar-controlled, which helped it lead the aircraft, making it scary accurate. It also carried four QW-2 Vanguard surface-to-air missiles. The little buggers didn't have a lot of range, but they were deadly to low-flying aircraft and helicopters, which was why the Air Force had targeted them.

Dice effectively jinked and moved out of the way of the anti-aircraft fire. Suddenly, the gun truck fired a pair of QW-2 missiles. Joker fired off his HARM and told Dice to get the hell out of the area.

The first enemy missile went after one of Dice's flares and blew up. The second missile got within range of its proximity fuse and detonated. The shotgun blast of shrapnel practically tore Dice's left wing right off her plane. In the blink of an eye, her plane spun in circles and slammed into the side of the ridge before she had a chance to eject.

"No, damn it. No!" Joker screamed. He'd known Major Lacey "Dice" Dickson for five years. She was a hell of a pilot. She was also a good friend.

Catching a quick glance in the valley, he saw his missile had scored a hit. They'd gotten the last of the gun trucks. Pulling his own aircraft up to twenty thousand feet, he saw his fuel gauge was getting low. He needed to head back to base or find a tanker. He'd left with four HARMs and he still had one left. He thought about trying to find a tanker and sticking around to use that last missile. Then he shook his head. The smart play at this point was to return home. He had a wing to think about and manage, not just his own aircraft.

****

Joint Battle Command Center
20 Kilometers Northwest of Beijing, China

President Yao looked at Dr. Xi Zemin with a bit of skepticism. "Doctor, what are the models telling you now?"

"The AI is still predicting that we will achieve victory," replied Xi.

Yao lifted an eyebrow at that. "Even with the losses we've sustained in Cuba?"

Xi didn't back down or flinch. "Even with the losses in Cuba."

"How? I mean, perhaps I am not understanding how this all works. The Cubans lost five squadrons of fighters—the five we sold them and trained them on. We lost two squadrons of *our* fighters. Last I checked, most of our air defense battalions were wiped out. Half of the 635th Brigade was destroyed. That constituted half of our CJ-10 cruise missile launchers, not to mention the 616th Brigade and our DF-15 launchers. These kinds of losses hurt, Doctor. This isn't a computer you can replace or a new software code you can write to recreate them," the President reminded the scientist.

"I understand that, Mr. President," Dr. Xi replied with a nod. "The AI already restructured hundreds of our factories to replace the military equipment and munitions expended and destroyed. It's estimating what future losses we may sustain and building new equipment to have on hand when the losses happen. We also have to keep in mind the losses the Americans have sustained. They cannot readily replace the aircraft they are losing or replace the enormous volume of advanced missiles they are using. Our remaining forces in Cuba and the Caribbean only need to bog the Americans down for nine to twelve months. Then we'll achieve our overall objectives."

President Yao then turned to look at General Li Zuocheng. "General, how ready are our forces to execute the next phase of the operation?"

Sitting a little taller in his chair, the general replied, "We are ready to initiate combat operations against Taiwan when you give the order."

The next phase of the plan called for the final annexation of Taiwan and returning the renegade island to the fold. Once the island had been subdued, the PLA would move to fortify it against future attacks and act as a shield in the Pacific against future American aggression. Then they'd move to phase three, the final phase needed to secure China's economic and military security for the rest of the century.

"Before we initiate this next phase, are our forces in Venezuela and their government prepared?" asked President Yao.

"We are ready," General Song Fu, the commander of the Chinese Caribbean Forces, replied confidently from the Chinese embassy in Caracas. "We have dispersed our forces across the country, as have the Venezuelans. If the Americans opt to fight to remove us, then we are ready. If they choose not to fight us, then we'll be able to make sure the Panama Canal remains neutral and unavailable to military traffic. That'll prevent them from being able to carry out operations in both oceans as easily as they have in the past."

The President nodded. "Good. One less item to have to worry about. OK, Generals, then I believe it is time to move to phase two of this operation," Yao declared.

In the coming days, the prodigal island would finally be returned to the fold.

Chapter Thirty-Three
The Long March

Type 95A
East China Sea – Northeast of Taiwan

Captain Lee Jian Ho sat in the Conn of his Type 95A submarine, the *Changzheng 30*—translated into English, Long March, signifying the long march the PLA Navy had gone through to create what Lee believed was the most advanced submarine in the world.

The *Changzheng*-class submarine was the pride of the PLA Navy and represented a true revolution in naval technology. She was the product of decades of technological innovation, industrial espionage, and billions in research and development. The result was the most advanced submarine the PRC had ever produced.

They had been underway for a month now as they patrolled the East China Sea between Taiwan and Okinawa. They had originally been part of a screening force for the *Liaoning* as she transited the Pacific to bring more soldiers and supplies to China's new allies in South America. That was until they'd stumbled upon something that caused them to stay in the area.

Several days ago, Lee's crew had come across an American *Ohio*-class ballistic missile submarine lurking in the waters off the coast of China. It had taken an enormous amount of restraint not to engage them. The *Changzheng* had the American SSBN dead to rights. Unfortunately, the war hadn't started yet, and his rules of engagement were clear—he could not fire unless fired upon by the Americans first.

Instead of sinking the American boomer, the *Changzheng* faded into the deep. They let the submarine pass over them and then followed in their baffles until it was time to rise to periscope depth and check in. They needed to see if the war had started. They were eager to start hunting.

When Lee ordered the boat to periscope depth, they received a shocking report of the battle that had taken place several days earlier. The war had already begun.

I should have raised our communications buoy at least once a day, Lee chided himself. *We might have been able to attack that American boomer had we known.* He was angry at himself for not following standard protocol and checking in, but he had been too busy trailing this boomer.

The *Liaoning*, China's first aircraft carrier, had sunk, along with three other ships of her strike group. One of their newer large amphibious assault ships had been damaged in battle. Even the new Type 60 *Dingyuan* battle cruiser had taken a torpedo hit. It appeared to have shrugged it off, just as they had been told it could so many months ago in their secret meeting at the JBCC.

Lee adamantly disagreed with this part of Operation Dragon Fire—ghosting the American electronics into thinking they were under attack so they would fire on the Chinese ships first. He understood the need to make it appear like the Americans and their NATO allies were the aggressors—attacking the peaceful people of China would play into people's sympathies. Still, as a military officer, it stung to allow it to happen—to know many of his fellow sailors would ultimately die or get hurt as part of this elaborate charade did not sit well with him or many in the upper echelons of the navy.

Lee's blood boiled at the thought of so many countrymen lost at the hands of the Americans. Even more troubling, it appeared the attack had been carried out by a single American fast-attack and her autonomous subs. If that was truly the case, then maybe that damn super-AI had underestimated the American Navy and its capabilities. Lee was determined that his ship would get their pound of flesh. They'd make the Americans pay for attacking their fleet.

"Officer of the Deck, set course to one-seven-zero, make your depth three hundred and fifty feet. Rig ship for quiet running." Lee straightened his shirt as he looked intently at his OOD.

"Setting my course to one-seven-zero, making my depth three hundred and fifty feet, rig for quiet, aye," repeated the OOD, setting the Conn about executing the captain's new orders.

Lee motioned for his executive officer to approach. As Commander Wu drew close, he could tell the man already knew what he was thinking—the war had started, and it was time to hunt. This pleased Lee considerably as he was anxious to strike back at the Americans.

Lee and his crew now had permission to rain hell upon any American vessel they came across because the Americans had drawn first blood. Lee grinned slyly, excited about the opportunity to demonstrate to the world the power of the Chinese Navy.

When they rose to periscope depth, they received the latest satellite imagery downloads from DragonLink. Satellite images showed the *Carl Vinson* and *Theodore Roosevelt* strike groups remained in a holding pattern around Guam and Saipan. The Chinese Navy had forced the Americans to position two of their carriers in the area by deceiving them into thinking the Chinese Navy would invade the islands.

Lee examined the map; he still wanted to go after that American boomer they'd let go. He saw the last known positions of the sub and the current position of a squadron of ASW ships.

There has to be a way to work them into the equation, Lee thought. Sinking a boomer would be a huge morale boost for China and a real blow to the Americans.

The other piece of intelligence they'd received in their data dump was an analysis from Jade Dragon's acoustic signature library, a priceless collection acquired over decades. The acoustic signature let them know the boomer they were after was the USS *Maine*. The dossier also included the file on the commander and as much information as they had on him and the crew.

Lee tried to look up the commander of the *Texas*. Unfortunately, China's intelligence on him was minimal. What little they did know of him suggested that his superiors thought him an extremely aggressive and capable ship commander.

He returned his attention to the *Maine*, the boomer he had to let go earlier, and a plan began to form.

Looking at the digital map, Lee saw the Navy had a small squadron of ASW ships he might be able to task. Prior to the start of the war, the Navy had grouped small groups of frigates and corvettes together in the East and South China Sea to carry out ASW missions against any possible American incursions. These little squadrons of ASW ships would hopefully finish off the American sub force the merchant raiders were unable to hit in the ports.

Having formulated his plan of attack, Lee had his sub rise to periscope level one more time. He transmitted a burst message to the *Sanya*, a state-of-the-art frigate, to begin coordinating the hunt of this American submarine.

The *Sanya* was a Type 054A advanced frigate. She was an exceptional ASW platform that could also engage surface ships if needed. The *Sanya* was the squadron commander for a group of two other Jiangdao corvettes, the *Luzhou* and the *Weihai*. They were the new Type 056 corvettes specifically designed for hunting down enemy subs. To round out the squadron, three Type 037I *Haiqing*-class submarine chasers were added to the mix. They traveled around the perimeter of the squadron or would race out to investigate a possible sub contact.

Lee would use the *Sanya* to help him identify where that American boomer had gone. If they were lucky, they'd either sink it or lead him right to it.

Over the next half a day, the *Sanya* and her squadron hunted the *Maine*. They started dropping sonar buoys with the help of coastal ASW aircraft and their helicopters as they pursued the hunt. It wouldn't be long before they found them. Then the fun would begin.
****

Fourteen Hours Later

Captain Lee observed his sonar operator place his hands to his earphones and tilt his head. Lee rose from his captain's chair and walked over to see what he had found. As he approached, the man turned.

"Conn, Sonar," he announced. "Contact bearing one-one-zero, range twelve thousand yards. It's passing through two of our buoys." The young sonar operator was as visibly excited as Lee was inside.

"Conn, Sonar. Contact designated Sierra 1."

"Sonar, Conn. Very well," answered the Officer of the Deck.

"Conn, Sonar, Sierra 1 is an American SSBN, probability ninety-six percent it's the USS *Maine*."

"Sonar, Conn. Very well. Designate Sierra 1 Master 1," replied Captain Lee with a slight smile. It was time to finish this hunt.
****

250 Miles Northeast of Taiwan
USS *Maine*

The junior officer of the deck was tense. The whole Conn was tense. They had received data from one of their Orcas, the *Bangor*, that the sub they had identified as a Type 93 had disappeared. Either it hadn't entered their engagement box or crossed the picket screen they established with their Orcas, or they'd simply lost track of her. This wasn't a good sign considering they had lost contact with Pearl and nearly every other naval asset in the region over the last couple of days. Something was up—they just didn't know what.

Captain Dale Redding saw one of the CPOs updating the master plot table with the latest information they had from the Orcas and their own towed sonar array. He got up and walked over to the master plot to see what kind of picture it was painting.

In addition to the possible enemy sub, they were now tracking a small squadron of Chinese surface ships that appeared to be headed toward the Senkaku Islands, a small cluster of islands currently in dispute between China and Japan.

Captain Redding figured this squadron of Chinese ships was looking for them. Not only were they starting to spread out in an obvious ASW formation, but sonar buoys appeared on the surface, which meant one thing—shore-based ASW support. His biggest concern right now was those ships getting in range of using their helicopters to hunt him. If they started using dipping sonar on him, he'd be in trouble. This would complicate their return to Pearl.

Despite what people thought about the Chinese systems, he knew if a dipper was dropped anywhere near them and an active sonic ping hit them, it'd light them up like Christmas. These weren't passive buoys. A dipping sonar in the hands of a good operator could find even the stealthiest sub.

The more Redding looked at the plot table, the more he felt the *Maine* was being pushed or chased into a kill box. On the Taiwan side, the ASW aircraft were dropping buoys, which meant the *Maine* needed to stay away from there. On the Senkaku side, this squadron of corvettes and frigates was pinging away. The big question Redding had was where that Type 93 they had lost was. He needed information—he needed help dealing with the situation on the surface.

Captain Redding decided to try one more time to make contact with the fleet. He had the *Maine* come up to periscope depth and raise their communications masts. Within seconds, they received a deluge of information. They were told the country had moved from DEFCON 4 to DEFCON 2 and that a de facto state of war now existed between the US and China. They also received a new set of orders: return to their old station off the coast of Shanghai and wait.

Redding didn't particularly care for these orders. After being on patrol now for nearly four months, they were starting to near the end of their stored rations. They had two months' supply left, which included eating into their emergency canned foods. They could go back for maybe a month, but then they'd need to resupply in Japan.

"What do the new orders say?" asked Commander Tom "Johnnie" Walker as he leaned in so only the two of them could hear. He read over the situation report, so he knew the general situation. The crew didn't, at least not yet. They'd have to inform them soon enough.

Commander Tom "Johnny" Walker was Captain Redding's XO. He was an intense officer, even by submariner standards. But he was sharp, and not overly zealous, a good trait to have as a boomer captain as their mission was more strategic than tactical in nature.

The unfolding situation on the surface suddenly made a lot more sense. The Chinese Navy wasn't just looking for them for training. They were actively hunting them. This made losing that Type 93 even more concerning. It meant it could be out there right now, stalking them, and they wouldn't even know it.

"Our new orders say we're to return to our old station and await further orders. There's also the USS *Stethem* and *Benfold* somewhere above us. They'll kind of stay along our path back to our patrol route as they head to Okinawa and link up with a larger task force being formed up. Other than we're now in a state of war with China, nothing else," Captain Redding said as he handed the orders to his XO.

"By the way, what are your thoughts on that sub suddenly disappearing on us a little while back?"

"Sir, it's damned odd. We had her at no less than ten thousand yards. Then she just disappeared." Walker rubbed the two-day stubble on his chin as if he was trying to remember something that was on the tip of his tongue.

Redding nodded his head in approval. "Agreed, XO. I've had sonar go over the tracks again and again. Even with the background clutter, she was there making ten knots, then she just faded away—not even so much as an echo. We really need those destroyers to stay out here with us and not head back to Okinawa. We need to keep this area buttoned up so more subs don't slip out, but we also need to get on station. We aren't a fast-attack, so we can't be out here chasing down enemy subs like this."

Neither of them said anything for a moment. Redding was deep in thought before he instructed the communications officer to send a VLF message to the fleet. He hoped to convince them to cancel the destroyer's order and have them stay on station in this gap between Taiwan and the Senkaku island. Their ASW assets would be a great help in keeping this area clear of enemy subs.

Walker looked at the digital plot, then at Captain Redding.

"Sir, if you were the Chinese skipper, where would you be?" Walker watched the captain as he made some adjustments to the chart on the display.

"I'd go beneath the thermocline and try to get my towed array above it. Then I'd continue to look for us to slip past their surface ships somewhere around here." Redding pointed.

****

Type 95
Northeast of Taiwan

"Engineering, Conn. Status of the thruster?" Lee asked pensively. The rim-driven thruster was a shaftless rotor that was attached to a band inside the propulsion shroud. The RDT reduced noise and cavitation by magnitudes. It had fewer moving parts and took up significantly less space in engineering, and it increased engine efficiency by fifteen percent overall. It made the *Changzheng* the quietest nuclear-powered submarine in the world, and by extension, the deadliest weapon in the ocean.

"Conn, Engineering. Engine is running at peak efficiency. We are steady at twelve knots," replied the chief engineer.

Lee could picture the man standing in the engine room, eyes closed, listening for the slightest imperfection in his engines.

"Very well," Lee said as he replaced the receiver in its cradle.

In the last seven hours, they had managed to quietly place themselves within twenty thousand yards of the two *Arleigh Burke*–class destroyers. The two ships had been doing overlapping concentric circles as they made the transit back between the Senkaku Islands and Taiwan. They had been relentless in searching for the *Changzheng*. Had it not been for the fact that the submarine they were looking for didn't exist, they would have put her on the bottom by now.

"Officer of the Deck, retract the towed array."

"Retract the towed array, aye, sir."

Lee circled the master plot and looked at his position relative to where he thought the *Maine* should be, then from where the destroyers most likely were, given their circling pattern. He pointed to a position on the plot and stared at it for several minutes. As he grew more certain of his attack plan, he felt his heartbeat increase.

"Sonar, distance to the destroyers, relative to the last known position of the *Maine*?"

The OOD replied, "Sir, the closest destroyer to *Maine*, relative to her last known position, is twelve thousand, five hundred yards from our current position. Second destroyer is eighteen thousand yards away."

"Are they still circling?" Lee asked with a little more enthusiasm in his voice than he'd wanted.

"Yes, sir, their circling is roughly three thousand yards. In that circle they advance east, approximately fifteen hundred yards at each circle."

"Are there any discernible patterns to their sprints eastward?" asked Lee as he tried to confirm something.

"Sir, other than the circles, there is no pattern discernible from sonar."

Captain Lee paced the Conn, deep in thought as they pursued their quarry relentlessly. The time to strike was nearly at hand.

He called the Engineering officer to make one last check to make sure that the submarine would be ready. Once Engineering confirmed the *Changzheng* was ready for combat in all respects, Lee draped the phone over the cradle, looking briefly at it. It made him smile. It was an unconscious movement. Muscle memory, not wanting to place the phone back in its cradle, possibly creating a metallic transient for an enemy sonar to hear. From this moment on, they would be rigged for ultraquiet until they fired on the Americans.

"Helm, increase speed ahead full, five-degree up angle."

"Increasing speed to ahead full, five-degree up angle, aye, sir."

It was time to test the rim-driven thruster and see how close they could get to the Americans before he fired a salvo of the newest YU-9 torpedoes.

"Weapons officer, load all tubes, make weapons ready in all respects. Set tubes one and two to wake homing. Load tubes five and six with modified YJ-7s," commanded Lee.

"Load all tubes, make weapons ready in all respects, set tubes one and two to wake homing and tubes five and six with modified YJ-7s, aye, sir," confirmed the OOD.

Retrieving the phone, Captain Lee took a deep breath and made an announcement that officially took his men and his boat to war.

"Battle stations, torpedo."

****

**USS *Stethem*
East of Taiwan**

Commander Tim Wade stood on the flight deck as the SH-60 was on final approach to touch down. He had kept his antisubmarine warfare helos aloft for the last ten hours. Wade, along with the USS *Benfold*, had been tasked to perform a screen as the *Maine* slipped back into the East China Sea and retake up their position off the coast.

He had been told that the USS *Maine* was on patrol in their vicinity and that she had been tracking a Chinese Type 93. Just prior to the USS *Texas* officially starting the war in the Pacific, a Type 93 had apparently vanished.

Wade had flown to the *Benfold* and had a face-to-face with her skipper. Commander Lisa Bell had been a classmate of his at the Academy, and he regarded her as a damn fine officer. She was a hell of a ship driver and had a keen tactical mind. Together they came up with a plan to make sure no additional Chinese submarines escaped into the Pacific northeast of Taiwan and Okinawa. It was likely that a squadron of corvettes and frigates would engage them now that the war had actually started.

They both launched their ASW birds and were dropping sonobuoys in a wide pattern, attempting to canalize the sub so that the *Maine* could find her and finish her off before they'd have to deal with these surface contacts and any possible air contacts that might join them.

They hadn't considered that the Chinese Air Force would do the same. There had been a couple of close calls with some Chinese J-15s at the outer perimeter of their air defenses. Fortunately, they hadn't tried to test their luck yet, and the Americans were looking to conserve missiles until a real threat presented itself.

As the SH-60 touched down, the pilot powered down the engines. The work crews rushed over and began refueling the aircraft.

While that was happening, the crew loaded a new payload of sonobuoys.

Lieutenant Chuck Nellis walked up to Commander Wade. "Sir, we've covered thousands of miles and dropped over two hundred buoys. If that Chinese boat is out there, she's running silent and she's got to be deep."

"Damn, Lieutenant. You look like hell," remarked Wade. "Let's get some coffee. You've got about twenty minutes before your bird is ready again."

"I feel like hell, boss. Are we really at war with China?" asked Nellis as he ran his hands through his sweat-soaked hair.

Commander Wade took off his cap as they walked into the hangar, not really believing they were at war either.

"I know it's hard to believe. They were warned and they crossed the Clipperton-Galapagos Line. The *Texas* delivered a hard blow. They sank a carrier, so yeah—I'd say that means we're at war."

As the two officers walked toward the wardroom, a sailor ran up to them.

"Sir, the XO sent me for you. One of the *Benfold*'s ASW birds may have something!"

The three of them ran for the CIC. When they arrived, a video from the ASW helo was on screen.

****

ASW Helo
Northeast of Taiwan

Lieutenant Sarah Mills lowered the dipping sonar and was hovering at one hundred feet while the sensor operator listened to what the AAQS-13F dipping sonar was feeding. This was her second pass over this spot of ocean. Her helo was running low on fuel and would need to return to the *Benfold* in ten minutes.

"Manny, we're nearing bingo fuel. Either you find me a submarine to kill or we go home." Lieutenant Mills found this cat-and-mouse game they had been playing frustrating.

Petty Officer Third Class Manuel "Manny" Martinez was her acoustic sensor operator or ASO. On their second run of the day, he thought he'd heard something when they'd made their second sonar dip. It sounded like a torpedo once it had acquired a target and accelerated to its terminal run. Once he found it again, the sound seemed to vanish.

"Lieutenant, I know, I know! This could be important, ma'am. I know what I heard. Just give me…"

He trailed off and stared intently at his screen, tilting his head as if confused, and suddenly he turned to Lieutenant Mills.

"Missile in the water!" Manny shouted.

Mills didn't have time to think. She launched flares, cut the dipper, and accelerated to full military power. Rather than gain altitude and evade, she nosed down and headed for the deck.

"Hang on!" Mills grunted as the helo pitched forward.

"*Benfold, Seahawk*, we are under attack! Trying to evade!" shouted the copilot into the radio.

Manny looked out the starboard door and saw the missile. It had arced high into the air and shot through the space they had occupied seconds before. As Mills dove for the ocean, she gained speed, but Manny knew it wouldn't be enough.

He watched in horror as the missile corrected its course and headed straight for the helo. For some reason, Manny couldn't look away. The last sound he heard was Lieutenant Mills saying, "I'm sorry."

The missile impacted forward of the rear fuselage. The sixty-nine pounds of armor-piercing high-explosives detonated, vaporizing Petty Officer Third Class Martinez instantly. The overpressure from the detonation ripped the helicopter in half and ignited the remaining JP5 in the internal fuel tanks. What little remained of the helo fell to the ocean in a fiery heap.

****

USS *Maine*

"Battle stations!"

The crew of the *Maine* sprang to life as they prepared the boat for combat. The tension had been building as the crew hunted for the Chinese submarine. The pressure and anxiety had gotten worse when they'd begun to wonder who was hunting who.

"Sonar, Conn, distance and bearing to that explosion?"

"Conn, Sonar, distance eight thousand, three hundred yards, bearing two-eight-seven degrees."

"Maneuvering, Conn. Set course two-eight-seven degrees, make your speed ten knots, set your depth to three-fifty feet."

"Conn, Maneuvering. Set course two-eight-seven degrees, speed ten knots, make depth three-five-zero feet, aye."

"XO, COB, get the crew ready. We will find that Chinese submarine."

"Sonar, Conn. I need you to find that submarine, son. I need you to find it now!"

"Conn, Sonar. Aye, Skipper, we're working on it."

****

USS *Benfold*

The combat information center of the *Benfold* was a hive of energy. Commander Bell set the ship to battle stations, as did Commander Wade. Okinawa was redirecting a couple of P3 Orions to come over and assist them.

So far, they hadn't had any luck in finding that damned elusive Chinese submarine. It had shot down their helo, and they were livid. Between the *Benfold* and the *Stethem*, they'd launched two hundred additional sonobuoys. The only result they had to show for it so far was the final words of what Petty Officer Martinez had said he thought he'd heard—something that sounded like a torpedo accelerating to its terminal run and then disappearing.

Commander Bell sat in her chair on the bridge. She looked into her empty coffee mug, realizing she'd had too much caffeine. Her head pounded from a stress-induced headache that was quickly turning into a migraine. She'd lost three members of her crew and there was no sign of that damn Chinese sub. She felt the anger fueling her migraine and took a long, slow, deep breath.

Everyone on board was on edge. There was no trace of that submarine whatsoever. The N2 could provide no information about the SLAM, or Submarine Launched Anti-Aircraft Missile. They had been caught completely by surprise by its sudden appearance. The aircrews were spooked. They were now taking extra precautions. Yet the fact remained that the sub that had launched it remained undetected.
****

Type 95A

"Enable the decoys. Simulate torpedo salvos at the destroyers. When they make their evasion turns, fire tubes one and two. Passive homing until they are within one thousand yards, then go active homing and sever the wires," Captain Lee ordered calmly, as if this were just another simulation and not the real thing.

The various stations, officers, and enlisted acknowledged the orders and put the attack plan into motion. Soon, they'd learn if their captain and that damned AI supercomputer were as smart as they all hoped.

Since the modified YJ-7 had taken out the American helicopter screening for the destroyers, the *Changzheng* had maintained twenty knots and had thus far remained undetected by their prey.

Lee watched his crew with pride. Every person was methodically running through their specific tasks just like they had trained and drilled for so many months prior. Looking at them and the technology they were employing made him swell up with pride. He was truly commanding one of the most powerful warships ever built.

Still, in the back of his mind, he harbored some doubts. The boasting Submarine Bureau proclaimed the *Changzheng* to be the most advanced submarine ever built. They'd spared no expense putting this boat to sea ahead of schedule and with the most advanced weapons China had ever produced. When Lee unleashed this sub on the Americans, there was no turning back.

The *Changzheng* or "Long March" would continue across the ocean to the very doorstep of the Americas. At least that was what he told the crew publicly. Still, privately, he couldn't help but wonder if, like the Japanese had in 1941, they were awakening a sleeping giant.
****

USS *Stethem*

"Bridge, CIC! Cavitation, two Type 93 submarines. Designated Sierra 1 and Sierra 2, bearing two-two-zero degrees and two-six-five degrees!" the tactical operations officer shouted excitedly.

"CIC, Bridge. Very well. Alert the *Benfold*, prepare to prosecute the target!"

"Bridge, CIC. Torpedoes in the water! Same bearing."

"Ahead flank, right full rudder, fire decoys!" Commander Wade steadied himself on an overhead handrail as he felt the ship accelerate and angle into the turn.

Damn, how did they get in range of their torpedoes so fast? he thought.

****

USS *Benfold*

The klaxon for general quarters blared throughout the ship, and Commander Bell dropped her coffee cup to the floor as she entered the CIC.

The TAO shouted, "Fire the ASROCs at the bearing of those Type 93s! Ahead flank, right full rudder!"

Benfold lurched forward as the ship increased speed and made a tight turn. The deck of the ship shuddered twice as the antisubmarine rockets fired off at the enemy threats.

As Commander Bell tried to steady herself and make her way over to her chair, she scanned the room to find her TAO had taken charge of the situation just as she had trained him. The man was standing at the sonar station, a puzzled expression on his face as he tried to understand what he was looking at.

"TAO, SITREP!" Bell demanded anxiously as she started walking toward the sonar station. The ship had stabilized now that they were no longer in a tight turn at flank speed.

"Ma'am, we hear the Type 93s, and the fish they put in the water, but we can't track them from the original bearing. It's like the torpedoes left the tubes and just… stayed there."

"What? That doesn't make sense. Get me a definitive fix on those boats, and their fish, and do it now!"

****

Type 95A

A broad smile crept across Captain Lee's face. Jade Dragon had predicted the actions of the American destroyers and their captains almost flawlessly.

As soon as they increased their speed to flank, he launched his wake-homing torpedoes. The wires were still attached, and they were moments away from going active on the two destroyers. They had taken the bait, and he was about to unleash the first-ever YU-9 torpedo on the West.

In its current mode, it would home in on the wake of a ship. When its magnetic sensors were in close enough proximity to its target, the wires would be severed, and it would go to active homing. The second phase of the torpedo would then kick in. It would accelerate to its maximum speed of nearly sixty knots. Once this happened, there would be no escaping. When the warhead impacted against the ship, the chemical mixture in its warhead was designed to burn right through the aluminum and steel of a vessel at more than two thousand degrees centigrade.

The weapons officer standing near Lee confirmed it; each torpedo had acquired its intended target. Lee ordered the wires cut and listened as they went into active homing, each less than 1,100 yards from their targets. The weapons officer gave him one last status report and confirmed the weapons were actively homing and accelerating. The XO instructed the torpedo room to load all tubes and keep all outer doors opened when complete. Once the destroyers were dealt with, the *Maine* was next.

****

USS *Stethem*

"Bridge, CIC, torpedoes in the water! Bearing one-nine-five degrees, distance one thousand, one hundred yards and closing at fifty-five… correction, fifty-nine knots!"

"Launch countermeasures! Left full rudder!" Commander Wade did the math. At 1,100 yards, a torpedo traveling that fast would be on them in thirty seconds.

"CIC, Bridge, report bearing for the first torpedo!"

"Bridge, CIC, the first torpedo is gone, sir. It disappeared!"

That made no sense to Wade. How could a torpedo disappear? Then it dawned on him—they'd been played. Ever since they'd maneuvered out here, they had been sailing into a trap of some new nuclear-powered Chinese submarine that was ultraquiet—that could shoot SLAMs and knock ASW birds out of the sky. All of it was a trap, and every action they'd taken had lured them further into it.

"Fire three ASROCs along that bearing. We aren't going out without—"

Wade was cut off by a massive explosion aft and beneath the ship. The back end of the *Stethem* was lifted out of the water as a massive fireball raged through the aft compartments of the ship. The shafts were completely blown apart, and the back of the ship looked as if it had been flattened by a sledgehammer.

The bridge crew were all thrown to the deck plating. Commander Wade's ears were ringing, and he barely heard the emergency klaxon. He couldn't focus. As he pulled his hand away from his head, he saw it was covered in blood.

Rising to his feet, he looked out the window just in time to see the *Benfold* shudder from an explosion beneath her amidships. It was followed seconds later by a terrible secondary blast as she rose from the water and then seemed to crack in half. She began to sink, her back broken. The ocean boiled all around her as flames reached into the sky.

As Commander Wade felt himself drifting into unconsciousness, he heard someone shout, "Brace for impact!" He passed out before the second YU-9 impacted the *Stethem*, at the waterline beneath the bridge. Mercifully, he never felt the explosion that killed him and the rest of his crew.

****

USS *Maine*
Northeast of Taiwan

Captain Redding and Commander Walker had listened to the *Stethem* and *Benfold* being struck by multiple torpedoes. They anguished at the sounds of them breaking apart as they sank, likely taking a lot of their crew with them.

The *Maine* had been running at ultraquiet for nearly twelve hours. The crew was tense but ready; all her torpedo tubes were armed with outer doors opened. Every sensor at their disposal was operating, searching for the Chinese sub that had just sent two *Arleigh Burke*–class destroyers to the bottom. They listened to the torpedo launch and thought they had a good bearing on the sub, but again she disappeared.

"Conn, Sonar. Sir, I think I have something." The sonar operator said it more like a question than a statement, but anything was welcomed at this point.

"Sonar, Conn. What do you have?"

"Sir, it's a slight metal transient. I've been listening to the tracks of the patrol box since the ASW helo was shot down, sir. I think I have it," the tech said.

Redding looked at Walker—finally, some good news. They called the sonar tech to the plot and he filled them in on what he had discovered. When they'd heard the ASW helo shot down, they'd all suspected a Type 93 had done it, and sonar had listened for a seven-bladed asymmetric propeller. On two occasions when the destroyers had been fired on by what they thought were two Type 93s, they'd recorded the boats. When the sonar tech had run it through the computer, he'd discovered it was the same acoustic signature.

When the captain said, "So what?" the tech emphatically replied, "No, sir, it's the *exact* same signature. Like the same submarine was in two places at the same time."

Seeing that he was starting to convince the captain, he pressed on.

"Captain, I slowed it down. It's a decoy, sir. It made the noise of a Type 93 and the noise of a torpedo launch. But that's all it did. It stayed stationary and made loud noises while our real Chinese submarine fired on the destroyers after they went to flank. Those torpedoes were wake-homing. The faster the destroyers went, the easier it was for the Chinese fish to acquire and sink them."

Redding took a moment to digest what he had heard. It suddenly made sense. But it also meant the Chinese were years more advanced than the Office of Naval Intelligence had predicted. For the first time in his naval career, it appeared the US was in the dark about their enemy's capabilities.

"OK, what else do you have?" Redding asked. He hoped that there was something he could use to find this submarine and kill it. Playing defense was no way to live, and he was getting tired of it.

"Yes, sir," the tech replied. "So I started to think, what if this was something new? There are only so many ways a submarine can move underwater—most of which we have a signature for."

"Yeah, if you have a point, mister, get to it," Commander Walker prodded. He hadn't slept in nearly thirty-six hours, and the fact that there was a Chinese sub trying to kill them had him on edge.

"Sorry, XO. Right, so I started searching our database for experimental propulsion ideas that worked in theory or ideas that had failed. I also looked at propulsors on surface ships that aren't on submarines. I came across an article from 2017 about a Voith Rim Thruster made in Germany. I found a recording of it on a commercial vessel that uses it for river cruises in Europe. I ran it through the computer and overlaid it with the last seventy-two hours' worth of transients, and the computer gave me this."

He laid down an image of two signatures. They weren't identical, but they were close enough that it made the CO and the XO grab the images. They stared at them for a long moment before either of them spoke.

"Can you find this sub?" the captain asked with an edge to his voice.

"Well, like the man said, sir. If you get me close enough, absolutely. I now know how to filter out the decoys. I can find that boat, sir," the tech replied confidently.

"Get to it, son. We have a new Chinese sub to kill," the captain said with a grin on his face.

The XO got the Conn shift changed with fresh crews at the stations. They'd needed a break like this. Now it was their turn to go on the offensive.

****

Type 95A

There was a soft knock on Captain Lee's door. Rising from his bed, he opened the door to his room. His XO stood there, smiling.

"We have them, sir. The *Maine*."

As the two men went to the Conn, the XO gave him a situation report and the disposition of the ship. They were steady at ten knots, bearing fifty degrees.

The USS *Maine* was 12,000 yards off their starboard bow. She was running at ten knots, roughly the same bearing, which meant the *Changzheng* was almost in her baffles. At their current speed, they could close with her in less than thirty minutes.

"Increase speed to fifteen knots," Lee announced as he surveyed the Conn.

"Increase speed to fifteen knots, aye," responded the duty officer of the deck.

Captain Lee felt the increase in speed by a slight increase in the vibration beneath his rubber-soled shoes. At the plot, he calculated his attack against the American sub. He planned to fire four of his YU-9s at her.

Two would go active at half the distance between the two boats. The other two would remain passive until she ran evasive. At 6,000 yards, the first torpedoes would go active. At fifty-nine knots, they would hit the *Maine* in under three minutes, leaving virtually no chance of escape. When she ran evasive, the third and fourth torpedoes would go active and close the distance. The *Maine* would have nowhere to go.

****

USS *Maine*

"Conn, Sonar. I've got something, sir. Designate Sierra 1. It's faint, about twelve thousand yards at two-three-zero degrees. The towed array picked it up."

"Sonar, Conn. Does it match the signature from before?" asked the Captain expectantly.

"Conn, Sonar. Sir, I can't give you a definitive answer. I'm just not sure yet."

"Sonar, Conn. Best guess, this may be our only chance at getting this sub."

"Conn, Sonar. Yes, sir. It's him, best guess, sir."

"Sonar, Conn. Designate Sierra 1 Master 1."

"Conn, Sonar, aye."

The captain's plan was simple. They would fire four torpedoes programmed to run aft at varied depths, ranging from current depth of three hundred and fifty feet down to seven hundred and fifty feet on bearing 230. Once the weapons had traveled six thousand yards, they would enable active search for the Chinese sub with a tight kill box of only five thousand yards. If they were lucky, they'd hit the sub. If they weren't so lucky, they would be able to come about and reengage her in a fair fight.

"Sonar, Conn. Status of Master 1?"

"Conn, Sonar. Master 1 has increased speed from ten to fifteen knots, same bearing."

"Sonar, Conn. Very well."

"Retract the buoy."

"Retract the buoy, aye."

Redding looked at the digital clock on the wall. It was going to be an agonizing couple of minutes until the buoy was retracted. All he could do until then was wait. The weapons control officer looked as if he was about to pop. The tension in the Conn was thick. Yet each sailor in the room was a professional. They all carried the stress as well as could be expected. Redding was proud of them.

The last few days had been like emotional crush depth. He had addressed the crew over the 1MC earlier, but the time for speeches was over. They sent a communications buoy to the surface to transmit the data on the Chinese sub in case they didn't make it. There was no sense in risking more lives should they not survive the day.

"Weapons, fire tubes one and two."

"Firing tubes one and two, aye."

Tubes one and two fired the Mk 48 torpedoes into the water. The fish dipped beneath the bow to ensure the wires cleared the sub at one hundred yards out. Then the wires were cut, and the torpedoes dipped to their track depth and turned around and headed into the deep toward the Chinese submarine chasing the *Maine*. Two minutes later, tubes two and four fired and repeated the process. Digital timers on the wall marked their time.

"Helm, make your depth four hundred and fifty feet. Increase speed to twenty knots, bring us about, bearing two-three-zero."

"Make my depth four hundred and fifty feet, aye. Increase speed to twenty knots, heading two-three-zero degrees, aye, sir."

"Weps, Conn. Get those tubes loaded and ready to fire."

"Conn, Weps, aye, sir. Conn, Sonar. Torpedoes running true, sir."

"Sonar, Conn. Very well."

Redding looked at his XO, and the two sailors locked eyes. The captain nodded.

"Let's see who flinches first, Skipper," Walker said, gripping an overhead railing as the bow angled down.

****

Type 95A

"Conn, Sonar. Torpedoes in the water!"

"Sonar, Conn. Have they acquired us?"

"Conn, Sonar. Negative, Captain. They are passive at depths ranging three hundred and fifty to seven hundred and fifty feet."

"Sonar, Conn. Distance to target?"

"Conn, Sonar. Target is eleven thousand yards and closing. Same bearing."

"Sonar, Conn. Very well."

"Fire tubes one and two, stand by tubes three and four."

"Fire tubes one and two, stand by tubes three and four, aye!"

The ship vibrated slightly as the two torpedoes left the tubes. The wires remained attached as the *Changzheng* fed corrections to the torpedoes while they were in passive mode. The fact that the Americans had fired on a true bearing was unexpected. The captain of that boat was a cunning opponent, but he had no idea what was in store for him.

"Cut the wires, set torpedoes to active homing."

"Cut the wires, set to active homing, aye."

As soon as the wires were cut, the YU-9s went active and their speed increased from twenty-five knots to fifty-nine knots. Within seconds, they had acquired their target.

****

USS *Maine*

"Conn, Sonar, enemy torpedoes in the water! Distance ten thousand yards and closing speed, fifty-nine knots. They're actively homing!"

"Sonar, Conn. Very well."

"Maneuvering, Conn. Ahead flank, thirty-degree down angle on the planes."

"Conn, Maneuvering. Ahead flank, thirty-degree down on the planes, aye."

Redding was surprised at the speed of those torpedoes. Fifty-nine knots at ten thousand yards gave them over five minutes if they stayed at the present course and speed. He had to increase his speed and go deep. He hoped that those torpedoes weren't programmed to go deep in active search mode.

"Weps, Conn. Status of our torpedoes?"

"Conn, Weps, our torpedoes are still running true at fifty-five knots. They are in active search. Time to impact, five minutes, ten seconds."

This was like a Wild West shoot-out. They both fired at the same time. Now they had to wait, evade, and see who came out on top.

"Launch noisemakers!"

"Noisemakers away!"

"Left full rudder, come to one-eight-zero degrees."

"Left full rudder, come to one-eight-zero degrees, aye."

The Conn angled as the sub made the turn. Redding was getting the *Maine* further away from those torpedoes. He deployed his noisemakers, attempting to give the Chinese torpedoes something else to listen to. If they got distracted long enough, he could put more distance between them.

"Conn, Sonar! It worked, sir. The torpedoes are going for the noisemakers."

"Sonar, Conn. Very well."

****

Type 95A

"Sir, she's changing course."

"Match bearing, and fire tubes three and four!"

"Match bearing, fire tubes three and four, aye!"

"Conn, Sonar. Torpedo contacts one and two have gone passive. They lost acquisition, torpedoes three and four have acquired, bearing eight-three and nine-four degrees. They are actively homing. Distance nine hundred and thirty yards and closing!"

Captain Lee clicked his stopwatch and listened as the Mk 48 torpedoes closed in on his submarine. They had thirty seconds before impact. He had one option and it had to be timed perfectly. He waited eight more seconds.

"Vent ballast, launch port decoys!"

"Vent ballast, launch port decoys, aye!"

The *Changzheng* shuddered violently as the ballast tanks were vented. A massive cloud of air bubbles vented, and the sub lurched upward as the decoys floated in the cloud of bubbles. The Mk 48s zeroed in on the bubbles, confused by the noise and the clutter of them. One of the Mk 48s collided with the other as it detonated.

The crew of the *Changzheng* were rocked from the explosion as overhead lights exploded and computer monitors blinked out.

****

USS *Maine*

"Conn, Sonar! Explosion in the water. Our torpedoes hit the sub!"

The sailors on the Conn cheered and Redding shook his XO's hand. He was about to tell the Conn to quiet down when they heard the pinging of an incoming torpedo.

"Conn, Sonar! Torpedo in the water. Bearing one-four-zero, distance…four hundred yards. They must have fired before they were hit, sir!"

"Maneuvering, make your depth seven hundred feet, forty-degree down angle on the planes, ahead flank!"

As his commands were echoed, Redding knew this was his last act as the captain of the USS *Maine*. At that distance and probable speed, there was nothing they could do. He listened as the torpedo homed in for the kill. He nodded to his XO and thought what a shame it was that Walker would never get to command his own sub—he'd have made a great captain.

The YU-9 torpedo impacted just aft of the boat's centerline. The explosion broke the ship as if it were a twig and the two halves of the USS *Maine* went to the bottom.
****

Type 95A
Fifteen Hours Later

The *Changzheng* had sustained damage, but she would live to fight another day. As Captain Lee sat in the Conn drinking his tea, he remained quiet as they rendezvoused with the sub-tender, which to outside eyes looked like any number of container ships that traversed the global trade routes.

Once again, the People's Liberation Army Navy had developed an ingenious way to tend to her most secret weapons in plain view. His submarine was directly beneath the ship and was ascending into her hold, which had been converted into a dry dock to repair and rearm China's submarines and get them back into the fight faster.

Once their sub was fully retracted into the artificial dry dock of the cargo vessel, Captain Lee climbed the ladder and emerged on the deck of the submarine. To his delight, Admiral Wei Huang was there to welcome them from a successful mission. The two briefly shook hands.

"So, Captain Lee, how did the *Changzheng* perform in combat?" Admiral Wei asked as the two of them headed to a set of rooms to discuss things further.

"Admiral Wei, she performed beyond all expectations. How soon will the others be ready?"

The head of the Chinese Navy smiled at his protégé as a father might upon his favorite child. "They are ready now, Lee. They are already underway from China."

Walking into the briefing room, Lee saw a myriad of things happening. He saw markings of where other PLA ships were, and markings for where the American ships were.

"I must say, Admiral, I am surprised to see you here, and not in Beijing," said Lee. "Is something wrong that has caused you to risk yourself like this?"

The old admiral ushered them to a more private part of the briefing room, away from the others. "Lee, I wanted to talk with you in person, and not through official channels. How well did Jade Dragon really perform?"

Lee nodded in acknowledgment of what his mentor was asking. "It performed remarkably. There were a couple of things it couldn't account for, like when the American captain had deviated from the original projected plan the computer had said he'd pursue."

Lifting an eyebrow at the comment, Wei asked, "Such as?"

"The computer predicted exactly what the destroyer captains would do to a T," Lee explained. "But when it came to the captain of the *Maine*, it was less accurate. I'm not sure if the *Maine* had found a way to detect us or not, but when we attacked the destroyers, instead of joining the battle and gunning for us as the computer said they would, they rose to periscope depth and transmitted a message. I have no idea what they transmitted, but clearly it was important enough for them not to press their advantage like the computer said they would."

Admiral Wei didn't say anything right away. He stood there thinking for a couple of minutes. "The computer has made a few other similar errors as well. Not so much in the Pacific, but over Cuba and with the Europeans."

"Really? What's happening with the Europeans?" Lee quizzed, hoping to tease out some additional information.

"Let's just say we aren't at war with only the Americans. The NATO nations have all joined in. All except for Turkey—they have opted to remain neutral."

"What about Australia, Japan, or even Russia?" Lee pressed.

A slight smile spread across Wei's lips. "Now you're thinking like an admiral, Lee. The Australians have sided with the Americans. The Japanese have remained neutral for the time being, but we expect them to declare war in the coming days. The bigger wild card I'm concerned with is the Russians. So far, they haven't moved their Atlantic or Baltic fleet to the Far East. When they do that, then we'll know they are preparing to fight us."

Lee looked around to make sure no one had moved closer to them. Leaning in, he whispered, "It's one thing to go to war with America. It's a whole different story to go to war with the world. I hope that damned computer knows what it's doing, or we're all doomed."

From the Authors

Miranda and I hope you've enjoyed this book. If you'd like to preorder Volume Two of the Monroe Doctrine and continue this action-packed military thriller series, please visit Amazon to reserve your copy. If you would like to stay up to date on new releases and receive emails about any special pricing deals we may make available, please sign up for our email distribution list. Simply go to https://www.frontlinepublishinginc.com/ and sign up.
If you enjoy audiobooks, we have a great selection that has been created for your listening pleasure. Our entire Red Storm series and our Falling Empire series have been recorded, and several books in our Rise of the Republic series and our Monroe Doctrine series are now available. Please see below for a complete listing.
As independent authors, reviews are very important to us and make a huge difference to other prospective readers. If you enjoyed this book, we humbly ask you to write up a positive review on Amazon and Goodreads. We sincerely appreciate each person that takes the time to write one.
We have really valued connecting with our readers via social media, especially on our Facebook page https://www.facebook.com/RosoneandWatson/. Sometimes we ask for help from our readers as we write future books—we love to draw upon all your different areas of expertise. We also have a group of beta readers who get to look at the books before they are officially published and help us fine-tune last-minute adjustments. If you would like to be a part of this team, please go to our author website, and send us a message through the "Contact" tab.

You may also enjoy some of our other works. A full list can be found below:

Nonfiction:
Iraq Memoir 2006–2007 Troop Surge
Interview with a Terrorist (audiobook available)

Fiction:
The Monroe Doctrine Series

Volume One (audiobook available)
Volume Two (audiobook available)
Volume Three (audiobook available)
Volume Four (audiobook still in production)
Volume Five (available for preorder)

Rise of the Republic Series
Into the Stars (audiobook available)
Into the Battle (audiobook available)
Into the War (audiobook available)
Into the Chaos (audiobook available)
Into the Fire (audiobook still in production)
Into the Calm (available for preorder)

Apollo's Arrows Series (co-authored with T.C. Manning)
Cherubim's Call (available for preorder)

Crisis in the Desert Series (co-authored with Matt Jackson)
Project 19 (audiobook available)
Desert Shield
Desert Storm

Falling Empires Series
Rigged (audiobook available)
Peacekeepers (audiobook available)
Invasion (audiobook available)
Vengeance (audiobook available)
Retribution (audiobook available)

Red Storm Series
Battlefield Ukraine (audiobook available)
Battlefield Korea (audiobook available)
Battlefield Taiwan (audiobook available)
Battlefield Pacific (audiobook available)
Battlefield Russia (audiobook available)
Battlefield China (audiobook available)

Michael Stone Series

Traitors Within (audiobook available)

World War III Series
Prelude to World War III: The Rise of the Islamic Republic and the Rebirth of America (audiobook available)
Operation Red Dragon and the Unthinkable (audiobook available)
Operation Red Dawn and the Siege of Europe (audiobook available)
Cyber Warfare and the New World Order (audiobook available)

Children's Books:
My Daddy has PTSD
My Mommy has PTSD

Abbreviation Key

1MC	One Main Circuit (shipboard public address system)
AA	Anti-Aircraft
ABM	Anti-Ballistic Missile
AEGIS	US Navy phased array radar-based combat system
AESA	Active Electronically Scanned Array
AI	Artificial Intelligence
ALS	Amyotrophic Lateral Sclerosis
AMRAAM	Advanced Medium-Range Air-to-Air Missile
AOR	Area of Responsibility
APC	Armored Personnel Carrier
ASAP	As Soon As Possible
ASO	Acoustic Sensor Operator
ASROC	Anti-Submarine Rocket
ATACMS	Army Tactical Cruise Missile System
ASW	Anti-Submarine Warfare
AUV	Autonomous Underwater Vehicle
AWACS	Airborne Warning and Control System
BAT	Baidu, Alibaba, Tencent
BDA	Battle Damage Assessment
BMP-3	Boevaya Mashina Pehoty (Russian infantry fighting vehicle)
C&C	Command and Control
CAP	Combat Air Patrol
CAPTOR	Encapsulated Torpedo
CAS	Close Air Support
CBP	Customs and Border Control
CCTV	Closed Circuit Television
CDC	Centers for Disease Control and Prevention
CI	Counterintelligence
CIA	Central Intelligence Agency
CIC	Combat Information Center
CIRO	Japanese Cabinet Intelligence and Research Office
CIWS	Close-In Weapons System
CMC	Central Military Committee
CNO	Chief of Naval Operations
CO	Commanding Officer

CPO	Chief Petty Officer
COB	Chief of the Boat
COCOM	Combatant Command
COMDESRON	Commander Destroyer Squadron
COMMO	Communications Officer
COMSUBPAC	Commander, Submarine Force, US Pacific Fleet
CONUS	Continental United States
COSCO	China Ocean Shipping Company
CNO	Chief of Naval Operations
CNOOC	China National Offshore Oil Corporation
CSAR	Combat Search and Rescue
CSIS	Canadian Security Intelligence Service
CUPET	Unión Cuba-Petróleo (Cuban Oil Union)
DARPA	Defense Advanced Research Projects Agency
DD	Death Dealer
DDI	Directorate of Digital Innovation
DEA	Drug Enforcement Agency
DESRON	Destroyer Squadron
DEVGRU	Naval Special Warfare Development Group (commonly referred to as SEAL Team Six)
DHS	Department of Homeland Security
DIA	Defense Intelligence Agency
DNI	Director of National Intelligence
DoD	Department of Defense
ECM	Electronic Countermeasures
ENDEX	End Exercise
EOD	Explosive Ordnance Disposal
ESM	Electronic Support Measures
ETF	Exchange-Traded Fund
EU	European Union
EWO	Electronic Warfare Officer
FBI	Federal Bureau of Investigation
FDC	Fire Direction Center
FLIR	Forward-Looking Infrared
FMS	Foreign Military Sales
FRAGO	Fragmentary Order
GDP	Gross Domestic Product
GPS	Global Positioning System

HAHO	High-Altitude, High-Opening
HARM	High-Speed Anti-Radiation Missile
HGV	Hypersonic Glide Vehicle
HIMARS	High-Mobility Artillery Rocket System
HQ	Headquarters
HS9	Havana-Scarabeo-9
HUD	Heads-Up Display
HUMINT	Human Intelligence
HVAC	Heating Ventilation and Air Conditioning
IBA	Individual Body Armor
IED	Improvised Explosive Device
INSUM	Intelligence Summary
IR	Infrared
ISIS	Islamic State of Iraq and Syria
ISS	International Space Station
JBCC	(Chinese) Joint Battle Command Center
JD	Jade Dragon
JDAM	Joint Direct Attack Munitions
JIOCEUR	Joint Intelligence Operations Center Europe
JLTV	Joint Light Tactical Vehicle
JOD	Joint Operations Division
JSOC	Joint Special Operations Command
JTF	Joint Task Force
KGB	Soviet Union's foreign intelligence and domestic security agency
LNO	Liaison Officer
MANPADS	Man-Portable Air Defense System
MCPO	Master Chief Petty Officer
MI-6	Military Intelligence 6 (British intelligence)
MiG	Type of Soviet Military Fighter Aircraft
MP	Member of Parliament *or* Military Police
MRE	Meals Ready-to-Eat
MSS	Ministry of State Security
N2	Naval Intelligence
NAS	Naval Air Station
NATO	North Atlantic Treaty Organization
NAVSPECWAR	Naval Special Warfare
NCO	Noncommissioned Officer

NIPR	Non-Classified Internet Protocol Router
NMCA	National Military Command Authority
NMCC	National Military Command Center
NOC	Non-Official Cover
NOFORN	Not Releasable to Foreign Nationals
NORAD	North American Aerospace Defense
NRO	National Reconnaissance
NSA	National Surveillance Agency *or* National Security Advisor
NSC	National Security Council
NVG	Night Vision Goggles
OC2	Orca Control Operator, Second Class
ODA	Operational Detachment Alphas (Special Forces team)
OLED	Organic Light Emitting Diode (TVs with thin carbon based film built into the screen)
OOD	Officer on Deck
OPM	Office of Personnel Management
ORCON	Originator Control (gives the office that classified the briefing control over how the information is disseminated)
OS	Operating System
PAVE PAWS	Precision Acquisition Vehicle Entry Phased Array Warning System (early-warning radar and computer system)
PEOC	Presidential Emergency Operations Center
PGZ09	Chinese self-propelled anti-aircraft gun
PIR	Priority Intelligence Requirement
PLA	People's Liberation Army (Chinese army)
PLAN	People's Liberation Army Navy (Chinese navy)
PM	Prime Minister
PO	Petty Officer
POTUS	President of the United States
PRC	People's Republic of China
RDT	Rear-Driven Thruster
RFID	Radio-Frequency Identification
RHAW	Radar, Homing and Warning
RIB	Rigid Inflatable Boat
ROAD	Retired on Active Duty

ROTC	Reserve Officer Training Corps
RTO	Radio Telephone Operator
RTB	Return to Base
S	Secret
S2	Army Intelligence
SA-19	Russian-made self-propelled air defense system
SAC	Special Activities Center
SAM	Surface-to-Air Missiles
SCI	Sensitive Comparted Information
SCIF	Sensitive Comparted Information Facility
SEAD	Suppression of Enemy Air Defenses
SecDef	Secretary of Defense
SEAL	Sea, Air and Land (Navy's primary Special Operations Force)
SIGINT	Signals Intelligence
SINCGARS	Single Channel Ground and Airborne Radio System
SIS	(British) Secret Intelligence Service
SITREP	Situation Report
SLAM	Submarine-Launched Anti-Aircraft Missile
SOAR	Special Operations Aviation Regiment
SOCOM	Special Operations Command
SOCSOUTH	Special Operations Command—South
SOF	Special Operations Forces
SOG	Special Operations Group
SOUTHCOM	Southern Command
SSBN	Ship, Submersible, Ballistic, Nuclear (Ballistic Missile Submarine)
STS2	Sonar Technician Submarine Petty Officer 2nd Class
SUV	Sport Utility Vehicle
SVR	Successor agency to the Soviet KGB
SVTC	Secured Video Teleconference
TAO	Tactical Action Officer
TEL	Transporter Erector Launcher
TF	Task Force
THAAD	Terminal High Altitude Area Defense
THREATCON	Threat Condition
TOC	Tactical Operation Center
TS	Top Secret

U	Unclassified
UAV	Unpiloted Aerial Vehicle
UK	United Kingdom
UN	United Nations
Unit 61398	Chinese cyberattack unit
USAMRIID	United States Army Medical Research Institute of Infectious Disease
USB	Universal Serial Bus (common type of computer port)
USD	United States Dollars
VIP	Very Important Person
VLF	Very Low Frequency
VLS	Vertical Launching System
VP	Vice President
VT-2	Training Squadron Two
WP	White Phosphorus
XO	Executive Officer
ZBD-04	Type of Chinese infantry fighting vehicle
ZSL-08	Type of Chinese infantry fighting vehicle
ZTE	Chinese telecommunications company

Made in the USA
Las Vegas, NV
20 May 2025

1a56735d-dff5-42ca-b04c-8a376f34a9f3R02